Dear QPB Member:

I am thrilled that you will find my novel, *Chang and Eng*, inside your QPB cat-
alog this month. The novel took me about three years to write and research,
and it has been such a pleasure for me to see the reception that it has received.
It meant a lot to know that QPB selected the book because I have always been
aware of their offering adventurous and discerning fiction to their members. It
is nice to be a member of their club.

   I hope you are as captivated by *Chang and Eng* as I am. They lived remarkable lives and were the first celebrated conjoined twins and the inspiration for
the term "Siamese twins." They escaped death at the hands of the King of
Siam, came to America and found great celebrity, married a pair of southern-
belle sisters, got caught up in the Civil War, and raised a family of twenty-one
children in nineteenth-century North Carolina. I decided that Eng—the
more bookish of the two brothers—would be the one to narrate the book
because I saw a longing in his eyes when I came upon his picture that I did not
see in Chang's. I felt Eng might offer a more interesting perspective of their
twinship. But I mostly wanted to investigate the lives and epic loves of this
extraordinary pair, explore the issue of identity, and celebrate two lives lived
firmly as their own men: proud, individual, yet bound together by love.

   (If you want to know the truth, I really wrote about the famous Siamese
twins because I wanted to be one of the only published authors who deliberately starts his novels with an ungrammatical sentence: "This is the end I have
feared since we were a child." Try getting that by a compulsive copy editor.)

Enjoy,

Darin Strauss

Chang and Eng

A Novel

 DARIN STRAUSS

A DUTTON BOOK

01-1379

DUTTON
Published by the Penguin Group
Penguin Putnam Inc., 375 Hudson Street, New York, New York 10014, U.S.A.
Penguin Books Ltd, 27 Wrights Lane, London W8 5TZ, England
Penguin Books Australia Ltd, Ringwood, Victoria, Australia
Penguin Books Canada Ltd, 10 Alcorn Avenue, Toronto, Ontario, Canada M4V 3B2
Penguin Books (N.Z.) Ltd, 182–190 Wairau Road, Auckland 10, New Zealand

Penguin Books Ltd, Registered Offices:
Harmondsworth, Middlesex, England

First published by Dutton, a member of Penguin Putnam Inc.

First Printing, June, 2000
9   10   8

 REGISTERED TRADEMARK—MARCA REGISTRADA

Library of Congress Cataloging-in-Publication Data
Strauss, Darin.
Chang and Eng : a novel / Darin Strauss.
p. cm.
ISBN 0-525-94512-1
1. Bunker, Chang, 1811–1874—Fiction. 2. Bunker, Eng, 1811–1874—Fiction.
3. Siamese twins—United States—Fiction. 4. North Carolina—Fiction.
I. Title: Chang and Eng. II. Title.
PS3569.T692245 C48 2000
813'.54—dc21   99–059198

Printed in the United States of America
Set in Bembo
Designed by Eve L. Kirch

PUBLISHER'S NOTE

This is a work of fiction. Names, characters, places, and incidents either are the products
of the author's imagination or are used fictitiously, and any resemblance to actual
persons, living or dead, business establishments, events, or locales is entirely coincidental.

This book is printed on acid-free paper. ∞

This book is affectionately dedicated to:

Ellen, Bernie, and Izzy Strauss
John Hodgman, a great writer, a cunning agent, and a true friend
And Susannah of the Meadows

Chang and Eng

Prologue

This is the end I have feared since we were a child.

    Eng wakes to find Chang cold against him. The smell conjures the muddy stink of the Mekong in this double-wide bed half a world from Siam. Chang, the left, is dead. Eng is the right.

Then I too am done, *Eng thinks, and his heart twists like a cluster of wild vines.*

For the last sixty-three years, the two (few doubt they are two men, though Chang and Eng share a stomach and more) have lived jointly, a pair of complete bodies held together by a cartilaginous band at their chests.

It is late. The open windows usher the Carolina weather inside. Papers that carry the light of the moon fly across the writing desk like little ghosts. A leaflet from the catastrophic final tour snares on a gift from Tsar Nicholas—a pair of gilded containers, one preserving the shrunken body of a mongoose, the other that of a snake. Over the desk hangs a sketch of the Siamese Double-Boy wielding a pair of rifles to ward off an enraged crowd.

This bedroom is Eng's. The twins have lived in separate households for almost six years.

I will never sail home again. I will never salute the flat green coastline of Siamese shanties in the rain.

Though he has not been back since they were children, if his head could spill open Eng would find the contours of the Land of the White

Elephant in the folds of his brain, the flooding waters of the Mekong trickling from his hollows, and a wealth of faces like their own. Chang's face has begun to show the green marks of a new-sprung mildew.

I am the son of a Mekong fisherman, seven thousand, five hundred twenty miles and fifty years from home, *Eng thinks.* Has everything been *Chang's* fault?

Eng lies on his side, facing Chang; his fingers find the wrist where the pulse would have been. Legs and forearms are twined beneath the quilt, Eng spasmy and prickling under their weight. He tries to pull free and his double dances with him—Chang's head flops about like the head of a rag doll. Eng collapses back, feeling each hair on his body acutely, and all the sweat underneath his wedding ring. Eng is alone. The smell is asphyxiating. Time is a fish caught in their father's nets.

Eng rubs his brother's chest as if Chang simply is cold. The bedsheet falls to the floor. Eng hits him with a closed fist, but Chang's breast will not rise. Eng is certain his own soul will go to heaven, but he fears his brother's is destined for elsewhere.

Eng's life full of leering faces, slander, and unlikely love begins to recede. Like an exile looking upon his native city as he sails away into darkness, he is seized by memory, it being the wondrous strange hand pulling him back to the fading shores of his past.

Book One

 All of man's unhappiness stems from his inability to stay in a room alone. —Pascal

CHAPTER ONE

When First We Met

Monday, December 10, 1842
North Carolina

"Chang-Eng," the children chanted. "Mutant, mutant."

Now and then the little innocents sprang from the dust cloud chasing our carriage to cry my name and Chang's. The path we traveled cut through a droughty careworn field, and to either side of us a fast-passing scene of blond grass and dead milkweed thirsted under the burnt sky of sunset. My ear tingled with the nearness of my brother, who picked lint off of my shoulder and knew not to bump my head as he did so. His dark eyes showed little reflections of me. I was thirty-one. My life was about to begin: I was entering North Carolina.

My brother and I did not know that love was soon to deliver us. But twenty-one children and three decades later, how obvious it seems that everything to follow was a consequence of that evening. When you know you are dying, self-deceptions fly from your bedside like embers off a bonfire. Alone in the dark with a final chance to bind together circumstances that have made you a peasant who sells duck eggs on the Mekong one day and the South's most famous temperance advocate the next, you see a curtain open onto the landmark moments of your past.

When Chang and I arrived in North Carolina, we were coming to the end of yet another tour, exhibiting the bond that the public could not see without assuming we two were so very different from everybody else.

The halfwit we'd hired drove at a quick pace. And now, jounced inside a rickety carriage that had the legend THE SIAMESE TWIN in chipping yellow paint on its doors, I was trying to nap beside Chang.

My eyes were not closed for long. My brother tapped my shoulder. "Eng?"

I knew better than to ask him to quiet when he was in one of his talkative moods.

"Maybe," Chang said, "you read out loud?" He spoke in a soft voice whenever asking me for something.

"Now?" I made a show of closing my eyes more tightly. "I'd prefer not."

"A Shakespeare speech from your book, make the trip go faster?" There was a shiver in his words from the bustle of our ride. I felt his half of our stomach spasm.

"Let me please catch a little rest," I said, opening an eye. "Why don't you read it yourself?"

"Me? You joking." The listlessness in Chang's smile suggested what it is to spend three decades within five to seven inches of one another. "Eng?"

Reporters love to mention that I am the "less dominating member of the pair." A man may be quiet, does that mean he is not assertive?

"Eng?" That we hadn't eaten in hours spoiled his breath.

I shut my eyes tight again. Nailing down a personality is about as easy as pinning marmalade to a wall. I faked a snore.

"*Eng!*" he said, patience being a luxury allowed those who have more obliging brothers. "I know you not asleep."

The dust of riding whisked us into Wilkesboro, the last stop on this junket of somersaults and smiles that had spanned the eastern seaboard. I could not have imagined that in Wilkesboro we would meet the women who would—for all the kings I'd met and the nations I'd been—make up the kingdom in which I'd walk.

Chang had the driver bridle our two horses to a stop in a grassy square near the center of town: a little commons that had not yet changed its name from "Union Square" to "Westwood Park."

This open space was blotchy with killed grass, its unused flagpole stood without purpose in the wind. A line of four threadbare trees gesticulated like marionettes behind the flagstaff.

Townspeople rushed at us from every direction. Dozens of unkempt children and their unkempt parents gathered round our carriage, pointing fingers. The rest of the population climbed on roofs for a better view. My brother grinned at them all. He delivered his patented wave, like a little boy proving with a casual flick that his hand is clean on both sides—the motion Queen Victoria used to greet her masses.

"Come down, carriage man," my brother called out to our driver, wetting my face with spittle. "Will you please open door?"

The driver muttered at us from his buckboard. I asked this idiot, "Did you say something?"

He let us out, his well-shaved cheeks pink as Mekong tuna meat. He said, "Nothing, sirs."

"You are addressing Eng alone." I accepted the man's hand, stepping from the carriage with my brother close on my left. "Do you hear my twin talking? You must say, 'Nothing, *sir.*'" I was tired and irritable. "When you speak to Eng, you speak to one '*sir,*' not two."

Far away, between the rough corners of Wilkesboro's buildings (small white Presbyterian church with no steeple, narrow white beer parlor, small white general store displaying all its stock in its window), rows of sleeping blue mountains hid in shadow, each more blurred than the last. And the full moon had begun its crawl across the sky.

Everything about this environment seemed animated by our arrival: the crowd gathering on all sides of us; the bandy-legged old man in a white suit who limped across Union Square with a yellow rose in his lapel, and the pair of young girls who ran over and walked him arm in arm toward our carriage; the slaves across the courtyard pitching straw and pretending not to look; the dirty little white hands poking our ligament as we stepped from the carriage. Several reached for my face.

"Chang-Eng!" Even the dirtiest of children radiant like they'd just been given candy. "Mutant, mutant!"

"Thank you," Chang and I said as the dust gathered on our

identical black suits—tight and crisply English in cut, the very ones Barnum had bought for us. Strolling through the crowd, my brother and I were two complete bodies affixed at the chest by a fleshy, bendable, seven-inch-long ligament resembling a forearm.

"Chang-Eng acknowledging you, good people," Chang said. We crossed Main Street side by side, in the calibrated rhythm of our united movement, arms sweaty over each other's shoulders. Like Chang, I wore my hair in a black braid long enough to curl around my head. I tied it in a blue silk tassel that fell over my brother's shoulder, as his fell over mine.

North Carolina was a welcome change from Boston, Washington, Philadelphia, New York, that series of East Coast cities that even before the War of Yankee Aggression had become as vulgar as a row of women of easy virtue on a street corner. Some believe the war divided America's history in one stroke, all at once advancing Northern manufacturing and the forward parade of Yankee progress. But by December 1842 the North had swelled so hastily it simmered with industry and crime and most of all too many people, while Southern towns like this remained in rural condition, natural as ever. Wilkesboro was among those bygone cheerful hamlets that were so numerous across the map of North Carolina they seemed like stars in the nighttime sky, before Reconstruction hobbled the South.

My brother kept his smile and hadn't quit waving to the townsfolk. Few returned his greeting. A yellow-skinned man and his conjoined twin may be admitted into a village in North Carolina, but will never be adopted by it fully.

Main Street was rounded, with a humped center and sloping sides, and it led us across town. Chang and I were silent as we walked; I rarely spoke to him. At all times, a wordless debate concerning the fundaments of movement traveled across our bond like a message across telegraph wire, and that was conversation enough. I called this the Silence, and I was comforted by it.

The people of Wilkesboro had begun to follow us at a distance: here two blond schoolgirls crouched behind a craggy black oak tree to stare; there, in the Law Office Building, under the pressed-metal facade, a few cheerful boys shouted taunts. One brave Negro walked near us before scampering off to giggle behind some wagons tethered to the Court House gallery; across the street near a livery stable a woman froze in her tracks to gape at the Twins, her face turning pale as death. A few townsfolk, however, did smile openly at us as we passed, and let fly a friendly giggle whenever Chang waved.

"Eng," Chang said, crimping his eyes as he often did when he found his happy place in the world. "It is exciting, yes?" With his free hand he smoothed the lapels of his jacket.

"Brother, I don't know what you mean."

Chang was taken off guard; he always managed to discount that we were miles apart in temperament.

"Well," he said, searching my face, "this, I mean!" Crooking our ligament, he drew himself in front of and even closer to me, and he looked over my shoulder at the now large crowd following at our heels. Chang and I continued to walk in this manner— nearly face-to-face, with my brother striding backward—as he flung his hand in the air and waved at the people. Everyone clapped. Chang swung around to face forward again.

It was this sort of pandering showmanship that I hated, and strove to avoid for most of my career. (Like most everybody, I am proud of certain accomplishments: that we never participated in, nor were in any way associated with, an American circus; my predilection for reading, which saved me from the manner of immigrant speech that Chang never lost.)

Main Street came to an end at the Yates Inn. A Southern community such as Wilkesboro, in its distant relation not only to the central government, but also to neighboring villages, believes itself an individual, free from all others. And yet, little inns just like this one were features of nearly all minor Southern towns, and by now Chang and I felt at home loitering by innyards, waiting to be admitted.

Wilkesboro's version of the Southern hostel was a two-story unpainted log house, its modest front yard overgrown with chokecherry. A giant woman sat on the inn's drooping front porch, fanning herself in the skeletal shade of leafless oaks. She was some five hundred pounds, if not more, this innkeeper. Moist patches of her scalp were visible under her thin gray hair, like peat bog spied through the reeds of a marsh, and her hairline gave way to a glistening forehead just as a marsh would open onto a river.

My brother and I came to stand before her, resting our two free hands on the porch railing. The lady innkeeper scrutinized Chang and me in our unforgiving black. "A charming creature"—her bassy voice wiggled the flesh hanging below her chin—"just about as strange as they say." I could not tell whether the woman's face was friendly or taunting. She wore a homemade dress of gray cloth-stuff made with no thought to style. Her skin refused contour. Birds shrieked in the trees.

I imagined this woman a courtier in His Majesty King Rama's palace, bejeweled, dressed in silk while four or five husbands danced around her, runty men with short life spans.

To her left stood a frowning boy in a straw hat with a crooked rim. To her right, a pair of blond women—her daughters, I guessed, though they were not so young—long-faced, flat-chested, and each with lip rouge on her front teeth. The taller one's eyes flickered impatiently, like the wings of little birds. The way she did not turn away in horror gave me the urge to saw through my ligament. It was the light at that hour, or my fatigue pressing in, but I believed she was smiling at me.

My brother's skin was mucky as the Mekong itself, his breathing a gasp.

The declining sun acted on the girl's fine hair, cutting it into elements of gold and pink gold and shadow. She blushed and bowed her head, but she continued to peek at me from under her brows with eyes the color of blueberries. She bit her lip. A young lady was looking at me, of all things, and smiling. I could not fathom it—looking into *my* eyes! I returned her stare, I don't know where I discovered the courage.

Only a few seconds passed, evidently, though I was sure the moment slipped from the calendar. For the seeming eternity I stood there, my heart pounded only once, a single thunderclap, echoing. This strange girl's clear eyes looked like safe worlds in which to escape the circumstance of what I was.

Chang's heart, too, began to go frantic for this tall blond innkeeper's daughter—I felt it. Was it me the girl was fixing her gaze on, or the twin close at my side?

The whole time, the girl's sister stood in shadow and chewed at her nails. But before long this one was looking up into my face, too, without smiling or frowning. The entire town had gathered behind us, watching everything. And the sisters' large mother leaned forward in her groaning seat and straightened her dress, patted her hair.

"Jefferson," the large woman said to her boy. "Go get your father." Daintily, she removed a little gnat that had flown into her mouth. "Tell him I found a pair of husbands for your sisters."

I swear the townsfolk cheered.

CHAPTER TWO

My Family in Siam

Of course, my life did not really begin when first I came to North Carolina. I entered into this world many years before that, nearly eight thousand miles east. In the Kingdom of Siam.

Everything about our birth is known.

When Chang and I were born in 1811 on a bamboo mat in our family's home afloat the Mekong River, there was not a soul outside, because of the hard rain—no one except for my father, who was fishing in the storm. Mekong was the outermost corner of the world, Siam's badlands. The men all wore thin, pointed mustaches, trying to look Chinese. The river perpetually overflowed its banks and drowned things.

Mother had been born nearby. She was beautiful, save her teeth, and thus had been given all the advantages. But ours was not a beauty-loving race, at least Father said it wasn't; serene struggling was the virtue Siamese loved best. Life was too strenuous, said Father, to celebrate anything as worthless as beauty. But he was known to miss an hour or more of worktime daylight just to pet mother's delicate head.

The details of my birth are known.

It was the beginning of a summerlike spring, a rainy midnight in the rainiest season of a rainy country. Living on the Mekong, we were a day's journey and a thousand years from Bangkok. Houseboats like ours formed a loose floating village up and down a half-submerged waterfront of muddy swamp and profitless rice field, interrupted by the occasional grove of coconut palm.

Rubber plants and vines lingered everywhere, handsome, fresh, dangling at unexpected angles over rocks, streams, and puddles, innumerable puddles. We lived in the shadow of two modest lime-stone hills, among snakes both harmless and deadly, as well as the infrequent tiger or leopard. Across the river, barely visible in the distance, stood the red sandstone cliffs of Kang Gee Hill.

Moored to the rank green shore, our houseboat floated atop a twitchy ribbon of moonlight that was bleared by the rain. We had a simple home, no more than marbao wood planks arching over a flat-bottomed centerboard, the planks thatched together with bam-boo and grass. Everyone was crowded inside its narrow, darkened cabin for the birthing.

The ceiling leaked on Mother's swollen belly, on her hare-lipped midwife Jun, and on our aunts, who had ringed themselves around their laboring sister in a human curtain. Mother was the youngest. Her name was Nok, and she was three-quarters Chi-nese, as was my father. Mother was a woman who would have been bored with a baby less singular and troublesome than we were. There she is—I imagine her clearly: long black hair brushed up high; praying to her ancestors, her forehead wrinkled from the strain of delivering a double-child; her unblemished skin growing blotches around cheeks so busy panting. I picture Father, also: outside, fishing through the downpour, too anxious to watch.

The houseboat pitched. Jun knelt at my mother's ankles on the hard floor, alongside a tree butt that supported a thick white can-dle. "I see it." She was reaching between Mother's legs to ease out the baby. "Nok, I see your child." Jun's slow-witted assistant, the cross-eyed teenage boy Deng Xu held a second candle and could not keep it from swaying. Light was scarce.

Mother was gasping. "How does it look?" New-sprung lines in her face spoke of what she was going through, what was about to happen. "What is it, a boy? Is it a boy?" She squeezed a little silk man, a rag doll she had sewn together two years earlier, the night before her wedding.

"I don't know as yet." The midwife had a happy face. "It looks well. All is well."

"Jun, I must know—"

"Quiet, Nok. Everything will come to pass."

Little Deng Xu inadvertently stepped on Jun's sarong, pinching the kneeling midwife's calf between foot and floor. "Half-a-dolt!" she yelled. The boy jumped, his candle went out, and Mother's wail was heard all the way in China, or so tradition has it.

Jun waved her hand over Mother's belly, a sweeping kindness meant to end Mother's pain. Then something sentimental happened.

Father flew through the door, let fall his empty fishing sack, and stumbled in a skinny heap to the floor beside Mother. "My poor, exquisite heart," he said, bringing his bony hand over Mother's sweating forehead. He soothed her skin. Father was soaked, dripping rainwater. His eyes were red-rimmed.

"*Now* Ti-eye comes inside," huffed Mother's oldest sister. Aunt Ping was a traveling barber who during work hours carried her stock-in-trade with her, including the chair.

Mother gave another cry, a final push. And Chang and Eng entered this life together.

Our mother now rolled to one side and fainted from exhaustion. She began an intense dream. She dreamed voices were singing outside, in an unfamiliar tongue, a singing that filled the cabin and lingered over the river and in the darkness; the song moved her to tears. She waked crying.

And so our nativity was peaceful, at first.

Chang and I lay closely crammed together, facing head-to-feet. Chang's face had wound up between my legs.

"Twins!" Jun exclaimed. "We have twins, healthy and male!" And this animated everyone. One spank to our bottoms, and our gurgles and cries meant we were alive and hearty. The midwife cut the umbilical cord with a candle-warmed knife. Father whistled, and looked at Mother with the coyness of a rascal. She handed him the rag doll and twisted toward Chang and me with open hands.

Jun told Mother to wait, to let her "right" the one who was upside down.

"I have merely to give them their baths." Jun was adamant enough to be imposing. "Allow me to perform my job, and later you can carry out yours for the rest of your life." But then the midwife saw she could not separate us—that nothing could right my brother and me.

Sometimes one learns too early, as I did, what the world is capable of.

Jun screamed. Father screamed, and our aunts, too, with a pandemonium that echoed about the trees outside, startling flocks of birds from their nests and out into sheets of rain.

Jun dropped us to the floor with a crash. The midwife saw Chang and me as a single monster, difficult as that may be to believe. Father looked at his crying twin boys and tried to vomit but produced no more than a taste of bile. He ran from us and cringed on the far side of the cabin.

We lay wailing at the feet of cross-eyed and cowering Deng Xu; Chang and I each maintained a full, distinct body—with two pairs of arms and legs, two heads and chests, hearts and minds— but everyone noted only that we were bound together at the breastbone by a fleshy, twisted ligament: not two children, but one curse on the family. No one bent to touch the double-child. But the witnesses should have seen—the baby was two.

While the world is not a place of widespread kindness, a few oysters thrive in a sea of clams. Occasional grace exists. Mother, knowing my brother and me for more than one child, kept her calm. The glimmer of two thousand years of Siamese superstition left her dark eyes in an instant. She cooed into my face and patted our cheeks.

Mother was a sensible parent. She sat up and took us into her arms, untwisting our ligament. We faced one another, Chang and I. Mother told everyone to leave her. Her dear friend Jun, her sisters, her husband—all were banished from her houseboat.

"But I *live* here," Father said in a panic, his palms up as he walked toward his wife.

"What does that mean now?" asked Mother, and she kicked

her leg up at him. "And don't forget to take your fishing net. Perhaps you can build a new fortune for yourself."

Once everyone had gone, Mother bathed us. Our ligament was short, and Chang and I could lie only face-to-face, not side-to-side. The pounding of rain on the roof had slowed and softened.

Now Mother rinsed our binding; a thin blue vein traversed its length. Our skin was covered in a sticky film like ooze on the shore where fish has been skinned. Contrary to reports, I did not coo along with my brother as Mother washed under Chang's chin.

Outside, Mother's sisters, as well as Jun, Deng Xu, and assorted townspeople, had gathered by our doorway to peek in. Mother did not acknowledge this. She was too busy drying us, drying her newborns in slips of palm leaf, and she was exhausted. Finally Mother said over her shoulder, "I have not failed to notice that you are all standing there like fools."

Everyone scattered.

Wearied as she was, Mother finished readying our home for us. She swept the floor with a broom made of grass and wood, and she placed us in the bamboo pallet Father had built for his expected child to sleep in.

And after a time Father came back inside. His hair was drenched and pasted to his forehead, his clothes so wet a picture of his bosom emerged through the fabric. He stood unmoving, drew in his lip, and looked at Mother.

"Nok." His bearing was shy as a beggar's. "Nok, I've never loved you more than today, and today never as much as right now." My father was not a big man, but he was sturdy. A wind came rushing in and curled around our bodies like a wet velvet blanket. We were a family.

The four of us lived a normal life for six years, until word came from Bangkok that King Rama wanted us dead.

Though our birth was deemed extraordinary, my brother and I were not the first of our conjoined kind. If one forgets that I am proudly both Siamese and North Carolinian, one might wrongly conclude I belong solely to a fellowship consisting of men and women we have never met.

The so-called Baby Vertical, 1470, Stuttgart, was fused at the back and able only to hop on the one thickset leg between them; the Identical Scot Monstrosities from Glasgow, 1660, joined at the hips, a pair from the waist up, were a single man below that; Eliza and Mildred Plumphead, approximately 1100, Kent, England, known as the Midland Maids, were bound at the cheekbone and possibly at the shoulders (they faced opposite directions and never saw one another without the aid of a looking glass); the Scandinavian Siblings, Helga and Uula Helpus, who shared a spine and had an immobile hand dangling from their lumbar region.

These so-called double-people, none of whom approached the kind of fame I share with Chang, were never the secret friends to me that they have been to my brother, who committed their stories to memory ever since *The New York Times* (announcing our fifth national tour) dug their names from oblivion. I don't believe I have anything in common with that community.

When Chang and I were young children of the Mekong, our world was an island of unknowing. Father's houseboat floated apart from any other by half a mile, but that was only part of it. A volcano would not have been a more isolating boundary to our world than Mother was: my twin and I were not given the chance to understand we were different from other children.

Still, in our ignorance we were not unlike most of the five million other Siamese peasants, a people who knew almost nothing. Not that a North Carolinian could be mistaken for Isaac Newton, but at least information is available in America—you don't have to walk all day with your shins deep in muddy water just to find someone who's been somewhere. On the Mekong, it was not possible to enjoy a breeze; every whiff was tainted by the stench of fish and physical struggle. Boggy pathways congested with bent-backed girls, their shoulders contorted under heavy yokes, their legs covered to the knees in drying mud: this is the philosophy of my native land. And the Thai language may be a honey-tipped tool for minstrels, but its lack of precision led to a puerile brand of science that almost killed Chang and me many times over.

Nevertheless, Siam is my homeland and I will always regret spurning her.

After Chang and I were born, news of the spectacular delivery brought droves of sightseers, and soon physicians came forward to suggest methods of separation. And though I was but a few months old, I can only assume I would have craved disunion, even then.

The first of the surgeons arrived one afternoon and poured a libation at our doorway. Then he closed his eyes and prayed to himself in a whisper. Not moving, Mother and Father watched this little man as he picked up his calico sack and walked over to Chang and me in our bedstead. Father and Mother tiptoed side by side toward the physician and waited for him to speak. Chang and I lay squeaking and playing with Mother's rag doll, named In.

Dr. Lau had thinning, braided hair, a trimmed gray goatee, and a freckled nose. He was a Bangkok sophisticate. Resting his sack on the sawed tree butt at the midpoint of our houseboat, he looked around before addressing my father: "Please take no offense at what I am about to say, sir." The doctor was squinting the way Father did whenever he noticed our band. "How does one manage to live in these conditions?"

Father blinked as he took a step back, letting my mother's hand fall from his forearm. He told the doctor that we enjoyed our home, speaking as if each word was a pain he wanted quickly out of his mouth. His hair was wild, a few tufts standing from his head while the rest lay flat, as usual.

"Please, mister." The doctor scratched his chin. "I do not mean to be rude—"

"What do you mean to be, then?" Father took a step toward the doctor.

"—it's just that I've heard you are half Chinese." The doctor had begun talking in upper-class Mandarin. Outside, reeds snapped like crickets as a sightseer tried to get a peek into our houseboat.

"Ask our neighbors, they'll tell you." Father continued to speak in the Thai language, drawing in air and exhaling through his nostrils.

The doctor gave a little shrug.

"I am a Mekong River fisherman," Father said. "I'm proud of my vocation and learning to be good at it."

"You see, mister," the doctor smiled, "I boast some Chinese

blood as well." He fingered his withdrawing hairline as if he was petting a prize animal.

Father stormed to the doorway, grumbling. The doctor seemed nonplussed. When Father walked outside, the sightseer could be heard splashing away through the reeds. Dr. Lau chuckled softly.

Mother wasn't the kind of woman to waste time caressing her husband's insulted pride. She turned to Dr. Lau with eyes prematurely old but unweary: "Sir, my babies?"

The physician examined us with a nod of amused distaste, and squeezed our band until we cried. He clawed at it, pummeled it like a Confederate lumberjack trying to chop through a Union log, then pressed an ear gently to our breasts. Next he circled the bedstead with his hands held out from his sides, and began purring.

"This is what we must do," he said finally, his head bowed in concentration, but he lifted his face when he heard Father shuffle back inside.

Mother, nervously jiggling her loose brown front tooth with her tongue, motioned *all quiet* to her husband with a finger to her lips; Father looked to his feet for solace. The sadness in his downcast face touched Mother.

"We must"—the surgeon furrowed his brow—"hang the boys for ninety days across a cord of fine catgut." The physician ignored Mother and Father's confused interjections, and said, "This will be positioned at the center of that connecting ligature so they will dangle like a pair of saddlebags."

Mother stood tensely, her expression like that of someone about to shoo birds from a window.

"This catgut cord will," said the doctor, "by the end of the term, bore its way through their ligature, by degrees, thereby allowing the severed parts time to heal as it progresses."

Mother's lips quivered. Father ushered the physician out the door.

"If you have a change of mind—" the doctor said, coughing. Flat green coastline stretched beyond our houseboat, damp and quiet. The river lay ahead.

Other charlatans came and went, each with a new inspiration: to cut the band with a scalding-hot wire, or to burn it, saw us apart (this seemed particularly prosaic), somehow to use termites on it, etc. Each procedure would have bifurcated the stomach we shared inside our ligament, and killed us, of course.

Perhaps it was the doctor, or the onlookers, because it took Father some time fully to acknowledge that, even with our absurd and, to his eyes, repulsive condition, it was his duty to hide his disgust. By the time the King's men came for us a few years later, Father had become caring, in his reserved way. "All right, children," he would say to us sometimes. "All right."

Mother was of a sweeter temper. She worked without end to ensure our childhood would be a pocket of softness in a callous life. She sewed our "clothes" herself, designing a makeshift drape with a pair of holes for our heads. We were raised as normal boys, not pitied or slighted. She kept us utterly isolated from other children, she taught us to sing, speak, to help out around the house. She had us do everything, that is, except feel unlike others. We quarreled as I imagine other brothers do, perhaps a little more, and a little more troublesomely, due to what's obvious. But I would say we lived a discordant concord, to quote Horace.

After some time we were deemed deserving of names. My name means "strictly, to tie strongly," in the Thai language; Chang means "tasteless."

My brother liked to tell reporters that he and I thought ourselves complete and ordinary, and that, when eventually we saw other boys for the first time (the day we were attacked), it was the separate children who were odd and lacking in our eyes. But I did not feel that way; even as an infant I knew that the onlookers came to visit for a reason. I knew we were different, that we were constrained.

Early on, Chang's frailty didn't make learning to walk any easier. Our little connector did not allow us yet to stand side by side. My brother's chin nearly touched mine, day and night. Facing each other like a pair of dancers, we walked in side steps. But managing simple daily maneuvers was a hurdle we eventually learned to clamber over. Taking a seat without breaking the chair, reaching for something just beyond my grasp and not being jerked backward, and, much later, making love—these seemed like locked doors before we built our own passkey. I have seen two rummies trying to support each other in an attempt to get home unscathed, and I doubt that act is as difficult as it is simply to move when you are the "*Siamese Twins*," unequal in height and temperament. I was always a little taller.

It took a while to become capable walkers. I scarcely remember the first time (we were about three) when we strayed outside alone, but years later a British pamphlet from our first European tour dramatized the moment.

Whosoever has been a Christian child and yet now and again wanted to take to one's heels and hasten off on the double quick; whosoever has thought it about unbearable, at least once toward evening in November, to stand pat, attending to his business and the like—he will understand the wanderlust agitating the yellow blood of the baby Siamese Twin-Monster. The Bound-Duo were toddling by the entry to their floating skipper when they were beguiled by some Oriental music from a theater drifting by; the Double-Boys embarked toward it, and fell, in a topple, into the river directly. Thrashing about like the oddity they are, the Twins must have made quite a fanfaronade! The crew of an aquatic laundry eventually came to Chang and Eng's salvation, and the Twins were evermore attracted to music!

I *can* call back some particulars about that fall—a commotion of dust, the tang of peat bog in my mouth, thick green water blocking my lungs, and, later, the boredom of lying next to Chang during his delayed recovery. He was sick and ashen for weeks. After days in bed like this, I began to cry. "I hate him," I said. "I hate him." He was meager and pale and the work of looking at me seemed too much for his little face.

Mother hugged me, and I could smell the salt in her hair. When she tried to release me so she could embrace him, I held on and would not let go. My twin leered as if a judge had whispered in his ear—Chang's turn to win.

"I hate him," I said. But Mother brushed me aside and sat up straight. "A double-boy must never fight among yourself." Her face was very serious. "Others argue and are capable of escaping each other. You do not have that advantage. You may as well cut off your own head." She brought her hand to my soft cheek and to Chang's pallid one, and she smiled. "All right, Bean Sprout?" she asked Chang. "All right, Eng?" she asked me.

Calm down, I said to myself. I am sorry.

I cannot calm down, I still have to linger in this bed, I said to myself.

Ignore it, I said to myself. And I am not sorry.

All right, I will ignore it.

I was acquiring the Silence, learning how to remain true to the talk that stirred in my own heart and, instead of articulating the tragedy of my situation, recount it to myself.

Chang came around and we were up and both healthy, and soon I spent the days pestering Father for the philosophies of Mekong fishing and Gung-Fu—his twin passions.

Father sat with us on the small dinghy he'd kept tied to the raft that formed the floor of our houseboat, and his eyes gleamed. Mekong fishing is an art worthy of the knowledge and practice of a wise man, somewhat like poetry. It is contingent upon great precision: in the sewing of the twine with a delicate needle and silk, and the fastening of the twine into perfect square nets, and in the positioning of the worm (imposing your arming wire through his top and out at his bottom, and then affixing him to the net, and doing so as though you loved him).

"Here, Eng." Father grinned, something he scarcely did, and it made his big teeth look odd against the rest of his face. "Here, Chang. Now you do it." Ten thousand tunas were whipping just beneath the glinting surface of the water, I was certain of it. But Mekong fishing is Humility; it has a calmness of spirit and a world of other blessings nourishing it. The strands of the fishing net are the very sinews of virtue. "Mekong Fishermen stay abreast of change," he said. "River men's judgment helps one to make the appropriate decisions at the appropriate moment and diminish the influence of fate."

Father also showed us how to use our condition to fight better than any one child. On the river, in the mornings and at night, before and after the day's work, he would reveal the warlike arts of

China's Shao-lin temple, and the history of the temple monks who had organized combat into five phyla, each based on the rhythms of a distinct animal: the tiger, snake, crane, leopard, and the dragon. When the Shao-lin temple had been destroyed by fire, two of the survivors founded a town called Kowlein Tang. One of them, named Hung, was an ancestor of mine. Hung and Lau, the other remaining monk, had studied the tiger and the crane forms, respectively, and throughout their lives they continued training together. Their dual-animal method of Gung-Fu came to be taught in my family for generations.

Awash in the glow of the setting or rising sun, his feet an inch deep in the Mekong, his hair a disorderly black nimbus, Father would school us, contorting his hands into an approximation of a tiger's claw to scratch or grab an imagined opponent by the face; or, as the crane—moving his arms in circles to block imagined punches, emulating a beak with his fingers—he would teach us to poke out eyes. Gung-Fu accommodates both iron and silk, it yokes the supple with the solid.

Father had us flip in the air together, the better to master rare grace and agility. Being off of the ground was a brazen maneuver, especially for conjoined fighters, and it urged the limits of our attuned movement. Father was wise to educate us in his Gung-Fu, because soon we had to use the fighting arts even at our very young age, the very first time we encountered other children.

One day five boys arrived on the shore wearing triangular straw hats. Chang and I had been playing by ourselves, eight-year-old twins laughing and swinging face-to-face from the lines of bamboo fishing stakes that made a half-submerged corral off the bank of the Mekong. The boys in the hats were some years older.

How odd these separated youngsters were, and how lovely! I had assumed disconnection was for adults only. And now, hanging from the fishing lines, Chang and I looked upon these creatures the way seafarers would their first mermaid.

"They are half formed!" Chang whispered. To me they seemed liberated. This world, I understood then, had been created without thought of me.

These boys ran around making a great noise until the tallest one saw us and stopped. He was too tall for his gray mackinaw and red pants. One by one the others adopted their leader's posture of frozen shock.

"Hello," I sputtered with unease and spittle, my brother and I still dangling together on the fishing line above the river. From the shore, about five feet from us, these boys inspected Chang and me, and we them. Each of their dirty faces was an ugly denunciation of our existence, of their own wretched existences, of the grimy swampland spread around them, even of this bright day because surely it would be followed by two hundred rainy days in a row.

"They are coming closer," Chang whispered, and many sounds crowded into that moment, the lapping of the river, passing birds, and the wheeze my brother's breath made from what was weak in us.

The lead boy had a wide gap between his front teeth that he dammed angrily with his lower lip. Though this was long before I knew about the Bible, I understood from looking at this arrogant child that the meek were placed on this earth to contend with the enemies of God. I wanted to be among the latter group; I wanted to be separated.

The five attacked. They rushed us in unison, advancing into the Mekong in a massed and splashy movement, leaning against one another as they charged. This human wall grabbed us before we could move, and hoisted us free from the fishing line and threw us into the air, where we stayed until the water sneaked up on us. I feared for our life.

The tallest boy, the leader, lifted one of the bamboo stakes up from the riverbed, snapping it loose from the fishing lines. "Hold the monster down," he ordered his playmates, pointing the sharp stake at us. The others seized us by our shoulders and twisted us around; our faces were now two inches deep in the water. My mouth filled with the sour Mekong.

They spun us so our shoulders were submerged now, while each of us had a cheek pointing to the sky. But before we could gasp for breath, the leader stepped forward and began chopping at our band with the sharp stake. He was trying to separate us. With each blow, a swash of water jumped from the river like a flying fish. He drew blood, thrashing Chang and me both.

"Snap!" the boy's face gnarled in rage. But our tie would not break. "Snap!"

After a minute of chopping, the followers released our shoulders and looked to their leader. The chief tormentor started to walk away. We would not split. The leader threw the cane down in disappointment.

It was soon in my hands.

Taking heaving breaths, cracking the cane in two, I passed a half to Chang. If the gang had attacked then, they'd have ruined us, but they hesitated; their mouths were open. We clambered to our feet—I was an inch taller than Chang, but he was strong in his own right. And we stepped forward and swung ferociously, in unison and with Gung-Fu. We likely made a scary sight, a four-armed little fighter holding two sharp poles, each with inches of fresh white bamboo shards for a tip. My brother and I targeted the tall boy, the leader, and the other four scattered, shrieking as they left the one to face the two by himself.

Our swift double-kick to the boy's face and neck threw him backward with a curious serenity. He looked like a bird landing; his arms flailed like a sparrow's wings.

He bounced on the riverbank, sounding a dull *poof* that echoed off the trees. I chuckled. My brother and I had known wordlessly to kick at the same time—we simply did somehow. That is the way it was with us; our natural awareness of one another created a spark that in its white glow smoothed differences, answered questions, brought the world into our rhythm. That did not mean we were of one mind.

We have him now, I said to myself.

My brother nodded.

Our adversary, still on his back, reached next to him and clutched one of the bamboo stakes poking up through the water. The boy leaned on it as he rose, listlessly, to his feet. He wedged the pink mush of his bleeding lip through the gap between his front teeth. And he wrenched the pole free and held it like a sword.

Face-to-face, Chang and I trained our pointed tips in his direction. He charged us. Three would-be swords clattered together.

Chang and I approximated the crane, using placid circling

to fend off the boy's haphazard blows, and the air was filled with staff sounds: *crack, crack*. Even with the smallness of our bendable band, a conjoined child could twist better than any one, and we were enveloping the boy in a cloud of bamboo. Two, four, eight times we struck. We were close to him now, and in the smallest part of an instant, I had a good look at the boy's young face, crumpled in fear. He fell back.

We spun the boy with a blow to his hip and forced him against the bamboo corral; he nearly tripped when one of its stakes caught him in the back of the leg, and his expression asked: *How did I become turned around?*

Another synchronized kick and the boy fell on his back, and got tangled in the fishing lines.

"I'm sorry," the boy lied. "I didn't want to hurt you." His tear ducts were clearly still in working order.

As Chang and I advanced, Father came running toward us. He was frantic and waved his arms. "Stop—stop what you are doing!"

His face was white as a Caucasian's.

Chang and I walked away. We did not look at Father, who had begun to help free the boy from the fishing lines. We did not ask his permission to leave, or look at his face to see if he was shamed by us. Or if he sympathized with the boy. This fight brought no satisfaction, no gush of relief. I did not cry, but I felt the tears collecting behind my eyes. I felt a great affection for Chang. That is not to say I did not still crave separation. From this point on, that is what I wanted more than anything in life, to be separate like the other boys.

Chang and I limped back into the seclusion from which we had come.

I used to say I learned little from my childhood, save fishing and fighting. Looking back, I realize those wonderful days taught me the art of not weeping, regardless the strength of the urge.

When we were seven, Aunt Ping the traveling barber came to tell us King Rama wanted the double-boy dead.

Our family was spending a balmy early evening out by the riverbank. Residue of an afternoon downpour wept off the tree leaves, cicadas chirped in their miniature crescendos, the semidarkness brought about tree-shaped shadows, and a faded moon dangled in the dark blue overhead.

Mother, Chang, and I were washing clothes in the Mekong as a floating theater skimmed by with its actors singing and dashing across a little stage. The birds in the trees provided background harmony, the trees themselves marked a soft tempo as some wind rustled through, while a leaf or two danced off the branches and alighted in rhythm. We all stopped working and swayed to the music, except Father. He was hoping to sell bronze trinkets from his stand. This was his strategy to take in money when he wasn't fishing.

All that morning there had been a fire in one of the Mekong villages a mile from the shore, and the faint smell of far-off smoke still spiced the warm air.

Chang and I stood by the edge of the river, sinking our small bare feet into the soft mud, arguing and laughing and picking at each other's ears, and listening to the fish jump from the river with swishing tails (this always prompted Father to look up from his trinkets and grumble).

Soon a large woman in a short loose green jacket and green pants rowed up to us in a narrow dinghy.

"Is Aunt Ping coming to cut our hair again?" Chang asked.

I repressed a shudder of annoyance; I always noticed things before he did. If ever trouble made Chang react, I had already responded moments earlier, the way a flash of lightning precedes the dull boom that rushes to catch up with its kin.

"Patience," I said, tapping Chang's head bones with my finger. I had to admit a fondness for his smile, knurly as it was and incorporating the whole of his face.

Now past the mossy tree that arched over the river of our floating home, our aunt paddled to a stop by the trough of mud that began a footpath toward the inland village a mile behind our house. Ping was out of breath. Our aunt was a wide woman with warm, tawny skin not handsome enough to leave much impression.

"Nok, Nok," she huffed, "I need to talk to you." She was restless, holding a hand to her face and squeezing her bottom lip, as if that were the only way to keep from blurting out her secret.

Father stepped out from the trinket stand and positioned himself between Mother and her sister. "What is it, Ping?"

"Ti-eye, you are the only Chinese I have ever met who never sees what's in front of him," sighed Ping. She motioned at Chang and me and rolled her eyes.

After the adults sent us off to play by ourselves, we scrambled nose-to-nose along the water's edge, stepping on the raspberry-red snail-egg pods at our feet, side-winding past the tree line and all the way up to the summit of grassy Kang Gee Hill. Even from this high point, little broke the monotonous sweep of the horizon; but in the distance we could make out the two-color current where the clear blue waters of the Mun ran alongside the muddy Mekong. We did not yet see the little girl who was coming toward us.

"Well, here we are," my brother said, and wrapped his arms around me as I brought mine around him. We were stepping on worms with our bare feet.

I had to agree; we were here. His forehead fit against the top of my nose. And then Chang tucked his head in the nook where my neck joined my shoulder.

After taking a breath and thinking of home to avoid seeing the muddy grass and the salt pits hundreds of feet below, I started to roll down the hill with my brother, leaving a double-trail in the mud. Ever since first we had fallen into the river, we loved to roll.

Chang and I bounced along and I could feel his breath in my hair with each laugh. "Yes, yes," he shrieked when we picked up speed. Our spongy, exposed band skimmed against the grassy loam at the underside of each rotation, my brother's little mouth emitted a staccato murmur that sharpened with every bump, and I sensed he wanted to stop.

"No," I managed in a shaky voice. "We'll wait until we reach bottom."

Inevitably, our speed and the hill leveled off. We lay there at its base, disoriented and tired, our dress curled up above our scratched bare backsides. The heat had become oppressive, the sky was already swapping its dark blue for black, and rain began once more to fall.

We spent a minute catching our breath. The back of my head

was burrowed into the earth, while Chang rested his face on my breastbone.

Looking up, I noticed her.

More than halfway down the hill, a young girl with small bones and little muscles and smooth skin stared at my brother and me from under a mass of delicate wet black hair. About our age, she stood some twenty feet away, bent forward and squinting. This was the first little girl we had ever seen, and she was an angelic sight.

The petite creature waited in place, then she turned, ran, and soon she disappeared over the hill, screaming as she went. Her cries seemed to grow louder as she raced farther away.

Chang moved to get up and give chase, and so I followed. We ran after her. Actually, Chang ran while I backpedaled to keep pace. We were surprisingly fast in that posture, and I could tell by the increasing volume of the girl's shrieks, and by Chang's widening smile, that we were closing in on her. The hue and cry of her crash to the ground was heralded by the sound of her stumbling feet, and so I was ready when my brother slowed us to a stop.

My brother smiled down at the girl. "Hello," he said, and bent us toward her. Her face was bloodless, her mouth an uncertain sneer, heartbreaking and thrown open as if in mid-scream. She wept as this double-child, still standing face-to-face, tilted in her direction.

The girl kicked at us wildly, and she scrambled to stand. Then she ran off, and regained her ability to scream at the top of her lungs.

Chang motioned after her a second time, but I put my hand on his shoulder. Again, I did love him at this point—not as a part of myself, as others have said and written, but perhaps as much as I loved myself. The dank smell of the riverbank rippled over us with the warm rain, and yards away, down the far side of the hill, a pair of partially eaten duck carcasses by the chalky lip of the salt pits called to mind human remains.

It was shadowy, nighttime, when we returned alone to the table of trinkets in front of our floating home. Against the green shoreline, far upstream, there were little white boats around which tiny flecks of torchlight lingered like fireflies.

Mother was crying and her hand was over her mouth. Father
hugged her. Our aunt was running a hand through Mother's
hair. Ping had announced the news: the King wanted to kill the
double-child, the bad omen.

The young sovereign, new to the throne, was said to be delicate. Although we didn't know it yet, His Highness had a reputation as a poet. He had translated the Siamese version of *Ramayana*,
and subsequently He wrote the ten-thousand-line-long *Harvests of
Siam,* two stanzas of which remain with me: "For our proud and
mighty nation/It is high time for jubilation/Meeting our jaded
eyes in an altogether special way/This land's double-pride Chang-
Eng was walking about today."

Mother had always been remarkable, not only for the absolute
harmony of her features but also for her measureless tenacity. She
had ostensibly to obey Father's every whim, of course, but she
never failed to seem magnificently fierce while doing so. Now her
wailing broke our hearts.

Mother wouldn't stand for any decree, she said, picking us up
with a grunt. Rain still fell, and as the weather pelted her cheeks,
the dust of the day began to run down the side of her face in
muddy rivulets.

She told Father we'd all escape to China.

In a soothing whisper, he reminded her it would take at least
two days to make the house truly seaworthy and to build a suit-
able oar.

"But it can be done." She employed the tone she thought nec-
essary to use with Father sometimes.

"Yes." His voice carried little self-assurance, and scant certainty.
"It is possible."

I felt that Chang, as did I, sensed that the plan was merely some
complicated adult joke. But I imagined how lovely it might be to
float with Mother across the sea, watching her row through the
night, barefoot, her hair thick and salty with the seawater and tied
in a braid as black as her eyes.

"We might not have two days to waste on fixing the houseboat," Mother said, as if coming out of a dream. At the same
time, a wall of fog had sprung from the river to ramble our way.

Ping said she knew of someone who had a navigable boat for

sale, in a Mekong village not far from where we lived. Her own skiff was too small for the four of us, she said. My brother and I started to cry.

"We will see if we can purchase that boat, then," Mother said, putting us down. "Now."

The shaky wall of fog slowed its approach, grew, hesitated by the trees that hunched over the river, shrank, and retreated downstream.

Father asked: "Leave the Mekong, just like that?" Mother did not answer.

Our escape plans progressed quickly, until adversity, as it tends to do, hit.

Mother, Father, and Ping were in our houseboat gathering belongings. Left alone outside, Chang and I stepped sideways toward a low pontoon bridge. Playing through our tears under the dark sky, we tried to hurdle it together, but my brother was a moment behind in our jump. We came down violently, with our connecting band left straddling one of the posts. We hung there, face-to-face. The pain was terrible. Neither of us could move. Chang's face was red and he could not breathe.

I don't know how old one has to be to understand death. Maybe the young can fathom it, maybe no one ever really can. But on that pontoon bridge, thinking—maybe hoping—that my connecting band had snapped like a bamboo fishing rod, I may have grasped the idea.

At this time, our connector was about two inches long, and Chang loved it. He called it Tzon, or ripe banana, and wailed if ever I mentioned severing it. It was more taut then, and would crackle like an old knee when we inched closer or father apart (no one had any idea the thing would grow with us, and one day allow lateral positioning). I often fidgeted with a stretch of brown leathery skin—a hairy birthmark—midway across it, and also a little brown dot, a charming dinky island that lived, insolently, just free from the shoreline of the larger birthmark. The dot tingled pleasantly when touched.

But now we stretched across that post. Chang was turning blue.

Finally, somehow, I got together the strength to heave myself over toward his side. We fell with a thump to the mud, I on

my back with Chang across my chest. I shook with his spasms.
And the pain continued as if hot lancet blades were raining down
continuously on our ligament. Chang's eyes were closed, and it
looked as if my brother were lying dead beside me. His arm was
snagged around mine, and my legs prickled under the weight of
his. I tried to pull free of him, and, limp and unconscious, Chang
danced with me. I coughed blood.

Rain was coming down hard. My chest was scratched up and
the ligament was a purple welt. Blood escaped from Chang's mouth
onto my shoulder. I was too tired to scream for help, so I closed
my eyes.

I waked as Father carried us to our houseboat. The rain had let
up; I'm not sure how long we'd lain there. "These two obviously
can't go anywhere," Father said, looking almost sanguine as he
brought us across the threshold. Chang was still unconscious, I,
half awake.

Gently, Father placed us on the rug, on our sides. Then he
took Chang's shoulder in his hands and cautiously shook us. The
candle on the tree-butt table emitted black smoke, and gnarled
shadows roamed the cabin. Mosquitoes buzzed by.

Mother pushed him aside as she came to sit by us. "You don't
know what you're doing." Despite the heat, she wasn't sweating.
"We have to fetch the doctor."

They argued. No one knew what to do. Should Father try to
buy a boat and then take a day's journey to see a doctor in
Bangkok? Or should Father alone paddle toward the capital city in
Ping's boat, in hopes of persuading the doctor to come here, to
tend to us before the King's men arrived? Maybe the doctor could
separate us, and the King's men would find no double-baby to
kill. If only Chang would open his eyes.

Father decided it would be best if he alone went to buy the
navigable boat; on his return, we all could sail off together. He
kissed Chang and me on the forehead and left. He hunched his
shoulders to walk out into the rain. He did not look back at us. I
wish I could recall what Father looked like at that moment, but as
with so much from those days, that memory seems now like a

boat off in the distance, a little speck that glints on the horizon before disappearing. I never saw my father again.

Mother paced as our Aunt Ping came to sit with us in our bedstead. Ping was shaky, and perspiring, and she looked at us for a long, long time. "I'm all right," I told her finally, and I meant it. A stench of something like rotten eggs had been streaming in from outside. "We are fine," I said.

And without warning Mother ran over to us and cried. Chang had gained consciousness, finally. "My bean sprout," she said.

He blinked, and stared at Mother with frightened eyes. She kissed his cheek, asked him how he felt. "Our band hurts a little," he said.

Mother and Ping comforted Chang and me. And after Ping had fallen asleep next to us, Mother sang and cried and massaged our band with warm water and palm leaves for hours. "Oh, you are so very brave, Chang," she said, stroking his smooth cheek with her tender touch. "And you too, Eng," she said, still petting my brother. I had exhausted myself saving us from the pontoon bridge, and it was I who had been awake for the bulk of the pain, and I who assured Mother and Ping that we'd survive. Chang awoke and received kisses.

Soon dawn surged and passed, and the morning hours too.

At noontime a woman came running to our door. I didn't know who she was, but she looked as if she could have been one of Mother's relatives. "The King's men are here for the little monster," the woman said, out of breath. She rested her arm on the doorjamb; she was small, and her lovely cheekbones seemed to come straight from Mother—and also her soft black hair and clear deep eyes. "They're in Mekong village and looking for this place," she said.

From there things proceeded quickly.

The knife's blade was wet; Mother and Ping had submersed it in hot water. Chang was crying; I was not. "Please don't," my brother said. I do not think it was only that he thought we'd die from trauma if they tried to separate us. He simply could not imagine the aloneness of a life apart.

Slowly she pierced the ligament with the tip of the blade, drawing out a dab of our blood. Tears streamed down Mother's face, too. I heard a modest crunching as the cutting edge slid into our skin. More blood. We panted reflexively. Our legs in a spasm of self-preservation clung to each other, a tangle at the knees. And we wept, in pain such as no child should ever know.

The knife was inside Chang and me, though only at a pinprick's depth. I tried not to scream but the howl caught behind my gnashed teeth was a fluttering tuna fighting to get free from a trap. It escaped.

"Please," I said. "Do it."

Mother towered above us, lingering, stabbing my brother and me for a moment that seemed to drain time from the air. I believe she would have carved us apart. The attempt almost certainly would have killed us, but that seemed less terrifying than the King's men, who would take our lives for sure. Mother never got the chance to finish the cut.

The King's men stormed into our home, striding in as if invited—two strong soldiers with tremendous arms fit to be thrust out, one at a time, to part a crowd. They wore exaggeratedly flared red silk pantaloons, along with silk vests that barely covered their bare, tublike chests. Both were shaved bald. They stared with green eyes at Chang and me as they swaggered toward us. Mother still held her blade thrust into our band. I could barely keep my eyes open from the shock and pain.

One of the men put his hand on Mother's shoulder. She simply withdrew her knife and stepped aside.

A King of Siam, and by extension anything associated with Him, receives more reverence from His subjects than does any sovereign I've ever met, from the Tsar of Russia to the Queen of England. No one dares ever to pronounce His name or to write it, and no one but His inner clan even knows what it is.

Siamese are told from birth that His body is a womb that purifies His noble human soul before elevating it to godly excellence at the moment of His death. The very fact of kingly status is proof of a thousand previous lifetimes of glory; but all that past glory is insignificant compared to this final mortal position of sovereignty, which itself will be insignificant compared to the holiness awaiting Him upon His final breath. Still, it is treason to ponder the

King's mortality, and consequently no heir is appointed during His lifetime.

So I was not completely surprised that Mother stepped aside for the burly officials of King Rama, though they had come to kill her children.

"This is the poorest house we've ever seen," said the man beside Mother. Through a hole in the ceiling, sunlight reflected off his polished head. Outside, despite the sunshine, the sound of rain enveloped our houseboat.

As imperturbable as these guards strove to appear, they could not keep themselves from gawking at us, the connected twins who were compelled to lie face-to-face. Chang kept his head lolled heavily to one side, and we were still panting because of the knife cut.

Turning to the window, I was startled to find that it wasn't raining at all. Instead, on the lip of the shore, bare-chested drummers were rolling a soothing beat out into the Mekong.

Mother braved back tears. Using one hand to support herself on our tree-butt table, she asked the men if they could just wait until Father returned. With a little mercy, she said, our family could be together for Chang-Eng's last moments.

"We must take it to the King immediately," said one of the sentries, eyeing our bleeding bond with distaste and worry; he could not return to the King with unbonded children. He said, "His Majesty desires a look at the double-monster before killing him. Them."

I felt certain I would die that morning, and if Mother had cut the bond, perhaps I would have died alone. Or perhaps by some miracle, separation would not have killed us, and I could have lived on that way—separate. Now I knew that, whether it would be today or some far-off tomorrow, I would be condemned to die attached to my brother.

Mother now grabbed her chest and cried. "No!" And she wept and she wept. I thought this would be the end of her. Death by weeping. She kissed our hands tearfully, one after the others.

CHAPTER THREE

The Yates Sisters

December 1842
North Carolina

The very day Chang and I first met Sarah and Adelaide Yates of North Carolina, as they stood blushing on the porch of their mother's inn, Wilkesboro had begun construction on a new church, one that might be called splendid for a small town. It was going to be the tallest building for fifteen miles and would boast four stately white Doric columns and a tetra-style portico that would make an impression on any traveler passing through. Plans were being discussed to import real stained-glass windows—from Virginia, if need be. This new and grand house of worship was the brainchild of Wilkesboro's Parson Hodge and Mayor Dungsworth, and the platform on which the latter had gotten elected weeks before. But on the day Chang and I first rode into town, it was nothing more than an ambitious pile of wood across the street from the Yates Inn.

The town itself was mostly without trees, except for the pathetic row of bare Carolina poplars in the town square, their leafless state blamed on some poor topsoil that the former mayor, Brett Martin, had imported—foolishly, and most unpopularly—from the North. At least that was the rumor; the disgraced politician claimed the dirt had been purchased cheaply from neighboring Mount Airy. Regardless—though Mr. Martin's father's father had

been born in Wilkesboro when the village hadn't yet had a name
listed in the Post Office annals—he'd been known ever since the
topsoil disgrace as "that Yankee mayor Brett Martin."

Despite years of performing before festival crowds, Chang and
I were overcome by bashfulness that day when first we stood before the Yates family, milling about their innyard with a throng of
strangers at our back and these two blond daughters some twenty
feet in front of us. These girls worked to dim the caressing light in
their eyes, but it shone against their will in those shy smiles.

Conscious of the crowd, the large innkeeper fixed her eye on
us and cleared her throat. "Now, boys, you say you came here for
a room?" Her big legs were bobbing. I thought she was blushing
as much as her daughters were, though maybe her skin was just
mottled with red blotches.

I glanced at the sisters quickly, but did not answer or move.

"Well," the innkeeper said with the vivacity of most truly large
people. "You'all look like someone hit you with a stob." Mrs.
Yates had a manner I'd encountered in hippodrome promoters—
heartfelt-sounding but not especially human. "Why don't you
come inside and enjoy our inn?" She tapped her fingers on the
base of her chair. "Don't be squirrelly, now, Chinamen."

My brother was apprehensive, too. But the Yateses' rickety
front door was open; we had only to walk through it.

Someone in the crowd at our back muttered, "Ain't nowhere
else in Wilkesboro for the Chinamen to stay, anyhow."

The front door was open; we had only to walk through it, and
that is what we did.

Not a word was spoken as the two sisters ushered us through a
little corridor to our room. Shyly, they walked ahead, and with
my left arm over Chang's shoulder, we followed down the little
hallway, shyly. I was five seven, Chang five six.

The Yates girls were not traditionally pretty. They had unsettled complexions and long faces that fell right into their necks.
But they were American women, modestly broad (they were
broad, no other word for it), and they walked with quick steps
that bore their large figures with a dignified lightness.

We reached the doorway of a lean-to room with flyspecked walls and chipped white paint on the ceiling. The four of us stood very close, looking at one another. "I hope you find it passable, sirs, it's the only choosing in town," the taller one said. "My name is Adelaide." This was the first American woman ever to speak to us so gently.

Chang said: "Is no need to call us 'sirs.' " He wore a smile I had not seen from him before, like a turtle's. And he was sweating on the back of his neck.

Was this flirtation? The shorter of the two girls—Adelaide's sister—was staring at Adelaide with the same look of disbelief I assumed was on my face. For a while we all stood in the doorway of the small bedroom, submitting to the respectful silence, creatures from distant corners of the same world. The Yateses' floor had been worn smooth by naked feet—even now, the sisters were barefoot, with stubby toes.

"All right, then," Adelaide said. "How should we call you, then?"

My brother beamed but could not think of anything to say. He just let his whole face stumble into a smile. He probably did not realize he was fidgeting his ankles against mine.

Finally my brother said, "Call us any way that please you, ma'am."

Had Chang gone insane? It is fine to enjoy a chance grin from an American woman on a porch, but to engage in flirtatious conversation with her would always remain taboo for yellow-skinned conjoined twins such as us. I could not be a part of Chang's co-quetry, I could not even bear to watch. I noticed just how scuffed my black shoes were.

"All right, then," said Adelaide. "Siamese twin." She sniggered, and I smelled from her direction the musk of a woman's perspiration mixed with a fine layer of dust, a subtle and lovely odor.

"I see our reputation has preceded us, miss," I managed, "but we are the Siamese *twins*."

How lovely it would be to shake her hand in greeting, I said to myself, to perceive that softness in a woman's skin that I've read is worth crying for.

But that is impossible, I told myself. Chang is a fool and disappointment will shatter him.

Then, all at once, as jittery as a boxer before his first punch, my brother propelled us. Without consulting me, he bent to the dusty floor and, stirred by the chaos his heart no doubt was, he began to go into a handstand near the doorway. I had no choice but to follow, amazed that anything of mine at that moment—my clumsy hands, my tense shoulders—worked well enough to support half of us. We stood on our palms in front of the girls, who looked at the conjoined twins before them as incredulously as if we had turned into a horse.

"We are the Twins," my brother said, huffing slightly enough that the girls may not have noted the strain. "Most famous in the wide world."

We stood upside down for a minute, then two, my throat thick with embarrassment, until I heard approaching footsteps. A pair of man's feet came to stand beside the sisters'. I don't know how long my brother would have let us linger there like inverted idiots, so I moved us from the handstand, and we jumped to our feet.

"A pleasure to meet you, sir," I said, and Chang smiled a greeting. The man's face was pale and agitated.

"All right, girls," the man said in a severe paternal voice, "you have shown Mr. Chang-Eng to its room."

The sisters turned as if to leave, but the man hustled all four of us into the bedroom, then followed us in and closed the door.

Mr. Yates wore homespun gray woolen and had graying, curly hair. His head was wide at its top, but narrowed sharply as it made its way downward, so—by his chin if not earlier—Mr. Yates's face was skinnier than expected. His mouth was tiny.

After a few moments his gaze became unnerving. The man shook our hands in his cold and damp grip. "Hello, hello." He walked to the bed and sat down solemnly. The four of us—Sarah, Adelaide, and we conjoined—stood waiting for the fifth finally to speak, but Mr. Yates sat on the mattress resting his chin on two fists, nipping his lower lip between his teeth.

He raised his head and lowered it again, burying his face in his hands for a moment. Then he reared up and inhaled a deep gulp of air. "It is an honor to have you two famous people in my inn," he said. A strange grimace crossed his face, half the distance to a smile, yet still a wince. "We charge one dollar three cents a night, and we're a good lodge, you'd have to walk many a mile before you'd find the beat of it, and we have very few rules here"—here he eyed his girls—"but I'm sure you'll be heedful guests, so I won't waste all your time spelling them *quare* things out to you. Please, won't you enjoy our hospitality."

In a single motion Mr. Yates stood, crossed the floor, opened the door, and ushered his daughters out of the room. Before exiting himself, Yates turned to us one last time, expressionless.

He closed the door.

That evening Chang and I sat side by side on the windowsill of our room in the Yates Inn. I read from the Bible and a collection of Shakespeare—and then I thought about unpacking our flutes and asking Chang to practice with me. Chang looked out at the few stragglers who were waiting around and hoping for a glimpse. My brother and I were not giving voice to the thoughts that flitted through our minds.

"Eng," said Chang at length. "What do you think that big woman mean by *husbands*?" His face was calm and inquisitive, but his anxious breath stung my nostrils. "Well," he answered himself, "it could only mean one thing!"

"Are you not forgetting an important detail, Chang?" I poked our band with my forefinger.

Just then, a knock on our door. Somber as the evening sky, the shorter of the two sisters—not Adelaide—let herself into our room. She looked at us, and we at her, and though hers was not an expression to make one smile, Chang smiled at her. Her long face was set not in a *frown*, exactly, but not in something more pleasant than that, either. "My name is Sarah," she said. And, after a while, "It's dinner now." Then she turned and walked out.

Taking that for an invitation, my brother and I crossed the hall to find the Yates family—Mr. and Mrs., the boy Jefferson, and, of course, the two sisters—seated at a little table that took up most of the space of a little dining room, waiting for us.

Mrs. Yates was smirking. "Won't you join us?" If unease had

been legal tender, Chang and I standing there side by side could have paid for this inn three times over. The lady innkeeper did not stop smiling.

On the odd occasions Mrs. Yates made the effort to stand, she measured some five feet two inches high, and seven and a half feet in circumference. Her exact weight was never measured—Wilkesboro had no adequate means of determining the number. Years later, reporters from Raleigh contrived a scale by securing four 150-pound anvils to a swinging platform; when Mrs. Yates tiptoed smilingly onto the scale the anvils flew up and landed to shatter one reporter's feet.

"I am love to join you," said Chang. "Yes, thank you," I added.

On the table rested a meal of okra, rhubarb, baked sweet potatoes, and turkey with red-eye gravy. The girls kept their eyes pointed downward, at the food. The boy Jefferson stared at our connecting band with a stupid look on his face. Mr. Yates, weary, sat sucking on his teeth. Mrs. Yates beamed. (When she died, undertakers could not get her coffin into the house until the door was widened.)

"Say hello to the twins, Jefferson," Mrs. Yates told her son, though she was looking at us as she spoke. The boy's smooth face was without sideburns, and he kept his blond hair wetted flat. "Hello," he said. "It's nice to meet you." His face conveyed about as much emotion as a drunken actor.

We pushed two chairs close together and sat down on them, which left one place setting at the table unfilled. Mrs. Yates pointed to it and said: "We're expecting another guest. He's important, too, and dying to meet you." She made a little clicking sound with her tongue. "But of course you'all are used to attention." She started to giggle, and no one else seemed to know what to say.

A few awkward minutes later, Mayor Dungsworth arrived.

Unlike the Yateses in their cotton and woolen homespun, the large Mr. Dungsworth attired himself in a cutaway wool coat, white silk socks, and high-waisted loose trousers kept tidy with black foot straps. He stood there, taking in my brother and me. "You must be those famous *Siamese* twins, Chang and Eng?" He continued to eye us. "From Siam?" Mayor Dungsworth had a young face despite a whitish beard. "Sure are a *quare* sight."

The lady innkeeper Mrs. Yates raised her eyebrows knowingly. "Twins, this is our mayor, Mayor Dungsworth."

The Mayor's face remained impassive, and as he shook our hands he looked over Chang's shoulder to catch Mr. Yates's eye.

As soon as the Mayor sat, we began to eat—in silence, save for the casual percussion of chewing and slurping.

The Mayor pushed the food aside for a moment, patted his belly, and looked at Mrs. Yates. "I like your grits," he said finally, with the hint of arrogance deemed appropriate when a mayor compliments a townswoman. "Ain't bad at all." ("Ain't bad at all" is the phrase that sums up the attitude of people in northwestern North Carolina. They expect little, and are happy to compliment something that matches their meager expectations.)

Turning to us, Dungsworth said, "Welcome to a North Carolina town." The Mayor had the alert eyes of a youngish man who had aged quickly; he briefly looked at Mr. Yates, then away. And didn't I detect the tiniest smirk creeping onto the Mayor's lips?

That night, after dinner, as Chang and I were in our room readying for sleep, again a knock surprised us, and again the door was opened before we could answer. It was the sisters, still in the dresses they had been wearing all day. Adelaide, the taller one, smiled; her sister did not. They each held a white pillow.

"You only had two," said Adelaide. "Our mother thought you might like another one each."

"Thank you," we said. I steeled our posture until it was rigid as King Rama's justice.

The sisters looked around our room. Sarah eyed the modest book I had on the night table as if it had had a gilded binding. "Sir?" she asked. "Do you'all really read Shakespeare?"

I was so floored by the word "sir" that it took me a moment to answer.

Sarah said, "I'm sorry—I saw the book . . ." She was embarrassed.

"Yes, ma'am," I said. "I mean, true, I am reading Shakespeare, or a collection of his greatest soliloquies, anyway. And, it's quite all right, no need to be sorry, is what I mean to say." On the far side of the window, the clouds were out, the sky gray.

"You won't make fun of us too much, will you?" said Sarah, her voice showing real emotion.

"I, make fun of you?" I was astonished at the thought. Without rouge, Sarah's skin was snow in sunlight.

Meanwhile, Chang was now stealing a smile at Adelaide. And Adelaide was herself holding back a laugh.

Sarah said, "You won't be putting on airs?" In all the wildest dreams I had scarcely allowed myself, no woman ever bothered to speak to me in such a way. The desire of a female was to me a thing inconceivable, like the hand of God, a magnificence that would never touch a man such as I.

"Oh, these Chinamen won't look down at us, Sarah," Adelaide said. "They ain't the trifling type." This one's staccato brazenness was lovely, too, but like her sister she seemed so unreal to me that I might as well have been staring at a Siamese palace on Main Street.

"Yes, of course," I said, trying to regain my composure. Going too far, I continued in an unintentionally chilly voice: "We would not do such a thing."

"Especially," said Chang, "because I not read that Shakespeare myself."

They all laughed, and I recognized that Sarah was standing quite close to me. The perfume from the bosom of a Southern girl's dress—as invigorating as a cup of coffee to a yellow-skinned peasant virgin such as myself—caused my face to flush. I said in a faltering voice: "Never fear, madam. I will never look down our noses at you." I must admit I began to revel in the pleasure of speaking well to women.

"I'm sorry, what did you say?" asked Adelaide.

Chang answered: "He say we never look down our noses at anyone"—here, my twin needed to marshal his courage before continuing—"anyone beautiful as you." And now it was his turn to blush.

"Sorry," Adelaide echoed. "What was that?"

Chang and I turned to one another with raised eyebrows. I was about to repeat my point. And then Adelaide declared, "What did you say? I couldn't hear," and she started to giggle. We were being teased.

"Is it me," Adelaide said with a laugh, "or, may I ask, do you two don't talk to each other much?" I felt a delicious and unfamiliar type of embarrassment.

At that, the sisters excused themselves and went out into the corridor, continuing to whisper to each other as they walked down the hall. I could make out Sarah saying something to Adelaide. "All right," I thought she said, "what do you want me to do?"

What was happening with the Yates sisters?

Later on, after we'd blown out the bug-swirled lamp on the night table and climbed under the sheets and blankets, Chang and I could not sleep. We did not really fit on this bed, which was very narrow—the only width of bed that would have fit in this modest room. Though we huddled close, lying face-to-face, my back hung in the air, aching, unsupported by mattress.

I caught Chang's eye and, without a word, we rolled together in my direction to get up, stood, yawned, grabbed our pillows, and prepared to lie on the floor.

His face an inch from mine as we knelt to the floorboards, Chang was breathing excitedly. "I like the one whose face is not as long," said Chang. "Adelaide."

I narrowed my eyes to see if he was joking.

How ridiculous to discuss which sister each of us "liked" better. Perhaps I "liked" Adelaide better as well, but I found it pointless even to consider. He *liked* her. How preposterous!

Not that I bore women malice—I even secretly surrounded the ideal of romance with much veneration, much tenderness, though I could not fathom what love really meant. The ladies of my fantasies were not of that real, mysterious gender, but a mysterious confederacy flattered by the mellow light of imagination. Chief among them was Mother, encircled at a deferential remove by King Rama's daughter Princess Xenga and heroines from romances I had read.

Chang's hand was next to mine, and he was absentmindedly

tapping his fingers across his half of our band as we pulled the blanket over ourselves.

I knew what he was thinking.

"You are mistaken," I said. "They are just pleasant people. Do not give their friendliness more meaning than it deserves. Brothers such as we cannot 'like' a woman."

"That mother say *husbands*. I see you look at them, too. Why you cannot admit it to yourself?"

I did not realize I was rapping my fist against the floor until after it became unpleasant. "There will never be any marriage offer presented other than as a jest," I said. "Besides, it's *men* who make offers. Not women's corpulent mothers." Had he forgotten the path our life had taken? Going from exhibit hall to exhibit hall in a cage, a thousand nights spent smiling while such words as "horrible" and "disgusting" made their way above the din and into our ears? To add hope to the unremitting current of derision, gawking, and distaste that was our equilibrium could only bring heartache. Not to mention, would any judge look kindly on bigamy—what else would they call it?—and would we not be liable to arrest? "Stop being ridiculous," I said. But hadn't the girls lingered with us at the door?

"I am looking for this my whole life," Chang said.

"What woman would expose the secret of her bridal bed—a single bed, as ours would have to be?"

He shook his head. "Does not matter." Then his confidence gave way to doubt that crept across his face.

"And what *about* their mother, then?" I asked. "Do you not find it strange, that this woman seems to want her daughters to—"

"You don't care?" he spat out. "If you no care, you take Sarah."

"I should do what?" I found Adelaide the more interesting of the two. "How absurd even to discuss it!" I laughed.

Soon Chang fell asleep. He always drowsed off first, and often snored.

The next afternoon, after some encouragement from Mrs. Yates, the girls took us for a walk. Jefferson, whose silent presence likely would have gone unnoticed had he not been gawking at our

band the entire time, came along as chaperone. I could not fathom
any of it—*What was happening with the Yates sisters?*—but I said
nothing as we started off.

Just a few acres behind the inn, a green forest began, verdant
and comparable in leafiness to the great Russian woods of Tsarskoe
Selo that we had visited while touring St. Petersburg four years
earlier; Wilkesboro was beautiful once you dug deep enough. Quiet,
a relief from the bustle, speculation, and the embarrassment of big
cities, she squatted beneath the Blue Ridge Mountains, which
looked down at the dusty, shed-pocked scene with an air of disappointment. Peaceful desolation surrounded the town, with un-
plowed land giving way—slowly at first, in rust-colored streams—to
the modest banks of the Yadkin River. Deer lived in the nooks of
the mountains, foxes in the fields outside of town, and the green
of the trees was more rich than the murky swampland colors of
the Mekong.

Within a half hour we were winding through the foothills of
the mountains, above the river. It was a bright blue noontime.
The sisters (and Jefferson) hurried ahead to show us the sights to
be had, and we followed a natural path tufted with poplars and
bordered by the summits of gray rocks, guarded by bending wild-
flowers, scented by sun-warmed forest, and I could not deny I was
happy.

Once we had reached a high bluff, the girls bid us to turn
around, and—beyond the dust-brown blemish of Wilkesboro
proper on the landscape below—we beheld the purple distance as
it rolled out as spacious as desire. Ten counties could be seen. I felt
I had never been so high, so near to the sky.

Do not forget your place, I said to myself. Do not mistake
feminine friendliness for insanity.

Look at your brother, I told myself. That fool grins like someone's tickling his insides.

Before long it was almost sunset, and the five of us were winding
our way downward, chatting, laughing—*What was happening?*—
walking a bit more, and then we rounded a clearing and I saw
something that told me to stay in Wilkesboro for the rest of my life.
The Yadkin River. Shrouded in haze with thin curls of white mist
hovering over the water like strands of goat's hair, and even on a day

of such sunshine, this place upon which we had wandered seemed to adopt the coloring of another country. Gray shadow washed out the drab banks, overhanging trees arched up from the shoals to dip their wet green leaves into the mucky green water, cicadas chirped, and, in places, the modest scale of the Yadkin gave way to somewhat wider shores. My memory fled America for home.

"Brother," Chang said, his eyes and mouth wide as I'd seen them as he walked us to the bank of the river. Big speckled trout swam in number through the blue-green water, waiting for Chang and me to resume our fishermen's instincts.

"Yes, yes, yes," I said, "I know." The fragrance of marsh brought my exaltation to a pitch.

Chang's breath bristled the hairs on my neck as he laughed. I patted the back of my twin's head.

The Yates sisters began to laugh, too—though their giggles were more lighthearted than the heavy, deep laughter my brother and I let out at the sight of this Mekong in miniature. With the pink light of sundown on the water, the Yadkin started to blush. The delicate turn of light was girlish and sensitive.

My brother looked at Adelaide as an orphan would a home-cooked meal, and she focused her charm on him, her face long and thin and her complexion like cream left too long in the sun, with her puckered nose being the perfect center of her coy grin. Feeling his hand on my shoulder—he did not even notice me—I felt a chilling weight of anxiety and bitterness. Adelaide avoided my stare. I did not know what to do. I turned to Sarah, who had the light in her hair and in her eyes. She caught me looking at her, and with a shy smile—maybe her first since our arrival—she tucked her chin into her shoulder. But she didn't take her eyes from mine.

What, if anything, separated these girls from those who laughed as they walked past our cage, arm in arm with their suitors, enjoying the "merriment of the fair"? And what pleasure had Chang and I ever experienced, what knowledge had we of the way people live their lives, people who are not beholden to each other, to a cage, to another nation, to the next gasping crowd?

Yet here we were, climbing mountains with the Yates girls and looking at a world so colorful it was like the view at the far end of a chromatoscope. We had arrived at a nearly identical match of our homeland—except this was a land free of pontoons, a place with blessedly solid ground only yards back from the banks of the river. I stood overlooking that scene, standing beside women who had not mocked us yet, at least not maliciously.

And why hadn't they?

Two weeks passed, with Chang convincing me to stay in Wilkesboro at least another week. This is when my brother changed—to all appearances, overnight. Christmas was fast approaching, and Chang had tacked on a new personality: that of Adelaide's suitor. He no longer craved the attention of the stage, going so far as to say he did not even want to tour until he had secured Adelaide's heart. "Everyone entitled to hope," Chang would sigh from time to time, paraphrasing, he claimed, advice from Mother (though *I* never heard her say it). "Everyone."

As for me, I was unruffled. I did not concern myself with my heart. What had it to say to me after all these years? Instead, I decided to prove Chang wrong. Let my brother make vulnerable his hopes and "court" Adelaide. I decided to be nice to Sarah, and I was sure she would not respond. I did not think to do any earnest courting, nor even to become fond of her. I wanted only to prove my hypothesis. And as for my brother and Adelaide, I had no doubt; she would disappoint him this week, she would disappoint him next week, then we would get on with our lives. That is how it had to be.

One Sunday afternoon my brother and I went for a walk into town looking for a place to eat our dinner. We crossed dusty Union Square alone, walking in step, side by side, with Chang waving at the few finger-pointing, whispering townsfolk who strolled the streets as dusk approached.

We came toward a tap house that read EATING HERE in big letters above its two swinging doors. But we did not make it to the tavern. "Mr. Chang! Mr. Eng!" we heard a familiar womanly voice calling from behind.

We turned to see Adelaide and Sarah Yates, in matching, spotless white dresses with blue sashes, kicking up dust as they rushed toward us. They ran past a red-headed man who was walking slowly in our direction. Beside the girls scurried Jefferson, his hand atop his straw hat to prevent it from falling off.

"Hello, girls," we said as they reached us. My brother looked at me, grinned, and made a haughty face. Meanwhile, the girls stood there, catching their breath. At length, they caught it—and we all smiled at each other. Except for Sarah, who neither frowned nor smiled.

Jefferson spoke to us in a soft voice. "My mother was thinking maybe you'all should want to eat with us again."

"Wouldn't you want to? Oh, please do," said Adelaide.

Sarah clamped her sister's enthusiasm with a severe glance. Adelaide bit her lip. "Mother would like it," Sarah said, fighting out of the drab of her shyness.

Soon the red-headed man had stopped about ten yards away to stare at us. He had big sideburns and a series of dueling scars across his cheek that looked like the weave of a fishing net. He held a toothpick in his fingers.

"What are you doing there, girls?" he yelled, as if chastising two pets. His shirt was too small for his chest.

Sarah blushed, glanced around, and began smiling uneasily. Adelaide, though turning pale, assumed an air of false confidence. "Nothing, Will—just talking to the twins here," she said, rocking back and forth on her feet.

The man stood stock-still, staring at the girls, at my brother and me, then at Jefferson. "Son," the man said to the boy, "you're only half grown, and these girls are going to need a *pair* of chaperones. That makes you one and a half men short."

I gave the man the eye. He guided his toothpick to and fro between his fingers.

Adelaide turned her back on the man. "Please," she whispered to Chang and me. "Come with us to our mother's supper."

Sarah, also in a whisper, added: "Careful not to give Will dirty looks." She could not even muster the determination to glance at the man. "*Especially* not Will."

My brother and I, however, continued to stare; Will threw the toothpick to the ground deliberately. His wrists were thick as baby tree stumps. Sweat ran down my spine. I was not afraid.

Almost to himself, the man grumbled: "Ain't you caused enough trouble in this town, Sarah Yates?" His expression was bleak. "Ain't you got enough shame on you'all?"

Sarah shriveled. Adelaide, meanwhile, whispered to Chang and me: "He's just our cousin, forget him." At that, Jefferson cocked his head, as if he'd been left out of some family secret. Adelaide kept her brother quiet with a stern look.

"Trouble?" Chang asked. "Shame?"

"Will didn't mean nothing except as a joke," Adelaide said under her breath. Sarah closed her eyes tight.

"Did you," the man snarled and pointed at the girls, having no idea of the damage we could do to him, "come to Wilkesboro for this?" His face was full of disgust. "You're not going to get that."

We could have struck then, but I wanted to remain dignified. I did say, "Look here."

As the girls led us away, I kept an eye on the so-called cousin. He returned my glare all the way down Main Street.

That night we did not talk much at dinner. Mr. Yates failed to join us. Afterward we sat on the porch, where each of us felt that there was little to say. All except for Chang, that is.

"My brother wants to marry," Chang announced, a smile across his face. "If any young lady would have him, we hold wedding today."

At his words my heart quaked all through its cords and vines.

I could think of no response. The sun was setting at a snail's pace before my eyes—the sky as pink as the now embarrassed cheeks of the Yates women before us on the porch—and it reached below the horizon before I managed, "The reason I don't marry, as Chang knows, is because I am stuck fast to him." I pointed to our ligament.

Chang said, "And I don't marry because am stuck to him," and hinted at me. "It is sad?"

"If anyone, it is *he* who wants to marry, not I," said I, swallowing, sweating, shamed.

"He putting it off on me," Chang said. "He marry at the drop of a hat. He drop it himself, if that help."

"Is there no chance for you to be separated?" said Mrs. Yates. The flap of skin beneath her chin seemed to quiver in my direction as she posed her question, as if her skin, too, were curious.

"We have decided," I said angrily, "that we would rather simply look upon pretty girls, chastely, than take up residence in a graveyard." I cleared my throat. "So the answer is no, we cannot be separated."

Chang, laughing: "He drop the hat himself if ugliest girl in town would say yes."

"What a pity," Mrs. Yates smiled. "You two men who obviously love womenfolk so much would have liked not to marry, and what a loss, because some two lucky young ladies somewhere are denied the good husbands you would have been."

Sarah looked at her mother with anger that seemed to rival my own. Adelaide was fixed on Chang, however, and for the first time I believed him; there was affection in Adelaide's eyes for my brother.

I leaned forward, indicating to Chang that I wanted to stand. "We are going to retire," I said, my breathing labored.

"Tomorrow I come downstairs," Chang said, rising and motioning with his head toward me. "I leave *him* behind."

As soon as Chang and I crossed the doorway of our bedroom, I asked my brother, "Have you lost your senses?" I swiveled, and we were face-to-face.

I wanted to chop him in his throat. We hadn't fought since we were children, but that didn't stop my hand from assuming the position of the leopard. His vulnerable Adam's apple looked particularly inviting. The fibber, he knew it was *I* who longed more than anything for that dream of disconnection, while he was the one who thought of marriage!

We stood just inside the door, half in shadow. "Sorry," he said. His wide, toothy smile showed me just how much he had meant his apology.

Later that night, before resigning to the inn's damp floor, Chang said: "I want to see her."

"What?" I said.

He made for the door and soon I found myself peering down the hallway cheek-to-cheek with my twin, trying to get a look into the far-off living room at the Yates family's evening activities.

The inn was mostly quiet except for the occasional creaking sound of an old hostel coming to terms with its frailty—or the occasional owl's inarticulate lament out in a nearby tree. The living room door was fully opened. Mr. Yates had fallen asleep in his armchair, his *Wilkes County Spectator* unfolded across his lap. The two daughters and their mother mutely admonished each other to keep quiet. Sarah bent low under the lamplight, sewing needlepoint. Mrs. Yates fanned herself. Adelaide seemed to rebuke her sister with her glance. Every once in a while, the father would shake himself out of sleep, and—as if trying to convince his family he had been awake the whole time—he'd clear his throat and nod, pretending to be part of the conversation that he assumed they were having. Then he would fall back asleep and the girls would smile knowingly at each other.

This comic drama of household repose seemed lovely, and I felt a pang for family as I never had before. Chang and I closed the door quickly, so as not to be noticed.

Two days later was Christmas Day.

When we woke that morning, it was to an inn as fresh and trim as a Yuletide pie; green holiday garlands decorated the banister to the stairway, and balsam fir wreaths and an evergreen Christmas tree decorated with pinecones, rose hips, and a red velvet bow made the anteroom pretty.

Wiping the sleep from our eyes, we entered the room and saw Mrs. Yates sitting in her special double-wide chair, beside the big Christmas tree. Adelaide was perched on a step stool, fixing the star atop the tree.

"Our guests is up!" Mrs. Yates called out. "Merry Christmas, sirs," she smiled.

Adelaide turned round on the stool to face us, holding her lace-trimmed yellow hat on her head with two fingertips to keep it from falling. And at the same time the soft sounds of far-off feminine laughter dribbled from the porch through the walls and open windows of the inn—it must have been Sarah's; I hadn't known her to be capable of it.

Adelaide stepped down off her stool, then bent to the base of the tree to pick something up; she approached us.

"Merry Christmas," she said, and held out a box wrapped in red decorating paper.

"W-we shouldn't—" I said, but Chang had already begun opening it. The box contained an embroidered needlepoint depicting my brother and me, and was crowned with the title "The Siamees Twins."

"This is lovely," I said, feeling derelict about not having gotten the Yateses a gift. "We haven't—" Then Chang stepped on my foot, silencing me. His yellow-gray eyes were daydreamy.

"We had not known you giving gifts in *morning*," he interrupted. "Wait, please." Then he began to run down the corridor. I had to collect myself just to keep up with him.

"Where are we going?" I wheezed.

When we reached our room, Chang turned toward our crate of personal possessions and bent us down beside it. He came away with a small jade dragon figurine that we had gotten from King Rama's palace many years before.

"What are you doing?" I asked. He did not answer. I loved that dragon.

Before I could say anything, we were speeding back to the girls in the other room. Sarah had come to stand next to her sister and mother. She too wore a hat, tilted high on her brow.

Trotting us to our hosts, Chang handed the dragon over to Adelaide. "Merry Christmas, Yates family, and Happy News Year," he said. "Sorry," he said, still out of breath. "It not wrapped." He swallowed. "For you—a present. From Siam. My country. Our country."

I stood dumbfounded.

The girls bent down to show it to their mother, and in the commotion of women's voices that followed I whispered to my brother: "This was *ours*."

Chang blinked at me as if I had spoken French or another tongue he knew nothing of.

Looking at the dragon in her daughter's fingers, Mrs. Yates said, "That for sure is quite handsome, boys."

"It obviously, obviously is, don't you think, Mother?" Adelaide gushed, although she wasn't looking at Mrs. Yates; she was peering at my brother, but not for too long, because every few seconds she would look down shyly, her long eyelashes lashing.

Until Wilkesboro, I knew what travel had in store for me: conjoined fraternity, beds too narrow for our double structure and few surprises. But now my brother knew love, that unfathomable word I would never even have said aloud, like the untellable name of Rama or God Himself. I understood nothing of what lay ahead of us—of me—and a panic gripped my heart.

Everyone around me was talking, and I missed whatever witticism it was that my brother had used to charm Adelaide, but she was laughing, saying, "Oh, Mr. Chang." She listened to everything he said and her eyes were bluer than the water of the Mekong had ever been.

I found myself noticing the gentle landscape of Sarah's face, which was troubled only by wrinkles she caused by chewing on her lip, and by the crow's-feet just starting to dawn around her eyes. Sarah's was a homely beauty, filled with a melancholy grace living in those places up and down her long frame where it was most obvious the end of her youth was drawing near: the doughy skin at the base of her neck, the slight hunch of her shoulders.

She caught me looking, and she turned her head quickly, offering a view only of her cheek, leaving most of her face concealed by her hat.

Could I be falling in love with her? I asked myself. Is this what tender sentiment feels like?

Perhaps you are, I told myself. It could be so.

This discovery, which would have reduced me to fear and despondency just minutes before, seemed now little more than a whimsical circumstance that somehow did not concern me directly. Rather than a flood of passion, love came to me as a curious and distant spectacle. But I shared my brother's resolve to marry like ordinary human beings, to experience the matrimonial joy less deserving men relished.

Now I had only to win her over, as Chang had done with her sister.

I smiled. Sarah once again looked away; I could no longer enjoy a glimpse of her face. Meanwhile, my brother's Adelaide, still looking down, gathered some stray locks of her hair that were sticking out from under her bonnet and tucked them lovelily behind her ear while she stared at my twin.

Later that morning, we had Christmas breakfast with the entire Yates family. The girls had prepared sweet potato butter and spicy apple preserve, which we enjoyed on sesame crackers, along with biscuits and hominy grits topped by sorghum molasses. And we sat across from Jefferson and Mrs. Yates. Mr. Yates perched himself between his two daughters, a strict planet with pull over this pair of dutiful female moons.

The dining room, however humble, was the heart of Mr. Yates's palace, and I read in his shining disdainful eyes an attitude of superiority toward all. All except Mrs. Yates, that is—the one member of the family who seemed not to bow.

The girls made a deliberate effort to avoid mentioning that gifts had been exchanged between us. In fact, when my brother started to bring up the needlepoint we had received, Adelaide and Mrs. Yates shot him a silencing glance simultaneously.

And Mr. Yates was inclined not to hear about it. With his wild hair and his abiding frown, he avoided looking at my brother and me, to escape seeing us look at his daughters.

Mr. Yates opened a prayer pamphlet: *The First Wilkesboro Presbyterian Church Christmas Meal Guidebook.* He bowed his head and began to read, if not well, then earnestly: " 'Jesus set foot into the world like each one of us, dependent upon others, vulnerable to hunger and thirst, to cold and to mischance. "The Word became flesh and lived among us," says the Gospel of John—the Word was a child, newborn and dependent.' " He paused for emotional efficacy. " 'Through the birth of Our Lord Jesus, God revealed Himself, and He was in the end dependent upon human beings. This God loved us so, that He elevated frail, flawed humans to the level of accomplice in our own salvation. We were, and remain, partners with the Lord.' " He cleared his throat. " 'Christmas is a story about those who believe taking possession of that which we most want, nay, that which we most need: love—rich, powerful, unreserved love.' "

Across the table, Sarah's face coaxed a soft-heartedness from ·me. I wanted to run my finger across the skin of her cheek. Yes, I found God for the first time that day. I had never known a woman's skin. Sarah's skin looked softer than Chang's, or mine.

" 'More than anything, the Christmas story enumerates the lengths to which God so loved us—*loves* us—that he asks us to be partners in cherishing the world and each other.' Amen." Mr. Yates put the book down.

The food was delicious, and no one spoke at first. But then Mrs. Yates said, "Would you be kind enough to tell us what Europe is like?" Though she was addressing Chang and me, she was throwing her husband a smile of the furtive kind.

Mr. Yates turned to my brother and me. His disdainful eyes had seized authority over his face. Chang did not notice. "You never see the Continent?" my brother asked Mrs. Yates.

"Europe? Oh, how I wish I could."

"Paris," Chang said. "So beautiful—" He was enjoying the role. "A lady."

"What about New York?" asked Adelaide, wide-eyed.

Mr. Yates stared at Chang staring at Adelaide. The father's face had lost its color.

"If Paris am a lady," Chang grinned, "New York . . . not a lady."

Mr. Yates moaned, though neither Chang nor Adelaide heard it, and the way he then glared at his wife, then at me, put a knob in my stomach.

Adelaide went on, "Well, *I* always wanted to see—"

"That city New York," spat Mr. Yates, "is filled with Yankees. That's the other world from here," he said. "New York is foreigners to us." And Mr. Yates continued staring and staring and did not look away, and the humdrum rhythm of life ceased. My brother's swallow seemed the loudest sound in history. Finally Yates said, "Maybe you would not understand that."

New York, that unforgiving galaxy of firelight, concrete, and shadow; Boston and Philadelphia and Washington, twinkling like matchsticks in feeble mimicry of New York's glow; the dripping gray beast that was London, making sport of all visitors; St. Petersburg, with its vast squares, cold palaces, and ruthless stillness; Paris, city of clever talkers and derisive beauty—these places, none of them were ever anything but foreign to me. And I to them. "Perhaps you are right, sir," I answered.

And then, in a series of quick, jerky movements—straightening her dress over twitching knees, resting her long and slender ringless hands on her chair for support—Sarah stood. She narrowed her eyes at her sister. Adelaide seemed so happy, and Sarah forced a smile herself (the feigned naturalness of that smile was the saddest thing about her face) and, turning toward my brother and me, careful not to look at us directly, she said: "I'm sorry, but do you'all ever just find this time of year a grim business? It absolutely upsets the stomach. I'm sorry, but I see this time of year as a grim business." Absentmindedly, she ran a finger down her chin, gently tracing its lovely length.

Mrs. Yates said: "Sarah apologizes for wanting to retire so early, but she gets awful tired on the holidays, don't you, dear—with your stomach? Jefferson, which Easter was it when she—"

"That's all right, Sarah," said Mr. Yates to his daughter, softly. "You go to sleep now."

She left the room without excusing herself. Mr. Yates stared into his hand, scratching his palm. "Well, I think the rest of us may be fixing to retire, too," he said in a defeated voice, and he stood up.

"I was wondering . . ." Yates continued, speaking softly to conceal the ragged edge on his words. "Wondering how long you boys plan to linger at our inn—no hurry, I just need to know for guests' list arrangements and details of that nature, that manner. And I'm sure you wouldn't have liked to stay too long in our home."

He took a breath. "It has been a pleasure having you two stay here, it has—showing you the way we live here in Wilkes County. But the idea is that we're Southern white folk, my family is Scots-Irish. She is"—he gave a slight nod to his wife, and then to Adelaide—"and *she* is, too; so's Jeff here, and my other one also is, and the idea is we've produced all the things that make up a culture—not *us*, but our kind, I mean—like art and science and the cotton gin . . ." His gruff voice trailed off, though it didn't seem he'd lost the thread of his thought.

He scrutinized his shoes and, as if he'd found the hour displayed down there, muttered that it was time for him to excuse himself. He began to walk toward the door. Jefferson followed behind.

Mrs. Yates did not stir; rather she sat more deeply in her chair. "It sure has been a pleasure to have you two famous, good Siamese brothers here at our inn!" she cried, turning to Adelaide, who was herself beginning to rise to join her father.

Mrs. Yates's squint implored Adelaide to stay seated, and the daughter did so, easing back into her reclining position.

The mother said, "They remind me of a—of a breath of fresh air. Ain't that so, Adelaide? A breath of fresh air, these two Siamese boys from Siam?"

Mr. Yates turned around and saw that his wife and daughter were still sitting. "Adelaide!" he said. "Aren't you going to help your mother out of her chair?"

"We are going to continue sitting here a time," Mrs. Yates shot at him.

The husband and wife looked at each other like strangers. The sound of Sarah closing a door upstairs echoed. Then Mrs. Yates gave her husband a smirk. "We are going to continue sitting here a time, Addie and me."

Mr. Yates coarsely said good night. When he and Jefferson left, Chang continued talking about Europe.

Soon Mrs. Yates had fallen asleep, however, an event that was greeted with giggles from Adelaide and Chang. Adelaide's smile, her voice, even her physical movement became more grand and energetic by degrees; she was like a balloon inflating, and as she grew the world shrank around her, until she dominated the room. She got up and sat next to us, by my brother's side. She was in her way the loveliest woman I had seen.

"I know what you're thinking," she said, removing a lock of

hair from her face and looking sidelong at Chang. It was as if I had ceased to be.

Certainly, she could not at all want for Chang to kiss her, in spite of her eyes, her slowly approaching shoulder, and the way she licked her lips shyly. Passion and platonic friendliness, often contrary siblings, frequently wear similar faces to hide the great distance between them, I thought.

Adelaide was breathing deep and quick. "I *know* what you are thinking, Chang," she said again.

"W-what I thinking?"

I looked away. But I could feel my brother's heart pounding through my own chest. His hand was sweaty and fidgeted upon the crook between my neck and shoulder.

Adelaide took his hand.

This bold gesture was a shock, of course. She is being friendly, I thought. No more than that. What was it like for my brother to be touched by her?

The creaking wood of the house in the silence of the evening, the gloomy candlelight in the room, the ice-studded black of the sky outside, all these could not have been more passionless, I told myself.

"Well," my brother put up a brave facade, began to smile, "Chang am thinking: 'Why this girl not married already?' "

His idea of a compliment fell short of its intended result; she recoiled and pulled her hand from his.

"I ain't married and I am here talking with you." She introduced frost to her tone. "There ain't nothing more to say." After a second, though, she exhaled her venom, and as she breathed in, she brought the smile back to her lips. "Besides," she murmured quietly, "that obviously ain't *really* what you was thinking."

Chang looked over at Mrs. Yates to make sure the old woman was still asleep. Then, after whistling to manufacture some courage, he said, "I love you," the words creeping out on little tiptoes like children stealing from their beds at night.

"*What* did you say?" asked Adelaide. She had heard him, without a doubt, though he had spoken delicately. She had heard. As for me, the only thing I could think was that my ears had lost their credibility.

"Adelaide, I love you." His mouth was a big grinning loop.

"Do you?" Hers was less a smile than a glower. "Swear it."

"I love you."

"*Swear* it, Chinaman."

"I swear. On, on—" He looked around the room frantically, then out the window. "On the moon up in sky." He smiled.

"Oh, don't you go swearing love by the stupid old moon, boy; that thing disappears every morning."

Chang frowned. He asked, "You— . . . love me?"

Adelaide looked deeply into my brother's eyes. *What was happening?* With one hand she haphazardly pulled on the top of her dress to situate her chest more comfortably under her clothing. She inched her bottom into a more cozy position.

"Yes," she answered. "I suppose I might." She was fetching, even to me.

Meanwhile, Chang had let loose a sound that was almost a tweet, and he laughed. At that moment they embraced, they did embrace. I was not blind to my own deep bitter want. I needed to say something, even some silly incongruous thing, but I did not—only because words failed me. I felt more isolated in that room with my twin and Adelaide and Mrs. Yates than I thought possible.

Adelaide hugged Chang and pulled him toward her; it yanked me nearly off of my seat. Chang and I were now halfway toward face-to-face, a position that stretched our band painfully. I cleared my throat to remind my brother of my company, and I slid us back to our original position. I tried to imagine myself in Chang's place and could not fathom it.

My twin sighed as he disengaged from their hug. Then he touched our band and continued to ignore me as he told Adelaide: "But with me . . . special problems—"

They both turned to look at me before continuing.

"But," she said, turning back to face him only, "if a love is obviously strong, even Fort Sumter can't hold that love out. You do love me, don't you?"

"Yes."

"What is the first thing about me that would make you stop loving me?"

My brother swallowed, then waited a long time before saying: "How long you stay in love with me?"

She screwed up her lips and thought hard for a moment. Adelaide smiled. "You really this charming all the time?"

"You always be this beautiful—never go fat?" Chang said.

"How many children do you want to have?" she asked.

Chang blurted out, "What is thing you loving least of me?"

I wanted to hear the answer to this one as well. Before she could answer, he went on.

"I like when you smiling," he said.

It is a bright, happy smile, I said to myself.

"What is it that you love about me, boy, exactly?" I thought I noticed a slight quiver at her upper lip.

"You make neat house?" he asked her, and they laughed.

"You love me?" he could barely get the words out over his guffawing.

At this she stopped giggling, which, in turn, stopped him from laughing, too.

She had lost her smile by the time she said: "Do you want me to tell you the truth always, about *every*thing? Because I will. If you want." She was serious as a preacher. She took his hands and squeezed them. "In what ways does this here woman come up short of your hopes already?"

Then she said: "Boy, that's a heap of questions." She resumed her habit of grinning slightly at the end of her remarks, an ironic and playful gesture. "Can you think of any others?"

"No," Chang said.

"I can." She looked ardently into my brother's eyes. Her face grew its fiercest, and her thirty-two years showed. "One more you ain't asked yet."

He understood, and began to kneel down, but I did not follow. He was left somewhat hanging between the couch and the floor, and he turned to me with a look of entreaty (*now* he remembered my presence). I went to the floor with him; in a second, we both were kneeling.

Adelaide, cheeks afire, tears rambling down the long terrain of her face, leaned over and shook her mother. "Wake up, Mama, wake up!"

"Huh?" said Mrs. Yates, and she shook her head. Ripples crossed her cheeks, wave upon fleshy wave over her face.

Chang turned to Adelaide. "Will you marry me?" he asked.

CHAPTER FOUR

King Rama III

January 1819
Siam

Gongs and flute players filled the air outside our houseboat with their high-pitched noise from the decks of the King's large junk. This lumbering ship that would bear us to Bangkok and the King and away from the safety of our family had a gilded prow and a hull of painted tigers. Chang and I were seven years old, and being taken to the King's court to die.

Nothing moved around us. No other boats floated on the river, no birds flew in the air. The only people who stood on the shore to see us off were Mother and her sisters, all of whom were crying. I tried to wave at them before the men brought us inside.

I was scared. I couldn't look any of the strangers in the eye, not the flutists standing erect in the official royal musician stance (legs approximating the profile of a longbow, with the hind shank straight, the front one bent), not the five sad-faced and scabby-knuckled rowers aligned along the length of the boat, and certainly not the stoic bald guards carrying us by our arms from our home. We were thrown in a dark little room with a little porthole. The chamber was seven of our footsteps by five of our footsteps. The door was locked. Our ligament was not yet long enough to allow anything but face-to-face positioning.

Without a blanket on the damp wood floor, the breeze from

the porthole swept up our homemade frock to bite our backsides. The bruises on our ligament pounded and the knife cut burned as if on fire. My brother and I decided to try to sleep. Neither of us voiced the questions we so desperately wanted to ask. A shriek of compressed air from flutes outside signaled a rude bon voyage. For an unknown fate we were leaving our home against our will. I closed my eyes and wept.

My imagination conjured a horrific King's court: skeletons wrestling fat women, worms shooting from women's noses, young children connected as Chang and I were—four, five of them bound by one ligament. After some time I was shaken from this nightmare. Chang's head was down, and he was convulsing. I thought he had again fallen into unconscious seizures. I called his name, and he looked up quickly, with wide eyes. He had been awake the whole time.

Chang jerked his hand out from between his legs. One of his despicable habits had begun.

A bolt of something, half embarrassment and half disgust, shot through me.

"If you must play with something, let's play with In." Appalled, I handed him Mother's rag doll. I had been clutching it since they took us away.

"I do not want to play with In." Chang made a face and began discreetly to slide his hands toward his groin, as if I would not notice. We were nearly nose-to-nose, and he was discreet at least two more times. His eyes were less than bright, the way they would get years later whenever he took drink.

The doll, In, meanwhile, was purple and unwrinkled, with dark stones for eyes. He was worn soft except around the seams. His left arm was bigger than his right. We pulled In back and forth, and before I knew what had happened, the fabric ripped. We had pulled him apart; I now held the head, Chang the body. We looked at it, and at each other. There was nothing to say on the subject. My brother and I considered the torn little man and then started crying. Water rasped against the hull. I actually had this thought: I am too young to die.

Our crying must have been loud, because the man who had taken us from our home opened the door to our cell and entered.

He was breathing heavily, wiping his sweaty bald head with his palm. The man's scalp was shaded where hair follicles had refused to clear fully away.

"Please," he said. "The King will not want to see you crying. I am to bring you to the King once we reach land."

We stared at him, and he at us. I stared especially at his round bowl of a stomach. He looked down at his chest.

"What are you looking at?" he asked. The room was dark except for a stripe of sunlight that stretched from the open door to the wall. "I am a sergeant, you know." He came in and half shut the door.

"We were not looking at anything," I said through tears.

He brought his palms together in front of his mouth, with his fingers straight and touching, the way an American child would pray, and he bounced his hands against his chin. "Are you trying to be clever?" he asked.

"No," we cried.

He screwed up his eyes. He was fixed on our ligament.

"Does it hurt?" he asked.

We couldn't answer. Tears were falling.

He asked: "May I touch it?" Leading with his outstretched hand, he had already started his descent. He petted us on our stabbed and sore band and shook his head.

"Is the King going to kill us?" More teardrops.

"Are we going to see Mother?" asked Chang.

"I cannot presume to speculate what His Majesty is going to do."

"We didn't do anything wrong," Chang said.

No response.

The guard breathed through his nose and squinted. Then he asked if we'd like to join him on deck.

Chang and I stood on the prow, wiping tears from our cheeks as the ship skimmed the shore. We neared our capital. Smells and sounds led the eye toward a herd of buffalo tramping at the edge of a rice field. At their side, two young elephants loped close across a clearing, mocking the hurry and relative insignificance of their smaller cohorts.

Our boat wound between rows of wide brown houseboats and little floating shops (whose patrons came out to wave at this royal craft), and overtook a fleet of huge Chinese junks just arrived from Peking.

Before long we entered Bangkok, the Village of the Wild Plums.

Golden temple spires formed an artificial horizon above mean huts and wooden hovels on piles and floating pontoons. Here and there the sea lanes were decorated with fruit trees, palms, and a sacred fig tree just like the one under which Buddha, we learned later, had found enlightenment. We followed the river through the center of the city, and on each side there were strings of houseboats, every boat bigger and more sturdy than Father's, each supported by a raft of bamboo and moored to the muddy shore.

This was all otherworldly to us. We continued crying for our mother.

The estuary of the river was mobbed with small, darting boats. The capital had no roads, just the Mekong and its canals, which were thick with bare-chested ancient vendors hawking their wares by screaming into the air, and with bald monks in orange cloth vestments. Further on, thousands of these holy men prayed from their knees on a small hill that had been furrowed into a series of steps and was now overlaid in orange cloth. Above and behind this tiered hill was a large golden Buddha sitting inside a painted-metal replica of a purple flower.

Our junk was met by a rowboat carrying another two representatives of the King. This rowboat guided us to a special landing by the wall that enclosed the palace. The wall seemed miles long, and was whitewashed and battlemented and tucked in from the shore. Multicolored spires and flat golden roofs peered out from within, and granite lions placed every few feet along the top of the enclosure roared at the world from behind red glass eyes.

It was all new to us, the spires, the outfitted hillside, even the elephants, but none of it impressed me; I was sick with longing and panic, and our ligament hurt. The gloom and dread in an abducted child exceeds the majesty even of the fiercest granite lion. Chang looked especially frail; his eyes kept closing.

He didn't respond when I whispered his name.

"Get off the boat," we were told. On the shore, the ground was so solid below my feet I felt I'd landed on another planet.

As we walked, Chang looked even worse than Father had when he'd agreed to sail away with us to China.

Four palace officials brought us under an old gum tree and threw a scratchy gray blanket over our heads. I heard a mewling voice: "His Majesty wants no one to see it before His Highness does."

The royal officials led us with the blanket over our heads through some kind of entrance, then around a short dank passageway.

They removed the cloak. It was dark. We could make out a pair of tall, roundish shadows in front of us—guards, likely, frightening as the unattached monsters I dreamt about. Even face-to-face, with our double width Chang and I spanned the unlit corridor—our backs scraped the chalky walls—and all at once, in sorrow and desperation, we formed the confused idea to get away. Thrashing around, skinning our knuckles, we started to run.

The men thwarted us before we'd taken two steps, grabbing us by the arms and squeezing.

The passageway opened into a wide, well-lit chamber. The scene looked as if it had been the site of some devastating fire. The granite floor was scorched black, with swatches of anomalous pinks and oranges. I thought I heard the whine of a cat from somewhere.

My foot suddenly felt cold. Chang and I were ankle deep in one of the puddles that lay throughout the room. Looking up, I saw the King himself standing in the chamber; I did not know at the time that He was royalty, but His three-foot-tall golden crown made it obvious He held an exalted position.

The King was staring at us in blinking disbelief, surrounded by a clan of green-robed subordinates. His Highness' was a fat stomach of a face, swollen and expressionless, with a small belly-button-shaped mouth. Despite the presence of King Rama, or perhaps because of it, we raced back toward the exit, running straight into the arms of the four men who had escorted us.

One of the bald attendants managed to grasp our shredded frock from behind, and another to take our arms in his hands.

Another man from the pack stepped toward us, and he unsheathed a saber with a curved blade. He advanced, blade first. At this, the King turned on his heels and withdrew from the chamber; His robed party followed. Chang and I were left alone with these three men—two holding us still, the other drawing near with his sword.

One of the men who clutched us said, "Approach from the middle attitude."

"No," said the man with the sword. He wore a long braid from the top of his stubbly head.

The swordsman stood before us with his sword high—the upper attitude, perhaps.

"This is it, brother." Chang closed his eyes but could not stop his tears.

No, I said to myself. Not yet.

One of the men behind us pressed my hand against my coccyx, and the guard squeezed harder. I tried to backpedal and failed.

The swordsman's open grin showed an incomplete row of brown teeth—(I thought briefly of Mother)—and he took the weapon in his left hand and made a flicking movement with his right.

I felt a sharp pain in my head, then came darkness.

We awakened to find ourselves in a dark cell, a smaller adjunct to the chamber proper, accessible through a trapdoor, which I did not learn about until later. The cell had no windows, no blankets or berth on which to sleep. What it did have was a locked door, and a persistent drip from the low ceiling. In the corner, a crouching cat meowed. I tried to sleep but could not. Chang, however, seemed to have no problem dozing off. After studying the cell for the fourth time, I turned to my sleeping twin and was disturbed by the changes of the last twenty-four hours on his face.

"Chang," I said. "Brother."

He looked even worse than he had when we arrived off the boat; his pallor was ashen, his eyes in a constant fight to open.

In fear, and also to comfort my brother, I began reciting something Father used to say when he was teaching us to fish. "Mekong Fishermen stay abreast of change." The adult words comforted me, even if I barely understood them. "Rivermen's judgment helps one to make the appropriate decision at the appropriate moment and diminish the influence of fate. Mekong Fishermen stay abreast of change."

"Shh," Chang said. He fell into and out of sleep. Our band was still sore.

After some time I managed to summon over the limping cat from the corner. I named the cat In. In the cat had only three legs. It staggered around, making water and defecating. The cell began to reek.

My brother opened his eyes and looked at me with a face unfocused from sleep. "When do you think we can leave here, brother?"

"How am I to know?" I chafed, rubbing at our inflamed band. "Tell me, Chang, how am I to know?"

Before I finished my question, Chang was back in slumber, his face contorted in pain. I petted his sweating head. I brushed a hair from his eye, which opened with a start.

"When do you think we can leave here, brother?" he asked, blinking.

After some time, an hour perhaps, I heard rattling from beyond the trapdoor. I nudged Chang awake. "Please don't," he said, and fell back asleep.

We will not leave here, I thought, until the King kills us.

Just then a bald guard entered our cell and closed the door as if he was entering his own bedroom. Wrapped in a black raiment, the man carried a tub of water and appeared horrified. Draped over his shoulder were what seemed to be articles of clothing. The man had to hunch his shoulders to fit under the ceiling, and as he did so I saw he was our familiar bald captor, round and tense-looking.

"There are things you must know," he said.

Chang waked. He asked the man, "What is your name?"

The man scratched at the back of his bald head. "Nao," he said finally.

"We are Chang and Eng," my brother said.

Nao stared at us, gathering the mettle to look into our eyes for the first time. "Always bow in the King's presence," he said. "And you are never to look Him in the eye, never to address Him directly, but, rather, to talk to the royal 'listener.' "

Nao put the tub of water down.

He gave us the least tender bath in the history of Siam, with warm water and leaves, and handed us black wool pants and green silk jackets modified to accommodate our ligament. The special hole in the jacket was a little constricting, but I was happy to have new garments; these were our first pants. Soon two other men came to brush our hair, which grew down to our chins. Three more arrived to supervise.

"Is the King going to kill us?"

We were given confusing, barked instructions in court protocol, told how often and when to make obeisance to the Throne, and how deeply; how to look away when addressed by the King; and how to sing the Song of Siam, which we most likely would have to recite on command.

"When is the King going to kill us?"

They had us practice genuflecting. We stretched our bond, painfully trying to synchronize our bows and touch our heads to the damp ground. We could not bow, but only wrangle into a position more lying than kneeling, with our faces chin-to-chin.

We were told it was time to meet the King of Siam.

I whispered Father's words to Chang and to myself: *"Judgment helps one to make the appropriate decision at the appropriate moment and diminish the influence of fate."* We were seven years old.

Chang and I were led through a trapdoor to the larger chamber, where more attendants who would not look at us stood waiting. These wore towering golden hats and held their swords before them in a two-handed grip. They were shirtless.

The men marched us outside, into the sunlight and beyond the retaining wall, to a twelve-oared barge on the banks of the river. The boat was piloted by sailors dressed in vermilion silk. We stood at the bow as the boat traced the perimeter of the outer wall of the palace, docking at a gate with metal spikes.

"Get on that," one of the bare-chested attendants said, and pointed to a large hammock fastened to four poles. A pair of giants carried the poles. And comely, large-breasted women wrapped in blue scarves handed us plates of prawns and told us to eat before we entered the royal gardens.

Never before had we reclined on a hammock, smelling a king's flowers that stood tall with the rising sun. My brother and I were very young, and not only according to the calendar; never had I imagined accepting prawns from the delicate hand of a winsome housegirl. We were carried over the spangled gardens and through a second gate patrolled by sentinels in puffed red costume, then along a sandy avenue flanked on either side by rows of black cannons, and past a grassland where wardens led a dozen gray elephants around in a circle. We finally came to the National Assembly Hall, and the third and final gate. "Get down from the hammock!" a guard roared.

Three buildings met us on the other side: the steepled royal palace, its golden roof shining in the sun; the Temple of the Emerald Buddha, a tableau of stepped red and green spires and richly gilded roofs; and the sprawling Hall of Justice, where the King was concluding a legal case.

We entered the Great Hall expecting to die.

The main parlor was a towering dome, the ceiling and walls a deep red embellished with friezes of gold. The floor was a dark gray marble that shone like river water in the morning. A string of two-story columns linked by engraved balconies spanned the rear wall, and stuffed lions snarling in an everlasting silent roar stood nobly atop ivory pedestals in each corner. There were more people crowded into this assembly than we had seen in all our lives.

The seat of state itself was raised high off the ground by a series of semicircular carpeted steps. This perch of honor was decorated in jade dragons and golden plates, and surrounded by red curtains, drapery that measured from the floor to just below the etched ceiling, where it met a canopy of twenty golden parasols hanging overhead like gilded cloud cover.

On the throne in His shapeless golden gown and red sash squatted chubby King Rama. At the King's side sat a little girl in a red silk cape, a princess probably, nervous and diminutive in the plush red seat of a petite throne, her coal-black hair in a loose train over her shoulder.

With His slightly jutting chin and a smile like a lackadaisical sneer, He spoke with the drowsy deliberation common to the cultivated classes of all societies. He was about twenty years old, and He was adjudicating: a legal hearing was in progress. The litigant, a short farmer, bowed his forehead to the floor when the judgment did not fall his way. The man was ushered away, crying.

The multitude of courtiers in attendance stared at my brother and me. This was our first encounter with the concentrated gaze of a crowd; the assembly, and all its eyes.

Don't look my way, I thought. Look at Chang.

My brother and I now had our turn before the Great Lord. At this point many strange courtiers strode up to us and whispered in our ears.

"Do not talk to the almighty King directly."

"Do not look at the almighty King directly."

"Nor at the almighty King's wives, either."

"The eternal sovereign has two thousand of them, you know."

"If the all-powerful monarch calls you 'Illustrious Dog,' meet the term with the utmost thankfulness."

"It means He likes you." (The King of Siam addresses His young prince as "Acclaimed Rat," so great is the divide between a sovereign and the most exalted of His court.)

We dropped to the floor before King Rama. Though we were forbidden to look at Him, I peeked. His Highness had no neck, and His hair was a slick black tidal wave surging high above His brow. His eyes were the color of sable.

A few steps below His Majesty's feet sat a serious-looking man with a smoothly brushed mustache, a rattan cane across his lap. This man was the King's listener. He would be the conduit for all conversation with the King.

As the King and this other man scrutinized my brother and me, a skinny boy of about twelve came running up to us quickly and jerking like someone in spastic paralysis. He whispered: "Repeat after me." Then he recited the proper way to address the King.

"Exalted Lord!" Chang and I said, parroting the whispering boy. "Sovereign of manifold princes! Let the Lord of Lives tread upon me, a slave who here grovels, and stomp upon this slave's spine! I am prepared to receive the dust of golden feet upon the summit of my simple head!" Meanwhile, the swarm of courtiers had gathered behind us, forming a half circle. I was afraid that if I closed my eyes, someone would chop off my head when I wasn't looking.

"So this is the challenge Nature has for me?" The King puckered His royal face as if He were referring to some noxious smell. Then, furrowing His brow, He said: "Scurrilous dog, ask them if they have eaten rice yet today." His voice an instrument that employed petulance and thunder and surprising tenderness.

The man sitting by the Royal Feet repeated His Highness's question. We replied that we hadn't had any yet. (Siamese make use of the rice question the same way the English initiate conversation with "It is a nice day today, isn't it?" Each greeting reveals a different national obsession.)

"Sniveling toad," the King addressed His conduit, "remind this double-child that We will gouge out its eyes if it continues to look at Us directly."

The King's listener jumped to his feet and ran over to us. He was much taller than I had thought. He struck us a blow across our backs with his rattan cane. We gasped for breath; Chang's skin turned white like a phantom's. The listener went back to sit at the King's feet.

"Tell His Highness we are sorry," I said. "Yes, please do," said Chang.

The marble was cold against my cheek. The Princess, too, made sure not to look at her father, instead watching the tapping of her own slippered feet.

"The twin has apologized, Your Highness." The conduit looked straight ahead as he spoke to the monarch sitting over his shoulder.

The King continued: "Confounded idiot, ask the twin: Has the Lord of Deaths sent it here to presage the destruction of our kingdom?"

"I don't think so," I said, the pain from the rattan blow subsiding. It had begun to seem less me with my head against the marble and more some other hapless boy in my situation. Chang smelled of sweat and days away from home.

"Can you be sure?" The King's voice now depended wholly on intimidation, all tenderness stripped away. The Princess sat at his side noiseless as a flower, and she dropped her eyes when they met mine, and she cringed.

The man at the King's feet said: "Can you be—"

"Siam can speak to this creature Ourself!" the King roared. Then He narrowed His raging eyes and allowed them to take on a penetrating shine. I did not look away.

"Do you deserve to live, double-child?" His tone was calm now, as if He were asking whether we thought it might rain.

"I think so," Chang said in a quiet voice.

"Analyze the process expressed in the words 'I think,'" the King sniggered. "You'll find a series of assertions that are difficult to prove. For example, that it is I who think, that there is a self, that this self knows what thinking is." His face twisted in a smile that held little joy. "You don't understand," He said, smoothing His sash. He was going to decapitate us, I knew it.

If this is the end, I thought, how will Chang handle our death?

"Get up," King Rama said. "Get up, get up, get up."

Chang and I hopped to our feet, making a squeaking noise on the marble.

"We are curious to see how you travel about." He let no sentiment into His voice or face now. "We question whether you will be fit to make your life a substantial contribution to Our kingdom." As He spoke, Chang and I began to tread a small circle before the throne.

"Cooperative syncopation," He murmured quietly. "We did not realize you were so graceful." Then, recovering the rumble in His voice, "Faster, now!"

We informed King Rama's manservant we could walk on our hands.

"But this is a surprise," the King said, laughing. "*Can* you now?"

"We'd like to show you."

"Come, come. We're watching." The King gave a knowing glance to the aristocrats standing behind us. Then came the shuffling sound of everyone looking away, careful not to meet His gaze.

The man at the King's feet said: "Come, come, Double-Boy." The King stamped His foot at the man. His royal face had reddened. The hall was in absolute silence. The conduit looked sadly at his own lap.

"We're *watching*," the King said finally.

And there, in that glorious court, Chang and I gave our first performance.

We bent toward the double-reflection rising at us from below the surface of the burnished marble, patting our four outstretched hands on the cold floor. Then we hoisted ourselves in the air with a flick of our hips and trudged ahead, like a pair of wheels connected by a small axle.

I swear the King clapped. He smiled, too. And so did the Princess. My brother and I had the ability to walk on four hands as assuredly as other children ran on two feet. Despite my exhaustion and loneliness, I enjoyed the pride I was feeling. Answering the applause, we began a string of backflips, cutting quick, precise rings in the air as we tumbled over and over. The Gung-Fu moves were painful, as our band was still compromised by Mother's knife, but we managed a four-point landing, and stretched our arms in the air, hoping to have averted our own murder.

King Rama cocked His head, grinned amiably, and threw up His hand. I felt a new-sprung twinge in my heart! The grin and the lissome gesture belonged to a frieze on the royal ceiling! The breeding and charm in the smile and movement were, at what could have been an awkward moment, pacifying. He knew how to captivate. He was kingly.

"Lovely," He said. "What a *lovely* creature." He nodded in the direction of someone at our backs; gongs crashed. All the courtiers in the Great Hall dropped to the floor in genuflection. People whooped and whistled; Chang and I held our ears. "I want to go to sleep," I told my brother, who could not hear me for the clamor. My excitement had soured into exhaustion. I could feel tears gathering behind my eyes. Attendants would not stop banging the deafening gongs. My brother hugged me. We were going to live.

The King stood and lifted His arms and nodded His head up and down as a number of manservants ran to close the curtains that had been concealed in back of the throne. In a moment King Rama and the little princess were gone behind the concealments.

The room grew quiet. The people of the court got to their feet and shuffled toward us. The King was done having His look; it was their turn. They crowded my brother and me. We had never been near so many people.

I thought I saw a familiar face, far from us, and deep in the crowd: Dr. Lau, the Bangkok surgeon who had come to our houseboat with plans of separation. He smiled, and laughed, and pantomimed the act of sawing through our bond. Before I could point him out to my brother, however, too many faces had swarmed around Chang and me, and the doctor was out of sight.

Another man, a fat aristocrat dressed in gold, stepped between us and everyone else. He crooked his neck and threw up a hand— the same gesture his monarch had used minutes before. The movement had little charm in this man's care: a royal gesture muffled by the charmlessness of an ignoble body.

And now a multitude of fingers touched our band from all sides.

"Does it hurt?" someone asked.

I began to cry.

"Does it *hurt*?"

"Not usually."

"Do you share thoughts?"

We said nothing.

"Do you share thoughts?"

We said we did not know.

"Do you relieve yourselves at the same time?"

My brother and I did not understand.

"The *toilet*. Do you use the toilet together?"

"Often we both have to go at the same time."

Another odd person stood back from the crowd, watching the excitement of the throng as much as he was watching us. His skin looked strange—it was white as rice—and his thinning hair was brown. He wore a black three-piece Western-style suit, and was the first Occidental I had ever seen. I thought him a freak.

Then a man who smelled of sweat and linseed oil took Chang and me by the hands and escorted us from the hall. This was the end of my childhood.

★   ★   ★

Though he kept many women, strictly speaking Rama had thirty-five wives. The other nineteen hundred or so were concubines. We were taken to see these women immediately after we had our audience with the King.

The linseed-oil man led us through a great mirrored hallway. The hallway was narrow and curled around itself like a nautilus shell. I had trouble keeping my eyes open as we walked. I had not slept since they had taken us from our fishing boat days before.

"Why are you crying?" the man asked me, mistaking my closed eyes for tearful ones. "You are going to meet wives of our King."

"My brother is tired," Chang explained. Then, as if by suggestion, the tears ran down my cheeks.

"Aren't *you* tired, then?" the man asked Chang.

"Not particularly." He shrugged. "When can we see Mother?"

We entered a large boudoir with blue silk curtains hanging in drooping arches from the high ceilings. There were no windows to deliver light into the room. Our guide disappeared as soon as he deposited us at the Queens' doorway.

Chang and I were alone with the women. These royal wives were young—ranging from twelve to twenty, I'd guess—and they lounged across lavish beds (we had never seen proper beds before), wearing golden gowns similar to the one the King had worn, except that their garments lacked Rama's royal sash. There were thirty-five of them.

"Look, a half of it is crying," one said. She could not have been much older than we were, and her arms were as thin as handrails.

The King's exquisite maidens bade us step before each bed and answer questions. I can't remember what most of them asked, harmless interrogation of the womanish sort, but I've never forgotten what happened as we came to the last of the circuit of beds that traced a line around the chamber.

The final queen was the oldest, the most regal and beautiful. She seemed uninterested in the spectacle we were making. Each of the others had sat up as we approached, but this one simply rested flat on her back with her nose pointed at the ceiling. She didn't even move her head; she just slid her eyes and looked at us with sidelong glances.

"I want to know if you have one sex or two." She was a woman of snarl and excess. "Strip yourselves naked."

She pushed herself up by her hands and sat.

We hesitated. In the years since, I have suffered heartbreak, been spat upon, been attacked, I have felt alone and anomalous in the gunmetal-gray cities of the West, but nothing has pained me more than the humiliation of that moment.

"You will do as I say or die," the Queen murmured. "I want to see." She pulled on the lobe of her ear absentmindedly, and she showed her nasty smile. *"Now."*

I might wish to blame my submission on lack of sleep, or on the timidity of youth, but the fact is that we stripped without enough protest. As an adult I would debase myself for no queen, no king.

My brother and I stood before her, bared. The other women, roused from their beds, flocked to us. We were twin bodies, complete and distinct and face-to-face, with two parts for every one found on an ordinary birth. Plus a single connecting ligament.

The Queen who had made us undress nodded at us for a while. The others watched her. Chang and I stood there, the cold air goose-pimpling our skin. The silk ribbons hanging overhead remained absolutely still.

Then the Queen pursed her lips tightly. Her cheeks distended and she began to heave like some drunkard holding back her own sick. The laugh burst forth, however, and proved contagious. The royal bedchamber began to vibrate with chortling feminine laughter.

Until I'd arrived in Wilkesboro, this was what I knew of intimacy with women.

Soon Chang and I found ourselves back in our unlit little cell, prisoners, with In, the three-legged cat. I could not sleep. I do not know how long it was that I lay awake, because we could not tell the changing of days or weeks in that cold and damp place. The cell smelled awful from In's waste.

Chang would not stop chattering when he was awake, asking the same questions repeatedly. "Do you think we can leave here, brother?" or "Will Mother come?" I did not answer him aloud.

No, I said to myself. And, no.

Every once in a while, Nao entered our cell, carrying a tray of rice and a waste-bucket. Chang and I grew accustomed to using the bucket; if only we could have trained In to follow suit.

Time passed slow as lava in that dank chamber. Our band started to heal.

"Not much in the bucket this morning, boys," said our bald attendant on one of the occasions when he came to remove our foul matter.

"How do you know that one day we won't attack you, Nao?" Chang asked. We were still wearing the very pants and jacket the servant had given us to wear before the King. They were now blackened and stinking. "How do you know we won't take *you* hostage?"

Despite the dark, I could make out a smile creasing the skin of the attendant's immense face. His scalp was smooth. The full curves of his body beneath the robe seemed to float in the shadow illuminated here and there by light stealing through cracks around the door. "You don't have it in you," he said.

Many days must have gone by, and still I could not sleep. And that's when I learned that the high spirits of malice may masquerade as kindness.

One morning or night, as Chang slept and I did not, the uncomfortable heat and my lack of rest made me sluggish and I did not immediately detect His arrival. But there He was when I raised my eyes. Did He really kneel His silk-covered knee to the damp floor and look at us? Yes, I did not dream it. I saw King Rama's soft, brown sandaled feet and heard and smelled Him. In our cell. His perfumes put me in mind of ginger and of a forest grander than any I'd seen.

I sat up in shock, pulling Chang with me. I looked around, but He had left. Or vanished. I begged in the direction of the slamming door. I needed Mother, and though I was a young boy who had never wanted to before, I felt so dirty that I wished desperately to bathe. Our clothes were completely in tatters now.

Maybe He had come to kill us.

I told myself to remain calm. *Mekong Fishermen stay abreast of*

*change. Make the appropriate decision at the appropriate moment and di-
minish the influence of fate. . . .*

Even sitting up, Chang slept. I hated him then, for sleeping, for
merely existing. If I could somehow have managed to separate
from him before all this, I would be with Mother now, I thought.

Time, as it will, kept passing. My brother persuaded me to play
games of our own invention, though I was beginning to tremble
with fatigue. We practiced handstands, flips, somersaults. It was
probably this exercise, and the fact that we were growing older
and bigger, that caused our coupling band to change. The ligament was lengthening, gradually, and after a few weeks or months
we were able to walk almost side by side, with our arms around
one another's shoulders like two men posing for a portrait.

I sometimes felt the concrete floor was about to open, and at
our feet an abyss bristling with—what? Sharp-toothed monsters
or downy pillows? The high spirits of malice, or kindness? The
marsh of the Mekong had always felt too cold and grimy between
dry toes. I tried to comfort myself with facts like that, when lying
awake.

Each time Nao cleared away our bucket, he gave Chang and
me instruction; we learned the *Hymn of Ramkhamhaeng*. We were
shown a map and told where Cochin China was. We practiced
genuflecting. And then Nao would leave, Chang would sleep, and
I would talk to the cat.

Once, while Chang snored, In limped into a bit of its own
stool, and then over to me. Gathering a little energy, I picked up
the smelly creature and for the first time told it, "I love you." It
looked at me, perplexed. I glanced at the space where its fourth
leg should have been, then down at the pools where the feline water was freshest, and where some cat dung had been steaming recently, and I said: "I have come to love you in spite of—"

"Do *I* want to be loved *in spite of*?" said the cat in a voice deep
and polished. "Does anyone?"

I dropped the animal, having reached a new class of despair. I
needed sleep.

Nao brought new green silk jackets and black wool pants to
our cell and had us put them on.

After that, accompanied by a noisy display of handlers, Rama himself began visiting our chamber just to talk with us. He came in silken slippers and flowing robes that two subjects at His back held off the ground. After entering, He would smile at us, say hello, ask how we felt, and leave. At first, we were still not allowed to look at Him, but over time we began to address Him directly.

Trying to re-create the atmosphere of this period for his readers, a journalist of questionable ethics invented for the German weekly *Der Uberfallen* a fanciful—and inaccurate—entry in an imaginary diary of a King Raima (*sic*) of Siam:

> I met again with my friends the Monster again. Are they two?
> As this is not a question that can be answered in more than
> two ways by a sensible man, let a King, who enjoys immunity
> from any culpability whatsoever, pass it over, and merely state
> that Chang and Ang are not indistinguishable. Ang is quiet
> and sullen; little Chang is a delight.

This passage—this *fictional* passage—makes me prickly with anger from head to foot. The writer answered his own question: we have always been our own men. Besides, the editor of *Der Uberfallen* committed a typographical blunder—I was Rama's *Freude* (delight).

This went on for a fortnight, then two, then time enough to make one lose count. I told King Rama I had trouble sleeping, and before I knew it we had pillows, and blankets to lay beneath our bodies and to warm us. Despite that He had us in captivity and was most likely still pondering whether to kill us—He seemed sometimes to be speaking with us as a way to debate the merits of keeping us alive—I was young enough to see His Majesty as friendly. He seemed enthralled by our band and stared at it throughout His visits.

Soon He moved us to new quarters. While small and austere, this house—slave quarters, by design—was lavish compared to our old cell, and also compared to our floating home on the Mekong. We had a bed, a real bed, and sheets, and it was aboveground and looked out onto the palace. Unfortunately, Nao would not let us take In with us.

I was able to sleep well there, but I always awoke saddened and wondering if I'd ever see beyond the palace walls. I sometimes imagined my parents calling to me in an exotic language I couldn't understand.

Even as my brother and I were awarded more considerate treatment, and despite the companionship of His Highness and the glimpse of palatial beauty that went with it, I more than ever longed for that grimy stretch of Mekong from our infancy, for the wind-riddled houseboat, and especially for Mother and her kind hand. In this cottage by the edge of the palace, taking long flights of imagination along the route of the junks to the bright brown mud and half-sunken posts of home, I was made less miserable by the august presence of the King, and by his royal handlers who brought prawns, rice, and white tuna. For some reason I look back with fondness on that time with the King. I suppose memory has at least two faces, and capricious ones at that.

By the time His Highness arrived for one of His visits, following drumbeats and a footpath of rose petals, the sun had already set. An hour earlier, His servants would have come to clean our cottage before slipping away silently.

Chang and I performed handstands for His Highness while He either questioned us or simply talked of the troubles only a leader knows. His men stood still and in a line, each with his gloved hands clasped behind his back (except for the one carrying the bushel of rose petals, and the other who held the food).

Once, instead of the robe of dragging red silk that covered the floor all around Him, He wore a costume styled more precisely than anything we'd seen Him wear before. The pants, long and straight, were cut snugly according to His royal form, and they were pleated. His strange shoes were made of shiny leather (a material new to us). His jacket, double-breasted, partially hid a gray vest with buttons. This was Western tailoring. The King wore this suit when He had us meet the Emperor of China, and again when He sent us home.

"You must join Us on a journey, Double-Boy," He said the first time He visited us dressed in this way.

"Where, Your Great Highness?" I addressed Him directly.

The King said Chang and I were to follow Him to the Temple

of the Reclining Buddha, where we'd meet the Emperor of Cochin China. "It will be a great honor for you."

"That sounds exciting," a frothy Chang said, tilting his head as though someone were stroking his neck. "Your Highness." Did he not miss Mother anymore? He did not talk about her at all.

Our King and His retinue left us alone in our quarters. Soon another group of servants entered carrying two sets of clothes: black silk robes made majestic by yellow tassels, and two pairs of red pants decorated with stitched flames. One of the servants, a sloe-eyed boy of about twelve, shrank away from us, repulsed. My twin stared at him with bitter half-closed eyes; I touched Chang's hand and brought it to rest on our ligament. We were laughing before the servant boys finished putting on our clothes.

Outside the door, two other of Rama's men arrived with a short gray baby elephant. The gray sky showed no sun, nor any clouds. Misty rain fell.

The first man, who was very short, and whose face was small and round and red like a fleshy pomegranate, sat on top of the elephant. The other man, very large and smelling of dried dirt, took my brother and me by the waist, walked directly behind the beast, and hoisted us onto its back, or tried to; each time the man lifted us high enough, Chang and I would reach for the elephant, but would fail to gain any purchase as the animal swatted its tail or rocked forward.

"Hold still," grumbled the man who clutched us. The other man, sitting atop the elephant laughed quietly. On the tenth try we were successfully placed on the creature's posterior.

Chang and I held onto the red-faced man as he drove the elephant across the royal grounds. He turned to us over his shoulder and sniggered: "That will be a difficult scene to describe."

Chang gave me a look that said he thought it had been fun.

"It took him ten times to lift you up here," the man said, turning farther around to get a better look at us. He took a second, and smiled nastily. "You will probably be able to survive in this world as long as you have servants to keep hoisting you up every day of your life."

When we got to the end of the royal grounds we were put in a little skiff. At our back, the elephant driver rowed; another man stood next to us on the prow—this was Nao, whom we hadn't seen for quite some time.

"Nao, it's me, Chang and Eng," said my brother.

"Yes," he said. He was squinting because of the misty rain, and standing, elegantly, with one foot on a pile of rope. Years later, when first I saw the famous painting of George Washington crossing the Delaware, I was reminded of Nao.

As our boat made its way up the river, people began to amass on the shore, rushing to the fold of marsh where the Mekong meets the land; they were pointing. Other boats started pulling up close to ours. Everybody started shouting.

"What is happening?" asked Chang.

"Rumors of your arrival have circulated," said Nao. "The paired-omen."

From behind us, I heard the voice of the other man, the red-faced rower. "These folk should have seen that thing try and get on an elephant," he snorted.

Meanwhile, the people were approaching.

They grew in number, and in loudness as they gathered, and under the clamor of gasps and ringing voices they soon made up a crowd.

Strange boats closed in and bumped ours, more and more of them. And from these circling skiffs, people leaned over, stretching across our prow—to reach for our connecting band. The screams in the air were loud now. More boats; more grabbing hands. Through a shifting curtain of jostling bodies, I caught glimpses of fishermen on the shore jumping up and down; between groping hands and lunging arms I could see men running out from the banks—the muscles and veins in their necks tense and bulging—as they yelled: "Look! Look!"

The swarm of boats now rammed our skiff and bounced off. Chang and I held Nao for support. Faces surrounded us, enough of them to conceal the sky, and it was like shaking in a hive, or in a swarm of wide eyes and desperate mouths and twitching noses. Even as we squeezed closer to Nao, a hundred hands grabbed me;

the heat of as many bodies terrorized me; a dense tangle of smells tainted the hundred individual breaths exhaled on me in unison.

"Back, back!" Nao was yelling as he slashed the mob at its heads, faces, and shoulders with his rattan stick. "Back!"

The crowd began eventually to recoil. Nao yelled over his shoulder to our rower (who was almost overwhelmed): "Move us, you half-a-dolt!"

We inched through the mad crowd. And we made our way downstream, past the mob and toward the Temple of the Reclining Buddha. And the sun started to shine.

The open-air Temple of the Reclining Buddha was composed of a circle of perhaps five thousand tall wooden poles that, as they rose, widened into arches like flower stems spreading into leaves. Every eighth pole held a watch station that, in turn, held a sentry. Inside, flower beds were arranged in huge concentric rings on the ground, at the center of which sat a Golden Buddha. The many flower petals swayed, though there was little breeze. As the flowers moved they sent red, blue, and yellow dust that had been spots of color on their stalks into the air. The muddy brown earth around the beds was, like the statue, stained by the delicate powder. Chang and I were brought to the center ring, in front of the Buddha, to stand in Rama's party.

This royal party was arranged in three columns. A step in front of us stood King Rama, wearing bracelets and rings of hammered gold and His Western-style suit; to His left, a few of His wives, including the queen who had made us strip naked. To His right was the princess we had seen at the Great Hall, Rama's daughter Princess Xenga, whose dark beauty stood out even among the exquisite handmaidens at her side. We stood with Nao, arms across his broad chest and frowning as he noticed me staring at Xenga. Behind us, a host of courtiers fidgeted and cleared their throats. The temple was empty other than we thirty or so members of Rama's retinue.

"What are we waiting for, Nao?" asked Chang.

Annoyance spread across the man's face. "Keep silent," he said.

Through the front gate, in marched an assemblage of a thousand soldiers wearing silver uniforms and wooden helmets. Close by trudged eighty elephants with dusty trunks. Forty drummers went by us, too, one on every second elephant, and a tiger growling in a wooden cage. And then in came a royal personage of some kind, sitting atop a throne carried on the shoulders of four huge, shirtless attendants.

"The Cochin Chinese delegation," Nao whispered to us through the side of his half-closed mouth.

Are they going to kill us now? I asked myself.

Look at your twin smiling nervously, I told myself. Simple and kind and what a shame you are attached to him.

The Emperor of Cochin China, chubby like Rama, stood waving and smiling at our delegation. He wore a green vestment and a golden hat taller than any of the tall hats I'd seen Rama wear. The hat swayed and bent as the Emperor waved.

Rama watched the Emperor and nodded at him without emotion.

One of the elephants kicked up its forelegs without warning. The drummer sitting on the animal was thrown, landing in a cloud of dust and color on one of the flower-bed circles; his drum crashed down next to him. King Rama exhaled through His nose. Meanwhile the elephant had broken rank, and the earth shuddered as the massive beast galloped around the temple avoiding soldiers. The Cochin Chinese Emperor wore a grimace. "My men shall catch the beast in a moment!" he cried to us in Chinese; he smoothed his robe. "Not to worry!"

The soldiers collared the elephant and brought it before the Emperor. One of the Emperor's attendants handed him a whip, and with a troubled smile he struck the animal as at least twenty men held it still. Then the bloodied drummer who had been riding the elephant limped to the Emperor and prostrated himself at his Lord's red-slippered feet. Another attendant stepped forward holding a sword.

"You failed," the Emperor said to the prostrate man in the kindly scolding tones that good-hearted parents use with their children.

The attendant beheaded the man with one stroke of the blade. From a distance, I saw blood spraying the flowers. A speck of blood stained the green collar of the Emperor.

Chang and I buckled at the knees. Again, Rama turned His head toward His queen, raised His eyebrows, and exhaled. He shrugged. "Very *strict*," the King whispered. Everyone nodded discreetly.

The Cochin Chinese Emperor walked across the fort to where Rama stood. His hand twitched forward in greeting and he yanked his head abruptly up, not unlike the elephant. The two leaders embraced, kissed each other on the cheeks, then laid hands on each other's shoulders. As they did so, the Emperor caught sight of us over Rama's shoulder. He looked away quickly, pretending not to have noticed. The Emperor returned to his supporters. The two parties—the Cochin Chinese retinue and Rama's—faced each other. Farther afield, the headless body had not been removed from the pool of its own blood.

Midway between the two parties, the Cochin Chinese lined up all of the elephants across from the tiger in its cage. Then two Cochin Chinese soldiers released the tiger. While Cochin Chinese soldiers stood in a circle around the two breeds of animal, we were treated to a mismatched battle between species.

The tiger, long a hated beast in Cochin China, had had its mouth sewn shut and its claws removed. It was also attached by rope to a pole the soldiers had planted in the ground. All of the elephants stood in a row before the tiger. Soldiers prodded the beasts, one by one, to fight the tiger, and one by one, the elephants shrank back. The giant beasts were afraid of the defenseless tiger.

The elephant keepers were flogged with bamboo until they fell unconscious. The Emperor wore his dignified grimace and smoothed his robe as he chuckled. Finally one of the elephants charged the tiger, impaling the smaller animal with its tusks. The skewered cat snarled and tried to scratch its attacker; the elephant shook his head, throwing the tiger high into the air. The tiger was dead when it fell back to earth.

Not to be outdone, King Rama stepped forward.

"We have prepared for our neighbors from Hue a demonstration, in honor of the recent revision of the Emperor's laws regarding trade between our two lands," he said.

Nao grabbed us by the hands and walked us to the King. Then

he stepped back and away. The King looked at us as God must have at earth on the Seventh Day.

"Behold the Double-Boy!" Rama cried.

Chang and I stepped forward in the little black silk jackets Nao had given us for the occasion—our band exposed—and we bent to the muddy floor and stood on our hands. We heard a roar, which was likely the wind. I wondered what would happen to us if we did not please our King and His guest. My gaze went to the flowers, which stood upside down and began to sway between us and the Emperor's party.

One stroke is all it took, I was thinking. One stroke to separate a man from his head so cleanly.

We flipped in the air and landed back on our feet. The only sound was that of elephants breathing. Everyone watched the Emperor, until finally he walked in his twitchy manner to the King and Chang and me. He stood face-to-face with Rama. The foreign emperor took an incredulous look at us and touched our band. He was very young, younger even than Rama.

Chang and I fell into a bow, and stayed there.

In a grave voice, the Emperor said: "Of course, We have several people in Our nation who are similarly united."

Rama said, "Is this so?"

"More than several, in fact." The Emperor jerked his head. "We did not know you prized them, King Rama. If We had, We would have conveyed the many double-boys from My kingdom to you as a gift."

"When We pay our respects to your country, We shall see them at that time," said Rama.

The Emperor's eyes narrowed. He regarded Rama. "Yes. That will not be difficult to arrange."

"They are a sign," Rama said. "Don't you agree?"

With the smell of flowers, a wind rose, carrying dust in itself. The Emperor watched the sand sprinkle.

"A sign of a blessed nation," said Rama. "No?"

The Emperor paused, swallowed, forced a smile. "Yes."

Nao stepped forward and escorted Chang and me back to our place in line. The afternoon's glow was now mixed with the light from torches on watch stations. After two more hours of tedious cordialities, Nao brought us home to our cottage. The mob outside had scattered, and we were hidden from view this time, ducking under a tarpaulin on the deck of a junk to avoid reigniting public interest. Public interest would come later, and too much of it to avoid.

CHAPTER FIVE

A Double-Courtship

December 1842–January 1843
North Carolina

Once Adelaide—or Addie, as my brother now called her—accepted Chang's proposal of marriage, we took an extended break from touring, and my brother changed into someone other than the man who craved the public eye.

It was not that Chang all at once began to act differently when he and I were alone together; rather, it was when he was with *her* that he unveiled himself as a new person. In his case, love was not really blind, but blinding. Here was a man who had entertained royalty with his, if not wit, then at least a facile drollery. But now love had so stupefied him, he had lost sight of the fact that the "clever banter" he had developed in the drawing rooms of Europe would serve him at least as well in the social settings of rural North Carolina. He was tongue-tied before country folk.

One noontime, just after she'd said yes to my brother, Adelaide and Chang and I sat on a blanket she had spread over the dusty, leaf-strewn grass of the Yateses' backyard. In that warm weather, the old longing to return to Siam was reawakened in me by the green treetops all around and the sunlight casting shadows and bestowing upon the leaves the bright transparency of emeralds.

Mrs. Yates was watching us from the back porch, out of earshot. Her husband Mr. Yates was trying to avoid being seen as he peeked out the window at his daughter and her two exotic companions. Yates did not know of his daughter's engagement; Mrs. Yates planned to hold off telling him for as long as possible. I couldn't understand why Adelaide and Mrs. Yates did not share Mr. Yates's opposition.

You owe it to your brother to end it, I said to myself. For his own good.

Expose to him the unlikeliness of his position, I told myself. It will spare both of you regret.

Adelaide lay flat on the blanket, facing Chang, her chin on her folded forearms. She and my brother looked at one another, each like a child eyeing a wrapped Christmas present on December 24. They both wanted to speak but did not know each other well enough to converse without restraint.

"You'all obviously have to stay right here," Adelaide said finally, brushing the dust off. "And I mean every night till we're married." She leaned close to my brother and looked fiercely into his eyes. "You've got to show Daddy how good your intentions are. How you going to do that someplace else than here, Chang?"

"Why?" I said.

My two companions turned their attention to me in a hurry, as if I had happened out of the air; I had not said a word in hours. "Why are you talking marriage with us?" I asked. "Why, why?"

My brother's eyes flash with anger. "Because she—"

"How?" I did not want to let my brother finish his thought. "Why would she love one such as you?" His face registered the effect of my words on his heart.

As for Adelaide, she looked away, but she may have had to suppress a smile. I found myself thinking: Sarah wouldn't do that, smile so nastily. I hadn't talked much to Sarah, seeing her daily but not summoning the audacity to engage her in courtship, and I surprised myself now by feeling delighted at the thought of her, and the infrequency of her sincere smile.

"Listen." Adelaide pointed a finger at me and she took on the conspiratorial, radiant demeanor of a schemer. "You know something, Eng." She was definitely smiling. "It's obvious you should get to know my sister."

I am not sure how successful I was at keeping my mouth from

falling open. She shrugged and I realized she was taunting me. Or was I wrong? I narrowed my eyes at her. "You think that I—"

"That's why I said it," she smiled. Chang looked at Adelaide as if she had just solved the mystery of flight.

She said, "It obviously don't make sense for me and Chang to get married if there's a single brother around." Her voice was composed of whisper and giggle. "Two plus two is easier than two and one."

"Yes," I said, still understanding very little of her motivations, but understanding that little sliver with rapture. I was a caricature of composure. "Perhaps I would like that very much."

From there, things proceeded quickly.

A few hours later, my brother and I were sitting on the Yateses' porch with Adelaide and Mrs. Yates. Chang and I were silent as mother and daughter considered how to arrange my future with Sarah. I sat mutely while these two near-strangers planned my life.

Adelaide sat stiffly on the edge of the railing. Mrs. Yates set her face as rigid as a marionette's.

"It's what that girl needs," said Adelaide. "She just don't know it."

"Ooh, I figured it," said Mrs. Yates, smacking her knee. "A Christmas quilting."

I was too embarrassed even to ask what that was. Chang's knuckles wandered across his lap, and his eyes were blank.

Mrs. Yates was saying: "Get all of our people together—get the *whole town* together—and everyone will be in a good spirit. . . ." The mother luxuriated in the excellence of her idea. "That girl won't know what hit her."

Adelaide added: "Maybe it will finally shut the town up about her for once—"

Both Adelaide and her mother froze after Adelaide stopped herself from saying more. I saw an unexplained bitterness in Mrs. Yates's face suddenly, the way you can sometimes catch a quick glimpse of a trout rising in the current of a river.

Chang did not catch the festering anger in Mrs. Yates's eyes, and so he smiled at his would-be mother-in-law. She regained her cheer and smiled at him, too.

How horrible my days and nights would become if, while my

brother lived the married life, I ended up unsuccessful in my quest for Sarah's heart! Whatever the outcome, I would survive, I told myself. Mekong Fishermen stay abreast of change.

"What is a Christmas quilting?" I asked, interrupting the others.

My question, however, would at least for now remain un-answered—no one told me a quilting was a get-together where a large group of women sewed while the men drank—because at that moment Mr. Yates stepped out onto the porch, putting a hasty end to this discussion. He looked at Adelaide, and then at Chang, and though he had been told nothing, he had to see the shipwreck of his family life. Holding his hat in his hands, Yates was smaller than he had been a few weeks before, and more pale. Unrest had caused that; grief had caused that.

Though Christmas had come and gone, Mrs. Yates began to arrange a Christmas quilting. She would invite the entire town to spend the following Saturday, January 3, in her backyard. Though ostensibly a belated celebration of the holiday season and, accord-ing to Mrs. Yates, a way for Wilkesboro to demonstrate the mean-ing of Christmas to its famous double-boy visitors, the plan was actually designed to force Sarah to spend time with me. That quilting would mark my sole chance to win her affections, I thought. My charm had to be in top form if I wanted to get to her—did I even want to get to her? I felt great stress.

On the porch one morning, we were sitting by ourselves when Sarah walked past us and into the inn. "Hello," I said as she went by; I did not hear a response. After that a strange fatigue came on, and I wallowed in it. An hour or so later, she breezed out the door and past us again, on her way into town with her sister. "Hello, Mr. Eng," she said this time, after I'd said hello first. And just like that I got sucked into some dead place hidden under the sparks and minerals of my own heart and mind. I had no pride anymore, no brain. Just a longing not to be left alone while Chang had happiness.

The night before the quilting saw a raging fight.

Adelaide and Mrs. Yates were off with Mr. Yates in one of the upstairs bedrooms while Chang, Sarah, Jefferson, and I sat in the living room. The noise of an argument crashed down on the air, with a clamor as distinct and as unhappy as a cannon's roar.

"I will not have it!" screamed Mr. Yates. "I don't care what people say about us, this is not the way! That's no reason. No reason to——"

At our side, Sarah looked at me. Her face was flushed with embarrassment. "Nice weather for Christmastime, ain't it?" I was not prepared for Sarah's words, and so did not hear this first attempt of hers to draw our attention from the sounds of the argument in the other room. *"I can't remember the last time we had such nice weather in January,"* she repeated, louder this time.

"Yes," I said, ready to play this game. "The—the temperature is splendid." I smiled at her, and she managed to return the favor. Her lower lip was trembling, though.

"Pa, you obviously don't understand what it's like!" came Adelaide's voice skittering through the wall. "I been punished for ten years," she was screaming, "and it weren't even my mistake!"

"Hush!" said Mrs. Yates. "Hush!"

"I'm a woman grown now, Pa, and have been!"

"Well, Sarah . . ." I cleared my throat, forced a smile. "Are you looking forward to the quilting?"

"I don't care who hears me!" Adelaide's voice resonated through the wall.

"Oh," Sarah answered me, though her eyes grew dim as she concentrated on both speaking and listening. "Are you coming to our quilting, Mr. Eng?"

"Mind your tongue, Adelaide Yates, I'm still your father! You liked to have said too much already!"

"I am looking forward to it," I told Sarah. I patted together my palms, which were sweaty. "The quilting, I mean."

Across the room, Jefferson broke his silence with a moan. "I hate a quarrel." He sat in his mother's custom-built double-wide chair, staring at his hands intertwined in his lap.

"Yes," said Chang. "Not good."

Sarah began to cry. A tear trod romantically down her cheek. The image of this weeping girl ranked with the true purities of this life, a flower wanting to open, a day with your family by the riverside when you are five years old, the lavarous sunset reflected by a hundred gleaming temple spires on your King's royal grounds, all happy memories. But she did not look at me.

Still, the morning of the quilting came in due time. Just as I never found highborn personages, sold-out performances, or a new city on the horizon quite as grand as I had been hoping, in my eyes the actual affair paled before the grandeur my imagination had bestowed on it.

Still, my disappointment was short-lived.

On what was a sunny morning hour, Jefferson and Mr. Yates helped Mrs. Yates out into the backyard, where they positioned her on her unseemly double-wide seat. Next to Mrs. Yates, the father and son set up a picnic table, upon which they put a big green Christmas quilt and numerous sewing needles. Beside that, a second picnic table enticed the guests—and some backyard flies—with a pig, a fatted calf, a large holiday turkey, cranberry sauce, and gravy.

Adelaide, in a bright yellow dress, talked to Chang and me. "Daddy will come around to our way of thinking." She was gleeful.

Sarah, on the other hand, was nowhere to be found, and so I put to my love's sister a few artfully veiled questions in regard to Sarah's whereabouts.

Adelaide, though she wore a broad-brimmed yellow hat to match her dress, put a hand over her eyes to shade out the sun. "Look at this one," she said to my brother, "he's nervous as a wet kitty." She shook her head at me, the kindest sort of mocking. "Don't you worry about a thing, Eng. I put a heap of thought into this. Chang and I can't have a wedding with just him and not you."

With the delight her words brought me, I began to feel an affection for Adelaide that was in some ways greater than what I felt for Sarah—at any rate different. Adelaide was bringing the object of my desire to me, whereas Sarah herself was still indifferent to my charms. Besides, it was Sarah that I *desired*, and who therefore made me nervous every time I saw her. Adelaide was a sympathetic collaborator. I tipped my head at my brother's fiancée to show my thanks.

"May I ask a question, Adelaide?" I cleared my throat. "Is there something that—happened to your sister? Something people are—reluctant to talk about?"

Adelaide's eyes got dismissive and hot. "I believe it's obvious to everyone you never will screw up the courage to talk to her," she snorted. "That is, on the outside chance that she decides to take a shine to you'all." Her lips curved into a smile.

Then Adelaide, an inch or so shorter than Chang and two shorter than me, looked over her shoulder to see if anyone was keeping an eye on us. Furtively, she brought her hand very near my brother's coat sleeve, whereupon he grinned like he'd won a sweepstakes and positioned his arm so the cotton of his jacket touched her fingers slightly.

Guests arrived, a few at a time. First a small number of women made their appearance, and then some tall ruddy North Carolina men joined the quilting, each one the owner of a broad set of arms and thick sideburns. The women's table soon clattered with the sound of busy needles, and before long tobacco smoke streamed in ribbons from each man's mouth to blanch the warm air.

Next to the quilting table, perched on top of her home-crafted seat, Mrs. Yates, with Jefferson quiet at her side, beamed delight. About ten yards from the guests, on the back porch, Adelaide still attended to my brother and me—Chang and I being too nervous to handle the social pressures of party conversation. "Try not to look fidgety, you'all," she said. She pulled at her hair and chewed her lip, and kept looking back and forth at us and at the party. "Adelaide Yates, Adelaide Yates," she murmured to herself, "Adelaide Yates, Adelaide—"

The partygoers did not talk much, opting instead to stare at Chang and me. Milling about with the men was the girls' "cousin" Will, the red-headed cur who had given us trouble in town a few weeks earlier. He was not related to the Yates family at all, I had found out, and he worked hounding escaped slaves as far as Canada, branding the ones he apprehended on the spot. He was shaking his head as he wondered at us.

Meanwhile, Sarah still had not made her appearance. Neither had Mr. Yates made his. I began to give up hope, but then the lady I may have loved strolled from the house onto the back porch accompanied by a tall and curvaceous girl with cross-eyes. Sarah nodded at me as she passed by on her way to the quilting table, a meager salutation.

Adelaide glared. "Go on, boy," she whispered to me, motioning in Sarah's direction.

Chang and I headed for the quilting table.

Before we got there, a man walked over to my brother and me, stepping between us and our destination. He was large and drunk, and his long frock coat hung off his round shoulders. He gripped a sewing needle that had been on the quilting table, and he stood a few steps ahead of us.

In a loud voice he said, "You those *Siamese* twins?"

I said nothing. My brother, too, held silent.

"Chang and Kang?" The man went on. He was also turning his head to look at his friends behind him. He tightened his grip around the needle. "From Siam? Tweedle-one and Tweedle-two."

My brother and I tensed.

"You really attached?" Even as he accosted Chang and me directly, the man spoke in a very loud voice, as if he meant to embarrass us before the whole gathering.

"Right again," I said. "Sir."

The entire crowd's eyes were on us. We held our hands against the sun to see our adversary. At the same time, Mr. Yates emerged from the house. He too said nothing as he watched from a distance.

Adelaide came over to stand by Chang. The three of us faced this man, who seemed to grow taller with every wordless second he faced us.

From the picnic table, Will, the cousin, barked, "See that?" He rose from his seat. "See that girl just make her way towards them attached Chinamen?" He headed for us until he was shoulder-to-shoulder with the man holding the needle.

"C'mon, Sarah, ain't you planning to join this little freak show? Or are Chinamen too white for you?" Will said, searching my eyes the whole time, contriving to look rugged. He put a thought to everybody: "Whatever it is they'all are doing, I wouldn't want to watch it."

At this Chang and I bounded right up into the faces of these

rivals—after one skip we stood an inch from them at most; my
nose was nearly touching Will's mouth. Thuggish as they were,
the men must have been astonished at the quickness of our united
movement.

"Keep talking," Chang whispered, "and my brother am have to
knock you down."

From out of the corner of my eye, I saw Mr. Yates—and
though I had no way of knowing if he was planning to say or do
anything, I raised my hand in his direction, indicating that he
should stay put and be silent. The guests rustled as they moved
closer to watch.

"Renounce what you said about Sarah Yates," I said in a very
soft voice. Slowly I reached across my chest and put my hand on
the wrist of the drunkard who wore the long frock coat, and I
brought my fingers casually over his sewing needle. His hand did
not flinch at my touch, nor did he oppose my hold as I drew the
needle from his fingers. He took a step backward, away from us,
and then he took another.

I held the needle now, and I raised it to Will's chin, where I
rested it delicately, with the point just under his lip. He stiffened.

"Just what do you expect you're doing?" His voice was all at
once high-pitched and girl-like.

"Do you understand my words?" I asked. The man smelled of
dirty clothes. If he makes a move, I thought, I will lance his face.
"Never, never again will you speak ill of Sarah Yates." I raised my
outside hand, the one not holding the needle, and—to my eternal
surprise—Sarah walked over to me to stand beside us.

Will slid his eyes to her and back to me. I put a bit more pressure on the needle against his skin. He swallowed.

I was very conscious of Sarah, who had set her lips; she looked
to be having trouble holding back from speaking. She placed her
fingers around my hand, the one that held the needle, and she
lowered it away from Will—her grasp was harder than feminine,
but this woman's touch was pleasant. She did not know what to
do next, I could see that.

Not saying a word, leaving the company at the quilting openmouthed, Sarah took Chang and me and led us away from the
party. After a few feet, Will cried at her back, "You finally caught

something else in your trap!" But it did not matter; she was leading us into the woods toward the Yadkin River. I saw a last face
before we entered the forest: it belonged to Mr. Yates, and he was
frowning.

Sarah did not quit shaking and muttering as we walked. Chang
and I shrugged our shoulders, not knowing in what direction we
were being led, but I was too happy to care.

Maybe I will have what you have, brother, I said to myself.

Does my twin feel the pounding of my heart? I asked myself.
The way I felt *his* when he asked for Adelaide's hand?

Sarah ushered us up a steep, thicketed hillside, to the crest
where the Yadkin first bubbled into the world, its clear water fretting down a series of bouldered steps. Abreast of the brook,
within a gathering of high trees, three colorless boulders surrounded a patch of flat, soft green about the size and shape of a
bed. When we reached this clearing, which was striped with
bright spokes of sunlight, Sarah sat herself down on the grass, her
back against one of the jagged dusky rocks. Not knowing what
else to do, Chang and I sat next to her. My brother patted me sub-
tly on the back, and I loved him without bitterness. We had lived
so much together, in our three decades and more.

Chang and I stayed like that for a while, not saying a word,
seated beside this woman whose face was coated with perspiration. She was not crying, but I may have heard a sniffle as she
dried her nose with the back of her hand.

A faint wind tickled, the light of day burned deep and clear,
and everything was perfect—the tips of rock emerging from the
narrow green wellspring; the soft grass; Chang on my left; Sarah
on my right, fingering the turf beside her.

"The setting is idyllic," I said.

"I always thought so," she said, looking off into the air and biting her lip. "I always thought so."

We sat for a stretch, our eyes on the modest source of the river.
Chang reached for something to say and came up with: "I loving
your sister."

Sarah laughed quietly, a single stream of air let out of her nose.
She did not look at us.

"Why do they tease you?" I asked, gently as I could.

She closed her eyes, which were dry and flinty, and she dropped her face between her hands. She inhaled as deeply as if she were about to plunge into water. And when she began to talk, her voice, already a near-whisper, was muffled further by her hands blocking her mouth.

Some time ago, she said, when she had been young and girls and boys her age hadn't yet begun to care about who had money and who did not, she had been popular, remarkably so, thanks to a yellow bonnet she wore around town—she had been called "Yellow Bonnet"—and she was made junior chairwoman of the church social committee. Her parents had owned a slave to make the beds of the inn and to help with the few rows of now-laid-by cotton in their backyard. Because she was too young to know better, Sarah became friendly with the Negro, whose name was Thomas. He was a tall young slave, and his knee had been ruined by a bullet when the "Underground Negroes' Railroad" was derailed near the northern Virginia border; his limp made him affordable to Mr. Yates. He had eyes unlit, she said. She had not known better than to trust a slave. Not back then. She had acted neighborly, she said.

"And he—took advantage of my neighborliness." It was the first time I heard her sound throaty and needing something from me. "Do you understand, Mr. Eng?"

I told her I did.

Of course it had been against her will, she said, and only once, by a slave, that horrible slave, and she talked of how her brother Jefferson had stumbled upon them in the woods. And of the subsequent trial, and of the hanging, which had been such an event for Wilkesboro that the school had been closed for the day. Children had been encouraged to watch it.

And then she stopped talking.

I did not know what to say to this woman, but I wanted to say *something*, and then I heard a person approaching us. It was Adelaide, walking out of the wood and climbing toward us. "I knew I'd find you here—Sarah's best secret spot by Moody Rock."

Adelaide stood regarding her sister; she put her hand on her hips, pursed her mouth, and looked at Sarah for a while, and understood.

"It was a horrible scandal," Adelaide said, addressing Chang and me. "Just tore Sarah apart," she whispered, and ran a hand through her hair. "A *slave*," she said, and made the face one does when eating a lemon. "Nearly tore me apart, too. Remember, I'm only a year younger than my beauty of a sister." She began to smile. "But he got took care of," Adelaide said. "They obviously got *that* buck," she said.

Sarah raised her head, and her eyes looked to her sister feverishly. "Gone is what's done," she said. "I see that." She breathed deeply, over and again, until she ceased trembling. Her hands were clenched against her forehead. "I see it gone." The day was silent enough to hear the river bubbling softly to life, and the wind, too, spoke its soft noise.

Adelaide sat herself down by my brother's side. We were a pair of couples bound together by circumstance.

Adelaide said to her: "Ain't that a nice thing Eng did back there for you, Sarah?"

Once she got control of her shaky chin, Sarah turned to me and said, "That was—that was a nice thing you did for me, back there." It took her a long time to face me, but she did. From the trees behind us, a bluebird chirped.

Sarah and I stared at each other. Then she looked away.

She had trouble getting herself to gaze into my eyes, but she continued to try. For the first time in my life I saw that a woman other than my mother was striving to love me. Sarah sat there almost looking into my eyes, under the North Carolina sun, her sister smiling beautifully behind her, and I grinned an awkward grin. A thick, warmish joy entered my heart. Sarah had a face of beautifully long length. Her blond hair was marvelously different from my dark own.

"Sarah," I said, my nervous lips surprisingly forming the words I wanted them to, "would you—"

"Yes." She was nodding, and touching her face lightly. Her hands did not look young in the light. They were fidgety, veined, and very thin, and now they were betrothed to me. They were mine now. I pulled Chang to our feet. We quickly made for the hills.

"Why do we go?" Chang asked as I climbed us over the rocks

and ran us down into the wood. "Why are you leave Sarah up there, just when she say yes?" I was out of breath from running, and the twigs thrashing past scratched my cheek.

I could not answer. I was taking my brother with me into the deep of the woods to hide my tears of gratitude.

CHAPTER SIX

The Sadness of Siam

1819–1825
Siam

The captivity Chang and I knew as teenagers at King Rama's palace brimmed with the habiliments of nobility. Temperate and pretty was our morning bath in the collapsible tub that Nao would bring by. Tar-black English soap was a friend we had not known during our life on the Mekong. Another friend was His Highness himself. At this point I was reasonably convinced he would not kill us.

One night, late, the King entered our cabin, waking us. He was, surprisingly, without his usual escort of handlers. He wore a long flowing red robe, with a tiger on the back and the sign of the sun on the breast.

"Wake up, double-elephant," He boomed from the doorway. "Did you know that the citizenry have begun calling you by that name in their new legends—double-elephant? No? Well, We know. We know everything."

I was too young to understand it then, but the King was drunk. "Get up," he burped. "We want to show you something." He directed us out into the night with hands as big as Buddha's.

It was very late. The crickets seemed unusually loud, and the twinkling stars bright and lovely. Shoulder-to-shoulder, we walked with the King, alone, the only ones about on the royal grounds.

He walked uneasily, wavering a bit, with the two of us a step behind, yawning.

He took us to a marble floor in the middle of an empty plot of grass, atop a green hill and encircled by rubble. In the center of this displaced marble floor, a naked man and thirteen naked children were confined in a huge iron cage loaded with thick chains. They were all gagged. The man was awake, and looked at us with the eyes of someone frightened to his core; the children slept.

"We want to tell you a story," Rama said to us, patting our heads. "Sometimes a man will think he is a shadow. And this man believes a shadow can flee the sun until the shadow is tiny in the remotest distance. But the royal sun sees things, no matter how small. Our eye is like a magnifier."

The King avoided looking at the prisoner. Swallowing, He told us that this man would be hanged by a hook from his chin in the morning; afterwards the prisoner would be made to sit on seven sharp pikes, each a foot long, then dropped in boiling oil, and finally pounded into pumice in an immense mortar before the eyes of his family. Rama wanted everyone to see the traitor now, He said, that is why all the walls blocking this view had been broken down. Tears filled the King's eyes as He told the story. Chang looked into my face with a fear I hadn't seen since we'd first been abducted.

There is a reason the King wants us to see this, I said to myself. We could still suffer this fate.

I took my brother's hand and held it, the way I would later take my wife's.

Rama brought us back to our cabin and gave us a hand-sized jade dragon figurine as a gift. "For you," He said. Even in the semidarkness, a white band of moonlight illuminated the tiny green figure, with its black stones for eyes, and its spiked tail, and its smile that seemed as though it might shift any second into a snarl. Chang and I thanked King Rama, climbed into bed, holding His present, and fell asleep. We held on to that gift for more than twenty years.

I thought He was going to keep us on his grounds forever and exhibit us whenever a foreign leader came to visit. I was wrong, but I could not have known why.

As two of the King's prized treasures, we started to receive schooling. Nao would come to our quarters to give us history and language lessons. This went on for some four years. In all of that time, King Rama himself instructed us in the manservant's stead on three occasions. On one of these days little Princess Xenga accompanied her father and listened along. Chang and I must have been about thirteen.

Beside us in our hut, the royal father and daughter sat on portable thrones held aloft by pairs of large attendants who gripped handles at the legs of the chairs. Held two feet off of the ground, Xenga, like her father, was gowned in red silk, and across the room I could smell the ginger that perfumed her hair. Below her feet lay fresh rose petals.

Somewhere between the rules of Thai grammar and the history of the battle of Ramkhamhaeng, the King instructed: "People remain young through faith in Siam." The words came out of the King's throat packed with emotion.

I tried to sneak glimpses of the Princess. Nervous and little in the plush red seat of her small throne, she had a resplendent loose train of hair. Like me, she did not know what to do or say in the presence of her father.

So many handsome children are exquisite because of their youth; their shape and demeanor are so different from those of adults that the youngsters seem almost part of another phylum. And with others it is different. This princess, at twelve already like the most elegant of *women*, had begun provokingly to carry her charm in her smooth face and graceful body; she sat there, her head cocked, with hands on undeveloped thighs, the bloom of youth approximating, through some extraordinary intuition, the full-blown flower of injurious adult charisma.

"He who seeks the best in life grows old and is crushed by the world," said the King. I sat in mute appreciation, knowing that even to steal another look at the Princess meant leaning forward, which would have stirred my brother too obviously in the direction of the royal child.

I did so regardless. Xenga was nodding her head at her father's words.

"Your Excellency?" My brother's voice had the same casual

note it carried when interrupting me. A shocked silence fell over the room.

"—and he who is always prepared for the worst becomes old yet sooner, with his worry," said the King, as if he had not heard.

Chang said, "Your Highness?"

Even though we were now allowed to look at him, we were not to address the King unless He asked us to do so. From his elevated throne, Rama glanced at the ceiling and sighed through His nostrils. His attendants shuffled their feet. The Princess deigned to eye me for the first time, with a fidgety glance.

One of the King's handlers leaned forward and whispered too loudly in His ear: "The double-boy has a question, Your Excellency."

"Yes, Siam knows that," the King said. "Siam *knows* that." His Highness wiggled in annoyance, and His throne swayed. The handlers worked to keep from upsetting the King's position.

"What?" Rama asked my brother. "What is it, that you break off the lessons of a Crowned Majesty?"

Looking at the floor, I groaned inwardly.

"Your Majesty." Chang had brushed aside safety. "Would it be possible to see our mother again?" That surprised me. He hadn't mentioned Mother in quite some time; then again, neither had I—not to him.

Rama's crown, a white oval with silver feathers sprouting from its summit, now lay a little tilted on His head.

"You wish to leave the royal grounds?"

The Princess snapped, "You are a guest of Siam." Her lisp was pronounced. Drops of sweat had formed on her little brow, and the black hairs that coiled out of the horseshoes of her eyebrows began to twitch. I wanted no more than to hold hands with her, because a handshake bears at least some aspects of intimacy, and I believed I would never travel any closer than that to a romantic kiss.

Rama lifted His hand calmly, held His forefinger pointing upward in a quieting motion, and looked at His daughter. "Sniveling Female Dog," He said in soft tones, "who gave you leave to speak?" The Princess lowered her head.

The King ordered his attendants to carry Him to the doorway. There, His Highness opened it onto His palace and grounds.

"Behold Siam," He whispered, and gestured outside to the kingdom of Him with a sweep of His arm that rocked the chair a little; the royal lifters scrambled to keep the King stabilized. At the lip of the river, boy soldiers stood guard here and there atop the palace wall, shooting arrows into the air for sport, distant missiles that looked ineffectual as pine needles in a breeze. Over the river a golden ray of sun was falling through a hole in the gray clouds.

Princess Xenga turned with a lover's thirst to the sweltering scene of green meadow, sunbeam, and the seven royal temple spires on the horizon. She grinned on her existence of soft and eternal tranquillity.

"Chang and Eng," the King barked. We turned toward Rama, who was licking His teeth like a serpent. Afternoon sunlight appeared about the doorframe, curling around the King on his throne, and He glowed with this light, this royal halo in which wars were raged, villages razed, temples constructed, sacrifices offered, and luckless conjoined subjects were taken from their homes.

"My young visitors," He said, "after loss the coarser soul is better off than the noble one; the dangers for the latter must be greater. King Chulalongkorn, Our forefather, said: *When a dragon loses a finger, it returns; not so with a man.* Do you understand?"

Far in the distance, I made out a patch of black clouds distinct among the gray ones covering most of the sky. Perhaps this marked the stretch of river where we had lived our old life.

"Put Us down," the King told his handlers. The two burly men looked at each other with raised eyebrows.

"Your Lord requests to be *put down!*" Rama's eyes were bright with magnificence and spleen. "Should We have your ears stretched to hear commands more easily?" The men brought the throne to the floor, gingerly.

Rama smoothed his sleeves. "Take Xenga and leave Us with the double-one. Now!"

The King's handlers directed the Princess and her subordinates outside. Wind rattled the doorframe, far-off trees danced, and the air promised imminent rain.

We were alone with the King. "We understand things about you." There was nothing in His face now but sympathy and apprehension. "Maybe you understand Us a bit, too. Maybe as much as any person can."

My brother asked, "Your Majesty, would it be possible to see our—"

I kicked Chang, and he quieted.

The King's eyes looked off as he spoke. "What I *am*, for the world I am *not*. In the Royal Hall of Judgment, a thousand faces before me, waiting for a decree, often I ask myself, Am I King, or another? Am I estranged from myself?" He blinked and gazed at my brother and me for a while.

The King cleared His throat. "It is coincidental that you mention taking leave of the palace now," Rama said, regaining his regal tone of voice. "Do you know what coincidental means?"

We nodded.

"There has occurred a reason for you to return to your family." Rama ran His palm along His throat from chin to collarbone. "News reached Us yesterday that your father has died. Perhaps We will let you see his funeral." And with that, he released us forever.

The next day, in the early morning, we were awakened by Nao taking us from our bunkhouse. He draped a black blanket over our heads and carried us to a pull-cart and had us lie down on it, the cloak hot over our sweaty bodies, the pull-cart splintery below. The cart seemed close to falling apart over each pebble. Chang asked, "Do you think it is true?"

Our cart stopped. When Nao lifted the blanket, we were beyond the palace gates, at a pretty green spot beside a big tree on the bank of the river. Birds stepped like tightrope walkers across the tree branches.

My brother and I stepped down onto the soft grass and Nao stood behind us, silently. Chang and I pressed against one another. River mosquitoes bit us. The birds took off and flickered into the damp afternoon. With the orange-yellow light of dawn flaming on the water, the Mekong was intensely sad. We stood looking at the river for hours.

At last I heard the sound of footsteps. Two of the King's attendants emerged, leading a third man toward us. This man's gray frock was the first peasant garment I'd seen in a dog's age. He was Uncle Xau, a relative of Aunt Ping's but a stranger to us.

Xau was craning his neck and looking all around. That, and the quick action of his thin legs, and the way his arms dangled loosely, thrashing about, flopping, made him look like a marionette. Before long Xau saw Chang and me for the first time in his life. He stopped as if the sight had hit him physically.

His mouth started to open and his hand came to cover it. The sadness and surprise in his eyes gave him a facial cast I'll never forget: heart-stricken and petulant. I looked over our shoulders to see what pitiable sight he was gawking at, but there was nothing behind us except sunshine and grass.

After a quick silent nod to Uncle Xau from Nao—who then threw a fleeting good-bye look in our direction—we were off, cramped in the back of our relative's small boat while Xau rowed across the blue and twinkling gold of the Mekong, toward home.

It was the peak of the hot season, and our little boat passed from light to darkness and back in quick repetition, keeping close to the shore, under the cooling shadows of the trees.

Nobody spoke. Chang and I stood contemplating the closeness achieved by certain psychic bonds. Once Xau turned around toward us to touch the lustrous black silk of our jackets. He nodded and grunted, and he turned back to rowing. The river had risen to its high mark and Chang and I lost our footing twice.

Father was dead. What of Mother?

We took the long route, away from the capital and down one of the Mekong's tributaries, to avoid crowds, and we kept looking over our shoulders until the spires and steeples and the tops of the statues inside the palace wall grew tiny; and soon we saw the entire city of Bangkok far behind us, too, with its tiny footbridges and hillsides adorned with statues and its empty boats tied ashore together and bobbing in unison with the tide—from this distance all of a piece, like some somnolent giant.

As we approached our familiar corner of the Mekong, I felt a thousand and one emotions swimming through my brain. I was hopeful and stung all at once. Anticipation fluttered in my chest, alongside loss.

When I saw the river in the distance, it seemed different. What looked like the curved backs of logs protruded from the water, one or two every few feet at first. The air was becoming heavy and musky in the hot sun, growing more so as we traveled nearer our old home. Soon the water breathed off a strong smell like old fish; it wafted up from the embankment across the river, over the trees. The stench clung to the dewy leaves and, slowly, to our clothes and our skin. Before long my nostrils were burning. The logs in the river were in truth the submerged bodies of the recently dead.

Xau paddled with one hand while using his other one to cover his nose and mouth. The putrid smell of the drowned grew more profound with every inhaled breath, more intense, and more nauseating in the summer air.

We continued on. The river was now choked with corpses, half submerged, dead bodies black with mud and earth, their frocks stirring a little in the gentle breeze as our junk kept running against them. The bright sun shone on the river, the warm sunshine played about the decomposing flesh. This was our homecoming.

It was late 1823 and cholera had gutted Mekong. The epidemic came upon the village like a hard clear light through the dark and when it had passed, those left living were unable to bury the many dead. A multitude was cast into the river. The current did nothing to move the putrid accumulation.

Soon we saw Mother, on the edge of the river, *our* stretch of river. Her skin was stippled like old newspaper. And a short bony man, a stranger to Chang and me, had his arm around her dainty shoulder. When Mother saw our junk coming, floating with the tide and around the corpses, she pushed the man aside and ran to the lip of the shore. She began to scream. "My babies!" she cried, and extended her arms toward our arriving junk in an ecstatic flurry, spreading her fingers wide. "My babies, my babies," she cried, over and again until we reached her. "Eng, and my Bean Sprout."

As soon as we were near enough, Mother lifted us with a grunt. We were much bigger than when she'd last held us, and she had aged a great deal; not only was her face as wrinkled as an old woman's, but her hair had grayed in patches. She stumbled under our twofold weight. But she smelled sweet, the way Father used to, like someone who works hard.

Mother left Cousin Xau on the shore—and that strange bony man who had caressed her shoulder, too—and she carried us inside our houseboat. How small our home looked now. The marbao wood planks slouching over the flat-bottomed centerboard, the narrow cabin semidark even in the middle of a sunny day, the sawed tree-butt table that was our least wobbly furnishing—it all looked so meager. We had *lived* here?

Father had been among the first to die in this epidemic; Aunt Ping was the scourge's last casualty. We'd missed Father's burial ceremony. Ping's funeral was to be later this day.

Chang and I wiped tears from Mother's cheeks, and she started laughing on top of her little sobs. "You are able to stand side to side now, the way real brothers do." In her smile lived the kindness that motherhood itself illustrates. "I always knew I would be reunited with my double-joy," she said, though her face told us she had not known.

On the way to Ping's funeral, I could only recall my aunt as a patch of piquant warmth and not as a clear, precise image. Once she'd brought us the hugest rice balls I had ever seen. The woman had liked music and would hum in a sweet-pitched voice when she'd cut our hair. I could picture the rice, hear the tune. And Aunt Ping had been the one to warn Mother that King Rama was going to take us.

"We still have Mother," Chang whispered

Chang and I followed Uncle Xau, Mother, and Sen—that bony man (he was her childhood friend, and his hair occurred in wisps above his skinny face)—into the courtyard of a temple in the woods. This shrine was low to the ground, a modest imitation of those in Rama's palace grounds—bamboo where the royal temples had been marble, and thatch where they had been gold.

Ping was coffined in a wood box perched on a high bier that was draped in thin red cloth. Above her, a white canopy hung down—white being the color of Siamese mourning—and the canopy was festooned with fragrant flowers. Mother was crying uncontrollably.

Chang started to weep. I shook with his tearful spasms as we waddled our way through the crowd. In the back of the temple, flutists and drummers began to play, and someone sounded a gong. People whom I did not know walked over to comfort Mother with a word or a phrase before moving on. "Sorry," they said, "sorry for your loss."

A bent old priest in yellow robes limped over to Mother, shook his head as if it gratified him to join her in reviling the fates, then he took Mother in hand and led us slowly to a little grassy courtyard behind the temple. As he tried to comfort her in his weak voice, the shriveled priest slid his eyes our way again and again, trying to steal glimpses of Chang and me.

The high-pitched music was loud now, and it sounded like wailing. Meanwhile, the modest crowd of mourners had followed us into the little courtyard. A light rain started to fall, but offered no relief from the heat.

The priest walked, bent-backed, to a low wooden platform. He climbed onto it, grunting and shuddering as if it were much higher than it was, and he turned to the crowd. At his old feet sat four young women holding lit wicks. These women were hunched over, too, but not from age; they were trying to protect their tiny flames from the rain as if their lives depended on candlelight. Mother, Chang, and I stood before this platform, with a small assemblage at our backs. They gaped at our band.

I stood there, frightened, believing that everything was somehow, if not my fault, then the fault of my predicament, the peculiarity of my connecting band.

The priest started to pray softly in a guttural voice. "Life is done. Life has begun," he said, grumbling the words, and he kept repeating this, chanting it, as four young clerics carried Aunt Ping's coffin through the crowd slowly on their way to us and the platform. The coffin was empty. Aunt Ping herself, her corpse, was nowhere to be seen.

A young priest stepped forward and presented Mother with the thin red cloth that had been draped over the coffin's bier.

"Your beloved sister's body is being washed and purified." He held the red fabric like it would shatter if he dropped it. Mother's lip trembled and broke my heart. "Thank you," Mother said, finally taking the cloth. The smile she managed was as rueful as misery itself, and I don't think she noticed it was raining. She rested her hand atop Chang's head, twisting his hair with her long fingers. I felt my brother sobbing. And I joined him.

Aunt Ping's corpse was making its way back to the empty bier, our aunt now balanced atop the shoulders of the four who had carried her coffin. She was glistening wet, and draped in white sheets as pale as her lifeless skin. Mother gasped when she saw her sister's body. I pretended to think kind, solemn thoughts but couldn't concentrate. The women sitting at the edge of the casket with their lighted wicks distracted me. They tried not to look at us as I was trying not to look at them.

Then the thought came to me that Aunt Ping was smiling as she lay there. But she was not; when I concentrated my eyes on her, Ping's expression looked solemn and drawn—the skin so tight the bones nearly poked through—and her naked body could be seen through the sheet in gray patches where her wet flesh stuck to the cloth. "Hello, Aunt," my brother said. Ping's eye sockets were hollowed. Her gray hands were crossed on her stomach, and her drab face looked angry, and huge, with black deep nostrils. The skin of her face was covered in white downy fuzz. Even in the rain, the smell was asphyxiating.

We backed away. The four sitting women threw their lighted wicks onto Ping.

Fire jumped to my aunt's corpse, engulfing her. Using my hand to shield my face from the heat, I stole a glance at her silhouette diminishing in the middle of that blaze. I felt ill. Chang leaned his head on my shoulder, burying his face. Death had stolen into the dancing flames, taunting both young and old, throwing the soot of Ping's remains into the air, where they brewed in ample circles over the fire.

Years later, as I read the Bible to prepare for my baptism in North Carolina's Yadkin River, a passage unsettled me, and brought me back to Ping's burning corpse: "For dust thou art, and unto dust thou shalt return." How to prepare for this, when, even now at the end of my life, I understand nothing?

We had grown, Chang and I, since we had last seen Mother, and so something had to be done about the living arrangements in the tiny houseboat. This was our old home, but it did not feel that way. Our first night with her, after Ping's funeral, Mother sat us down on the floor and asked us about our time with the King. She contrived a grin that went to the core of me. But her chin had trouble.

"There were things about the palace that were pleasing." Chang was trying to comfort her, but spoke as nervously as one of Rama's courtiers before the King himself. "Look at the jade dragon His Majesty gave us, Mother," he said.

"I missed you," I said. "Yes," Chang said, "we missed you, of course." The sky was raining into the cabin.

Mother looked into my eyes. A frown passed over her face quick as spilled water. "Please," she said. "Stop it." Chang and I did not know what we had done wrong.

"I know what you are doing." Her voice was soft and even. "You are pitying me. And yourselves. I am sure of it."

"No," we said.

She managed another smile. She seemed half our size now—I could not believe that.

"When your father first got ill," she said, "he was leaking from his body." Her eyes got impassioned. "Life is not a jade dragon. He was leaking everywhere. And Ping, too. So do you think that is disgusting?"

I felt my brother swallow at the same time I did. Everything inside the cabin was getting rained on. Mother breathed loudly out of her nose. I looked to my brother for comfort from Mother— one more awful turnabout.

It was not always like that. Sometimes she would forget herself and smile, and I would feel again like a six-year-old with a father and a happy mother and a home I did not realize was preposterously meager, I was laughing again and not thinking, talking affably with my brother and listening to his talk. But Mother's smile would die, or I would hear a fish jumping from the Mekong, and I was back to sleeping on the unpleasant floor, next to inconsolable Mother's berth, sweating together with Chang on a rough hot straw mat.

The nights were sweltering and an inky blue. Sometimes Chang, who usually nodded off before I did, would curl even closer to me and lay his arm across my hip. This made the nights even hotter.

"Good night, brother," I'd say. He'd snore.

Mother, her head propped on her hand, would moan and whimper in her sleep.

The repeat visits at our doorstep by Sen became upsetting to Chang and me. An austere widower, thick-browed with dark bags under his eyes, Sen was, in his own words, a "most successful merchant," and he carried around with him a bedraggled carpetbag filled with fishing hooks he'd once taken "all the way to Hong Kong to make an honorable living."

Sometimes, if Mother left him alone with us, his eyes would flash a moist whimsy and he would, in a hush and with a grin, refer to women as "the lower gender."

We would nod.

Sen tried to look paternal. "May I tell you something, Double-Boy? To such a man as myself, and to the brand of men you will be—if I can be of the help that I think I can—hardship isn't the exceptional thing it is to lesser people." Unlike Father, Sen used a loud voice to pass along what it was he thought he knew of the world. "Calamity is no more unusual to my day and night than are torrential rains to Kang Gee Hill, children. Do you think I always had so little hair on my scalp?" He drew us close. "No, no, keep quiet for a moment, Double-Boy. I shall tell you a story. My late father, a man you would have done well to meet, lost his eye when he was a young priest. But he kept the eye in a hollow box, covered with cloth, or he told people he did. The word spread that this eye could see into your soul. And so it was that my father was beloved by all." As Sen spoke, I focused on his teeth, even and full and white. "And, I may add, prosperous."

"Your father sounds interesting," I said.

"You may see yourself as a double-boy suffering strenuous times." He did not look at us as he talked. "I see you starting the climb up the mountain marked 'opportunity.' Hardship is what makes a man, it is exciting."

The lack of Father seemed less than an opportunity. Mother spent her time crying, or sitting with Sen, or both. We lived in deep poverty.

Father's and Ping's funerals had cost Mother everything; our tuna nets had been sold, our trinket table discarded, our spirits broken. Chang and I sat for days on the dinghy tied to our houseboat, trolling the river with our hands. But few fish wanted to swim around the corpses of the fallen of our village, and the few that we *did* catch were valuable to us as food, and for that reason we had nothing to sell.

Yes, Sen—it is always an adventure to lose one's father in the first blush of high fishing season; and when one's meager family savings lose all their flesh in the course of a few weeks, then that too becomes instructive, an "exciting" misery. Mother's moans and cries would often drive Chang and me from the houseboat. She was right there with us after all this time, and I found myself yearning for her anyway, and new pains gathered around my heart.

Rain fell and irrigated the earth, fell and irrigated, and fell and at last flooded. Wet days passed and then weeks. Chang told trees and rocks and the dripping mud our troubles, hoping to enlist helpful spirits. None emerged.

Sen slipped Mother tiny gratuities here and there.

I began to dream of Princess Xenga, and of her fragile hands. A year passed like that; we were fourteen. If we had been two separate boys, we might have gotten work, the better to help Mother—this is what I thought.

And then something happened.

As they had done ages before, strangers began to visit our houseboat.

It started with a lone sightseer. A woman arrived one bleak day from Bangkok, elderly and lean and serious, her forearms thrust into the pockets of her frock, halfway up to her elbows. She stood before the houseboat and stared silently.

"Why did you come all this way?" Sen asked her, scratching the top of his bony head. He had been sleeping, and the few hairs he had stood tall. "Just to see *these* boys?"

"They have met the King." The woman closed her eyes as if trying to imagine what such an honor would be like. "And I wanted to encounter them. The double-elephant. The double-happiness of Siam."

This woman poked her old head in the doorway, caught a glimpse of us, smiled, nodded, and left without another word.

Soon people began turning out in hordes. They came just to glimpse. One visitor, a man who had lash marks across his neck and face, handed us a bushel of duck eggs, and then a large black duck that bobbed its head and squawked. A moment by our door, and the man turned on his heel, walked down the shoreline, then twirled again and waved.

That was when Chang and I began our business of raising ducks and selling their eggs.

We sold the eggs to local merchants for cash, and then borrowed Uncle Xau's boat to go upstream and buy another few ducks. Merchants were close-lipped and wide-eyed as we peddled our cargo to them.

With the money from the eggs, we increased our flock, and then we negotiated the whole business again. After a short time, Mother said, "What is this? Have we become duck vendors now?"

"Yes, we have," we said.

I hated her new pallor, her weaker voice, and her new expression because I saw them somehow as groundwork for the lack of maternal interest. Her brown front tooth had at last fallen out; she concealed its absence behind an everlasting grimace.

At any rate, on the shore beside our houseboat, Chang and I had built a fenced bamboo-enclosed circle in an afternoon (we had grown quite strong for our age). Inside it, we dug a basin and filled it with water. We kept our ducks on this little pond as pure as any in nature.

Chang and I looked out for one another then, and each had answers for all of the other's questions.

What if we do not succeed at this? he asked.

We will make an appropriate decision at the appropriate moment and diminish the influence of fate. As Father said.

What if Mother or Sen stops us from fishing? I asked.

A Mekong Fisherman stays abreast of change.

"We should only ever work together," Chang said. "Nobody else knows things the way we do." He winked. "Don't ask me to say what that is that we know, but we know it."

We rolled on the riverbank and hugged each other because we could not stop laughing. Who could say when last we had laughed like that? Or the next time that we would?

Every morning we mixed clay and salt in a bamboo tub and preserved the eggs in a clay-salt compound that conjured the muddy stink of sweat. My right arm and Chang's left were becoming strong from blending this sinewy clay and salt mixture, stronger than misery. My brother and I still did not talk to each other much, but we shared this accomplishment. Contrary to Western accounts of our life, our business was successful *not* due solely to a morbid curiosity on the part of our customers, but thanks to our hard work. We sold quite a few eggs.

"Let's keep one," he said one hot, sunny day.

"What do you mean?" I asked. We were bare-chested, mixing the compound. Arms around each other's shoulders, we each had a hand on the pole we were using to stir the paste.

My brother pointed to a small thin white duck circling the pond in need of a bath. "That one. As a pet." We named the duck In. He had a long bill and a fetching hop.

Then once upon a Mekong morning we saw two men walking side by side over the hill, marching toward us. One was small and the other was tall. We did not know then that this day would change our world forever.

"Right this way," one of them was saying to the other.

The first, dressed in a dirty Siamese peasant's frock and wringing his hands while he walked, tripped over himself as he led the second through the mud to our duck pond. It was raining, of course, and the first was holding an umbrella over the taller head of the second. "I think you'll find that the double-elephant is this way, sir," the first said, dripping, raising the umbrella like a beacon above his taller companion.

The second man looked strange; he was a giant, with skin not only pale like Ping's at her funeral, but at the same time vaguely pink like animal fat, and his hair was *brown*—a freakish color! He shielded one eye with a round piece of glass, leaned on a white walking stick, and under his greatcoat had on a suit like the tight-fitting and oddly cut suits Rama had sometimes shown off. The man also had a bushy mustache, like a scraggly brown puppy above his lip.

I remembered that I had seen him before: when we'd first met King Rama in His court, this odd man had been there, standing apart from the crowd.

Chang and I waited for this white man and his companion to approach. Ducks waddled around us, shaking water off their wings. The men stepped around our flock and came before us.

"I have searched for you," the strange man said, his tongue not quite conquering the demands of the Thai language. He was puffing at his pipe, despite the rain, and the smell of cherry tobacco reached my nose in smoky ringlets.

"We are Chang-Eng," said my brother, and I asked, "Who are you?"

"I am Captain Abel Coffin," the tall man said, in booming voice. He smiled at us smugly, as if he'd been our confidant forever. And he percolated with energy, and from under his balding dome his broad nose seemed to occupy the center of his face by force.

"Are you unwell?" my brother asked him.

"I'm sorry?" he asked.

Chang pointed to the Captain's light hair and then his too-pale cheek.

The man laughed and said: "Have you somewhere inside where we can chat?" And he handed his subordinate his cane as he began walking toward our houseboat without waiting to be invited.

What was it about Captain Coffin?

His voice was a foghorn, his steps wide as nations.

But was that enough? How could a man—even such a man in such a place—have persuaded Mother to allow him to do what he did?

We followed Captain Coffin and his companion into the houseboat. Even in the daytime, with little or no sun getting in through the one tiny window-hole, our small cabin was hazy with a dusk yellow light, amid which the candles looked like pale thin ghosts as they fought the drizzle. Mother was sitting with Sen, silently, their chairs facing one another, her hand in his. They turned toward the Captain slowly, without a start.

"Hello, my good lady," the white man said, his Thai shaky but loud.

"Hello," echoed Coffin's man, a step behind the Captain and very wet.

Mother examined the Captain for a long time. She said nothing, focusing on his mustache.

"I am Captain Coffin." Then, more slowly "Coffin. Cof-fin, it's an *English* name." Chang and I moved out from behind the Captain to see what Mother's reaction was.

"Are you unwell?" she asked him.

Coffin turned to his man, confused.

"He is a foreigner," the man told Mother, gesturing toward Coffin's skin and hair.

"What do you want here?" she asked.

"I want to change your lives," he whispered, filling the sentence with the white cadences of his foreign speech. Air from between his lips ruffled the bottom half of his mustache.

The Captain wheeled around toward my brother and me, taking us by Chang's arm and putting us between him and Mother.

"I want to make them rich, and you too, by, by—what's the word in this backward tongue?"

"By extension," the other man said.

"Yes, by extension." The Captain rolled his monocle between two fingers of his free hand. His other still grasped Chang's arm.

I felt the jiggling bulk of his entire frame behind the slightness of ours—he was as broad as Chang and me both—and he now clasped my wiry bicep with his large hand. As he held my brother and me, I could feel the tugging and closing of his ringed fingers, and despite his height, I was unable to avoid the smell of his breath—which was unmoving and heavy with tobacco smoke.

"Do you fathom what I am offering you?" he asked. The houseboat was steady as he spoke, as were the muffled calls of the ducks outside in their pen. "I am offering you glory." The pale skin of his hands looked even more unwell in the gloomy light. The flickering candlelight of the houseboat were slender indifferent ghosts playing on his knuckles. And Mother's weary face was just another of the particulars of the scene that could not have been more inexpressive, more indifferent to Captain Coffin.

He told of his plan to take Chang and me to America and England, republics of which we had never heard. Coffin said we would be made rich beyond our dreams.

"Savages?" Mother said. "You want to take my babies to savages?"

"No," said the Captain. He spoke the way men do when they understand that the world bends to their own vigor; it was the way Rama spoke, low-pitched and with heft. "The people in these places are like me," he said.

Mother shrugged her shoulders.

"The people there are not like you," the Captain said. "They are like me."

Mother frowned.

"Chang and Eng would be rich?" Sen asked. "Are there many ducks that need tending in these lands?"

The Captain smoothed his greatcoat. "People will pay money to see these brilliant creatures." He took a breath. "Allowing them to be a circus attraction would bring great honor to your family, and your nation, that the world may behold what the most blessed woman in the favored empire of Siam could alone offer."

Mother looked confused; there was no translation for the word "circus."

The Captain spun us around to face him, and he knelt before us. The spinning entangled my feet with Chang's, and the Captain had to catch us from falling. His huge bent knees touched our chests, and he looked into our eyes. "Of all the nations of the earth, of all the families, Siam and this family alone have the double-creature, the living wonder."

"They are just children, no different from other boys," Mother said. "Except they are attached."

Captain Coffin assured her that we would be treated with respect, and that the money we earned would go directly to her. "And they will be back in a year's time. Two, on the outside," said the Captain.

"Two at most," the Captain's man said.

The Captain rose.

"You can trust in me, I am a friend of your king." He told us about the cities of America, places of tall stone and solid pavement and gaslights and electricity and locomotives and horse carriages and glass, and of steamships that could outrun any junk on the Mekong.

The room was filled with skeptical silence.

"You will never have to work again," Coffin told Mother. A different kind of silence fell upon us.

The Captain snapped his fingers. His man stepped forward and handed Mother a pouch filled with jewelry. "Your sons will be treated feelingly," said Captain. "With great dignity."

Terrible, helpless anguish spread in my heart: We were leaving again.

The *Sachem*, the 397-ton sailing ship under Coffin's command, was the most impressive I'd ever seen. Two masts at either end of the boat held five huge white sails, and a taller third mast between the two held six. A network of ropes connected the sails and met at the conning tower atop the mizzenmast. A hundred feet long and thirty feet wide with two shining decks, she was unlike any junk afloat. At the prow, a huge pointed pole lanced the air ahead of it. Large white sailors on the lower decks jostled one another against massive sacks of rice. Even the cabin rats were colossal.

The first time we saw the ship, Chang and I were in Xau's rowboat with Mother and Sen and our pet duck In, weaving our way up the Mekong, and there in front of us, where a row of old houseboats bobbed like wreckage between our boat and the mouth of the Gulf of Siam, and where the eye was met with an excess of familiar sights—the green rice fields flanking the river as it emptied into the gulf, and the network of clotheslines mimicking the fishing nets below them, and the glut of little boats like ours carrying fish or prawns or silk—was the grandest sight of all: behind the jumbled angles of roofs and walls and beyond the gray Siamese peasant frocks dancing on their clotheslines were the masts of the *Sachem*, standing amused above it all, the way adults loom over children at play. The sight caused a bristling shiver to rake out from my spine like internal lightning.

I heard Mother sniff. I looked up at her and saw she was smiling through the tears that streamed down her face. "How beautiful," she whistled inadvertently through the space where her tooth would have been.

"We don't want to leave Siam," Chang said. We sat next to Mother; Sen paddled. Quacking In was jumping from Chang's lap to mine.

"You have beheld more in your young lives than I ever have," Mother said, her voice splintering. "And you will behold even more now."

"We don't want to," Chang said, close to tears. Sen made a grumbling sound from behind us.

"We will be all right, Mother," I said. Chang hit me in the chest, hard, just above where our band flares out into my body. I slapped him across his little ear and we fell to the floor of the junk, wrestling. In fell along with us and flapped his white wings.

"Shh. Stop it, now," Mother said.

Leaning on the starboard rail of the ship, Captain Coffin was waiting for us. We could make out his mustache from twenty yards; waxed this time, coming to sharp points on either end, it was wider than his face, probably wide enough for people behind him to see both greased tips.

So much higher than we were, standing with his hands behind the small of his back, Coffin wore his red tunic puffed out from under his blue captain's jacket. His golden buttons glinted in the early sun, matching his epaulets, and his white breeches flared out by his thighs. Even among the huge masts of his ship, he seemed a giant. The tip of his hat seemed from our angle to buss the clouds.

He waved when he saw us, and let out a hearty laugh. He bid us a deep hello in the Thai language. Mother hugged Chang and me and said good-bye. "I'll see you in a year's time, my babies." The morning sun was casting orange disks on the water.

"This is for the best," Sen told us.

Then came the ship's whistle, and Chang and I left Mother and boarded the *Sachem* with In, our pet duck, and headed off for America.

CHAPTER SEVEN

A Wilkesboro Wedding

1842–1843
Wilkesboro

Our double-wedding was set up very quickly. Not that the town had sanctioned it, or Mr. Yates, either. But I wrote Yates a letter, spelling out my feelings and intentions, and sent a copy to the *Wilkes County Spectator.* I was chaste and a Christian, and would continue to be both, my pen informed them. And so Mr. Yates capitulated to the will of the three women in his life, and fairly gently at that. That is not to say that he could yet look at Chang and me, or speak to us. But he did not say much against us, either. And so Chang and I found ourselves one day arguing before a North Carolina court that neither Sarah nor Adelaide would be committing bigamy by marrying conjoined twins. The judge, the Honorable Patch Meadows, somehow agreed.

We were careful not to break other laws. In North Carolina, a free white woman could not marry anyone with Indian, Negro, mustee, or mulatto blood down to the third generation. I felt lucky that North Carolinians hadn't any legislation forbidding Siamese, though the looks and hisses we caught let us know that there may soon have been such an addition to the court's ledger.

We were also told to choose a last name. Wanting to appear American, I came up with Bunker, after the battle that started this

country on the path to freedom. Chang agreed, and we became
Chang and Eng Bunker.

Just when it seemed everything was coming off easily, life again
became a hardship. In the eveningtime before my wedding ceremony, we were summoned to the rectory of Wilkesboro's Parson
Hodge, a man we barely knew. Sitting in the parson's study, with
books of God gaping down at us, we had to explain our intentions to this thickset young minister who had hairless pink cheeks
and Benjamin Franklin eyeglasses. The town of Wilkesboro, Hodge
said, demanded it.

Think about what it is these people want from you, I told
myself.

Perhaps, I told myself, it is the same thing that you want.

I said to the Parson, bringing his teacup to my lips, "If it will
save Adelaide and Sarah from disgrace"—I took a calm, gentle-
manly sip, then put down the cup—"then my brother and I will
be split asunder."

"Yes, we will do," said Chang, though he did not look happy
about it.

Surely we knew the dangers, and yet here we were, discussing
disunion. This was not the first time we'd considered attempting such an operation with a Westerner. In London, New York,
Philadelphia, and Paris, doctors had asked to evaluate us for a possible separation, and always they convinced Chang it was too unsafe. I wanted to try it, despite the risk—especially if it meant
winning our right to wed. If I could be married *and* separated,
what an unhoped-for bliss my life would become!

"Listen, Mr.—Eng, is it? You don't understand," Hodge said.
The young parson looked mussed, as if he'd spent the whole day
fully dressed in his wrinkled brown suit and sprawled in bed. "The
town is very upset. And people are ready to—"

"Oh, we understand, Parson Hodge," I said. "I know that it
presumably will kill us."

I couldn't escape our double-reflection in that little room. It
lived in the smudged mirror on the far wall, in the spoon I used to
stir my tea; it was undulating in the tea itself, in the burnished
wood of the table, in the Parson's eyes.

"Yes, we understand," said my brother. "We so very different, the town people all afraid of us. I have wanted to be disconnected never in our lives. I like Chang and Eng the way he is. But still we make a decision." My brother leaned us forward. "We understand."

The murmur of a crowd assembling in the distance had grown loud. Through Hodge's front window, on a dark hilltop yards away, single glowing dots bobbed toward a large body of light— men with torches joining a throng under the stars. The town had its demands. That is why Chang and I had brought guns with us.

"No," Hodge told us. "You don't *understand*. These are the sort of people, they couldn't care so much that you are born quare. We have a town of mountain people here. Wilkesboro is isolated, and that's so by choice." He was whispering to peel away the meanness in his words.

"We're uncontaminated by the other world," he said. "Picture these Southern highlands as a sort of islet, left alone for generation on generation. Maybe now you recognize us. We don't see many outlanders from beyond. People here are not used even to people from Savannah or New Orleans, and we call *them* foreigners." He was kind-faced now and positively grinning. "So, what the people don't want—they don't want these Yates girls marrying near-niggers from the other world. Especially these girls, especially after—" He looked at me a long time.

He knew I was a Christian. We had talked about God when Chang and I first arrived at his door, and I had impressed him with my knowledge of the Bible.

The Parson spoke in a soft voice. "Perhaps you've stayed too long in Wilkesboro." He smiled. "I know what you are thinking. We are not a backward people. We have a powerful ambition when we see something to win out over, and we have the sort of heart that's fair. We just like things the old-fashioned way, as it was for Daniel Boone a hundred years ago, and the way it was before him. Time doesn't scoot along here; it stays on." He was not finished. "The point is that you're Chinamen, that you got lemon-color skin."

Outside, the crowd began its approach. I did not believe Hodge. Surely what they were protesting, I thought, was the idea that the husbands were one, the wives two. The Yates girls, it had been hissed, were after lustful perversion.

The throng's murmur was now a roar.

Conclusions, not deliberations, propel action. Reason cannot bring strangers to one's perception of the world. No dialogue can bridge the great divisions. Chang and I decided to fight. A man must remain a man.

"Excuse us, Parson."

We took our shotguns and walked to the porch. We had never fired a gun, but how difficult could it be? I held my left arm fast around my brother's shoulder. We kept the firearms down, at our sides, and loaded. Parson Hodge came outside and stood by us. I remember thinking he was a brave American.

That night was warm for January, and as black as the crows in the Wilkes County coal mine. The crowd, a ball of light that spread as it approached, was fast separating into individual torch-bearing men. The throng numbered about twenty fellows strong; one or two men were armed with guns, a few others with pitchforks, shovels, axes. The rest carried just their torches, spitting and swearing and wiping their foreheads on filthy shirtsleeves. Most of them concealed portions of their faces with kerchiefs. They came to a stop before the parson's porch and stood in his front yard.

The crowd was close before us in firelight and shadow. Chang moved his arm from my shoulder and used both his hands to lift his gun. Doing this, he had to pivot toward me, and so we stood toe-to-toe; he pointed his weapon at the crowd. I felt myself sweating from my armpits. My mouth was dry.

"Slow down, people," Chang yelled, though nobody was moving. The thick wooden butt of his gun was an inch off my cheek.

"Parson, you liked to stand down," said a man in front of the throng with a straw hat. "Our beef's with the Chinamen." I recognized this man's half-covered face. He had been among the first to wave and say hello when we'd arrived in town.

"I ain't sure this marriage is right, either, John," blinking Hodge muttered as he scratched his head. "But one thing I know is wrong is violence." He pointed at this man: *"Violence!"*

Another man, bigger, a thug with bushy black eyebrows, walked forward out of the thick of the group. He closed one eye and lifted his gun, pointing it directly at Chang. The tip of his weapon was about three feet from my brother's. "It ain't natural," he said calmly.

Using both of my hands, I directed my shotgun toward this man's head. He didn't move. Black flies buzzed between us, on their way to the horses that fed on grass in the neighboring stable. The knuckles of my left hand touched the knuckles of Chang's; the barrels of our guns came to a point. Chang, this masked man, and I stood there, our weapons forming the letter Y in the air.

How have you ended up here, Eng? I asked myself.

You followed your brother, I said to myself,

"We will die," I heard myself say to the crowd, "before we give up the right to marry—" In my voice shook desperation and splintered courage.

The thug did not move his gun from my brother's direction.

"—and at least some of you will die before we do," I said, "I can promise you that." What was I doing? I had no grudge against these men. I imagined pulling the trigger—nothing won, all lost, everything finished. I had never focused so hard on something as I did on that man's gun.

Do not back down, I told myself. This is what you want, too. A chance at happiness.

"We'll burn your house, Parson," a voice wheezed from the crowd, "don't think we won't."

A rock came flying and broke the Parson's front window. "God will strangle you dead."

Hodge shook his head. "I know these Chinamen are good men of their kind, upstanding *Christian* men." He held his hands in front of him, palms out, fingers spread; his voice wavered.

Chang and I continued to aim our weapons at the man before us. I could feel the smallest tremor in my brother's hand. "Steady," I told him. "Yes, I know," he said. I felt my internal organs pushing their way up toward my throat.

In the periphery of my eye line I noticed a carriage coming toward us, down the dirt road adjacent to Hodge's yard. It was Sarah and Adelaide. I tried not to look, not to draw attention to their imminent arrival.

Someone from the throng implored, "Parson, move." And I gripped the gun more tightly in my hands.

A second rock was thrown, and struck me in the chest; it knocked us down, onto our sides. Both our guns went off as they fell from our hands. My breast was throbbing; the rock had taken my breath. I was left wheezing. The bullets whistled off into the distance.

The thug charged up on the porch. In two steps he reached us, aiming his gun at me.

As the man started to squeeze the trigger, Chang and I brought two of our knees to our chests in one shared motion until they abutted one another. And then we kicked him in his gut, the heels of our feet striking as one.

What happened next is immortalized in a drawing by a North Carolinian artist named John Ray, Jr., who was commissioned to illustrate the pamphlet accompanying our last tour. In the sketch by Ray Jr.—who may have been there, a kerchief over his face— the thug sails backward and his gun discharges harmlessly into the air. The thug is shown to be about five feet off the ground, his arms splayed. The force of two kicks hitting simultaneously was portrayed with accuracy. I did not come out well in the portrait, caught as I was in the blur of the instant, but Chang, sitting some- what higher than I, can be seen smiling. What the picture could not capture was the next moment, when the man crashed into the rearmost pillar of Hodge's porch and landed with a thud. He was unconscious by the time he'd touched down.

With a unified yell, the throng rushed forward, bloodlust in their eyes. A few dragged their torches as they went, scalding the ground beneath them. The rest held their flames in front of them, set to burn the parson's house to the ground and kill us. Their shadows were giants.

The thunder of a gunshot stopped the mob in its tracks. Adelaide was standing on her father's rig and pointing a rifle in the air. She was girdled by gunsmoke. Sarah, my own Sarah, was there, too— holding the reins and keeping the bucking horses from running.

"Don't you'all realize I can tell who you are?" Adelaide was cry- ing. "Did my father put you up to this?" There she was, standing there, a tall young woman with a broad chest with large hips, a fighter. Her hair was very tidy. "I recognize you—Jed! And Steven Thomas!" She pointed her gun at a different man with each name she called. "David Cooper," she shouted. "Tyler Brody! I see you through that little muffler. Did your mama knit you that?"

"Let's get to our weapons," I whispered to my brother, and, crawling, we managed to seize Chang's rifle while the crowd was focused on our brides. As Chang and I got to our feet, my brother leveled his gun toward the crowd. I held my hands before me in squeezed fists.

"You rascals!" Sarah yelled. I hadn't thought she'd had this passion in her. She turned slowly toward the men. "You rascals!" she screamed, shaking the reins in anger.

The crowd stood still. The one named John, calm as the weather that night, said: "These Chinamen, these quare Chinamen, can't have you girls." At this point John turned and saw my brother, and the gun leveled at his head, and the cur jumped back.

"Go home," said the Parson. "Just everybody go home."

Nobody reacted.

Be brave! I told myself. *Be brave!* I caught this man John's eye. A heartbeat, and then he looked away.

The men grumbled as they limped back from where they had come. I turned toward Sarah, but she was still looking ahead into space. It was time for our marriage to begin.

The next morning marked our wedding day, a gladsome sunny afternoon in Wilkesboro. Our ceremony was held in the sizable living room of the Yateses' boardinghouse, and as any wedding is still a wedding, Wilkesboro had put on its white shirt. It seemed there were more in Wilkesboro who were willing to celebrate a high-profile union than to try to prevent it by force. And so, a crowd of townsfolk was clustered around the house, decorated for the affair. Those not invited, especially the women, decided to throng in front of the first-floor windows, pushing and wrangling, peeking with their noses against the glass, hoping to be granted admission. A few strange men paced in the yard, grumbling. Sheriff Bishton stood by the front door ready for trouble.

The townswomen who actually were our brides' guests entered through the front door wearing flowers and holding their trains. Unwelcome newspapermen milled about, in ill-fitting coats,

white ties, uniforms and broadcloths, and white gloves. Chang
and I had invited no one.

I was hopeful that, despite the fracas of the previous night, it
would be an excellent event; the Yateses had spread roses along
the living room couch, straightened the painting of daisies on the
living room wall, and placed a silver candelabra atop the makeshift
dais at the far end of the hardwood floor in front of the two rows
of wooden chairs—and all of these ornaments beamed in the sunlight. Strings of popcorn decorated the ceiling and swung from
the rafters like fancy spiderwebs.

Chang and I, in our trousers but still not yet wearing our coats
or waistcoats, stood at the top of the carpeted staircase hiding behind the edge of the wall; I spied the scene downstairs. "What's
happening?" my brother asked, his hand squeezing my shoulder.

Rising from the swarm of velvet and satin, of hats, hair, bare
necks, and arms, there was discreet but lively conversation that
echoed under the low ceiling. The level of anticipation was higher
than what was appropriate for a wedding. Some members of the
Yates family tried to look as if they were not thinking of the impli-
cations of united bridegrooms.

At last one of the ladies of the crowd, in a red dress with massive puffed shoulders, said, "It really is strange, though!" and all
the guests began expressing their wonder openly.

Then Thom, a shopworn Negro, maybe forty-five, who was
our wedding present from Mrs. Yates, came up behind us and said:
"Masters, it's time to finish getting your dressings put on." He had
an eye patch and shoulders so tired from years of exertion that he
could not lift his bowed arms as high as his head. Still, the slave
placed a hand on my right arm, and his other on Chang's left. We
had met him only that day.

Making our way back to our dressing room, I caught sight of
Chang's betrothed across the hallway, through the crack between
her not fully closed door and its doorjamb. Adelaide was looking
out the window, biting her pointer finger, and wearing her white
dress and long veil and a wreath of dogwood blossoms. Someone
inside her room closed the door.

Chang was hunched a bit and grimacing like someone was stepping on his head. "I hope I been a good brother to you," he said.

I laughed slightly, told him to relax.

"I think you been pretty friendly to me, considering," he said.

"Let us get ready."

It was not easy to dress because Chang kept trying to pace the floor. We were to wear identical black tuxedos, keeping the three buttons at the center of our shirts unfastened, along with the top two buttons of our black silk waistcoats, to make room for the bare ligament.

"The ring—you have?" Chang asked me, frantic, waving his hands.

"Yes," I said. "And you have not lost the other one, I presume."

He winnowed through his pockets, then screwed up his face in despair.

The slave Thom cleared his throat. "The second ring is just right there on the dresser, master," he said with a placid smile. The ring was where Thom said it was, next to our ever-present checkers board.

"Anybody else acted foolish as this, ever?" my brother asked me. I stopped in my tracks, planting my feet firmly; I had had my fill of walking to and fro. Chang halted with a snap.

"All right," I said. "You were stupid to misplace the ring. But there it is on the counter. Relax yourself, brother. You are my best man—come, let's put on the waistcoat." I said, "Thom, help us."

"But the shirt!" Chang cried.

"You have a shirt on, Chang," I said.

For a long moment, Chang stared down at his own chest without saying anything. Then he said, "Well, this one wrinkled!"

Thom stood scratching his head. The slave was looking at our ligament despite himself.

"Your shirt is *fine*," I said. "Let's finish dressing."

There was a knock at the door and Mr. Yates entered, his curly hair standing out on both sides of his head. He looked at us for a long time, squinted, then forced a smile. "It's time, boys."

"There they are!" "Which is which?" "Why, my soul, those old girls look more scared than happy," were some of the whispers from the crowd.

Chang and I stood before young Parson Hodge. The guests sat

at our backs, and we waited for Mr. and Mrs. Yates to bring Adelaide and Sarah to us.

I could not take my eyes off my bride as she walked the aisle. I saw nothing and no one else; I didn't care what people whispered; her face was long, longer even than Adelaide's, but that's what made her so beautiful, I thought. There was grace in the swoop of nose shooting out of her white veil in such a maidenly way toward her long pale neck. The longer the face, the better, I thought, and I pitied my brother for marrying his woman who had only a long*ish* nose.

It was some while before the girls and their parents could figure out the logistics of what they were to do. Mrs. Yates was breathing heavily and waddling her immense body one slow step at a time. And when the girls' parents reached us, Mr. Yates took me by the wrong arm—as if he thought he could walk *between* Chang and me—and Mrs. Yates forgot she was to step aside so Adelaide could stand by Chang.

The crowd shifted in its seats, arousing a rustle of skirts.

At last things were set right, with each bride taking her husband-to-be's outward hand in her opposite palm. The girls' eyes betrayed the same questions that were living inside me: *What am I doing? What do I expect will happen next?* I had recently turned thirty-two years old.

It is puzzling, I told myself, but bringing more people into our connection will make attachment easier to bear.

Chang had been right, I told myself. And you owe him for that. I wanted to tell him how thankful I was to him at that moment.

Mrs. Yates stepped before us and tried to say something but couldn't speak. She began to cry, and then laughed, sending waves through her chins. Meanwhile, rumpled young Parson Hodge, his shiny wet blond-gray hair parted down the middle of his head, began to lean on the makeshift dais between him and us (actually an end table, covered by a red sheet, atop a dining room table). He moved the silver candelabra to one side so he could see the two couples.

Mr. Yates leaned toward Sarah cautiously, whispered something, and, making a sign to his wife, took two steps back. With a bit of difficulty, Mrs. Yates followed him.

Can this be happening? I thought, and I turned to my bride, toward her face in profile, and from the scarcely perceptible quiver in her lips and eyelashes I knew she felt my eyes on her. Sarah didn't return my glance; her veil, caught on her little pink ear, trembled.

I beamed at my brother, who was blinking, and at his bride. Adelaide held back a sigh in her throat. Her little hands were shaking in their long white gloves. She caught me smiling at her and looked older than her thirty-one years.

I was filled with joy and dread. I was not some famous Siamese oddity now; I was a bridegroom marrying sisters from Wilkesboro, North Carolina.

"Let us stand," Hodge said, and the crowd did. He prayed for us, for peace, and the house seemed to breathe with his voice. He prayed for understanding from an unreasonable world. The speech impressed me. How did I believe I could go through life alone? I thought. I smiled at my wife and touched her gloved hand with my finger. These girls came to our aid with guns at night, I thought to myself.

Hodge invoked God, North Carolina, and the United States, then turned to us with the Book: "Eternal Jesus, that joinest them together that were separate," he read in a gentle but piping voice. "Who hast ordained this union of holy wedlock that cannot be set asunder, Thou didst bless Abraham and Sarah and their many descendants, according to Thy Holy Covenant, leading them in the path of all good works."

"Amen" came rolling from behind us.

I looked at my wife. She was nearly smiling, and staring dimly at nothing. A vein on the side of her face was pitter-pattering. Chang and the two girls had stopped listening to the preacher. With eyes glazed over, each had missed the meaning of the words of the service—a fact I found vexing.

Not that I wasn't swept up in things. On that day, at that moment, there was taking place a complete severance from my old life, and a different, normal life was beginning for me. I lifted my hand from my brother's shoulder and patted him lightly on the back. He didn't notice; he'd shifted toward his wife, stretching our band as far as it would go.

But this new life I'd envisioned was not yet, and I could not even picture it clearly to myself.

Suddenly I realized the talking had stopped. I had lost track of what Hodge was saying; there was a moment of hesitation, of whispering and smiles. My brother was holding out my ring, and apparently I was supposed to give Chang his.

Chang handed me the trinket that I was to put on my bride's finger, and I returned the favor. We both tried to rotate toward our brides, but ended up in a ridiculous back-and-forth tug that staggered us. That hadn't happened once in the thirty years since we'd learned to walk. The crowd murmured.

After Chang put his ring on Adelaide's finger, we shifted in my bride Sarah's direction. I heard groans urging me to get on with it as I turned toward the smile of happiness on Sarah's radiant face. That smile was reflected in everyone who was looking at her. A geyser of emotion exploded from the mud of my insides.

"Put it on!" she whispered, showing her strong American teeth, her eyes open wide. "Put it on!" Meanwhile Chang's panicky hand was tapping my shoulder with all five fingers.

I was struck by what I took to be the jubilance in my bride's long face, and her feeling infected me. I took her delicate gloved hand and slipped the ring around her finger. Sighs and teary chuckles from the crowd feathered my ears. The spark in my bride seemed to have kindled the whole gathering.

And I had never before seen Sarah look as she did. The glow on her cheeks was bewitching. I wanted to speak to her but didn't know if the ceremony was over.

"You may kiss the brides." Hodge was smiling grandly, too. "And, girls, you lean in and kiss your men."

On tipped toes Sarah bent toward me. I kissed her smiling lips with timid care, and the side of my brother's head pushed against mine as he weathered his bride's forceful kiss.

We offered the sisters our forearms and walked up the aisle, overcome by a strange new sense of closeness. It was only as I met my bride's—and her sister's—awed and timid eyes that I believed it was true, because I felt that we were one. I barely knew these girls, but it did not matter. They had saved our lives last night, and were saving them again now.

Later that evening, everybody danced the Virginia reel. But before that we had a big supper.

At the main table we dined with our wives, along with Jefferson, Parson Hodge, Mayor Dungsworth, and Mr. and Mrs. Yates. Other guests filled the five tables positioned around us in the dining room. I looked around me and wondered if any of these people were among those who'd tried to kill us the night before.

Just as Chang and I were, Mrs. Yates was sitting on a custom-built bench. To our right, Hodge was constantly laughing and making conspiratorial faces. He seemed to think every utterance was an inside joke.

"The slaves are saying that this is a spirit marriage." Hodge's voice was starting to crack and tremble in advance of the laugh coming in his throat. "*Voodoo.* Now whether that's good or bad, I don't know." He batted his eyelashes.

"Slaves," said Mayor Dungsworth, "need their rumors of spirits."

"But so do I!" Hodge cried, and then shrugged his shoulders to exonerate himself from any charge of impropriety. Mr. Yates turned away from Hodge.

"I don't feel what we are doing is *that*, you'all," said Adelaide, shaking her head. "A spirit marriage."

Sarah looked downward. "I don't feel that, either."

Hodge looked at her a long time, as if he wanted to say something but knew he should hold back. "I just mean to say"—he leaned in to whisper—"I sometimes get silly and think I'm not any more civilized than they are. Well, not *really*—" He chuckled at the thought of being uncivilized, and looked into the space between my brother and me. "Do you ever feel that way, twins? No more civilized than the other nonwhites in Wilkes County?"

Chang opened his mouth but didn't speak. He was waiting for me to say something. The house creaked sternly.

"Excuse me?" Chang answered finally. Everybody laughed. Chang began to smile, and he nicked me with his elbow as he wiped the sweat from his upper lip.

"Chang and Eng are brilliantly smart," Mrs. Yates said to the Mayor. "They picked up English themselves, and Eng reads Shakespeare."

Mayor Dungsworth's whitish beard, young-looking face, and

clear blue eyes gave him an almost regal air. He pursed his lips at Mrs. Yates and nodded. Meanwhile, my father-in-law breathed through his nose, producing a sort of soft, bitter chuckle.

Mrs. Yates waved her meaty hands to get the attention of someone sitting at a table across the room. Then she smiled. "What are you'all laughing about over there?" she shouted. "Everyone's having such fun at your end, and I'm here with these stuck-in-the-muds," Mrs. Yates went on with mock peevishness, in a baby's tone of voice. She pouted for an instant, then exploded into a laughter that shook her whole body as she laid a weighty hand on the Mayor's wrist. I looked away.

Thom and two other Negroes, young Harriet and Brett, who another slave owner had lent out for the night, brought out dinner—green beans, mashed potatoes, roasted duck, and turkey gravy, the latter being presented separately, in silver boats. Thom, as wobbly as he was, had the two slaves shuffling tableware so hurriedly that Harriet's kerchief was stirring behind her as if she'd been facing a breeze.

I told the Yateses that I found the food delicious. My father-in-law looked at me, his eyes very baggy, but he managed not to frown, then resumed looking at his plate.

"You'll be getting used to this sort of cooking," said Dungsworth.

"We were going to prepare some rice for Chang and Eng, isn't that right, girls?" said Mrs. Yates. "But the twins wanted good food, like we was having. Were having." She grinned and huffed—breathing did not come easily to her.

"I'll bet this's an improvement on rice," said Hodge. He pouted, and waited until he got our father-in-law's attention before continuing. "Bet it's an improvement," the Parson added.

"I'll venture it is," Yates muttered. He gripped his fork with a vigor that spoke volumes about his thoughts on the subject.

"This gravy is especially delicious, girls," I said, not really knowing what I was saying, focusing on my smile and the heartfelt air I could lend it.

"Not that anything wrong with rice," Chang said.

My wife kept her head down as if her long chin were an extension of her collarbone. Our choice to marry had consequences, I thought. She probably knew this.

"Jefferson likes rice," Mrs. Yates said, looking at her son. "Isn't that right, Jeff?"

Jefferson scratched his head.

"Please, Mother," Adelaide and Sarah said in unison.

"It's true." Mrs. Yates nodded with determination. "Not like a Chinaman, but the boy likes rice."

"I believe I do." Jefferson's voice was wobbling on the opening of adulthood. "With chicken sometimes."

I was not listening: I thought of my hopes that for years had gone unnoticed like bubbles coming off hidden treasure at the bottom of the ocean. I seized on them to feed my appetite for the coming adventure. And my fear of it. Outside the window, mist sat on the front lawn.

After dinner, everyone gathered on the grass and danced the Virginia reel by lantern light. While Hodge stood on the veranda playing the fiddle, the crowd split itself into clapping lines, one of men, the other, of their partners. The pair at the bottom of their respective queues met in the middle, joined hands, and do-si-doed through the space between; and then the next couple echoed the ritual, and so on. This propelled the lines. The ground rumbled. Mist curled around dancing calves.

With our wives, Chang and I retreated to the porch, by Hodge and his fiddle. It was understood we would not dance. We four newlyweds looked out into the dark, mild universe, clapped, smiled and nodded at the bouncing guests occasionally.

Hodge's fiddle music was high-pitched, based on the pentatonic scale. I thought of a wind slowly blowing through dead trees when Hodge played in the lower register, and when he scratched out the highest notes, it sounded like the regret that left Mother's lips when she was grieving.

My wife shivered by my side, though it was not shivering weather. "Do you know we play the flute?" I said. Delicate-necked and wondering about the mystery of love, Sarah looked back at me, her eyelashes flittering like butterflies lighting in a meadow.

"I am an abominable dancer," I said, feeling a warm trickle in my chest that I took to be the start of my future, "and have never in my life asked anyone—"

"And we not even any good at it," Chang said, turning to his bride on his elbow.

"—But I'm asking you now." In my wife's eyes I saw my own smile. "May I have the pleasure of this dance?"

When it was our turn to skip between the rows of guests, there was some confusion. Kicking up more dust than previous dancers, Chang and I skipped out to the center, our hands squeezing each other's shoulders; and we waited for our brides. The two girls waltzed toward us together, smiling and blushing, facing their new grooms; but when it was time to turn and start dancing through the makeshift lane, Adelaide followed her instincts and tried to take her husband's *inside* arm. She realized her mistake and skipped to the outside, but it was too late. People had seen.

My brother's face showed a pathetic nervous smile; I could feel my own cheeks going flush. The clapping was disrupted and uneven now. Still, we four newlyweds began to dance between our guests. I succumbed to the rhythm and the melody. I closed my eyes. I felt my wife's sweating and shaking hand in mine. I began to dance.

It was lovely, and with my eyes still closed, I thought it was an exquisite moment—except for the "excuse-me"'s I heard. I opened my eyes and saw people shuffling to move out of our way as we danced up the lane. The lines had been too near one another, the lane too narrow for a double-couple.

The columns billowed out, widening our path: the bedlam of rearrangement. Hodge's music kept on, though, and the clapping rhythm with it, and I closed my eyes again. A tepid breeze felt good through my hair. My wife was fondling the heel of my palm with her thumb as we danced. All that bustle, and wasn't she pretty to stroke my hand lightly in hers. I opened my eyes. Everyone was smiling under the lantern light. I knew love. All I had ever wanted was to be alone, and I had gotten just the opposite of that wish. And I was happy for it.

Book Two

CHAPTER EIGHT

The Mysteries of the Bridal Bed

1843
Wilkesboro

Our double-wedding coincided with the end of the most blessed age of the variegated American South. Chang and I, two immigrants thinking just of the pursuit of happiness, had been immersed in our own lives and had failed to notice the portents and discontents of America. But after settling down in Wilkes County, one could not fail to mark the emotion in the air, even as early as 1843.

The preservation of the Union, while it seemed less and less possible, had become the golden goal—even, at that point, of most Southerners. The nation was building the roads and canals that Carolina's favorite son John Calhoun himself had called "a most powerful cement to hold the parts of the nation together." In time I would fall under the sway of the great politician Henry Clay of the Whigs, whose belief in a high tariff on imports would increase the value of the corn and hogs I would come to raise— but I admired Calhoun as well. His allegiance to states' rights, the belief that the self-governing components of this body politic should have the power to do as they pleased, was a position for which I of course felt a natural affinity. The seeds of secession were already being planted, however; South Carolina had gone so far as to threaten to secede eleven years before, but she backed down once President Jackson raised an army to head off the defection. No one believed she would yield again, if ever there were another confrontation. And another confrontation seemed inevitable.

It would be some time before I really got caught up in the current of politics. At this point I felt an uneasy kinship with an America that had been my home for as many years as had Siam. Sometimes I looked at my skin and felt ashamed. How far removed were we from Thom in the Yates family's estimation?

After the wedding, Chang and I decided it would be best if we stayed away from our wives while our new home in Wilkes County was being renovated. This we financed with the money we'd saved after years of touring. My brother and I passed the first weeks of our married lives alone together in the Guion Hotel in neighboring Mount Airy, North Carolina, making minor modifications to our plan regarding how best to decipher the special questions of our marital bed.

This is the method Chang and I decided upon, and told the newspapers about: Whenever one of us needed privacy with his wife, the other was to become "insensate" for the next hour, to become unconscious, allowing each twin to enjoy his wife in seclusion. Though our situation seemed immoral and shocking to the outside world, it was through what we called an "alternate mastery" that we would be certain to remain pure. I would pass immediately into the highest loftiness of trance, trying to raise my spirit out of our bodies, like a mist, to circle the world and vapor toward Siam. In this way we would avoid allegations of improper relations between our wives and ourselves.

Soon enough, what would soon be known as "our house" was said to be ready, and my brother and I went excitedly to examine it before our wives arrived. Our carriage reached the little home well past dusk. Our new residence was on Trap Hill, a knoll outside of town named after an old hunter who had had a predilection for setting snares to catch wild turkey. The house was a stunted white square, unassuming, sturdy, crouching on a stretch of dust and hillock set back from the dirt road. ("No angry townsfolk would bother us here," I'd said to Chang.) It had been

built with rocks and wood taken from the banks of the Yadkin
River, and it had a kitchen, dinner room, and a small parlor on
the first floor, as well as an extra-wide stairway for Chang and me.
There were two sleeping quarters on the second floor—one with
a bed built to accommodate three, and one in which our wives
would alternate spending every other night alone—and two more
bedrooms for any children we might have.

Leafless, skinny birch trees corralled the house, which had a
brown curb roof and two chimneys, one at each side. It was a
desolate, peaceful scene, a home blending into the tableau of cotton wagons, wayward livestock, and tottery churches that was
Wilkes County. Next to the house stood a barn in which we
would shelter our animals and store hay and corn and firewood. In
the backyard, Thom's shed completed our modest estate.

It was dark by the time Chang and I and Thom arrived at this
new residence, and no one had been there before us to light any
of the lamps inside. With only the full moon lending its light, the
dry earth of our property spread out lumpish and gray like cooling lead around our home.

Thom gathered boxes of clothes and books for us and set them
down amid the dark oak and hickory furniture.

That first night, alone again at least for one more evening,
Chang and I lay in the biggest bed we had ever seen. We had not
yet put up shades over our big new windows, and the room was
full of moonlight, lending the floorboards the color of white
sand. My brother's green-striped nightcap kept sliding off his
head, and he could not sleep either.

"I cannot believe our good fortune," I said.

Chang answered as if he had been in the middle of a mono-
logue. "That these sisters do this, that they excuse—" His emotion-
filled voice was thick as if his mouth were full of rice. "To become
a mother is so important to them, that they—" He smiled and we
huddled closer together to keep warm. Beneath the blanket Chang's
feet were wandering, silently, like moles digging underground.

"Few other girls would be so—refined," I said, my nose filled
with the sweet smell of the pomade in Chang's hair. "They saved
our lives," I sighed. The word "wives" slid around in my brain.

How many times had Chang and I lain like this, afraid even to talk of marriage?

"Yes, *extra*ordinary," he said, shifting his arm beneath my neck and absentmindedly tapping my shoulder three times with his hand.

I'd given up trying to find an explanation for our newfound love. Though the sisters were dissimilar in many ways, they were like most siblings in that their conduct, in respect to one another, was baffling to everyone other than themselves. Some sets of siblings adhere to their own ethics, like a society of two.

"Suppose we hadn't found them," I said. "These lovely sisters."

"Why I want to think of that?" Chang did not open his eyes.

"Only this," I said. "It is odd that we could have needed something so badly and not known it."

"I know it all along," said my brother. "I know it all along."

I could not help wondering about the pleasures and mysteries of the bridal bed. "We are about to receive something else I didn't quite expect."

Chang did not respond. He'd fallen asleep.

That night I dreamed I was Sarah and myself at the same time. I knew this was impossible—and impossible to put into words—but I felt I was *two genders at once*, though I knew a person had fully to be one or the other. I was both, somehow man and woman, she and myself.

The next evening Adelaide and Sarah arrived after supper. It was a cold weekend night; the stoves were heated. We gentled our wives from their carriage and down the path to their new home, while Thom gathered boxes of their cosmetics and clothes and notions and brought everything inside. Church bells were clanging on the other side of Trap Hill. For some reason I felt in a great hurry.

"How are you, Adelaide?" Chang searched his wife's face before allowing himself a smile.

"Isn't it obvious?" she said. "Excited as I've ever been."

"How are you, Sarah?" I asked.

"Very well, thanks." Her voice cracked. "Only I have a bit of a bother in my stomach."

The girls wore toques and identical long ruffled white dresses with red trim. Above the frilly neckline of their attire, the tops of their chests were more visible than usual, and I admired the tightness of their skin and the little plots of childish freckles scattered across their collarbones.

Their dainty hands in our sweating ones, we brought Adelaide and Sarah to the soft gray couch in the den. Before they'd sat down, Chang and I turned on our heels and ran out of the room, toward the kitchen. Adelaide yelled to us. "Where are you two going?"

We were sprinting down the hall now. "We'll show you," I called over my shoulder. "One minute, please," said Chang over his.

While we rummaged through an open drawer and found our battered oblong flute cases, I could hear the noise of an animated whispering session between our brides in the other room.

In an instant, Chang and I knelt before the girls, facing one another to free our arms. "For you," we said. Chang, not following our agreed-upon script, added, "For love," shaping the words around the jagged cadence of his accent.

We'd spent the day practicing for this moment. We opened the instrument cases and fit together our flutes expertly, laying the two instruments side by side like two silver-gilt eels. Then we played. Sarah took her toque off and brought it to her lap. Her blonde hair was parted down the middle, pulled back into a chignon—a perfect, golden setting for the angular splendor of her nose, which seemed carved by an old-world sculptor too covetous to stop sculpting. Her sister was a variation on the same theme.

When Chang and I began to play "O Susannah," my wife's eyes took on the respectful focus of someone watching a passing parade. The high notes jumped quickly, free of vibrato, their throaty elegance receding before the greater elegance of my wife. I tried to concentrate on the airholes, my mouth, and the oscillations of breath, but my notes fell to pieces around her.

I noticed Chang was feeling the same as I was. We stopped playing.

"Don't stop," our wives said, holding their toques.

It was agreed by the flip of a buffalo-head nickel that Chang and Adelaide would have that first honeymoon night together in the three-person bedroom. As we decided to turn in, I said good night to Sarah and leaned toward her, pulling Chang with me, and I kissed her. I had given my lips to my wife before, at the wedding, with similar enthusiasm, but now it felt more familiar, and I found myself importing visions of our future life together into the feelings of this first good-night kiss. I divined the laughter of our unborn children, and the warmth of a thousand kisses to come, each to be more familiar than the last.

I kissed her lips once, twice, and then simply kept my mouth pressed—tenderly, softly—against hers, not moving, and a crowd surged in my chest. My bride pulled away, blinking. "Tomorrow," she said, wiping her lips on her forearm, turning to walk to her bedroom, swaying in a way that hit me physically. And then Chang, his wife, and I went to the main bedroom and the riddles therein.

Adelaide went to freshen herself in the little washbasin next to the main bedroom, while Chang and I remained in the bedchamber and got into our usual rose pajamas, which we unbuttoned at our torsos to allow the band freedom and exposure. Chang wore his nightcap.

When Adelaide entered the room, lit by the single candle she carried with her and by the radiance of her nervous smile, Chang and I faced each other on our sides atop the bed—the comfortable way for us to lie down. Chang fidgeted more than I. Adelaide placed the candle on the night table and picked up a big hand mirror. She gazed into it while troubling with her hair, unable to disguise an aspect keenly curious and nearly panicked.

Chang's head trespassed on my pillow. His nose nearly touched mine; I felt the hurry of his heart.

"I've often wondered what this moment would be like," my brother's wife was saying softly to her reflection. Eventually she placed the mirror facedown on the dresser and shuffled toward us. "Maybe I'm wicked," she said. "Ever since I was a girl I've been wondering. . . ."

My brother's wife glanced at me, then her eyes darted away. She seemed to be talking to both of us through the anxious disappearance and reappearance of her smile.

Adelaide looked to Chang, and she let out a laugh she did not seem to trust. She tucked her blond hair behind her ears, but wisps fell about her cheeks and forehead. Falteringly, she crawled onto his side of the bed, and kneeling over her husband, she kissed his temple—not gently, or with any ease, but like a chicken bobbing after some feed.

Chang blinked his eyes. He said something, but his lips were too taut to shape the sound into a recognizable word.

"Maybe I'm wicked." She reached for him.

I closed my eyes—the method Chang and I had decided upon—to become "mindless" for the next hour. But with each bounce or jolt or kick of Adelaide's leg, my eyes opened instinctively, as if against my will.

Eyes closed tight again, hoping to find innocent thoughts, I couldn't ignore the substance that exists in men only to hasten the flow of blood at the sound of a woman giving herself for the first time. Her scent was light and poignant.

Adelaide's fingertips accidentally swiped my groin. I found myself looking at Chang as he lifted her white frilled dressing gown, and when my eyes were unfortunately opened again, he was taking off her white cotton undershorts and pulling her, naked, to him. We were on our backs, stretching the band. After another trespass, I think a poke to my shinbone, I saw her sitting cross-legged over Chang, unbuttoning the top of his pajamas and frowning. She had small breasts, very pale. The hair in the place where her lower body divided into her thighs looked like a furry valentine.

Her skin was lacking muscle, almost hairless; she was thin. I had not expected the naked female body to look like that, but it seemed perfect in its femininity, its weakness and oddity. After trying to close my eyes again, I felt a third unintentional brush of her hand—along my chest this time—as she fumbled with Chang's buttons, and again as she struggled to remove his red cloth pajamas. For a moment she stared directly at me, with soft eyes, just as scared as I was. Adelaide touched our connecting band hesitatingly, almost caressing it, a strange novelty.

She has pale breasts, I thought, very small.

I shut my eyes tight. The sensation of her leg touching mine was faint and natural. Her throat was flecked with talcum powder.

Adelaide didn't look Chang in the face; she touched his chest, though, rubbed his skin, and let loose a snort when she uncovered his manhood—she was shocked, likely, by the hair of Chang's pubis, which was (like mine) half black and half gray, divided vertically. And then my brother and his wife began to have relations.

Chang stirred me yet again as he climbed on top of his wife and me. He was touching her breasts at the nipples as if he feared he'd never get the chance again. My arm was wrapped around my brother's shoulder, and to make this positioning possible, our band extended farther than it should go. The inopportune logistics meant I had no choice but to curl against Adelaide, to cover her body partially—at the curve of her hip—and move along her leg as my brother rocked back and forth. Chang saw my eyes were opened; he turned away quickly, and I closed them. As tightly as I could.

After some rolling of the three of us, Adelaide's soft blond hair came tickling across my neck, simultaneously gift and ordeal. I strained to keep my eyes shut as knees, elbows, fingers poked or bounced off me. Our band ached. Though my eyes were closed, I knew she was still on top of my brother because her hair gladdened my neck once again. I let my stare glide over her coloring face, following the swerve of bone in her exquisite cheek. Another accident, her fingers ran involuntarily against my palms before she could withdraw her embarrassed hand. She was alarmed and self-conscious and nearly crying. I felt alone and exposed.

Meanwhile, Chang, eyes closed, perspired, bit his lip, and then began triumphantly to smile. I felt something, too, like a feather dragged lightly across the length of my body, chin to feet, and I shivered. I began gradually, instinctually, I hoped imperceptibly, to approach the cheeks of my brother's bride with my own lips opened in an O. I cut their journey short at the last moment. The wind made a shrill noise through the magnolias outside, and the mattress sounded its own creaky song.

That was it. Yes, I eyed my brother's bride now, and I hoped to see in her a new knowledge. I assumed that by seeing her unclothed I would be able somehow to comprehend everything about this woman—to locate the secret that made her an individual, and to draw out what was essential about her from the inessential, like a box within boxes. But of course I could not contain anything at all about this person, just the opposite. It might as well have been ten Adelaides I saw now. The one sister-in-law as ten-headed mystery.

When she and my brother were finished, it took Chang a moment to separate himself from his wife. He was panting like a mackerel plucked into the air. And then Adelaide, smiling, was covering Chang's mouth with her tiny hand, resting her head on his breast, and staring back at me.

In our pajamas and bare feet the next morning, Chang and I waked alone in bed. Seeping into the edge of my dream, the smell of the fat and the meat of breakfast sausage told us it was time to rise and enjoy the first full day of our marriage. Chang and I put on our matching suits and entered the dining room to find Sarah in a simple blue dress, and Adelaide in a gray one. We went directly to the long rectangular table to eat, and Thom began serving us the tomato-onion omelet and the sausage he and our wives had prepared. Our wicker double-chair creaked as we eased into it. The girls came to sit stiffly at either side of us with their eyes downcast.

The dining room itself, with its heavy mahogany furniture and its big window looking onto the dusty junction of two forgotten trails that now formed our backyard, did not yet have the familiarity of a home; that would take time, if not other things as well. Beyond the back fence, dark bushes separated our strip of lawn from the highroad.

"Did you sleep?" I asked my bride, daubing wet egg from my lips with a napkin.

Sarah put down her fork and sat for a while, chewing in a hurry so that she could answer. "Yes," she said, swallowing. "Very well." She nodded her head, and then stopped. She looked around the room. Then she picked up her silverware again.

After my wife resumed eating, she asked softly: "And did you'all sleep?" She was sawing at her eggs with her knife and looking shyly into her plate.

My sister-in-law shot a look at Chang, then lowered her eyes.

The look was directed at my brother, I was fairly sure, but for an instant I believed she had stolen a peek at me.

My wife, meanwhile, waited for my answer. It was my turn to set down my silverware. "I slept fine, my dear," I said.

Chang said, "This going to be beautiful." He smiled. "Marriage."

After breakfast it was a slow day. Though we were planning to begin a life of less frequent touring, Chang and I practiced our routine in the yard, playing our flutes, somersaulting across our dusty plot, doing handstands, breaking twigs over our ligament, improvising banter with an imagined audience. The girls arranged the house and knit and did needlepoint, and waved from the window from time to time. In the evening, we ate the chicken and rice Thom had prepared. Then, as the four of us strolled under the trees and aimlessly up and down the deserted stretch of Milburry Lane that met our yard, I was thankful for the feel of Sarah's soft hand, which I managed despite my nervousness to bring to my lips.

That night it was my turn in the bedroom with my wife.

As I waited for Sarah to join us in the bedroom, my brother whispered in my ear, "Do not be nervous."

"Thank you, Chang. I am not nervous." We were on the bed, anticipating Sarah's arrival.

"Do you have questions for me?" He was cheery.

I took a breath. "No, brother." I wiped the sweat from my lip and tried to calm myself. "Thank you."

"Ready, then?"

"I am ready, Chang, yes."

"You are prepared?"

I was thinking about my wife, and how things would be in twenty years.

"I think you might have questions." Chang made a long face. "Because you never done this before."

"I do not, but I'm sure I will be less—obtrusive than you were."

The time came, and when it did Chang and I lay facing one another on the mattress. I wore my most reassuring smile, but my heart pounded as I watched Sarah undress. I had not realized how difficult it is for a woman to undress. She struggled with the hook-and-eye clasps of her corset, and no doubt it was now, before I had even begun to touch her skin, that I felt the greatest pleasure. The delicious mystery stretched each second, and raised my expectations in the direction of the limitless. My wife's hair was fastened in a precise twist atop her head.

Chang closed his eyes, and I hoped he would not speak and shatter the rare and fragile impression.

My wife, however, talked and talked as her dress fell to her feet: "Mother said it would be an odd experience, you'all. 'It's quare enough when there's just one of them,' Mother said. Not that she meant, I mean . . ." Sarah stammered. "I don't intend any offense to you, to either of you'all—"

To avoid hearing her chatter, I focused instead on the sounds of her undressing, her hands fumbling with countless fasteners, catches, strops, and stays. It reminded me of my months on the *Sachem*: if I closed my eyes, there I was, among moaning cord, buffeted sails, and—as the cotton of her underthings rubbed whispering against the softness of her flesh—the sound of waves lapping up to the prow. I rolled us onto my back, distending our band as I wiggled my arm beneath Chang's head. He opened his eyes for a twinkling, then closed them tight.

Sarah reached the foot of the bed, stopped in her tracks, and scrutinized us with a confused sad look across her face. She was tall, and her body seemed more corpulent when naked. She raised her arms and freed her blond hair to cascade down her cheeks, framing her light eyes. Her chest grew taut as her raised arms lifted her breasts so that they resembled pale oranges with pink tips. My brother's eyes were closed, but he wore an inexplicable and bothersome smile.

Sarah climbed onto the bed and shuffled to me on all fours. And she kissed me. I savored it with my entire body. A spasm fired in my lower half, my stomach filled with thunder and lightning, my head was in a spin, and I swore my ribs were cheering like the court of King Rama. I kissed my wife.

Lest I should do something wrong, I considered my own body of no importance aside from hers. But at the same time I realized that what I was feeling bore little resemblance to the bliss I had hoped for—it held not enough magic, and an excess of wheezing and melancholy.

Sarah was expending so much energy that when I opened my eyes to the sight of her reddening jowls, I grew alarmed she'd grow faint from overwork. She bit my bottom lip—by design?— and as I flipped all of us over, my brother moaned as if he'd been kicked or slapped inadvertently. But Chang could not have been, because all of Sarah's hands and feet were touching me.

My wife's eyes were open and linked with mine as I coupled with her. We moved together, in cadence. I was on top of her, with my brother bouncing to my side, straining the bond. The tight round globes of her breasts had widened into soft flat saucers.

I felt my wife had become a strange part of me, not integrated fully—but not fully only because this new part of me was experiencing its own pleasure. In my hand, her hand, trembling and weak, her fingers hooked around mine—and the only way to describe what I experienced is as a new-sprung void in my chest, sucking out a solitary life's worth of loneliness and wanting now to be filled with something new. I tried hungrily to fill it with the images around me: her throat arched as if yielding to the hangman, the curve of her naked hip, the shape of her open mouth (all my life, I told myself, I will remember her open shuddering mouth), the urgency and the tears welling in her eyes.

And then, without warning, this new outgrowth of my body that was Sarah lost all tenderness, even as she was contriving to bring across her face a dramatic expression showing not only passion but something even more significant. I felt cold suddenly.

A jolt, a sigh, and it was over, almost as soon as it had begun.

CHAPTER NINE

At Sea

1825–1826
On the Sachem, *Bound for New York*

The sun was bright, flickering on the water, white at the sky's apex, and the heat had come. We were fourteen years old and had begun our journey to a place called New York, but in the distance behind us, a lone Siamese trinket vendor could still be heard yelling, his calls traveling across the water, and I imagined he was summoning all the junks, all the houseboats, every last one, and the coastline and the sky, and Mother, to come after us, and the Mekong, too—that would be our rescue. From the moment we stepped on the forward deck of the *Sachem*, our new life at sea was difficult and lonely.

Our ship rolled sluggishly through the sea. The trade winds whispered us away from our home, and by the ship's main rigging there must have stood forty crewmen in a row, all white-skinned, all at attention; each held his hands behind his back—the same position in which Captain Coffin had been standing when we arrived. The Captain addressed the crew in what sounded like gibberish, then turned quickly to Chang and me. "I will introduce you to the finest seamen in the world," he said in his unnatural Siamese.

The crew raised a collective eyebrow at the sight of us.

I looked in their faces for some future to weigh against my past.

The crew did not see this, they did not understand the vanishing monuments of my life: the gray rocking Siamese houseboats that seemed to bleed into black mud under the rain; the sunshine reflecting hotly off the golden skin of one of Rama's palace domes; a flying fish shaking off the current to twitch in the air, sunlit, before falling into the next Mekong wavelet; Mother's eyes, filling with tears before we left to meet King Rama. I did not see anything to match these in the odd white faces of the crew of the *Sachem*.

But eventually my insides settled. The decks had their curiosities, and my brother and I were allowed to roam freely under the cloudless sky.

At first Chang and I kept to ourselves, crossing the decks uneasily, like men dreaming of walking on clouds, certain they'll fall through with each hesitant step.

A day passed in silence. We had just about given up eating the first night for fear of sitting down with the crew. We stopped communicating altogether. Before this, whenever we'd encountered people unaccustomed to our uniqueness, we'd had only to stay among the gawkers for a short while before either walking away or fighting. On a ship a double-boy is under scrutiny at all hours.

Eventually, though, we had to eat, and on the second day we sat down to dinner with the crew. The dining cabin was fairly large, and lit by silver lamps. We sat at the Captain's table—the longest. The opened wooden shutters ushered in the sea breeze and the smell of salt tides. The lamps threw the shadow of the wall crucifix across the white cloth of our table, where it curled around the bottle of wine and the platter of roasted duck that stood at the center of the spread.

Coffin sat at my side. He held up a saltshaker, poured some salt into his hand, presented his open palm and its contents to Chang and me, whispering in English, "Salt."

We were silent. The room was silent; the whole world was silent. Except our duck In, who quacked from his seat on my lap.

"Salt." Coffin scrunched his brow and spoke more loudly, ignoring the duck sounds, splaying the fingers of his open hand as if showing us a grand diamond. He brought his palm toward his monocle and pretended to examine it. *"Salt."*

"Salt," I said.

"Salt," echoed my brother, though not as well around the *l* as I had.

The crew, of course, laughed. The Captain licked his palm and nodded. "Good," he said in his weird Thai.

From that evening onward, whenever he was free of the burdens of command, Coffin was at our side, teaching us English and walking the two decks. If he was occupied, the crew would take to educating us. Despite our newness to the language, they taught Chang and me to play checkers.

Why did they all wear vests and coats—surely they were not all royalty? Did they *never* eat rice? Why were they so pale? Were their hands so clumsy that they needed to use knives and forks?

These questions were slow in the answering, because Chang and I spent most of our time at play in our cabin, on our bed—which was about six feet by four feet, attached to the wall. The cabin was situated in annoying proximity to the clanging handbell of the poop deck. Our only possessions were our clothes, our pet In, and the jade dragon King Rama had given us.

Passing the hours, learning English, learning checkers, I was kept occupied and fell into a kind of numbness. Every few hours, each time a surprise, my homesickness opened its eyes and rose again to life, and there was nothing but the familiar agony. "We need to think up a plan," my brother said, his face filled with wanting, "about how to get back home."

Yes, he was right—a plan. "As soon as we get there, we will figure a way to escape," I said. We would work together and return to the Mekong before we knew it, he said.

But, my brother, it is my very togetherness with you that ruins everything, I thought.

"Eng?" Chang asked. We were alone playing checkers one night before bed. I heard my own softened voice say: "We are going to be fine, brother."

Chang's eyes fell to his lap, and he put his hand on top of our connecting band. The game was positioned midway between us, and as we were unable to sit far enough apart to station ourselves at opposing ends of the board, our sideward view gave my brother and me a complete enough picture of the contest easily to defeat the sailors we often played. But now it was just the two of us at the board; he slid his lone king into a position that would surely lose the game for him. I corrected his move, sliding his piece into position to jump three of my checkers. He did not look up as I did so. The ship rocked, her hull creaking and cables singing.

That night we slept soundly, and I dreamt Chang and I were dressed in white, lying on a white bed in a white room; hundreds of fat pink twigs were poking at us, into our chests, stomachs, eyes, into our band.

I awoke with a start, unsure where I was, but I saw Captain Coffin standing over us, his pointer finger extended and hovering just over our ligament. Behind the Captain stood a sailor holding a dim candle and a journal.

"Hmmph?" Chang muttered, opening his eyes. My leg began to cramp under my brother's. His body next to mine felt strangely small; this cabin was not my home.

"Back to sleep now, double-boy. No one was ever here," Coffin whispered in Siamese. He and the sailor backed out past the porthole, which was rimmed with sea salt and moonlight. Our duck In awoke and began to quack in the corner.

I had picked up enough English to piece together what the Captain had recited to the sailor on their way out: "Experiment A: When one twin is touched, both awaken simultaneously."

"As soon as we arrive in New York, understand?" I said to Chang.

"We will be back home soon," he said.

Early the next morning, as sunup was starting in and the sea just applying its sunshine rouge, Chang and I stood at the center of a ring of sailors. I tried to concentrate not on the situation at hand but on the lone cloud fenced in, from our viewpoint, by the random corral of the *Sachem*'s masts and cables. Directly in front of me, the situation at hand: Captain Coffin, and, next to him, a sailor holding a thick rope. The sailor had a neck thick as a pontoon and a great living puff of white-blond hair. Around us, every face in the circle was stupid with anticipation. The sailor's rope was wrapped around our connecting band like thread over a spool.

The Captain wore his pants pleated and white in the summer sun. He held his white-gloved hand high over his head. "On my signal, Mr. Lawrence," he said. He seemed twice as tall as the sailor.

"Aye, sir." The blond Mr. Lawrence could almost be called a boy. His face sweaty and sallow from sea- or heat-sickness.

"Now," said the Captain, dropping his hand.

I took a quick breath and held it. I dug my nails into Chang's shoulder, as he did into mine. My brother squeaked as the sailor tugged the rope. Come apart! I thought. Come apart!

"Gave it a sharp yank, did you, Mr. Lawrence?" the Captain asked. I opened my eyes and exhaled.

"Aye, sir."

"And again, Lawrence."

Another tug. Squeak. And a burning feeling.

I panted. The lone cloud overhead was impaled on the mizzenmast.

The Captain turned his attention to Chang and me. He fiddled with his monocle. "Double-Boy, did you feel that?" In his wobbly Thai.

"Yes," my brother and I answered.

"Would you characterize the sensation as . . . uncomfortable?"

"Yes."

"Would you say painful?" He tilted his head toward us as he spoke, as if he wanted his face physically to accompany the words as they left his mouth.

"Yes," we said. My brother's eyes were glassy. "Yes," he repeated.

Captain Coffin considered this for moment, scratching his whiskers thoughtfully. The rope still chafed our skin, though the sailor held it less than taut.

"Mr. Smithers!" the Captain called. A skinny sailor stepped forward from the circle, carrying a journal. "Smithers, note that neither twin completed the experience free of pain."

The Captain turned to us. A wide smile crossed his face. The crew nodded their heads, turning to one another approvingly like relatives after the birth of a healthy baby. One sailor applauded, realized he was the only one doing so, then stopped abruptly.

The Captain touched Chang and me on our cheeks. "I am very tall, and perhaps that is why the only thing that has ever loved me besides the sea is the sky. But the whole of the New World will love you."

We were again free to roam about the ship.

And roam we did; the decks were the only playing field available. Our synchronicity had become a delight to the crew, and often they played games with us, mostly in good fun. One sunny day found us scampering at the stern of the ship, on the poop deck above the main deck. We were being chased around the fore-topsail mast by Mr. Lawrence, the sailor whose disheveled hair looked like a tousled white lapdog stretched from his scalp to his neck. Other sailors stood here and there, shirtless, blond mostly, doing work scrubbing or folding cloth and ropes. They looked up to smile at us. "Get the Chinamen, crony," they laughed as Chang and I, never out of step, fretted our way through the labyrinth of men and ropes and masts and rails. I could hear my brother almost chuckling through his heavy breathing when suddenly we came to an open hatch in the deck.

What happened next was as natural as birdsong in a North Carolinian wood, but it left the sailors openmouthed, as if we had lifted the very ship in our hands. When conjoined people are running and suddenly there is nothing underfoot but twenty feet of uninterrupted air, a moment's disharmony—when one twin hesitates and his brother jumps—could mean death.

But it is different with Chang and me. Our intrinsic appreciation of one another's body creates a spark in our shared blood that smooths differences and brings the universe into our own current.

The two of us vaulted together with the grace and harmony of a bounding deer and its reflection in a still pond, clearing the open hatchway in unison and landing safely on the far side to continue our run. A look over our shoulders revealed that our pursuer was standing before the hatch, wheezing and resting his hands on his knees.

Mr. Lawrence was the one who had become chiefly responsible for teaching us English. Every day after breakfast, he would come in and sit on our bed and read to us. He was not much older than we were—maybe four years older—and very tall and unsophisticated. He'd instruct us by drawing simple concepts on a pad: the word "house" and then a crude representation of that idea.

He sat there for what must have been hundreds of hours while we lay on the bed. Chang complained of a toothache and learned slowly, and I waited for my brother to pick up what I had grasped hours, days, weeks earlier. The ship would rise, and my porthole—with the sun setting in its lowest quadrant—looked like a guillotine after a beheading.

Once Mr. Lawrence had had to repeat the word "examine" more than a hundred and fifty times before Chang understood it, and "help" at least two hundred, and I began to hate English not only because it was an odd tongue spoken by strange-looking men from a land that I was unhappy to be visiting, but also because of the slug's pace at which I had to learn it.

As soon as we get there, I told myself, I will devise our escape.

The evening of one of our lessons, when my brother and Mr. Lawrence were bringing to an end an hour-long dialogue that consisted of the word "house," I felt some shift in the position of our vessel as it sailed, and even through the hull I heard the buzzing excitement of the crew outside.

"We are dropping anchor soon," said Lawrence. *"Anchor."*

"Anchor," parroted Chang. I could hear the shouts of the sailors as they crowded each other and leaned on the mahogany rails. Laughter too.

"St. Helena," said Lawrence. "We're at St. Helena. It's an island." He started to sketch the ocean on his pad, and then drew a dot.

"Herena-it's-an," said Chang. "It's-an."

The Captain entered our cabin, the smoking meerschaum bowl of his pipe in his fingers. He wore his deep blue captain's coat spotless and pressed, his monocle fixed in his eye socket as if by magnetism; Coffin seemed dressed for some formal event. He was too tall for the cabin.

"You are relieved, Mr. Lawrence. Go."

The Captain brought the nub of the lacquered pipe stem between his teeth, dragged, then withdrew it and aimed the stem at us.

"This will be the last conversation you have that is not in English," he said in Thai. "Even amongst yourself. It is important you can speak the language well when we get to New York." The

pipe smoke filled our cabin, smelling like a flower bed in smoldering decomposition. "Do you understand, Double-Boy?"

"I can't sleep, and my tooth hurts," Chang said in Thai, rubbing his eyes. "What is New York like?" The wings of his nostrils
were raw and glistening.

"You are easily excited, little half," the Captain laughed. Then
he began to speak in English: "The city of New York is like the
Garden of Eden."

We both looked to him for help. Coffin put his hands on our
shoulders and bent his huge bulk forward as if he were leaning
over the deck rail, and he stared at the wall as if it offered a de-
lightful view. He was back to speaking our tongue: "New York is
radiant." And then again in English: "A great eddy of terra-cotta
and stone."

"What are we to do there?" I asked.

And the Captain raised his eyebrows, parted his lips. "You are
to do nothing." He brought the pipe to its home in his mouth like
he was doing it a favor. "And the world will watch."

Coffin turned and went out, presumably to the island of St.
Helena, in the Atlantic Ocean, some 3,500 miles west of Siam.

Once again, Chang and I were left to lie alone together

Eight months had passed at sea. The captain was letting us spend
our afternoons and evenings in the crow's nest atop the main mast.
Solid on the crown of the sail pole, the crow's nest contained a
comfortable seat, and a leather rack for maps and speaking trum-
pets. The crow's nest was where we were sitting when we saw our
future.

It was the early watch; the sky was darkening with eveningtime. Below, the seamen were standing in a cordon near the
taffrail, looking out into the distance. Only the occasional flap of a
sail broke the silence, or the infrequent rasp of the advancing keel.

A rangy seaman named Tyrone Miller who was slouched
against the after-hatches jumped straight up and called out, "Hark!
Do you see it?"

After traveling seven thousand, five hundred and twenty nautical miles, the *Sachem* was approaching New York Harbor.

Even after two hundred and fifty days at sea with Captain Coffin, we were not prepared for the first sight of Manhattan. As much as we would come to see in our traveling life—and within a short time Chang and I would seem always to be on the move—nothing would ever compare to that moment.

The shoal on the horizon came into view. I had never seen a city lighted up before.

As the *Sachem* curved around in a long arc toward the city, her bow gliding past flat Brooklyn, Chang and I climbed down to the deck to get a better view: a glowing city of narrow concrete mountains stretching sixty and seventy feet to the sky! With their steep wedge-shaped walls and sooty cupolas and with their glass windows, these roughcast peaks were blinking from summit to base with the reflections of streetlamps.

Burning piles of wood formed a string of pearls up and down the docks far into the night; with flanks steaming, enormous animals called horses pulled queer conveyances along the waterfront. "Look at it!" Chang was bouncing us up and down. "It's wonderful!"

I disagreed. It was the buildings, the very solidity that the city conveyed, despite being right on the water, and the pervasive grayness of the place—the smokestacks exhaling gray breath; the gray leafless trees slouching up from the gray concrete in the gray evening; the smoke that fled the burning piles of wood; the clouds, gray in the receding light, hiding in the clefts and angles of this tall horizon—that led me to imagine Manhattan as a herd of freakish elephants that assembled to congeal in stone along the water's edge.

We were standing by the *Sachem's* mast, wrapped in a blanket—even at Rama's palace we had never seen glass windows before, or brick, or a horse—as the skysail poles sailed into the spires of the port. Where were the junks? I wondered. There were none. Even at the docks, people sat on benches, strolled idly, they rode in carriages, four-in-hands, or in crowded streetcars. And oddest of all were the elegant, well-fed, well-dressed, white-skinned men and women loitering, come to watch the ships. On the far side of the spyglass that I was pressing to my eye, ladies held lorgnettes between their fingers, gentlemen sat balancing silver-topped canes over their knees. When could we go home?

The *Sachem's* sailors were readying to lower our sails on their masts, and, with her foresail swelling like Captain Coffin's white-shirted breast, the ship slithered into place in the landing pier. The *Sachem*'s decks moaned with the lowering anchors, her unfastened chains squealed toward the ground, and her sailors began to cheer.

At our side, the Captain laughed and grinned at our disbelief. "This is New York." His great cheeks were quivering. "Neither you nor she is ready for the other." He did not look thrilled so much as frightened. "That will change."

Captain Coffin had us ushered off the *Sachem* under a blanket. When the cover was lifted, Chang and I found ourselves beside the Captain on a darkened stretch of dock, beside stacks of crates and bales, out of the sight of any passers-by. From out of the shadows, a man came toward us.

"Well?" Coffin asked the gentleman when the latter reached us. "Was I not telling the truth about our boys?" There were four of us now standing in the shadow of the ship's hull, which was a deeper shade of darkness against the sable night.

The Captain lit a match and held it near our connecting ligament. Mr. Hunter screwed up his eyes, touched the ligament, smiled. "Yes, people will come in droves." He was a tall, lean middle-aged man who wore a neck cloth and gaiters.

I could feel Chang growing antsy. We stroked each other's shoulders. In, our pet duck, was inside a basket at our feet and starting to quack. I looked around at all the shadows; how would we escape?

"Quiet that duck." Coffin looked back and forth, making sure no one could see us, and he shook his match until its flame died.

"Hello, mister," my brother blurted out, his *l*'s bending under his heavy accent.

"I am Eng," I said, "and this is Chang."

The man answered, "Hello, double-boy. I am Robert Hunter."

Coffin started to belly-laugh. "Hello, my golden egg."

Both men cackled. Perhaps we could stow away on one of these ships?

"Hello, life of velvet and clover," Hunter said to my brother and me, once he caught his breath.

"And how do you do, you fluke of my good fortune?" The Captain was giggling now. As well as bouncing a bit.

And now it was Hunter's turn: "Hello, millions in the bank!"

And the Captain: "Salutations, my heavy purses of Fortunatus!"

"And good morrow, answer to my prayers of cash and coin!"

"Pleased to meet you, loaves and fishes fallen into our laps like manna!"

"Good evening, *argent fait le jeu!*"

"Come and relax your bonnet on my chair, you happy combination of fortuitous circumstances!"

"Greetings, you good bet on ice!"

"Why, hello there, my twin pot of gold!"

"Welcome to New York, my coupled wellspring of boundless booty!"

Both men laughed and laughed, until Hunter recovered command of himself, looked at his pocket watch and said: "All right, literally enough of this."

Coffin left us in Hunter's hands, and we said good-bye to the Captain.

Hunter's horse-drawn carriage took us through the vivid agitation of nighttime in New York. We clip-clopped up Broadway (it was like a Mekong in cobblestone), past the green-shingled Cortlandt Street ferry house and the marble City Hall building, which had on its roof a miniature skyline of turrets, columns, and gables. We passed the towering Franklin House Hotel with its countless windows, which gave onto Bogert's bakery with frosted cakes on display. Landmarks passed in sequence, the stone and brick of Hanover Square followed by stately Putnam Booksellers, followed by the squat gray theaters on Chatham Street, each flying its own flag. Theatergoers, top-hatted and white-gloved, their complexions so much fairer than our own, had gathered to compare the evening's entertainments.

"Close the curtains," Hunter hissed as we loped by. "People will literally *see* you." I pulled the thick maroon drape across the carriage window.

"Everything will come in good time, what?" Hunter said, smiling and sucking on his teeth. He was a little deaf. His nose turned upward at its midpoint and aimed high. Like Coffin, Hunter wore a monocle, but unlike Coffin's, his lens enlarged the view of his left eye to the point where it looked as if he had tacked a giant eyeball on his face. "But now we must get you ready before anyone notices your existence." He had a high whining voice meant for a frame smaller than his. He kept looking at his pocket watch and sighing.

We spent our first nights in New York in seclusion.

Hunter brought us to a place known as uptown, a landscape of isolated farms just ahead of progress, to one of his buildings, on Dutch Hill, at the eastern edge of Forty-second Street. It was a ruined two-story house with a garden—or rather, a dusty plot aspiring to cultivation—encircled by a ditch.

He escorted us into the anteroom, where we met Mrs. A. C. Sachs, a widow whose sagging, half-shut eyes no doubt exaggerated her age. She had no eyebrows.

"I'll be." The woman gave a little laugh. "These Chinamen sure are a sight."

She and Hunter gazed together at us. We stood there, with Chang holding In.

"Exactly the point, my good widow Sachs; they literally *are* one of Mother Nature's blemishes"—Hunter attempted a gentle tone—"and people cannot turn their eyes from Mother Nature's blemishes." He handed the woman a purseful of change.

My brother and I hadn't seen an American home before. We gazed about the room, examining everything in detail—the doilies on the shining tabletops, the plump couch, the lamps.

"Two at once." Mrs. Sachs shook her head. "Look at it."

"Eh?" Hunter asked, cupping a hand around his ear.

"Two at once, I say."

"Yes." Hunter looked at his pocket watch. "Just about time for me to—"

"And just what are they doing with that creature?" she interrupted, pointing to our pet. My brother was holding In out of its basket, wrapping his arms around the duck so its head relaxed against my chest.

"Our duck named In," said Chang, and he petted the animal's neck.

The widow Sachs turned to Hunter and tilted her head slightly. The skin where her eyebrows should have been was raised expectantly.

"I'll take your pet for now, Double-Boy," said Hunter. He took a step toward us and flung his arms around In, trying to get a hold of the duck, which reared, looked around, and started to quack. Its wings flapped into my face. Hunter couldn't get a good grip on the animal. "I'll have this duck returned in literally no time, Double-Boy." The man grunted and grabbed, his face flushing dark, his monocle becoming dislodged from its perch in his eye socket. "Just give it here, what?" He smiled through his agitation; he couldn't get hold of In, and was losing the struggle. "Just give it, please, boys."

My brother and I handed over In.

Finally, duck in hand, Hunter took a moment to compose himself, and to return the monocle to its spot in front of his eye.

"Ensure that no one hears of the Double-Boy, not even your daughters," he instructed Mrs. Sachs, as In flapped her wings beneath his chin. Holding our quacking companion, Hunter departed, telling the widow never to allow Chang and me outside. "Never. And speak of this literally to no one."

Mrs. Sachs walked us to our room, a warmly lit space on the first floor, cramped with dingy white piles of dirty sheets, linens, bodices, and undergarments. (Later, when first I saw a snowfall in New York, I thought at once of the mouse-colored drifts of dirty laundry in our room at Mrs. Sachs's.)

"All right, now," she said on her way out the door. "Chinamen, that upstairs bedroom is mine." She shook her finger at us. "I don't know what kind of Oriental fiddledeedee you're expecting, but you stay down here." She drew a long breath. "You sure are a sight," she said, and left.

We slept on the floor.

New York loomed in the distance outside my window, uneven, the buildings in various states of construction. The dim light and the shadow of a cloud chiseled new ridges and hollows into the cityscape, continuously amending their handiwork, to reveal a cleft or conceal a ridge there, revealing and concealing, while five or six disconsolate little fires scattered across Manhattan's half-lit jagged horizon flickered beneath stars that twinkled with the same lonely intimacy found in the Siamese early morning. (New York before daybreak was constantly alight with at least a handful of small, lonesome fires.)

"Eng?" asked Chang. He was shaking his head at the preposterous city beyond our window. I pretended to be asleep.

"I know you are awake," he said finally, in our native Thai. When I did not quit my snoring imitation, Chang said, "It could be worse, brother." If my twin was right, I did not see how.

"We will leave, run away, maybe tomorrow," he said.

I opened my eyes. "Let us plan now."

Then the door creaked ajar, and with a jerk, we turned and saw two pairs of bright eyes peering into our room from the dark— just two sets of eyes, floating brightly in the shadows, seemingly detached from bodies of any kind; these eyes hovered there a moment, incorporeal, accompanied by gasps. Then the door closed, and through the wall we heard women's giggling, and the sound of dainty feminine feet running up the stairs.

Hunter was at our door the next morning. He brought two white sailor's suits and a pair of sailor's caps. "For your performances," he said.

He rocked his tall, lean frame back and forth and blinked his eyes sweetly. "You can't just literally stand before the crowds, what? You do have an *act* of some kind planned, correct? A show?"

Chang turned to me. We shrugged our four shoulders.

"I won't deny that I am a little out of temper," Hunter said, pulling out his pocket watch and shaking his head. "I do not have the time for—"

"We play checkers," my brother said, struggling into his sailor pants. "Do you have the duck, mister?" he asked.

"Checkers?" His left eye—the enlarged one behind the monocle—was intense, the only sign of life in the drab context of his face.

"It's a game," I said.

Chang's eyes were welling up. "You have the duck?"

"I *know* what checkers is," Mr. Hunter said. He smoothed his neck cloth with the tips of his fingers. "And, *yes,* boys, your pet is safe. We are going to be friends, right? You will see your duck soon enough. Friendship's the best thing, what—?"

"So we can have our pet, sir?" I asked.

"—literally one of the best things, friendship is. One of the very best. Now which side of you is Kang and which is the other?"

Two minutes later Chang and I were standing on our hands among the linen on the floor, and Hunter was saying, "Yes, yes, Double-Boy—that's it," and laughing. "Back tomorrow," Hunter said on the way out the door. "Excellent, boys, literally excellent."

That night, as soon as we made our spot between two piles of linen, we heard gentle footsteps approach. As it had the night before, the door to our room creaked open just a crack, and again two pairs of eyes hovered there, watching. And then two women peeked in through our doorway. One was tall in a golden-brown dress; the other, also tall, but less so, wore gray. In the semidark, it was hard to distinguish anything more. The two women stared for some time, and then they walked toward our bed slowly.

"They're horrible," said the taller one. Her face was a perfect oval underneath black bangs. She seemed almost a grown woman.

"Shhh," hissed the other, some twenty years old or so, a shapely girl with the jowls of a bulldog.

"Don't quiet me! They can't understand—they're *China*men," said the first.

Chang and I said nothing, holding silent with tensed muscles, feigning sleep.

"I think they are funny-looking," said the jowly one.

"Horrible, I say."

The jowly one approached. She peered into my eyes and grinned.

Her companion gasped. "What are you doing?" Then she giggled. "Get back from there, Martha."

"It's my sweetheart," bulldog-faced Martha said, laughing. "No. My sweet*hearts.*"

Then the two ran cackling out of the room.

"Could any woman ever *imagine?*" one asked the other as they ran up the stairs noisily.

All women were the same. It was women who were the more frightened of our condition, the more inclined to give voice to nausea when in our company, I thought, and I missed my mother.

Our first audiences fell into two halves—either they frightened easily, or they did not believe. And then they returned.

Coffin and Hunter had set up a huge tent next to the wooden palings in one of the meadows of Madison Square and placed a small barred cage beneath it. Beside the tent sat an old cannon that signaled the start of the festivities.

It was a balmy night, and torch flares flanked the tent; the four poles supporting the canopy each bore a crude rendering of my brother and me standing under palm trees. Inside the cage, we sat down among straw on the ground, dressed in our white sailor's suits, our band showing through two holes cut into the torso of each of our outfits. Our long hair was tied into braids that we curled atop our heads and tied with silk tassels—his were blue, mine red—and we held each other's hands as a throng walked by: openmouthed children and nodding adults, frowning old men and blushing young women, paupers wearing ripped blue stockings and rich gentlemen leaning on canes, everyone had to pass quickly to move the long lines that had formed undulating chains and stretched the length of the tent. Chang and I felt the accursed peering eye, the concentrated gaze of a crowd, and I could not stop shuddering.

Together with the casual visitors there were relays of professional skeptics—doctors, newspapermen—who stepped up to our cage, not content with the dim lighting, like nearsighted proofreaders getting as close as possible. From the front of our cage hung a large and gay placard that read THE MONSTER.

In full seafaring regalia, Captain Coffin stood at the side of the cage, his jacket bunched and clinging tightly under his arms. For his part, Hunter stood in front of the cage with a speaking trumpet, wearing a tunic stretched to breaking that turned his face an unnatural red. Outside the tent, bare-armed teamsters gripped the halters of horses that reared and neighed; beyond that, the bumpy horizon of New York.

"Ladies, gentlemen," Hunter boomed through the trumpet, "I should like to treat the civilized world to a creature of Magick."

Let's run and get out of here, I thought to myself.

"Do you promise we will?" I asked Chang.

"Yes."

"From the shores of a backwater known, good people, as Siam," Hunter was saying, "this creature literally had two fathers—but one mother . . ."

I turned to my brother in disbelief. *Two* fathers?

Chang looked back at me, his face fallen.

Hunter brought the speaking trumpet closer to his lips, and he lectured in hushed tones. "But, ladies, gentlemen"—he closed his eyes in ecstasy—"this is a mild-natured beast; in fact it may even be said to be two beasts—both kind, both intelligent—"

I thought of Father, the good fisherman, the proud fighter.

"And lo"—Hunter spoke in the pinched tones of a man aware of the money he's making—"not only do they play checkers, they perform tricks!"

The promoter turned to look at us. Louder this time, he repeated the words, which were to have been our cue: "They perform *tricks*"—he coughed a little. Chang and I did not move. "Such as *walking on their hands*," Hunter said, and there was pleading in his voice now. Someone—a man, probably drunk—yelled from the crowd that we must be mannequins, he knew it all along.

The flame from the torches of our cage bowed under a breeze and left Hunter shrouded in darkness for a moment. In that prolonged and transcendent instant, the authority was flowing palpably from Hunter to us like electric power through a telegraph wire.

Chang and I still did not move. When the flame righted itself, the panic in Hunter's eyes was unmistakable. And Chang and I, together, calmly and in English, said: "We had only one father."

Hunter's big eye twitched. He swallowed, and began to breathe quickly through his nose. In the darkening evening beyond the torches, the crowd appeared a single gray element.

"And now!" Hunter achieved a broad smile. "The freak child of two normal parents, Chang and Eng!"

From our handstand, in the low light, I had trouble making out the audience, but I could hear what seemed like thousands of voices raised over so many noisy feet scrambling to get closer to us, voices raised in shouts and snorts, filling the tent with declarations of disbelief and wonder.

We flipped, in unison, across the stage, almost losing our synchronicity as my hand came down from one of the rotations onto a sharp rock. I gasped, and shuddered, but we managed to recover, and landed squarely on our feet after three full revolutions.

The crowd rushed the cage, at least the men did. They pushed Hunter aside—all the while the promoter yelled, "Please, gentlemen, please!"—and they plunged their hands through the bars, trying to grab at our connecting band. We shrank away, leaning our backs against the bars. People were surging forward, screaming, straining to reach us, extending their arms, hands, fingers, inching closer with each attempt; it looked as if they were throwing invisible darts at us.

A thin teenage boy lost his balance during the push. Caught in the human tide, this blond, nattily dressed young man slammed into the bars with his head. He let out a groan. His face extended farther and farther into our cage with each push of the crowd. His ice-blue eyes opened wide, his cheeks chafed against the bars, and he looked at Chang and me. He tried to say something, but the breath wouldn't come to his open mouth, so he squeaked.

Soon there did not seem to be a spot on the boy that was not scuffed or bloodied. Then unseen hands pulled at his back, and he was swallowed into the crowd. And my brother had begun to smile, in spite of—or because of—the peering gaze of the audience. With great effort, Hunter wriggled his way between the throng and the cage, his arms extended over his head, his knuckles white as he gripped the bars behind him; he was moving from bar to bar as a trapeze artist would swing from rope to rope above a net.

Hunter screamed. "Please!" he said. "One at a time! The queue forms to the left!" The surging continued unabated.

Then a gunshot, immediately followed by the sound of a ball ripping a hole into the tent. Captain Coffin, still rooted to his spot beside our cage, was holding a pistol in the air, its smoking barrel pointed upward. He stood like that, not moving, and slowly the crowd arranged themselves in a column to the left of the cage.

The audience, now orderly, filed by until one man stopped in front and held up the line by refusing to continue on. He was old and stood bent over—with his crooked back, fully a foot shorter than anyone around him; he was wearing a black eye patch.

"A fake!" he said.

"Please, sir." Hunter dusted himself off, returning to his place in front of our cage. "I assure you . . ."

"Fake!" The old man shook his head. "I want my money back."

The crowd—which had been murmuring until now—quieted. The old man patted his eye patch nervously. "A fake . . ."

"Sir." Hunter gave a disappointed smile. "We cannot extend a ref—"

"No refunds!" snapped Coffin.

"Give him," my brother said, "half money back."

Coffin and Hunter whipped around in disbelief. "What's that?"

"I say now is this," Chang smiled, "he only have one eye; he only see half a show. He only pay half!" The crowd exploded in laughter. My brother grinned.

Though he had hit upon the right tone of unctuous confidence, Chang's gestures and manner were not as showy as they would come to be. He was young yet. Later on, when he had had years to practice obsequiousness, he became as polished in spurious gesture and speech as in attitude. I had never seen this side of Chang. He had caught the sideshow bug, a temptation as addictive and (almost) as loathsome as alcohol.

I find nothing wrong with enjoying the hurrah of the crowd, but when one goes about becoming another person in the freak cage—when one has two identities, oneself and one's stage self—then life has gotten out of hand. Years later, if I had remembered Chang's first, quick capitulation to the bug, I shouldn't have been surprised by his affair with the bottle.

Eventually two young ladies appeared at our cage door, local girls who had won in a newspaper drawing the honor of being Hunter's assistants for the night—blissful creatures who seemed friendly until their cruel eyes darted from ours in horror. Dressed in red gowns, the ladies took Chang and me and walked us to Coffin's carriage. The belle at my side was careful not to touch my hand with hers, and so I did not experience her skin as she guided us into the carriage.

After drawing the curtains, Coffin, Hunter, and we, conjoined, rode off, and the crowd followed, running after us for at least a minute.

※❧ CHAPTER TEN ❧※

The Newness of Marriage

1843–1844
Wilkesboro–Waveland, Louisiana

After the first weeks of our marriage, I thought Sarah and I made fairly happy newlyweds. To her credit, she worked hard to warm our union. For example, one night as we lay in bed, I was startled by Sarah's hand, which reached gently for my own. Chang was snoring. What was odd was that this caressing hand did not feel odd. The other, lonely existence I had led until just a few months before felt so far away that it and my wedded present seemed separate, the lives of two distinct people.

"Marriage will be wonderful for both of us, Sarah," I said to her, because her darting eyes looked unsure, and I gave her palm a little pinch before slipping my fingers out and away from hers. Chang wheezed beside me, his nose in my ear. Oh, could it be that this arrangement might actually turn out happily?

My wife—I still could not believe the sound of that—was now asleep. I pulled the covers over this woman I barely knew, kissed her lovely hair, and blew out the candle on the night table. The unease I'd had about marrying a quiet stranger was now replaced by a wave of nervous contentment that seemed to make my body dissolve. I heard myself murmur something about loving her. I wish I had more memories as joyful as this one.

As brightly as I felt the newness of love, Chang seemed to feel it even more so. He had no trepidation whatsoever. Whenever I brought up the idea of touring again, this man who had once flown to absurd peaks of joy at the applause of strangers now seemed upset at the thought of leaving Wilkesboro even for an hour. But I was not surprised. As much as ill health or retirement, love can exchange a first life for a second—once a man assumes a new role, the charm of the old loses its allure. Being a newlywed was giving Chang his cherished rations of attention, and he had forgotten the similar nourishment he had once drawn from performing.

Still, we continued to spend our days and nights practicing feats.

We were out on our property one afternoon, vaulting from our hands to our feet and back again. My wife was inside with an aching stomach; Adelaide sat with us on the grass, watching.

"Where'd you learn to do that?" my sister-in-law asked after a time.

"Our father," Chang said, from our downside-up situation. "Ti-eye the great Mekong fisherman," I added. We flipped and were back on our feet. And then we flipped again.

"That's a trick." Adelaide was trying to whistle. "That is some trick." We were not talking seriously, just the repartee of new intimates. "I can't even whistle, and you boys can do that."

Adelaide shifted her weight. "My father never showed me any tricks," she said. "Once the old man tells us, 'If you was boys, I'd show you how to hunt.' But that's it for tricks."

"That sound nice," Chang said.

She lost her smile. "What's that supposed to mean?" She looked us up and down. "I just said he never showed me anything."

We somersaulted again. Chang said, "I was just—"

"What somebody promises and don't give you, that's what you take away from them," Adelaide said. "That's my father's line, he's always saying that."

"Then he did pass something on to you," I said, upside down.

We jumped back to our feet. "You know I make promises to you, Adelaide," Chang said. "I keep my promises to you."

"You know something about your brother, Eng?" she asked me. "He's quite a talker. He says he ain't never been around a woman before, and it's obvious I believe him." Adelaide shook her head. "But how come he knows the way to be such a talker?"

My brother and I remained in our standing position for a moment, catching our breath. "Perhaps Chang obtained the mouth," I said, "and I, the brain." She laughed. Back into a handstand.

"Eng!" Chang whispered in my ear, not amused. He had never heard me tell a joke before, not successfully, whereas that was all I'd heard him do when we were on tour.

"You know"—Adelaide was sitting on her hands in the grass— "my father always said not to trust big talkers."

I could have attempted to be funny again, or not. "Another gift he gave you," I said. Into another somersault.

"You can do it, Adelaide," Chang said. "I can show you."

"What are you talking about now, boy?"

"To stand on hands," he said. "Easy trick, I give you."

"Hey, Chang." She was gazing at something above our heads and squinting. "Don't be squirrelly. Do you want a wife or a circus attraction?"

Supporting half of us, Chang's arms began to show strain, his shoulders shook a little, and his neck craned forward awkwardly. He panted when we got back on our feet.

"Yes, let us show you." I tipped a nod to Adelaide. "All you would have to do is fuse yourself with your sister, and we would have twice as much money in the family."

She laughed and I laughed, and even Chang laughed, in a manner of speaking.

"Please, just let me be a mother," she said. "That'll be enough, obviously."

"Okay," Chang said, frowning. Why couldn't he enjoy it when I finally made another person laugh?

Adelaide walked up to us, coming within a few inches from our faces. "Stop bobbing, you'all, for a minute," she said, and when we stopped she rested her hands on our shoulders with affection. "I want to do something," she said, smiling as wickedly as a gambler who's just cheated profitably. "Just go along now."

And she took Chang's hand and mine, slowly, gently, with a womanly delight that surprised both Chang and me, and left us speechless. But we were not frightened; we were smiling. She began to move the three of us in a delicate waltz for three, perfect in its rhythm despite the absence of music in the afternoon air.

"What are we doing, there is no song?" Chang said in a tremulous voice.

"We're dancing, boys," she said, "ain't that obvious?" My head was nearly brushing against one of her cheeks, and Chang's brushed against her other one, and she asked us didn't we find this fun. Yes, we did. It's lovely to dance, I said. See, boys, if we waited for music, we'd miss the chance for a lot of good times around here. You are absolutely right about that, I said. Eng, maybe you can teach your brother to dance as well as you'all. Chang said he did not need teaching from me. But his feet were getting tangled, and Adelaide held us upright, her hair fragrant with soap and near my nose and I found myself smelling.

That evening, we retired very early. I was reading in bed silently with Sarah at my back and Chang facing me, both of them asleep (I rested the spine of the book on my brother's forehead). At least I thought they were both asleep. But Sarah whispered: "Eng, are you'all reading that Shakespeare?"

I looked over my shoulder and squinted at my wife. I had been reading from the Bard every night of our marriage, and she knew that.

"Do you want to read to me, Eng?" She was blinking, her smile toothy and delicate.

"What's that, my dear?" I was using Chang's head as a placeholder.

"I would sure like to hear you read to me, Eng." She kept up that smile; I couldn't help seeing there was desperation in it. "It might help my stomach. Would you please?"

I never enjoyed performing; my brother was the showman, not I. But a husband should work at marriage, I thought, and I was as lucky a man as any in history simply to have the chance to attempt that work.

For the first time in my life I began to recite a passage aloud, the second sonnet. But I did not read it well. My voice was high and stumbling where it should have been deep and certain. I kept my eye on the page, even as I could feel her staring at me. Out of the corner of my vision I saw my brother's eyes open, and I felt my sleeping half twitch awake slowly, with the covers bunched over his shoulders. He groaned extravagantly before closing his eyes again and snorting a bogus snore.

That was one indignity too many. I stopped reading. The words had lost their meaning, and the syllables lost their elegance. I leaned over Chang's body and put the book down on the night table beside him.

"I am sorry, Sarah." I pulled the sheets up and across Chang and me. My eyes felt very heavy, and itched as if I had grit inside my lids. "My dear, I—"

"I thought it sounded well," she said.

I realized how loudly the breath whistled in and out of my nose as I thought of how to respond. "Good night," I whispered, facing away from her.

A long time passed before she asked in a soft voice, "Eng, are you asleep?" She nudged my shoulder tenderly, shaking my brother and me a little, but I did not know what to say. How to explain why reading like that was so unpleasant for an attraction as exhibition-shy as I was? My wife lay there for a bit, curled up against my back, quiet and still, breathing softly. I could feel that she was trying to emulate the pattern of my breathing.

But she could not sleep, and she kept me awake with her loud inhaling and exhaling, and her turning, and also the little squeak in her nose. It sounded like she had begun to cry, her face against the pillow. But I did not turn around to see if she was, because I would not have known how to react if I'd found her sobbing. Whatever was making her cry must have been more substantial than my failure to read to her, I thought. I would begin again to-morrow the work of making my marriage happy, I told myself.

The next evening, Chang and I were going through our ledgers in our study, figuring out exactly how far our savings would carry us, when the girls came back from town. Through the hall we could hear them giggling as they undid their bonnets.

"Adelaide is home," Chang said, as if he did not know by now that if he observed something, I probably had, too. He skipped us out of the study and over toward our wives.

"Hello," he smiled.

My wife looked at Chang and me. "Ain't that *so* sweet?" Sarah cooed uncharacteristically, trying to make her demeanor more winning by adopting the voice of a five-year-old. She turned to her sister. "Your little boy"—she substituted the *l* in "little" with a young girl's *w*—"is happy to see you." Then my wife directed her gaze to me. "I wonder if my little man's as happy to see *his* mama?"

I had never heard a grown woman speak in that manner, and it confused me. I had to look away from her, and I found my glance resting on Adelaide's face. She commiserated with a smile.

"Well, obviously, you don't want your husband *too* happy to see you, Sarah," said Adelaide, rolling her eyes. "Keep a little mystery in a marriage; the man can't be a puppy, now." She patted Chang on the shoulder.

Sarah asked if we'd gone over our books. I told her we had.

"Good," said Adelaide, taking her sister's hand and beginning to lead her to the kitchen. "Sarah and me already tried poor." Our wives stepped past us.

My brother had a look on his face like that of a whelp. I do not think he had moved a half inch since his wife quit talking. "What she means, 'puppy'?"

"Probably," I laughed, "she was speaking in jest, Chang."

"Oh," he said, still whelp-faced and looking into my eyes as if he wasn't sure whether to trust my gaze. "What we do when they do that?"

I stopped chuckling. I did not know the answer. We had never learned how to comport ourselves with women.

Since we had decided not to tour for a while, we needed some way to raise money. I must admit that my father-in-law, though he had opposed our marriages at first, was helpful during this time. The townspeople, too, seemed to grow accustomed to the sight of us on Main Street. Fewer in Wilkesboro sneered.

My brother and I decided to farm, as we had done years earlier in Siam, and Mr. Yates presented us with so many tables, tools, fertilizers, almanacs, and dictums to memorize that we became immersed in modern farming. Yates told us that after years of intense use and misuse, North Carolinian soil produced diminishing returns. Most plots in Wilkes County were less than thirty acres and consisted of corn or tobacco, but Chang and I raised hogs mostly, although we did plant a few rows of corn as well. Chang and I purchased three more slaves, Nathan, Basel, and Guillaume, and we became strict taskmasters.

Meanwhile, my marriage was beginning to feel like a house from a dream, pleasant at first but shrinking a bit every day. "Eng?" Sarah said one night as she was sitting on the bed and brushing her hair before sleeptime. She had been brushing it for minutes and was still not ready for bed. Chang and I were under the covers and I wanted to blow out the candle.

"Eng?" Sarah's voice high and in the nonsensical tone some people use to greet little animals. Though we had been married only a short while, I hankered for some time apart from her. I would feel more certain of my affection for her eventually, I believed. I just wanted to do it at my own pace.

"Eng?" Her voice still singsong.

"Sarah calling you." My brother nudged me. My temples throbbed, and I did not want to open my eyes.

"Eng?" (Why hadn't she let me know—before the wedding— that that was the way she sometimes spoke?) "Eng, my stomach feels not bad tonight." She winked in a way that made me not like myself, for the animosity it aroused in me. She leaned over to place her brush on the chest of drawers, and her dressing gown traveled up her thighs, which were ashen and doughy.

"All right, dear," I said, and smiled. I tried to make the smile affectionate, but it was not easy to overcome the foolishness of her tone. I didn't stop smiling until my cheeks ached. "All right."

During this time, my brother and his wife were so ardent in their copulation, I tried to be the same with Sarah—loving and enthusiastic about affairs of the flesh. But the strong current that had swept me up at the beginning of my marriage had started to dwindle. Love was now a mild streamlet that advanced in drips around my feet; despite how hard I worked at tenderness, I could not drown in a thing that shallow. And so, of course, I would still caress her—out of affection or some other substance—but after a few months I was reaching less and less often for my wife, who never asked why. I hoped for some other sort of connection, some additional intimacy to arrive and fill the absence. Sometimes I imagined Princess Xenga in Sarah's stead.

More often I found myself an unenthusiastic bystander during the nights when my brother was familiar with his wife. The trance I attempted rarely held for as long as I would have wished—nor as well—but on occasion I discovered myself finding Adelaide's accidental touches not as entirely unpleasant as one would expect. And Adelaide herself was agreeable, too, especially in her manner toward my brother. She fell into the habit of teasing him, amusingly exposing his foibles—in a good-natured way, of course, with an ironic twist and that smile at the end of her sentences. Usually his expression around her was meek to the point of unintentional comedy, until she would tell him she had been kidding.

Soon came the morning of our six-month anniversary, a Saturday. Chang had the idea that we should have an outdoor meal on the Yadkin, and as he began to convince us with talk of warm clear air, I found myself envisioning bright flowers abuzz with insects; I could feel the gentle radiance of the summer sun he spoke of, and was easily persuaded.

But the idyll described was not at all the way the Yadkin appeared that forenoon. Sweltering humidity overcast the air, the flowers neglected to sound with life, and the water was brown. We sat on the banks of the river. The ground was covered in a drab dry dust. Though fall was months away, a few of the trees were starting to go leafless. Dust and hot wind got in the eyes. We spread out our lunch blanket as close to the river as possible.

"Well, it's obvious to us all what a good idea *this* was, Chang," Adelaide said, breathing out through her nose and frowning with enough spite to make Chang fall apart. "It's only about one *hundred* degrees out." Chang looked down into the grass.

"Shall we eat?" I asked, and grinned at our women. Each wife sat with her legs gathered under her hips. Sarah was flushed and sweaty, her skin blotchy where it emerged from under her dress. Adelaide did not perspire as noticeably as did her sister.

"We shouldn't have even bothered to *cook* this chicken." Adelaide gave Chang a sidelong look as she reached for the food in the picnic basket. "You'all know we've got the kind of sun to bake everything right here." I hadn't heard her use this sarcastic tone with anyone else.

"Sorry." Chang's voice sounded as small as if it had sprung from a body two feet tall and shrinking.

I asked my own wife to hand me a piece of chicken, but she did not hear. She wore a babylike, innocent expression about her big blue eyes, her long, straight, and crinkled nose, and childishly sucked-in lower lip. She glanced at me a second before looking away as if she hadn't noticed my gaze.

"Isn't this just the kind of excitement you had in mind?" Adelaide was saying to Sarah. "Get yourself married, see the world. A picnic by the old Yadkin where it is obviously ninety-nine in the shade."

"Maybe we just stay and eat and try smiling?" Chang said, startling the girls, who seemed not to have expected him to respond. "Just stay and eat and talk?"

I would have sworn Adelaide's slanted frown was a look of embarrassment had I not seen the same expression on her face when Chang first slipped the ring on her finger six months before.

"It's too hot, you'all," said Sarah. "Excess sun messes my stomach."

"Stay and talk about what, Chang?" Adelaide's eyes burned with emotion one hopes not to see in one's loved ones. "Some people can talk well, some people can *walk* well. Obviously *he* can't do neither one." She pointed a disparaging thumb at her husband.

Sarah laughed, and so Adelaide went on reciting: "Most men lose their sense of taste when they're drinking, and those who always talk are no good at thinking." Then she looked at me and smiled, anger gone from her face. "That's another one my father passed on." But before long Adelaide saw her husband pouting, and she said in a playful tone: "I'm just *joking*, Chang."

She rested her hand in his and leaned in to give him a quick kiss on the cheek. Adelaide was one of those country women people usually write off as fools when they first meet them. She neither knew nor cared about the events of the world beyond Wilkesboro, was crude in conversation and bored by the majority of it, and had been unmarried for too many years before Chang and I arrived. But I was coming to see that, underneath the leavings of decades of obscure small-town life, she had a whimsical soul.

Now I found myself saying: "It *is* quite hot today. If you ladies prefer to leave, that is fine with me."

Chang leaned toward his wife, pulling me with him, as he attempted to kiss her. But she bounced up and said in a loud voice: "Look! What is that?" She pointed to a butterfly hovering over a dandelion. Chang and I almost fell over as Adelaide eluded Chang's grasp.

"It only a butterfly," Chang said, gloomily. He righted our position.

We packed away the uneaten lunch and started back toward home. The air was hot, undeniably, and the sky offered no hope of cooling rain. My wife and my sister-in-law walked ahead of us, talking between themselves, and I looked at my wife's figure descending the hill through the trees. Was wishing for love as hopeless as looking for rain to fall out of this cloudless sky?

Adelaide looked over her shoulder at my brother, who still wore the expression of a dog given too little to eat. She stopped walking, and stood under a tree waiting for us to catch up to her. She poked Chang's chest and said, half mockingly: "It's obvious I'm just having fun with you. He is good, ain't he?" She kissed him on the cheek, which she could scarcely do without leaning on me a little.

Adelaide had been my greatest concern when first I considered matrimony, an obstacle I had believed insurmountable. I had thought, What will be worse than a sister-in-law always present? It's never going to work. Had two couples ever survived such a close, unhappy predicament? A shadow wife not of my own choosing, always in my hair—how could that not change our life forever, in impossible ways, until sooner or later I would end up hating her and she would hate me.

But that was not how it was turning out at all.

Before long Adelaide was pressuring Chang to go on tour. In addition, she wanted to come along. She had "never been anywhere." Sarah, though not as eager about it as her sister, said that she too wanted to see the world, or at least as much of it as you could in the Southern United States.

Our farming was going profitably enough at this point, and our savings had not really been dented, but Chang, because he was getting to be the kind of man who feared crossing his wife, said he'd be happy if the women would accompany us. Though I hated the accursed peering eye of the crowd, I complied and arranged a modest expedition, a jaunt through the American South. People stared anyway, I thought; they may as well be forced to pay for the privilege.

Our fame had not diminished much, and we were able to set up exhibitions with no advance promotion. The inaugural show of this tour was in Wohl, North Carolina, a tiny community in the shade of the Leatherwood Mountains some thirty miles from Wilkesboro. It was to be the first time the girls would see our act. The thought of it made my brother and me nervous, Chang especially.

The Wohl Theater was new and small, like the community it- self. Prior to the late 1840s, few roads had come to the shaky homes that were in the midst of becoming the township of Wohl. Chester Wohl had built the Wohl Theater—and the town—after he had found a glistening thread of gold in the stream that coiled around Oxford Hill before disappearing into it like a snake slither- ing into a tunnel.

It was night when we first made our way to the theater. Mist and shadow encompassed Oxford Hill, and even the faint light failed to show that any building was there until we were right upon it.

Inside, the theater was dusky, despite the best efforts of a set of three weak torch flares abutting the stage. Also, our damsels of the front row, Sarah and Adelaide, were the only spectators. Perhaps our fame had diminished due to our lack of touring.

And yet, the show Chang and I put on then! Acrobatic feats, and feats of strength, rehearsed and improvised—the spontaneous moves hazardous to perform, vaulting, painful twisting, the more splendid for their severity; the rehearsed actions executed with an unprecedented authority and freedom from error. Chang and I swung from the bars of our cage; we gyrated on the cold floor.

At the end of the vigorous part of the performance, Chang

and I clamped together like a vise. His sweat ran toward my body, and his heart rattled my ribs. And then the vise disengaged, its halves going shoulder to shoulder. On the far side of the bars, our wives were applauding—not too loudly or vigorously. There was a play of light from the torch flares on their cheeks.

Mr. Wohl stepped in front of our cage and cupped his hands over his mouth. "Step right up close and examine the ligament!" he yelled into the empty theater. "Do you want to see if it's real?"

Adelaide hollered back: "We don't need no more proof!" Then she threw her head back in laughter. Her eyes were tearing and quite pretty. The shadows of moonlit branches outside threw jagged patterns on her face and body, dark lines in the near-dark. Sarah did not really laugh and looked tired at Adelaide's side.

We took in no money from that hastily arranged show, and not much from the few performances that followed. When you rush into a tour with little promotion, it's bound to start off sourly. Not much improved when we got to Windy Gap, North Carolina. At that town's lone hostelry, eschewing the normal routine, Adelaide and Sarah stayed in one room, Chang and I in another—at Adelaide's suggestion.

It was late. As we dressed for sleep, I noticed Chang had turned white. In that little room, its low ceiling just higher than our heads, we were standing face-to-face leaning against the dresser for balance as we were taking our pants off, when he looked at me as if he'd just noticed he was missing a limb.

"What if Adelaide stop loving me?" he said. "I think she stop loving me."

"Chang." I took a deep breath. "Has she not spoken of wanting to have a child more than anything?"

I put my arm round his shoulder so we could walk side by side to the bed. "Brother," I said, "you and I were never meant for love, and so we don't want to fail it. But do not fret over nothing." I gave his arm a light squeeze. One minute he was overjoyed about the glory of trying to be a husband, the next it was all anguish.

"Eng, you never worry?" He was blinking at me, nearly in a panic.

"I am a creature of habit, you know that, brother," I said. "I've come across some—crimps in my own marriage, but I go on, I work to get everything calm and smooth," I said as we climbed under the sheets. Chang cocked his head toward mine like a rooster.

Why is he talking to me this way? I said to myself. Of course I have concerns, attached at the chest and attempting what we are.

Why can't he do as I do? I said to myself. Is it not easier to live without sharing one's fears?

What I was coming to know about my marriage was that it afforded me a glimpse of the normality I had never understood before—but just a glimpse. I knew I had been right to caution Chang when first he began falling for Adelaide. The insignificant flat hanging appendage of flesh that linked us was stronger than the tally of its soft tissue, because it could ward off love, and all thoughts of happiness. I was lonely, maybe as much in marriage as ever.

Soon we found ourselves in Waveland, Louisiana, a port town just outside New Orleans. We stood one late afternoon on the banks of the foul-smelling Mississippi, waiting at the end of a very long line of people preparing to board, one by one, onto the *Ivory Eagle*, a white steamboat bobbing on the river. It looked like a wedding cake that belched smoke. I thought of the floating musical theaters of home.

Once aboard, the queue of riverboat travelers was divided into two classes—the Main Deckers, who cramped against the engines, barrels, baggage, random scatterings, live chickens, and derelicts; and the Upper Levelers, those lucky few who had paid to climb the baroque spiral stairway that led to a row of individual rooms, all of which featured a Southern porch and a mulatto maid to attend to any lady passengers. Our two couples were supposed to have been Upper Levelers, but because my brother had written the wrong sum on the check we had sent—I could not look after *everything* he did, despite our nearness—we four now had to stand on the main deck.

Gingerbread fretwork dangled everywhere, and the windows were of colored glass. Some of the boat's steam had condensed into beads of moisture that winked on the brasswork like tiny diamonds in the sunlight—but beneath these elegant cosmetics the steamboat was squalor set afloat. The loud hissing never softened, the funnel coughed out foul black clouds of smoke one after the other, and the deck shuddered with the hiccups of an inferior engine. All of these inconveniences paled before the detestable inhabitants of this world between paddle wheels. The fat, cigar-smoking gambler, in the market for a tourist to fleece; the stoop-backed farmer, clutching his modest harvest and looking nervously about; the crewman, sneering as he passed; the lady of the evening in her narrow bonnet, at work in the uglying light of day; the sightseer eyeing this harlot before turning back to his wife and children with displeasure; above all, the whole of this mass of shabby-clothed unfortunates, casting furtive glances around, reeking of threadbare unclean clothes and the perspiration of close contact, chatting or sleeping or making way for any and all flotsam being pushed aboard—these were what gave the main deck its particular character. Chang and I had not traveled in such conditions since we'd made our own modest fortune.

I had an uneasy feeling walking the decks with our wives, moving shoulder-to-shoulder with my brother, our band peeking through the vests of our suits. Hissing through their dirty pink-white mouths, the Main Deckers, ladies and gentlemen both, surrounded us, poking with sweaty fingers and pulling to see with frenzied wide eyes if the band was real. Treading lightly beside Chang and me trying to find someplace to sit, Sarah and Adelaide were stiff as statues and gazed straight ahead, putting forth great effort not to look upset. Chang and I used Gung-Fu to thwart the rude hands as best we could, pushing back the crowd with our precise circular strokes. Our wives were whispering between themselves throatily, "Please get us away from here," saying "please" over and again.

Finally the four of us found space on a secluded bench near the helm. The boat chugged across the water, which the prow cut through in a double-lather that dragged from the stem of the boat like a pair of foamy comet's tails. Everyone around us continued to stare, and pointed, calling out to Chang and me. Adelaide seethed under a wide-brimmed hat whose pink tassels wafted behind her with every breeze, while Sarah stood motionless beside the helm, hatless, without the lip rouge her sister always wore. Our wives were not used to this sort of reception. Adelaide would not look at her husband, and so she sat next to me. She laid her parasol across my knees. Sarah stood beside the helm, her shoulders sagging under the attention, worry lines springing up around her eyes from fighting back tears.

"Well, Eng," Adelaide said, making a show of addressing me instead of her husband. "I guess it's obvious to us all your brother here is a moron."

"Sorry," he muttered.

"I heard you before, Chang," she said, hot-tempered now. She imitated my brother's accent: " 'So*lly.*' "

"They're all staring at us—it's just terrible," said Sarah, slouching her shoulders and looking over the railing at little shanties bobbing to the rhythm of our passing boat's wake.

"Well, Eng," Adelaide said again, "it looks like we're both bound to the same moron." Her laugh could not have sounded less affectionate. I smiled at her.

She looked away from me quickly.

Sarah, meanwhile, had begun to cry. Her face was growing mottled, and she leaned over the rail of the ship and opened her lips into the breeze like she was trying to guzzle a drink of air. She wore her clothes as if they'd been flung on with a hayfork. "My stomach," she said, the loose skin under her jaw shaking. "What a squirrelly life you'all lead. Oh, my stomach."

I had to turn from the sight of my wife. And so, had my sister-in-law been the ugliest woman in the world, at that instant she would have appealed to me. She was not the ugliest woman in the world. She put her tongue briefly to her lips to moisten them.

As Adelaide was looking down at the colors of the sun on the water, I realized I had never noticed the perfection of her nose. I understood now that Sarah's nose was *too* long, a grotesque of Adelaide's. She looked away from me quickly, and I felt as if kicked in my suddenly disgraceful heart.

"Please, Adelaide," Chang said. "What the matter?"

Adelaide picked at her fingers distractedly. Does she suspect my feelings? I wondered.

"What the matter?" Chang said, morose.

This was the first time I had admitted my desire to myself.

"Can't a girl think about something," Adelaide said, "without a Chinaman asking, 'what, what, what?' " She cocked her head to the side. "What do you *think* is the matter? It's obvious this is not what I had in mind when I wanted to see the world."

"I make mistake." Chang exhaled from his nose, and I could feel his discouraged air on my neck.

"Chang, forget it," Adelaide said. "Forget it." She rose from the bench and began walking in the direction of a card game being played farther along the main deck. "Forget it." The phrase, which she now started to sing in an invented melody, formed a trail behind her. *"Forget it. Forget it. Forget . . ."*

Chang called after her: "Adelaide, sorry, I sorry—"

She spun around to us. "Shh! Chang, it's nothing."

He smiled nervously and swallowed his breath. "It nothing, Adelaide?"

"No. Yes." She began to laugh. "I was mad, but I ain't now."

She walked away again. He called to her once more— "Addie!"—but she did not respond. And my brother looked at me, his face flushed with helplessness, with sadness.

As for me, I was wounded by the image of Adelaide frolicking away from Chang, and also the warbled but lovely melody she had invented just seconds before. *Forget it. Forget it. Forget . . .* It did not bring me happiness.

Even now I felt Chang's stare.

Never allow yourself to surrender to this longing, not at all, I thought.

Adelaide will be a close friend, the closer the better, for that way I can enjoy her company. All else is lunacy.

I could hear Adelaide's refrain playing in my head, speaking to me, too: *Forget it. Forget it. Forget . . .*

At that moment Sarah, blinking and pale and not yet fully free from the hold of nausea, came over to sit down next to me and touch my forearm. "I don't know how you'all can stomach it all the time—staring and pointing." She was shuddering but managed to regain her babyish tone. I was startled by my wife's hand. I had forgotten about her.

After a few minutes, Adelaide returned, accompanied by a smiling red-shirted young crewman. The wind had curled one of the pink tassels of Adelaide's wide-brimmed hat down toward her neck. The sight of that lucky thread cambering from the hat faintly to touch her bare skin gave me a physical pain. Jealous of a tassel?

In any case, the smiling crewman at my sister-in-law's side shook his head at Chang and me. "This is Mr. Butler," Adelaide said. "I convinced him to let us stay in two of the vacant rooms of the upper deck."

Mr. Butler picked up our bags and shepherded us toward the stairway that would lead us to more agreeable facilities. After a few steps Butler had vanished into the steam and smoke and the thick of the rabble. Chang and I were a step behind our wives, fighting off invasive hands, and though the girls seemed to think we were out of earshot, we were not. They were talking, in hushed tones, about how Adelaide had convinced Mr. Butler to bring us to the upper deck. "What did you say to him?" Sarah was asking her sister. "I'll never know what to say to a man like you do."

"Don't be squirelly with me, Sarah Bunker." Adelaide was incredulous. "You obviously know exactly well how to talk to a man. Maybe if you hadn't known to sweet-talk so well, you wouldn't have gotten us ruined in the first place—"

Sarah turned her head away as if she'd been smacked. "Adelaide Yates," she hissed. "That was different." Then she shot Adelaide a look containing more cold steel than I thought Sarah capable of. The wind tore at what she said next, but I was almost sure this is what I heard: "Well, I married them, didn't I?" Chang looked not to have heard, or pretended not to have.

Walking up the stairs, I was overcome by shock, then rage. What did that mean, *Maybe if you hadn't known . . . ?* Had my wife lied to me about the slave? I was in such a state that I barely registered the black smoke that beset us from the belching funnel as we climbed the stairs. Had she lied to me? How dare she! The groundwork of our marriage was shown now to have been flawed from the outset. What about all of the effort I put into love and matrimony? But there was an underbelly to my anger that was almost agreeable. Sarah had lied, and I did not want to forgive her.

★ ★ ★

I was not able to savor my anger for long. As soon as we were shown to our rooms, a yelling came from below. I thought at first that a fight had broken out around the "grub stock"—the enormous metal container that our ship's stewards would fill with broken jellied meats, game, ragouts, and fish, in order that the main deckers could scramble for their dinner all at once—but no, the food had not been brought out yet, though by now it was dark and quite late enough for it. Looking over the rail, I saw what the commotion was about soon enough.

The *Mirrorglass*, another steamboat—this one about three hundred feet long, adorned with American flags and a cursive insignia painted on its colossal paddle box—roared toward us, flanking to the right of our *Ivory Eagle*, trailing us by no more than twenty yards. My fellow passengers were screaming taunts at the other steamboat. And they were demanding a race.

The stretch of Mississippi on which we were traveling was quite hazardous, and though steamboat races were common, that did not mean they were safe. The great river was always changing her form. New and surprising junctions appeared and disappeared with the rain, swells and ties emerged or vanished, slices of land became linked suddenly after having been divided for years. An inch of difference in the river's level from one day to the next could bring disaster.

Our captain screamed instructions to the pilot, who in turn shouted frenzied commands to the engineer and his assistants in the fiery engine room below. Everyone on the Main Deck was cheering and jumping up and down. We were going to race.

The river was narrow on every side of Waveland, and it also keeled into a fierce bend, none of which prevented the *Mirrorglass* from closing in on our right. The banks on either side of us were cluttered with half-submerged trees that poked their sharp claws out of the water, ready to snare us like bear traps. Careering together down the narrowing river at an unsafe speed, the steamboats creaked and lurched, but kept right on downstream.

"How terrible!" said Sarah, her shrill voice now a pain in my ears. She looked even more nauseous than before, which I wouldn't have thought possible.

Everyone on our boat was standing up and facing the *Mirrorglass*. People screamed into the wind: "Down with the *Mirrorglass!*" "We'll make quick work of you!" "We're for the *Ivory Eagle!*" My eyes rested on long-faced Adelaide, and her smile. "Go!" she laughed. "Go!" And I laughed, too. Her hand excitedly gripped her fan. She was holding her breath. I looked away. Before my heart had a single beat, my eyes were drawn back to her.

Meanwhile, the *Mirrorglass* was gaining on us. As she pulled even with *The Ivory Eagle*, her passengers began to throw food and balled-up newspapers at our Main Deckers. Our fellow passengers responded in kind.

Racing through the water, almost touching, maneuvering for position, and then actually coming to little brushing collisions, the two steamboats jockeyed like trotters after the starting gun—two nearly indistinguishable boats where there was room for only one. I could see the faces of our equivalents on the boat across from us, and they were filled with frenzy.

Our main deck below was bedlam, too, as hundreds thrust about, pressed against the rails—people of every age, of every size and class—screaming and crying and rasping against their limitations. Crewmen hurled spoiled meat and tallow into our boilers to raise the pressure. Engineers tied down our safety valves, the cry of the steam rose to a lunatic pitch. Faster we raced, much faster than any steamboat should have dared. The river was no wider than a boardwalk.

And my wife was now caught up in the excitement. She clung to the rails, laughing and calling out encouragement to our pilot below, her eyes rolled back in delight. I still fixed my stare on Adelaide, mindless of the wind and pitch of the race.

You are a wicked man, Eng, I thought.

I will never act upon it, I thought, because I'd never be a liar.

As for Sarah, I thought, she's an untrustworthy back-stabber.

The boats were shoulder to shoulder now, the smoke from their funnels merging in a great black cloud just overhead, and we were near enough to the passengers of the *Mirrorglass* to witness their jumping and heaving, the veins that swelled their necks, and in every face the particular ecstasy of competition. As fast as we were going, the *Mirrorglass* was passing us. The engines of both boats were shrieking for mercy, and the flimsy woodwork of our ship began to creak at the last limit of endurance. "Go! Go!" shouted Sarah and Adelaide. "Go!" Chang shouted, hoping Adelaide would hear that he shared her enthusiasm.

For a few seconds I looked without bitterness on Sarah's flushing cheeks and her tittering mouth. How insignificant I must have seemed in the measure of her life. She smiled at the thrill of the race, her hair twisting in the wind, and I was watching as if I had never kissed her or touched her. Her flushed face, her wiry blond hair—how must these have looked when she was in the thrall of girlish love? I felt sorry for her now, this sympathetic woman with stringy hair, her face more wrinkled than when she had loved the slave. When she was caught with him, no one knew the truth except her sister; the Negro had been hanged for it. Sarah knew how to talk to men, certainly she did. How terrible the tumult of emotions she must have been keeping inside her, and how sad.

My attention was pulled abruptly back to the boat race as wind lashed my face. The *Mirrorglass* roared more loudly than we did. Bright and innumerable sparks bolted to life on her main deck, a glowing fountain that set a quick fire. Screams flew on the air, horrible and immediate, and a shudder of horror passed over our boat.

The *Mirrorglass* flared up and burned as kindling. Her pilot steered away from our boat, toward the bank, but the *Mirrorglass* did not reach the shore, lurching instead to a groaning fiery stop as it snared on a sandbar. As our *Ivory Eagle* kept on down the river, the passengers of the *Mirrorglass* were screaming and plunging into the water, men and women diving from the upper deck into the shallow Mississippi, aflame. An explosion lit the sky, a dazzling holocaust, and the *Mirrorglass* blew to pieces. Muffled cries and a hundred magnificent comets shot toward the sky.

The pain of memory needled my heart. Amid the screaming, I had a silent recollection of the bodies of the Siamese dead—Father's body, and Ping's, and countless others'—that had clogged the Mekong decades earlier, and again I breathed in the odor, like burning excrement, and though I closed my eyes, the morass of Siamese corpses came horribly into view. But when I look back on our time on the *Ivory Eagle*, it is not that accident that springs first to mind.

"Finally, some excitement to get the heart pumping," Adelaide was saying to no one in particular a few hours after that tragic race. "Of course, it was terrible. It's obvious to all that it was terrible, but how my heart was going!"

She, Chang, and I were very uncomfortably in bed in one of the *Ivory Eagle*'s sleeping compartments—Sarah slept alone in another. And soon, much as they had been fighting earlier, my brother and his wife began having relations; she must have wanted children desperately. But she went about it with unusual zeal. From the candle that was burning, light flickered about their bodies; I did not want to see this, was not sure I could stomach it. If what I wanted more than anything when I was a boy was to be detached and alone, what I wanted now amounted to the opposite: love.

Adelaide's hand happened to brush my forearm, which was, admittedly, lying close to the thick, fleshy part of her leg, above her knee. She pulled her hand away very abruptly, shooting a nervous glance in my direction before looking at the ceiling.

I moved my arm from hers, but as she rocked slightly backward, she touched me again. My thigh this time.

I thought maybe she was doing it on purpose.

The sheets felt warm. Adelaide's skin was ghostly in the semidarkness. Once more, her knuckles brushed me, and gooseflesh rose on my arms and legs. Was it possible she was doing it on purpose? This contact seemed an impossibility coming from Adelaide, and as long as the experience of her skin touching lightly against mine felt so unlikely, it gave me no pleasure. Still, the sensation made everything about me seem unreal, as if in my shocked and half-trance state I were free from my body and from Chang's, a perception strange and wonderful.

Had she touched me on purpose?

CHAPTER ELEVEN

Fame, and the Movement of Our Hearts

1826
New York–Boston–New York

The night after our first performance in New York, we sat with the promoter Hunter in our room at Mrs. Sachs's house. He congratulated us on "a good beginning." Still, he muttered, things needed "to get quite better."

"First, our little financial question," he said, pulling from his pocket a large leather wallet. He took out two bills, unfolded the joined halves, showed the money to us, and put them in his pocket carefully. "These I will send to your mother." And then he fixed his eye on us strangely. "And now I need to talk with you two," he said, "for literally about three minutes."

Hunter took a hasty step toward us and, winding up, smacked Chang across the face. Chang yelped, fell backward, and I followed, yanked along. We landed, in a stack, on one of the piles of laundry in the opposite corner. I could feel my brother's chest heave as he fought off tears.

Hunter adopted the stance of a pugilist posing for a daguerreotype after a match—knees bent slightly, striking arm still extended, his hand above his head, as if frozen in the last moment of the slap—but his eyes gave him away, especially the left one, in which indecision was magnified through his monocle. Hunter was not comfortable with brutality.

"Do not contradict me, ever," he hissed, bringing down his arm to wipe his lips. "Especially not during a performance. If *I* say you had three parents, you had three parents."

Chang and I got to our feet slowly. My brother was moaning.

"You boys understand me, what?" Hunter asked, a catch in his throat. Meanwhile, Chang and I assumed the tiger and crane positions. Hunter could not keep his eye on us for more than a second. We took a step toward him, another.

He seemed to realize his size advantage suddenly. He stepped toward us. He was a grown man. We were fourteen.

But he did not understand much about Chang and Eng. With our smaller girth came a quick agility no adult man could match. Not to mention that we were two, in sailor's suits maybe, but ready to strike in perfect synchronization. Hunter's face was mottled red. He was shiny with sweat.

When I started into my flip, I knew Chang would be doing the same. As one, my brother and I tumbled shoulder-to-shoulder through the air toward Hunter. Each with an arm around the other, we both touched the ground with a hand as we somersaulted to our destination. Hunter likely could have moved out of the way or at least put up his fists in defense. But as Chang and I were cutting circles over the drab fluffy mountains of Mrs. Sachs's underthings and in the direction of his head, he did neither.

At the apex of our last rotation, we twisted in mid-flip and kicked at the same time. We had judged the original distance between Hunter and us perfectly, and our kicks—mine angled a bit downward, toward Hunter's throat, Chang's straight out, hitting Hunter across the face—struck at the same moment.

Hunter's raw, frightened cry buffeted among the peaks and valleys of Mrs. Sachs's underthings, and by the time Chang and I had alighted on a corset, Hunter was lying on his back with his four limbs in the air, stiff and groaning.

The door was locked, the window bolted. We could not escape just yet—but this was good news: we could handle him, and that would make for an easier getaway. But for now, we needed Hunter even more than he needed us.

Chang and I shuffled over to our vanquished master and helped him to his feet.

* * *

The New York newspapermen were smitten with us. The next day's *Herald* was one of a bushelful that printed a long editorial about my brother and me.

> We are set to pondering by our Yellow Visitor in two costume sailor suits, about the whims of Dame Nature, and about how men keep score, when they are forced to show the sign of "Two to one," and hang it over their door? We expected to see them pull their cord in opposing directions—it is for this that the spectacle under the tent in Madison Square is well worth seeing, most especially for learned masters of metaphysics and theology, not to mention divers into other scientific departments. This pretty yellow enigma poses Knotted Questions: What would be the implications for their unholy, double-freak souls were one half to remain a disciple of the Great Buddha and the other half should be converted to the true Gospel? Learned men of the Law, would ye indict two heathens as one heathen? Dare you send little Chang to jail if his brother shall happen to disregard the letter of the Law? Could one half sue its double if a falling out occurred 'tween the halves? And, metaphysicians: can ye tell us in this case how sorcery can turn dark into light? how Chang and Eng can settle the philosophical quandary of what's what, who whom? Despite the justified excitement surrounding the unholy, double-freak show, their unholy, double-freak intimacy is repugnant to any strong Christian investigation, and we support the possibility of effecting a separation of the unholy double-freak by surgical operation.

The morning after our fight, Hunter arrived early and awakened us. He was dressed neatly, the bruises on his cheek and throat not too visible for the most part. Handing us two black suits cut in the Western style, he said, "Hurry and get dressed." Then he averted his eyes. "We're going for a ride, if you please," he said to the floor.

As we piled into his carriage, Hunter drew the curtains, looked at his pocket watch, and sighed. "It's seven forty-four," he said. "I wanted to be on our way by seven-forty. Now, we'll be five minutes late." Obsessed by the way one second detaches from another, Hunter corralled each day into precise tracts; the mental fences he was always building seemed painful for him to cross.

"We are going to a meeting arranged for the press, north of Mount Vernon." He tried to hide his irritation with a kindly tone as he returned his chronometer to its pocket. "Do you know anything about God?" he asked. "That is something the reporters may ask, what?" He looked again at his watch. Seven fifty-three: time for a smoke. "I remember the exact moment I started to believe," said Hunter, pulling a cigarette from his coat pocket.

"I was literally a great runner when I was a boy. Quite a good distance man, I was. Like an Indian, the schoolmaster said." He traced the outline of the bruise on his throat gently. "Alone on the track, all alone, you are different than other people, what? Not bothered by anything, do you understand?"

He didn't wait for an answer; he was trying to teach my brother and me something. "Perhaps I'm not expressing it correctly, but that feeling of solitude, it's almost a paradox if you think about it, but being so alone in front of all those people showed me that there was *something* that was all-powerful, in its absence. Does that make sense?"

"No," said Chang.

Hunter ground his teeth. "I'll get you a Bible," he mumbled. The heavy scent of tobacco lolled around the carriage.

"So," Hunter said, "you had a father."

"Yes," we answered.

He thought about this for a moment. "You miss him."

"Yes," said my brother immediately; I did not answer as quickly.

"No," I lied. Chang turned his head toward mine with a start. The carriage bucked over an unlevel patch of street.

Once the carriage ride had ended, Mr. Hunter opened the door to see if the street was empty. After a few moments, he ushered us quickly inside a two-story white building, a small college.

In the center of the Irving Wallace Medical College, a circular observation room was scalloped into concentric, ringed tiers. Beside Hunter and a doctor who wore a white lab coat, my brother and I lay naked on a cold metal operating table within the inner-most circle. All but the uppermost rows were filled to capacity with gazers; the press, along with a smattering of medical scientists, sat in the benches that ran along the successively larger ascendant rings. Neither Chang nor I yet saw that there was a familiar face hidden among them.

Standing near Chang and me, pale, lean-faced Dr. David Rosen was in his forties, tall and thin, a mere skeleton with hair. He had shaggy brows over bright gray eyes, and a fine spray of curls on top of his head.

"Good men of the newspaper world, fellow doctors, and circus enthusiasts," Rosen read from a piece of paper with a creak in his voice that belied the ostentation of this display. "The highly respectable gentleman Mr. Robert Hunter wishes me to examine these yellow twins of Siam, in order to ascertain if anything fallacious or indecorous exists in their bondage, a task which I am proud now to perform, under the aegis of God and Hippocrates." His words carried an echo in this large chamber. Chang shivered at my side; the room was cold, the metal of the table colder.

"I miss In," Chang whispered to me.

A Mr. Nick Reding, of the *New York Herald*, wrote in the next morning's paper that the "diminutive-statured doctor" seemed to enjoy having an audience. Reding described how the doctor put his right hand under our connecting band and—with his left—"punched his fist hard against its flank." The punch hurt. Chang and I screamed; the crowd gasped. Dr. Rosen looked at us and blinked.

"This bond, it is not particularly sensitive, I don't think." The doctor placed his palms on our chests. He stood motionless for a second, his lips shaping words noiselessly, his sweaty hands moving about us. "The movement of their hearts seems not to coincide."

Dr. Rosen's pale hands were spotted, and crossed with ropy blue veins. His fingers squeezed the bond. "Also, their connection is—more complicated than I expected."

He turned his back on us now, to face the crowd. "The . . . link, as I'll call it, seems to be cartilaginous, a mass somewhere about five inches long at its upper edge. Also it is able to stretch to greater length; it is thicker up and down than it is in the horizontal direction. So it is quite—*loathsome* to the touch, full of gnarled cartilage below the flesh." He took a fortifying breath. "Not to forget the web of connecting vessels, lymphatics, abdominal viscera, and small nerves intersecting therein. The boys may share a stomach."

The doctor looked even more pale than when he began. "So, I am surprised to find it extremely solid. It's not as firm on the lower edge, not to forget there's a single umbilicus, through which passed a single umbilical cord that would have served to nourish the children in the fetal state. It is my opinion that, despite the protests made in print by your colleagues, separation is not the answer. True, that seems the humane solution, but the peritoneal membrane that lines the cavity would rupture the intestines, liver, stomach, and spleen."

Hunter smiled brightly: *Separation is not the answer.* How many times in my life did I have to hear that terrible news?

"Also, I would only advocate an attempt at separation in the case of the death of one," the doctor said. "Then it would be worth risking, true, to prevent endangering the life of the other." He gave our band a slap. "But only then. So in closing, I paraphrase Montgomery: These boys are 'distinct as the billows, yet one as the sea.' Thank you, hold your applause. I judge their health to be at present good. It is probable that the confinement of their situation, not to forget the sudden shift from their barbaric habits, will bring their life to a close within a few years. Thank you so much, so now I turn the floor over to your questions."

One reporter, wearing a tight-fitting brown suit and holding a little notepad, stood and asked us: "Do you both speak?"

"Yes, they do," answered Hunter, leaning with his good ear to the crowd.

I tried to gain Chang's attention. What was it the doctor had said about our lives coming to a close?

As the first reporter took his seat, another man stood.

"Are they the same age?" asked this one. "If not, which one is older—and by how much?"

Hunter chuckled. "Yes, of course they are the same—"

"No," Chang interrupted. Hunter, surprised, nervous, turned to my brother. The crowd was suddenly transfixed. Chang smiled.

"We are not same age. Two years different, because one day I am twenty years old, and Eng will be twenty, too!" I did not know how Chang could joke at such a time. Had he heard what the doctor said?

The crowd, meanwhile, was laughing as one. Brushing his hand through his hair, Chang was covered in bravado, as a tuna, just netted from the Mekong, is drenched in a skin of gleaming water. But the bravado was bound to evaporate before long. Remembering he was naked, my brother quickly hid his groin with his hand.

After a few more questions, a man sitting alone in one of the highest tiers rose from his seat and took a step forward, and everyone gasped as he did so. The man wore a red silk cravat over which a great fold of skin drooped. His hair had retreated to the top of his head in two tufts, leaving in its wake a strip of exposed flesh running wide atop his sizable head, out of proportion with the squat face beneath it.

"Barnum," whispered Hunter, after which his mouth fell open.

"I have a question," this man, P. T. Barnum, said in his loud, deep voice. Next to him sat a black-haired man, with a face and skin like ours, and what looked to be a peasant's frock.

"Mr. Barnum, I did not know you were here." Hunter was trying to regain his composure. "Our invitation was extended only to—"

"Fellows, my question," Barnum said, his jowl dancing, "is a moral one. . . ." He let his sentence trail off for effect. "I promote acts. Big Frenchie de Bouchamp. Little General Thaddeus Pinky. Strange? Of course. But my acts are Christian men. Foreigners, sometimes. But Christian men. What about these twins? Are these God-fearing attractions? I'll bet not. Just what are we subjecting the families of New York to?"

"Yes, exactly what are we doing?" asked a man sitting in a lower tier. With suspicious quickness, this "reporter" had spit out his question just before Barnum finished speaking.

"Well, yes, they are God-fearing," said our promoter Hunter. "My attractions are in the process of conversion to the Presbyterian faith, and are set to read the Bible." Hunter turned his red face to Chang and me with eyes that begged us not to contradict him.

"Good," said Barnum. "Interesting to behold, that'll be." He smoothed his cravat. "The good newspapers of this fair country have an obligation to follow that. Check on its veracity."

Barnum tapped the head of the yellow-skinned man seated beside him. The man stood up and stepped forward: the doctor from Siam who had tried to separate us, now moving restlessly from side to side. He had shaven off his goatee, and looked considerably older.

Barnum pointed to the physician. "A genuine witch doctor from the city of Bangkok, country of Siam. He doesn't speak much English. Dr. Lau. Arrived this morning. Barely a word. I got the yellow fellow a ticket myself. Lau says that they grow these double-boys on trees over there. Is that not right?" he asked, and patted the doctor on the arm. The physician looked at Barnum as if the bigger man had spat on him. The promoter tapped him again, harder this time.

"Yesh," the doctor said. And he gave his thinning braided hair a nervous tug.

Barnum said: "And it is also true that they—" Here Barnum paused for dramatic weight, at which point panicky Dr. Lau said "Yesh," which ruined the tension.

Barnum continued anyway: "—*can* in fact be separated."

Hunter looked at Dr. Rosen with pleading eyes. Rosen understood, and took a step toward the stands. "Mr. Barnum, I doubt your claims." The physician pounded a fist into his palm.

Hunter, smiling, saw his cue. "Gentlemen," he said, "do you take the word of a witch doctor over an American physician?" The room erupted in laughter. Hunter went on: "I think you would all agree that these boys are not little General Thaddeus Pinky, what?"

As the last snicker quieted, and before Barnum could think of a reasonable reply, Hunter looked at his pocket watch. "Thank you for joining us for our little spectacle, gentlemen—and Mr. Barnum. But the time has come to take our attractions home."

Traveling back to New York City, after hours of riding, the road curved away from the quiet countryside hills and toward an open view of approaching Manhattan. Hunter was asleep. Sitting side by side, Chang and I did not speak to each other, each no doubt thinking about what Dr. Rosen had said—that we only had a few years left to live. Chang's chin trembled.

I cleared my throat. "I'm sure that the doctor was just playing his part in their little show. Think, brother, did we have two fathers? No, but isn't that what they said to make our act 'better'?"

After a moment Chang answered in English. "How come you not scared?" He rubbed his chin with a clenched fist. "How much is few years?" His words trembled. "How would it happening if we—die?" Tears were forming in his eyes.

"What good could it possibly do to be scared?" I said. "Quit crying, now. And why don't you speak in Thai?"

"We am in America, what?" He looked over at Hunter as if to indicate I was about to get us in trouble for talking in a non-American tongue. "I am not scared that we'll die. It just that—" He narrowed his eyes at me and stared long into my face. "Why are you not scared?"

I turned away from him to look out the window. "Did Father not say that in the next life we would return as something better?"

The carriage creaked, and not so gently. Chang's nose nearly swiped my brow as he shook his head. "I am not believing you. Are you idiot enough to think death is a way to get what you want?"

"What do you mean?" I asked. Out the window two sections of a forest opened like a shell onto a narrow clearing as we approached. I could hear Chang's breathing and feel his stare on the back of my neck.

"You wanting to be alone," he said, "that is all you thinking about."

He whispered in my ear, with intimacy and surprising tenderness. "How come you never ask if I want to be separate? Do you think I do?"

I don't care if you do, Chang, I said to myself.

"I do not think of it, ever," he whispered. "Do you want to know why?"

If I were to speak openly, I thought, I'd say that I would not want a life after death if *he* were present, that I hated him from time to time, and that now when I closed my eyes I was fantasizing that we were a shell opening, its two halves being let apart. As if even daydreams could not go unshared from him, Chang snorted, "Why try wishing to separate if that not possible?"

I stared out at the countryside. As we approached dusky Manhattan, I was like some inverse counterpart to Lot, prudent enough to look only behind me, and not to the jumble of firelight and frenzy ahead. What fine, careless rapture it must be to live your days alone, wholly alone.

"Tomorrow, we escape," I said.

Fully dressed by the time Mrs. Sachs came in with our breakfast the next morning, we said "Good-bye, missus" as she opened the door, and we slid past her, skipping out into the hallway in our sailor's suits.

"What are you boys doing? You're not allowed to—"

We had the front door opened—and shut behind us—before she could finish her sentence. My brother and I were going to walk south toward the docks and then find our way back to Siam. That was our plan, such as it was.

The weather was cool and the air smelled as though it had been sweating. Uptown lay a grassland in the distance upon which a few cows still grazed. Shoulder-to-shoulder we walked south, down one of the spacious cobblestone avenues that was shaded by weeping willows and lined with wooden and brick buildings in varying degrees of completion.

We came to a populated section of town, and people stopped whatever they had been doing to point at us. Chang and I continued walking, not looking at anybody else, nor even at each other. We passed a newspaper-print house, a tavern with high plate-glass windows, an inn four stories tall, a tobacconist, a laundry, a chemist's shop with its green and red and blue bottles displayed, a locomotive that ran right down the street, a fire tower taller than anything near it. The sun was throwing its harsh glare in shafts on the ground between the shadows of buildings and unlit gas lamps, and I thought that even the daylight was different here, not at all like the soft warm gold of the sun as it slept on the lilac-colored Mekong. We walked down a street whose name I did not catch, with marble estates and granite mountains. Where this avenue crossed Broadway, traffic began to increase dangerously. Policemen stood in the street, helping carriages narrowly avoid collision.

Even at this time of weekday morning, people were heaped into taverns, drinking. "Just let's continue walking," I said, uncertain and improvising (at times I could be impetuous). The atmosphere of general blight had grown worse; the air was impregnated with wretched smells, and drunken fools—men and women—were wallowing in the filth of the ever-narrowing streets.

"Do we go back to Mrs. Sachs?" Chang's voice conveyed fear and regret.

I did not want to go back. Even if the taller and taller buildings now cast shadows more like sections of nighttime across the sidewalk on this clear morning.

From several of the doorways, great, mean-faced men emerged, shielding their eyes from the morning sun before wagging a finger at my twin and me. This was why I feared people's eyes, the nuisance of being stared at.

Now the entire street noticed the conjoined boys, and a community crowded around us in a circle. Chang's forearm behind my head felt heavy, like the arm of a deadfall.

We continued scuddling ahead, and the circling crowd moved with us. People began piling out of doors to join the circle, and those who did not screamed from the inside of buildings.

"Look at the people." Chang was suddenly smiling, his eyes as far from me as Siam. He began to wave to the people like he was greeting friends. I recoiled from the muttering crowd, but Chang responded to the noise, drifting toward it, and—for the first time since we were children—my brother and I tried to go in opposite directions, and we almost lost our balance as our band smacked us together.

A loud huzzah erupted. Maybe the crowd took our awkward lack of harmonized movement as proof that our condition was not a hoax. A call came for "The Siamese boys!"

"They know us!" Chang said (Hunter had been hiding the truth; without realizing it, we had become very famous while we had been cloistered in Mrs. Sachs's apartment). The hoop of people crowding around us grew.

The human circle closed in. I caught the eye of one boy who

stood directly in front of me, snub-nosed, flat-browed, dirty, and with the dull little ugly black eyes of an old man. He walked backward on his heels under the sunny sky, the calm breeze stirring his collar. The coat he wore was too large for him, and his hat was perched at such an angle that it barely stayed on his head.

This boy stepped toward me, touched our band, shrieked in mock horror, and then ran into the heart of the laughing crowd. People behind us started scampering ahead to get a look. The circle closed in on itself. A hundred hands, two hundred, grabbed at my brother, pulling back his shirt to get a look at our body. And then it all moved in, punching.

A lost animal would have perhaps been shown some kindness; we had to kick and to claw, two teenage boys felling six or seven with each blow, but it wasn't enough. The crowd swallowed us, the air around us went black, and we were knocked unconscious.

This was New York, and Captain Coffin had been right; neither she nor we were ready for the other.

My brother and I awakened in a police station, having been taken into a third-class waiting room. We made an interesting problem for the police. The law as interpreted in Manhattan trains an officer of the peace to apprehend burglars, or to harass moldy tramps—what was the protocol for handling a bruised double-boy? The reporters arrived just before Hunter did.

Chang had trouble keeping his eyes open, and when the police helped us to our feet, we found it hard to stand.

We told Hunter we had just been going out for a walk, wanting to see New York.

He shook his head. "A man gets what he deserves, and maybe a double-man gets double, what?"

Still, the publicity generated by our beating would be precisely what we needed, Hunter said. He was right. Our notoriety grew with each performance. A few more shows in New York and then it was up to Boston for a week's stay at the Exchange Coffee House.

The shows in Boston—which, after New York, we found a little underwhelming—went well, as did our conference with the local press, at which a reporter from the *Daily Courier* asked if we felt particularly close to one another.

"I thinking we about five inches close," Chang said.

After the press conference we returned to the Tremont Hotel (its eight toilets were the first of their kind in a public building in America—it took Chang and me, face-to-face, and then side to side, quite some time to navigate that device). We slept on the floor of Hunter's room, and before allowing us to retire for the evening, Mr. Hunter sat down, a solemn look across his face. He opened his mouth as if to speak, then stopped to clean his monocle.

"You have been steady fellows, boys—literally superb," he said. "If things continue and I remain satisfied, we will work out fine together. Here are four dollars," he said, holding up a black velvet change purse. He smiled as if he loved us and returned the purse to his pocket. "I don't want any of this business about you going into the streets on your own, so I'll hold on to these wages, eh?"

I opened my mouth to ask a question.

"—Your mother has been sent her share of the money." Hunter sounded irritated.

My brother started to say something, but Hunter held up his hand to silence him. Hunter's eyes flashed. He seemed about to stand but remembered himself, and instinctively he brought his fingers tenderly to his throat. He looked like one of the drunks who had come from the taverns of New York to flog us in the middle of the day (I was developing a hatred for alcohol even then).

With all this talk of Mother, I thought of her for the first time in—oh, I don't know—minutes. Her hazel eyes, her dark hair, and her reedy convincing frame. I felt a sort of gladness, too—at the thought of the improvements the money we were sending her would bring. Perhaps she had moved from the riverbanks and into a village, and it could be that she had gotten rid of Sen, and maybe she was happy again.

"Where is In?" Chang asked.

"Eh?"

"Duck."

Hunter bent his head quickly, as if he had thought Chang was issuing a command.

"Your pet?" he recovered, smoothing his hair as he brought his head back to its normal position. "The creature is safe with me." Hunter wiped a bit of perspiration off his right eyebrow. "I'm having a trip out tonight. I'm sure I don't need to remind you not to leave the hotel, nor even to open your window shades, what?"

We heeded his warnings, and went to bed early.

Before I dozed, I turned to my brother. "Chang?"

"Yes?"

"Don't you want me to help you with your English?"

He blinked at me. "Help why?" he asked. "My English no bad, what?"

We wished each other pleasant dreams and went to sleep.

Though our Boston shows drew ever-larger crowds, generated increasing newspaper ink, and, thanks to our expanding ticket sales, brought forth even a few smiles from Mr. Hunter, I was doing poorly in my attempts to pretend to be content.

Chang would chat playfully with any splinter who would break off from the body of the crowd to speak to us. "Back in line," he'd joke, "or you have to join us." He entertained the reporters and talked in soothing tones to the frightened schoolchildren (wan-faced nitwits) brought to see us as part of their science studies. "Do you know where Siam is?" Chang would whisper. "It beautiful, but not like America." And his face would beam when he made jokes with the contingent of Massachusetts-based doctors who in their white lab coats visited the Exchange Coffee House in a gaggle—they quacked and poked our band, and quacked again while they jotted notes. At this point Chang picked up the title "the More Dominant and Charming of the Two," while I lapsed into periods of despair and even complete disgust. This was a wretched career, we were not seeing any of the benefits of our success, and I yearned for home.

When we got back to New York and Mrs. Sachs's, the widow began to treat us better. She began to serve us, along with our usual bread, maple syrup that coiled around our spinning forks and slithered in a golden mass down to our hands, where it stickied our suddenly delicious fingers. Then she showed us into her water closet, handed us a bar of English soap—black as tar—and after she left, we bathed in her collapsible tub. I found nothing suspicious in the improved way Mrs. Sachs treated us. We had not seen her spying daughters in many nights, either.

One day Mr. Hunter came into our room holding a piece of folded paper, a pen, and a book. The paper diagrammed the twenty-six letters of the alphabet, the book was the Bible. It was a handsomely bound edition, the gilt edge of which beguiled me immediately. We had had very little religious instruction in Siam, beyond Father talking about reincarnation.

With an overflow of lazy sighs, Hunter ran through the written letters of the language, had us write the phonetic approximation of each one in Siamese, and—as I used this linguistic key—I applied my prior knowledge of English (I knew all the words by sound already) to discover how the Western utterances I had been making actually looked on the page. That is how I learned to read English in such a short time.

The following morning Hunter returned to read from Genesis, and he had us follow along. "I'm going to ask you questions about this the next time we are in public," he said. "We'll start with a little interrogation about this first part, about the Lord literally creating the world in six days, you understand. Continue reading, get to know the book. That sounds agreeable, right, Chang? Right, Eng?" He patted us on the head. Something had changed in his character. He too was showing us more respect.

After Hunter left, I read through much of the Old Testament, well into the evening. Though it was painstaking at first—consulting our chart for each letter, then shaping the clauses in my mouth, and enjoying the frisson of recognition each time the jumble of letters suddenly transmogrified into a familiar phrase—I was captivated.

Chang, who wearied of the words hours before I did, said, "Enough, brother, let's make flip onto laundry pile."

I ignored him and kept my nose in the book. For personal reasons, the allegory of Noah drew me in. The narrative of the Ark crossing the seas, the paired animals, the lone outcast looking for a new land, it all rang in my soul at full peal. My thoughts, elevated by the ancient and oddly familiar tale, began wandering in imaginary space. Other favorites: *And if thy right hand offends thee, cut it*

*off and cast it from thee. For it is profitable that one of thy members
should perish and not that thy whole body should be cast into hell.* But
even more than the pious magnificence of the Bible, it was the
thrill of learning, it was *reading*, that had me spellbound.

"Put Bible down, I want to play," Chang said, looking at the
ceiling.

"Hush!"

The legends, the characters so vivid and solemn, the language—
how could I stop reading? Our little room at Mrs. Sachs's house
was at that moment a fine cathedral. The altars of dirty piled-up
clothes assumed radiance, the musk of the laundry was redolent of
God. Eventually Chang fell asleep, leaning on me; refusing his
weight, I steeled my spine and read into the night.

Later, just as I was descending into dreams, our door opened.
The two young Sachs girls who lived upstairs—bulldog-faced
Martha and her oval-faced companion—had come back for another furtive look. Martha, who had been the braver of the two
during their last visit, walked up to our bed. Her companion
waited at the doorjamb. Chang was asleep.

The sky was not so black that night, with moonlight weeping
in through the window, and, though in the low light Martha's face
seemed a patchwork of shadows of varying darkness, I could see
the whites of her eyes, her wide-opened eyes—they were yellow-
ish white, like abscesses. As she finished her approach, her patchy
skin looked made up of cheese parings.

"Hello?" I said.

She jerked a hand to her chest and screamed; this woke Chang.

"In?" he muttered.

"It *talks*," whispered the other girl, who was now cringing by
the door in a yellow dress. Martha stood frozen on the spot, hand
still against her chest, mouth still opened in fright.

Chang, now almost fully awake, said: "Hello."

After a long moment— quiet seconds slinking like the maple
syrup we had enjoyed earlier that day—my brother and I sat up
in bed.

"W-what's your name?" Martha asked finally.

"Chang and Eng."

"You speak?" asked the girl in the corner.

"No," I said. No one laughed.

The woman thought a moment, then said, "I'm Ada, and this is Martha."

In a hollow presentment of hospitality, Martha, composure un-regained, stuttered: "Charmed, I'm sure."

Neither Chang nor I knew what to say. "Mrs. Sachs is your mother?" I asked.

Ada said, "Yes." She swallowed a number of times, looking more nauseous after each gulp.

I had been lost in the desire to shake their hands, to touch their skin with my skin, but I managed to recover and ask, "And you are sisters?"

"Yes," Ada said. "Originally from Tennessee." She swallowed hard again, and stared at our band. "And are you brothers?"

Chang and I smiled, "Yes." We kept smiling, until it felt un-natural and my cheeks began to hurt. The sisters were not smiling with us. Ada's hands, her long ringless fingers, looked elegant and touchable even if they quivered, or perhaps because they quiv-ered. Martha, pale as a ghost now, pivoted and raced out of the room. Without a word Ada followed, her yellow dress puffing up behind her, and before long, soft footsteps sounded their quick re-treat up the stairs.

Things are more divine if they seem unreal. When you cannot view an event except with the perplexed eyes of an outsider, when you covet a connection to a world that you believe you can never touch, the most basic facts of life seem miraculous; women appear as miraculous as the cosmos does to a stargazer.

Chang had the sad eyes of a whelp at that moment, and we shared the belief that we would never enjoy any sort of inter-course with the fairer sex other than to witness women screaming and fleeing.

CHAPTER TWELVE

A Last Lingering Clasp

1844–1846
Wilkesboro

We had been two years in Wilkes County and in marriage. Adelaide and I had brushed hands two times in the intervening months, never for more than a second. The touches were on purpose, I thought—but I could not confirm it. She and I never could speak of it, or the why of it. The immorality of the situation was not lost on me, and neither was the absurdity: Her husband always inches away, a one-hundred-and-fifty-pound shadow of flesh and bone, my future an endless labor of guilt and closeness to my goal— banish the thought, I told myself.

I wanted to believe in my ability not to think about the joy my brother's wife's hand gave me, and to fight that selfish indulgence with loyalty to my marriage, even though I knew that Sarah had lied to me about her history. I conceived of ways to tell her I knew the truth about her feelings for the slave, but whenever I deliberate about something for too long, it revolves within me until it sinks deep down and I can't pull it out—and what good would it have done? The only course of action in this situation, I thought, is to trust oneself. Not easy when one is a hodgepodge of fits and pangs, weak and lacking consistency—but oneself is all we are given. Despite my best efforts, however, I found it difficult to remain amiable to Sarah.

I was getting to know all the private little gestures she declined to hide from me. By now I marked the open and close of each day by watching my wife brush her hair every sunup just before she'd fully awakened, and again at night as she began to fall asleep. Slouching, drained either by the demands of rising from bed or by the burdens of a long day, she'd sit on the edge of the mattress, her face bare and tired, and she'd look at the top of her brush. Then she'd clear her throat and wait there, still as ice. What was she waiting for?

She'd stare into the bristles until almost the end of time, and sigh with emotion I could never figure out, then bring the brush to her head, let out another breath as if Chang and I weren't there, and after hesitating, she began the drawn-out and apparently painful process of brushing. She contorted her face as if she was enduring—barely—the amputation of a favorite limb, she slowly dragged the brush through her hair, and there was the ripping sound of roots unprepared to hold up under pressure. Pouting as though it were someone else forcing her to undergo this tribulation, as though she had never brushed her hair in this way before to know it would hurt her so—

"Why do you trouble yourself?" I'd say. "Please, no need to do it for my sake." I tried to appear husbandly. "Just let's go to bed."

Sarah would turn to us then and look at me as if I'd spoken too softly to be understood. And she'd begin the whole process again, the slouch, the minutes of staring into the head of her brush, the throat-clearing, the sigh and its double, and, of course, the drawn-out, painful brushing. She did this yet a few more times, and I could predict each move in the routine before it happened. In the morning, I could get us up and leave the room to avoid seeing it, but at night I was a captive audience. I'd have to take a deep breath for relief.

One day, when Chang and I were on the porch, I heard Sarah whistling in the kitchen through the open window. She was watching Thom cook and she was improvising, if you could call it that, making up a tuneless song, and it hurt my ears.

"Please, Sarah," I called over my shoulder and toward the window, "you are out of key."

My brother raised his eyebrow at me.

"Don't be silly, you'all," Sarah said. In that singsong voice. "How can I be out of key if I'm making it up?"

"You are," I said. "And please stop using that *manner.*"

She did not say anything, although the sound of feminine footsteps scurrying out of the kitchen conveyed its own type of message. Chang was still looking at me.

After a minute, Adelaide opened the door to the porch and came outside. "You're bad-tempered on my sister," she said in the tone she used to upbraid slaves. "It's not fair." But then she gave me a half smile. "Sarah's upstairs, her stomach in a bunch, I'm sure."

I wanted to tell her that she was a fine one to talk about being bad-tempered with a spouse, and that I was more than fair in silently watching Sarah struggle to beautify her hair—for whose benefit?—every day and every night. If I could not disengage from my brother, did I have to abide excessive closeness with my wife as well?

I told Adelaide that she was right, and that I'd apologize later.

At the onset of 1846, the country was filled with new tensions. John Calhoun, the separatist South Carolinian politician, introduced his idea of a "concurrent majority" under which America would have a pair of presidents—one to represent the slave states, and another to represent the free—each having the power of veto over the other. I knew better than anyone that this double-headed system would surely lead to secession. In my heart I was not wholly an American, however, and I was too consumed with the knots of my own domestic situation to care much about politics.

We were now thirty-four years old, and our hair was graying (though his more than mine). We also owned a double-plotted farm—one parcel a fertile twenty-six and a half acres, on which we grew corn; the other measured thirty-seven and a half acres, and had proven sufficient for the raising of hogs. But as long and hard as my brother and I worked, and no matter how much we spent on the finest tools and slaves, our costs always exceeded our profits. Farming was filled with hidden expenses. We owned some twenty Negroes, with Thom acting the part of our eyes when we could not watch the other nineteen slaves to make certain they all were working, which they did, for the most part, because we treated them sternly and because they feared our double-shape. We'd paid quite a lot for our slaves, as much as six hundred dollars for a seventeen-year-old boy named Soren.

And so Chang and I began to find ourselves wanting for money. Adelaide had expensive tastes, and Sarah followed suit. And Chang, who had taken to wearing black silk cravats, and who had become more attached than I had to the high-priced sets of argentine combs and brushes we used on our hair—which we wore short in the front and braided in back—Chang now wanted to return to constant touring. But the climate had changed since the time of our last tour.

Chang and I had our own problem with slaves. Our farm was not producing nearly as much corn as it should. After talking to Thom about it and hearing the amiable old Negro's vague answers, I decided that, rather than purchase more workers, my brother and I should buy more land. Land never has the desire to run away.

Using the little money we'd received from our most recent tour of the South, we acquired another few acres for the farming of tobacco. Actually, it was I who acquired it; Chang had had his own plan to raise money—selling the slaves—which I rejected as worthless by pointing out that we needed the slaves to do the bulk of the work on our crops. "Why is it that your brother got all the brains?"—that was how Adelaide expressed to Chang her dislike of his idea.

Our property had grown large now; our house looked across a green pasture and manicured golden farmland to the foot of the Blue Ridge Mountains. It was a good time and place to farm, though Chang, as I suppose I also did, allowed thoughts of his wife to distract him. He and Adelaide now fought continually. He would do something to annoy her—it could be a kindness he'd extend to her in some awkward embarrassing way, or some idiocy such as his incorrect use of a word—and she would roll her eyes and look at me. And then I'd picture her in a royal silk garment.

We spent a lot of time sitting on our back porch, talking. But mostly we gazed out past the green pasture to the foot of the Blue Ridge Mountains. I enjoyed sitting there, looking at my slaves off in the distance working in the field, and at my land, my home. Despite all the difficulties we still faced, I could not deny the satisfaction I felt now and then. I still had trouble believing that we had done it. Chang and I were American farmers sitting with our American wives.

Adelaide was more restless than her sister was. While Sarah would sit there not wanting to disturb her stomach by moving about, Adelaide from time to time would walk into the house and back, getting something to occupy her, a needlepoint for example. I watched her walk. I watched her sit down and manipulate the sewing needles in her long fingers. I watched her put down the needlepoint and stretch her long frame. Then she would sit down again to fiddle with some lint on her dress, her hands strong, and I would watch that, too.

One morning we were sitting on the porch and talking about the girls' cousin Emily, who had nearly been hit by a runaway buckboard in Mount Airy a few weeks earlier. Chang and I sat in one wicker chair, the girls in another.

Chang was shaking his head, laughing, and saying, "In this country, carriages everywhere, if you not careful you getting trampled over. It make you crazy."

"Ain't 'this country' been pretty good to you'all?" Adelaide turned toward him as if he had dropped a china plate. "Obviously you don't appreciate your good fortune in 'this country.' What about me and Sarah here?"

"Oh, Addie," said Sarah. "I don't feel well enough to be drug into your fight." She had a wet washcloth over her head and sat with her eyes closed.

With a strained smile and a weak voice, Chang said, "I am appreciate America, Adelaide, I—"

"—It just makes me so crazed, he is such an ingrate, Sarah," said Adelaide. "*Your* one isn't as bad as that."

Sarah raised a skeptical eyebrow.

"I only happen to mention about America," Chang was saying, "an interesting point—carriages everywhere. If you not careful you getting trampled over." He swallowed, then said, "Sorry."

Adelaide, knowing she had won the round, refused to look

away. With the fingernail of her thumb she absently gave little jabs to her neck. And my heart.

Chang asked, "You are crazed at me?"

"Obviously, I just said I was." Adelaide's eyes lit up when she fought.

Like the stillness after a crash, the hush that followed was obtrusive. The four of us listened to the sounds of our lawn for a while, to the sounds we sat there not making, and then Sarah stood, leaving her wet washcloth on the wicker chair.

"My stomach," she explained, crossing the porch and heading toward our house. Before going inside, she turned to her sister, pointed to her stomach and pantomimed crying. After all this time, I had not unraveled any of her puzzlements, the little mannerisms that would come into view just when I imagined there were no more annoyances to discover.

The porch got a little warmer after she left. Chang was looking at Adelaide. She did not return his gaze. "I'm in a hellacious mood today," Adelaide said, giving a hint of a smile at the end of her sentence and patting her long hands together.

I hazarded a response. "Well"—I tried not to sound too eager—"at least you have some fight in you."

"Oh, have I?" she said. She brought her slender hand to her throat.

"Yes," Chang said softly. "You have."

"Listen, I still have more fire left, Chang, if you provoke it." She snickered, then pointed a finger at him. "I'm in a hellacious mood, and miserable to boot."

"If I may say so, it doesn't seem that way." I tried to hit a balance in my smile between the appearance of platonic modesty and ardor. "The heat of the fight seems to brighten your aspect. 'Bright Phoebus in his strength,' as Shakespeare would say."

"You, Eng, hush now with your flattery. I think my husband might be near." And we laughed on this awhile. Of all the people that now made up my world, she was the only one I could joke with. My brother was not laughing.

With no money coming in, Chang and I bought a tract of adjoining land that had come up for auction after the death of a local widow. But Chang's frequent dejection made it hard to motivate him to work on the farm. This was a problem. Our new acres were in no shape for cultivation. And the slaves were slow to clear and prepare the land, which meant my brother and I were forced to work side by side with these Negroes for three sunny weeks. We cleared away the stones and underbrush, fertilized the soil, dug ditches and plowed, turning under peas and clover. Around us, our sweating slaves popped up and down with their pitchforks and shovels to the cadence of some crude work song— one worker would sing out a phrase, and the rest of the men would repeat it, black men slaving in a row that meandered toward the wood bordering our land. Their voices were dark and foreboding, resonant like thunder on this sunny day.

Concentrate on the work at hand, I thought. And not Adelaide's hand.

One young slave boy sweated along with his elders. Piles of grass and rocks grew higher and higher to the left of our tillage as we and the slaves made progress in the harrowing of this dark brown soil. Thom leaned on his cane as he walked up and down the row of Negroes and bade them to work harder. Even as they toiled, my slaves were watching Chang and me in wonder. I pitied them for the hopelessness of their position. And fleetingly I thought that the most awful thing about slavery was this: Servitude was brought upon them only because they were different, as my brother and I were. They were different, though of course also dangerous. That was the point of the whole situation, I remembered. From the bloody insurrections at Santo Domingo, to the short-lived rebellion led by the Negro Gabriel in Virginia in 1800, to the conspiracy of slaves in Charleston in 1822, and especially to the bloody and stubborn Virginia insurrection led by Nat Turner in 1831, I was not unaware of the historical evidence. Slaves had to be kept under control. Plus, abolition was a Northern movement, and I had no love of the North, especially after it had given birth to the political party of antiforeign bigots called the Know-Nothings.

Chang and I worked days on end, morning and afternoon with no rest, and then one Wednesday Chang and I allowed ourselves a late start because our wives' cousin Emily had come to visit. When we came downstairs that morning, Sarah and Adelaide were already having breakfast with our guest, whom we had never met.

"Oh, hello, boys," said Emily. "We were just discussing what a lovely home you'all have, lovely if I may say so." She was a very wrinkled woman, but you could see the elements of Adelaide's looks in Emily's long jawline, thin blond hair, and in the light of her eye. "Won't you sit with us?" She took a gulp of her tea. "Oh, listen to me, telling you what to do in your own home."

Chang and I eased into our chair at the head of the table. Emily sat to the right of us, our wives to the left. Chang reached for Adelaide's hand, but she did not allow him to take it. "Did you wash yourself before you came down, Chang?" she said. "You smell as healthy as the barnyard." Then she turned to Cousin Emily. "My sister obviously got the cleaner of the two."

"I never knew Wilkes County could be so lovely," Emily said. "In my day we never had such lovely tea. Mind if I ask where you get this lovely tea?"

I was the only one who noticed the look in Chang's eye. It reminded me of the squirm of a fish after it's hooked and hauled into the morning.

"We buy our tea in town," said Sarah. "Just like everybody else."

"Really, it's lovely," said Emily. "Last time I came to see you'all in old Wilkes—it's better than an old mansion here, your lovely home. You'all know I'm simple folk, we have a small . . . I've heard so much about you two boys—oh, goodness, I've finished all my tea, do you mind, Addie, if I have a sip of yourn? Anyhow, I've heard so much about you boys. Never thought any Yates would have such a lovely home—"

"Feel free to stay as long as you want, Emily," I said. "After a carriage scare like yours, you must like to relax a bit."

She was finishing Adelaide's tea. "That's very kind of you, Eng. You're Eng, correct? I thought so. And you're Chang then? Oh, as plain as day, you are. What a silly question, if you're Eng, then you're—"

"You'all want to know how you tell them apart?" Adelaide said. "One makes you angry when he talks, the other's a little better on the nerves, but he tosses around so much Shakespeare it can put you to sleep. If you're angry and asleep, it's a sure bet they're probably both talking."

Had circumstances thrown Adelaide into a different life, into the drawing rooms of London, say—and lent her a bit of a refashioning—perhaps her natural wit would have garnered her some admiration, and maybe her long face—had she been given the benefit of doubt accorded heiresses—would have been considered a fetching irregularity. And now she traced her collarbone with the tip of her finger.

Sarah was grimacing. "I think you may have got it wrong, Adelaide, I think you may have got it the wrong way round about these husbands."

Emily waved her hands in the air, trying to wipe away any disparaging words about Chang and me. "Well, either twin, thank you for your— I appreciate your lovely hospitality—don't you want your tea, Sarah?"

"It doesn't agree with my stomach, in fact I think I may go up and—"

"In that case, can I have just a sip of yourn?" Emily looked at Chang and me mischievously as she drank from my wife's teacup. Then she said, "I don't mind telling you, I for one don't think anything of it that they married you twins. If you can make my cousins happy, I always say. And that's all we talked about this morning before you came down, Addie especially. 'Well, Eng says this, Eng says that'—I thought *you* were her husband, and not you, Chang."

Adelaide couldn't help wearing a mischievous half smile that seemed to say I'd be able to crack my desire for her. I had to check my breathing.

Later that afternoon, Chang barely helped at all when we bent in unison to pick up stones, letting me carry the bulk of their cragged weight. Thom came over to us and said, "Well, this will all be cleared soon, masters." He used a hand to shield his eyes from the sun. "We've got almost half the land cleared since breakfast." Even amid the sunshine and sweet-scented grass, he smelled of the very old, and of labor. "Why don't you rest, masters?" He was the only slave whose pants fit well enough to cover his ankles.

"The whole point, Thom," I huffed as my brother and I struggled with some underbrush, "is to work quickly and not to stop. That is what you should tell the others." Chang and I kept pulling at the underbrush, the soil scattering darkly against our boots. I had done most of the hard jerking. I looked at my twin askance, thinking, It is no wonder Adelaide is always snapping at him.

Just then the young Negro boy walked to one of the piles of rock holding a few pebbles.

"All right now, son!" Thom called to the child.

"Who is that?" I asked Thom.

"My sister's boy." The old slave let out a chuckle.

Chang and I stopped working for a moment, to catch our breath. "I did not know you had a nephew," I said.

"Well, Master Eng, I do," he said, and walked up among the other slaves.

Thom may have whispered something in passing to one of the Negroes working a few yards ahead of us—a vigorous adolescent slave who flung rocks to his side with ease—because the young man laughed aloud after Thom walked by. I had the irrational thought that maybe all the slaves, with their voodoo, somehow knew of my feelings for my brother's wife, of my stupid hope that the smile she had given me before had a sign in it, that the strokes of her hand on the *Ivory Eagle* and afterward had been intentional. I shook those thoughts from my head and continued to work, but I had trouble looking at Chang as I did so, and I suppose that was due to a kind of guilt.

Later, when the sun was soon to set, my brother and I went to work on building the fence for this new parcel of land. We chopped wood, something we were renowned for doing well. We had invented the "double-chop" method of woodcutting—a technique that is used today across North Carolina whenever two men want to fell a tree. I'd strike with my ax angled in one direction, and Chang would strike the other side of the trunk by slanting his at the opposite angle. This practice allowed us to cut straight through the tree, neither brother needing to change the angle of his ax. When cutting, I would imagine chopping through our band every time.

On this evening, our method was not effective as usual because my brother was hitting the tree halfheartedly. My work had created a wedge that was twice as wide as the one made by my brother.

After Chang gave a particularly weak chop, I looked at him. "What is it?"

"Before, she touch my hand," he said, as if we had been in the middle of a conversation. He took a perfunctory hew at the trunk.

"What?" I asked, swinging heartily.

"Before she touch my hand, at dinner, in mornings, wherever, she holding my hand like a wife." His face looked devoid of emotion. "Adelaide." He laughed, almost. "Now she pulling it away," he said, and took his biggest cut of the evening.

This absurd thought shot through my brain: How dare *he* think of her.

"Maybe she have eye on somebody else. On American man!" he cried. My heart skipped a beat even at the mention of this. I imagined her nuzzling some tall redheaded American beau with thick sideburns.

"No!" I said. "No, no, that is not possible." We quit our chopping.

The veins in his neck showing now, he said, "What else explain it, brother? I know she will never love me again. Before we laugh together; now—" He took another cut at the tree. Wood chips jumped through the air. This was the anger and heartache that would before long lead him to the bottle.

"But you have—relations at night," I said. I truly was trying to be a good brother.

"She want children," he spat. "It mean nothing."

My mood brightened. "You do not think that she will ever love you?"

"No," he said. "You see the way things is, why you have to ask me?"

"And so—you really think she would love another?"

"Yes! What I saying to you all this time?"

My great joy, like an ax at chop, cut through all my thoughts. She would *never* love him; even he admitted it. I made him repeat his fears several times. I thought of nothing but Addie for the rest of the evening.

★　★　★

That night, when I was alone with Sarah and Chang, I could not stop talking about Adelaide, though I knew I shouldn't be doing so. I looked for any excuse to mention her—("Do you remember," I found myself saying to my wife and brother, apropos of nothing, "what Adelaide said today about circuses, about how the real oddities are the people who pay to see other people?")

Though I lived so close to my brother, and secretly wanted his wife, Chang and I saw the world completely differently. It was obvious that my twin, for his part, had visions of regaining the Adelaide who had existed at the time of their wedding, the Adelaide who had yet to cool toward him; meanwhile, I had been pining for an Adelaide who after years still did not exist—the Adelaide who would one day love me. And the result of all this? Chang's vision suffered from seeing too much of Adelaide as she really was, and mine from seeing not enough.

The next evening, at slumbertime, Adelaide, Chang, and I were in bed in our main room, and much as they had been fighting earlier, my brother and his wife were having relations, proving nothing more—I was consoling myself—than her desperate want of children. Again, candlelight flashed on their bodies.

I deliberately placed my forearm close to the thick, fleshy part of Adelaide's leg, but her hand did not brush mine. My band flexed and stretched as far as it would go, my face near enough to my brother's closed eyes that I could feel his breath hot in my ear, I left my hand close to Addie for some time, in the perfect spot for her to touch it if she'd wanted. But my hand remained untouched—nothing against my discouraged knuckles but cool naked air.

I decided to bring that hand to graze hers, which was now flat on the mattress and propping her up. I did so, and she moved away from me as quickly as she could without alerting my shut-eyed brother. Adelaide did not even look at me.

So I had been wrong; it had never been more than a mistake!

She'd never intended to touch me, and I'd misread her smile. I, positioned under the window, tried now to concentrate on the song of the wind as I was rocked back and forth. I did not want to watch. My heart had grown a canker.

I brushed my hand against hers again. She did not move it as quickly as she had the first time; I was unsatisfied with this Pyrrhic victory. All the pleasure I had earlier gleaned from such accidental caresses was gone.

Chang moaned, red blotches on his cheek and neck.

I had to take hold of her hand, actually squeeze her flesh. It would have to be executed in the same way as a military operation.

—But what if she pulled away? To grasp her hand, to squeeze it—this would not be a brushing of skin, it would be an undeniably intentional act. If she rebuffed it, if she screamed, all would be lost. I began literally to shake with fear. As well as a wretched person, I was a coward. I couldn't do it.

At the count of ten, I'll place my hand atop hers, I told myself. And squeeze it when Chang isn't looking.

If you do not, I swore to myself, I will kill myself in the morning.

Ten blinks of an eye rushed by and vanished. I was in agony.

After a minute and twenty-two seconds, each counted to the rhythm of a pounding heart, and while my brother contorted his face in oblivious bliss, I resigned myself to the fact that there was no way I could reach out and take Adelaide's hand.

But reach and take it is just what I did.

She made a shocked little noise, and pulled it from mine, almost losing her balance in the process. Chang did not notice, his mouth still open. Adelaide returned her hand to its position on the mattress.

She would not look at me; she was gritting her teeth.

Scarcely in control of my actions, in a new-sprung surge of courage I took her hand again. I noticed it was trembling, and I squeezed it over and over, like a man in an epileptic fit. Adelaide made a feeble, halfhearted attempt to wrest it from my grasp, but finally she did not struggle. She looked me squarely in the eye like a statue, her mouth open slightly, the candlelight dancing on her face. She squeezed my hand in her own.

I was in a state of ecstasy. I listened blissfully to the wind, trying to separate its music from that of her breath. I held her hand.

After a few short seconds, Chang was about to open his eyes. Adelaide sensed this, I think, because she began to pull away. I gave her hand a last, lingering clasp. She wrenched it from my grip.

The happiness that had flooded my heart now drained away.

What I had gained tonight may be lost forever. I had been lucky to summon up the audacity this time, but would I again, and when would I next get the chance? I feared the ground I had just gained was forfeited.

Poor Chang opened his eyes and petted his wife's head.

Adelaide held her fingers far from mine, and, the candle put out, she rolled over to sleep beside her husband, who now was positioned between us and facing me. In the cool blue dark, Adelaide and I eyed each other over the rising and falling side of my brother's body. She drew her lips into her mouth. She blinked a few times as she stared at me, and then she looked up at the ceiling, gathering a bit of blanket in her hands in an absentminded way. She would not look at me any longer.

For some time after, I did not get much sleep. Often, after either Sarah or Adelaide had blown out the candle, depending on with whom we lay, which itself was determined by the days of the week, I would watch the snuffed candlewick until it had quit smoldering, and listen to the seething wax even after it ended its tinny plopping on the tray. I would look at the bodies in bed with me. When I did dream, it was of remorse and guilt and hankering for another touch. Days were no easier.

I knew two Adelaides: my brother's bride whom I saw in the sunlight every morning, a woman I stole a conscience-smitten glance at whenever I found myself in a position to address her in a tone neither friendly nor unfriendly; and the other Adelaide, Addie, whose hand I would on very rare occasions have the luck to hold at night, under covers, when I was ashamed even to be looking at all.

Ours was a silent compact, to clasp hands infrequently and nothing more, least of all to acknowledge it. And then, the next morning, we'd sit at table for breakfast. Chang would say, "Everybody sleep?" and I'd feel like the villain I was.

Adelaide made a point of smiling and keeping her eyes on Chang. "Yes," she'd answer. "You ask about sleep so much, you'd think you was Rip Van Winkle." And I might catch Adelaide stealing a momentary glance at me and my heart would turn over in regret and bliss.

If I was never able to know her physically, then I would cata-logue all that I could come to know about her: that she was head-strong. Passionate. Cutting. Elegantly long-chinned. That she had been a precocious child given to spontaneous handstands, and that every little boy in Wilkesboro had taken a shine to her in the years before she had grown to her full height. That she enjoyed turkey more than chicken, that her laughter was always loudest on its third trill ("ha, ha, *ha*"). As for the unknowable turns of her pecu-liar mind, at least I could come to fathom those attributes that the rest of the world had somehow missed—or, if they had caught them, sneered at—and I could treasure them. Yes, she was coarse sometimes, but, though I wanted to help her lose that coarseness, I became attached even to that quality in her. I was able to have an affectionate silent laugh about it, just as I was able to do with my own foibles. That is what I learned about devotion: The bonds of love are best when you embrace the same outlook in judging your lover's flaws as you do your own. That is the key to forming the sort of attachment through which one chooses to unite oneself to another human being.

And that is how my love created an additional person, different from the woman people in Wilkesboro knew as "Adelaide." I sup-pose I knew it foolish to spend my life pining for *my* "Addie," whom I had invented, made up using as many parts of my person-ality as her own. Still, I could not help expanding her feverishly to proportions that would seem ridiculous to those who knew the Adelaide familiar to the outside world.

As for Sarah, I thought I could still be true to my wedding vow if I tried to treat her as a friend, a platonic associate. I was a hypocrite.

Soon this would all become complicated. I was about to be-come a father.

CHAPTER THIRTEEN

Celebrity

1826–1829
New York–London–Europe

By 1826 my brother and I were almost sixteen years old and still living at Mrs. Sachs's in New York, our act had become a huge success, and we had seen not one cent from Hunter. The idea came to us that it might be possible to persuade him to give us a better accounting of our prospects and maybe even some money of our own. "And our pet duck back, too," Chang reminded me. Also, he and I started to talk about another try at escape, a more finely planned attempt than our last effort. I wanted so badly to see Mother again, it was almost all I thought about.

The shows were becoming routine. There is a performance from that time, however, that stands tall in my memory: the day we performed in Tompkins Square Park.

The show was uneventful at first. Our cage was outside, on a hillock, and the sky was overcast. Hunter talked into his cupped hands, as usual, and we ignored him, as usual—from the perspective of our handstand, we watched the people walk by. Then something unexpected occurred. "Are they Christian?" someone boomed in a deep voice.

Hunter stopped speaking for a moment and looked into the crowd. He said: "Yes, in fact they are. They can quote scripture literally, all you have to do is ask it."

We flipped onto our feet and saw in the audience a man wearing a red silk cravat, a rogue with a drooping double-chin and a hairline receding to the top of his head: Barnum.

He stormed right up to our cage. His face was lit by torchlight. Hunter ran over with skipping, goosey steps to stand between Barnum and us.

"What do you think you are doing, Mr. Barnum?"

"Is he paying you, twins?" Barnum stood on tiptoes to talk to us over Hunter's shoulder. "Is he?" He bobbed his head around the impediment of Mr. Hunter. Chang and I walked toward the bars.

"All right, now, Mr. Barnum, that's literally enough." Hunter leaned against the larger promoter and tried to push him away from the cage.

Barnum shouldered Hunter aside; he leaned his face into the bars. His jowls curled around the metal poles. The skin on his nose showed wide black pores. "I can guarantee you a better life." Barnum's voice was almost a hiss, and with that he turned on his heels and left.

Hunter stepped into the space where the other man had been. He was red-faced, and swallowed vigorously for a while. Then, with a nervous laugh—"Can you believe that man? What a liar!"

At home that night, Hunter was locking us into our room when I told him we needed to talk. "Your allowance?" he said. "You will get that. But it is meaningless, anyway, for the next few months. Because you two and I are taking another trip."

And that is how we found out we were going to London.

Hunter, Chang, and I took a fast steamship to England, but if we had been expecting more perfect quarters than we had been used to, we were disappointed. We traveled steerage, which meant small, unlit accommodations, meals with the crew—a bland diet of potatoes and salt beef—that contrasted sharply with the sumptuous banquets I imagined Hunter was enjoying in the dining cabin. The crossing to England took twenty-six days. Chang and I decided that if any chance presented itself, we would make a getaway and find passage home somehow.

Our first night in London was a silent coach ride along Cheapside, through the runnel of the capital's gray attractions: Covent Garden theater, the Baker Street bazaar, Grosvenor Square, each hooded in fog and drizzle, and dingy even in gaslight when situated in mind beside the more newly built, fire-specked landscape of Manhattan. We traveled along the cobblestones of Whitechapel Road, among the drovers who walked herds of cattle to Smithfield Market. Soot covered so many faces. Pointing at the stars stood the arch of London Bridge, sickly lighted up in man-made light, and by the time the coachman gave his command of "Whoa, horse," St. Paul's was steady up over the mist, unlit, a great shadow in stone.

We stayed at the Beautiful Meadows, a hotel on Drury Lane, near the Theatre Royal where we would be performing. Hunter had alerted his London connections of our arrival in advance, and the Beautiful Meadows was crowded with gawkers: pallid English newspapermen, cringing and quick as a group.

London was another success, professionally. We charged an admission price of one crown. We had no idea, of course, that the one-crown price was—in part—to be responsible for the even greater notoriety we were soon to receive.

London, being so close to the Continent, was more cosmopolitan than anyplace we'd seen in America; along with manifold Englishmen (from the ash-cheeked chimney sweep to the fair-skinned nobleman), a smorgasbord of races came out to see my brother and me; elderly French ladies, voicing a "tsk, tsk" and squinting through their lorgnettes, leaned toward us like flowers curving under a light wind. Russian princesses blushed in front of our bars and mustachioed Spaniards scratched their chins. Our crowds were enormous, countless phantoms huddling by, knees knocking, and like a woman shopping for a dress, I'd imagine trying on one body or another: of that little blond boy, twisting out of his mother's grasp; or this buxom English woman with her frilly parasol; or that old clergyman, hunched over his cane.

As time passed, theater and throng became no more than a second greatcoat that I would put on with little joy or trepidation, every few nights of my life. I was growing impatient because Chang and I hadn't yet seen a chance to execute our escape plan.

What did I do when not performing? Back in the hotel, our two single beds pushed together, Chang and I fashioned a checkers game out of the effects located around the room (paper and pen, inkwell, a lamp), we practiced walking on our hands for a while, and ultimately, with Chang napping beside me on the bed, I read the Bible. I was able to recite chapter and verse—usually to an audience of one, and that one quite uninterested.

The Book offered flashes of stinging, personal poignancy: "I have been a stranger in a strange land" (Exodus 2:22); "Am I my brother's keeper?" (Genesis 4:9); the story of the child who would have been divided in two by Solomon.

Hunter would stare at my body then, and I could tell he saw in me nothing more alive than money in his pocket. "I know I gave that book to you, boy, but you're literally reading the Scriptures line by line, aren't you?" There was shame all over his voice. "I mean to say"—he sucked on his teeth, his rendition of a warm-hearted smile; he was embarrassed for me—"I wonder, do you think for a moment that you are going to heaven?"

I was left to question: If God feels the loss of every creature that dies, mourns without exception each pigeon that falls, would He not feel doubly sad at our passing?

The quality of kindness, I reminded myself, is better in Siam.

One dark and foggy morning in London, Chang and I had to give a special performance at the residence of the Duke of An-goulême. "These are more appropriate ensembles in which to meet dignitaries," Hunter said, handing us two short loose green silk jackets and trousers in the fashion of Siam, or, rather, made by an Englishman to look that way. "We are retiring the sailor's suits."

The Duke was the son of King Charles X of France, the monarch who had been dethroned in a coup. As a result, the Duke, who would one day have ascended to the throne had all things gone according to plan, was now living here, an exiled would-be regent suffering from gout, dropsy, and chest inflammation.

The Duke's residence was a small carriage house by Regent's

Park, and when we arrived a French valet whose little face wore a terrifyingly void expression announced us as "The Chinese Twins." He ushered Hunter, Chang, and me into a simple drawing room where the Duke had surrounded himself with his ragtag retinue of shaky footmen, untidy devotees, and two sad-eyed little girls in pink dresses. Also, there was a woman in the room, ignoring us and loitering on an overstuffed chair in the corner—a red-haired belle, the long, lissome shape of her an acute reminder of what I was and the suffering it caused me. Three or four men stood around this beauty as she leaned back, as if she were beckoning them to dive toward her.

The drawing room was carpetless and worn, its one displaced ostentation a crystal chandelier that lingered overhead like some small-scale galaxy, packed dense and glimmering all the brighter for it. A dreariness clung about the place, a deadness to the air like the space between conjoined twins' faces after one of them yawns.

The Duke idled on an old divan beside a fireplace that was, I was cold and unhappy to say, unlit. "Your Highness," Hunter bowed. "May I introduce the Twins?" And then our promoter skipped to the side of the room, leaving us before this almost monarch.

The scarlet sash that ran slantways down the Duke's bosom underscored the outrageous bloat of his chest and great loss evident even in his bearing. I wondered whether it is worse to lose a kingdom than to be born a serf.

Behind Angoulême stood his two little sad-eyed daughters and a man whom I later found out was Dr. Peter Mark Roget, secretary of the Royal Society, originator of the world's best-known thesaurus, and, at this point in his illustrious life, a dwarfish and balding medical doctor.

"*Venez vite,*" said the Duke.

A handstand led to flips, and flips to a flawless four-point landing, and Angoulême brought his hands together at a leisurely pace, a sort of half clap, and his people followed suit. All except for the red-haired woman in the corner and her admirers, who disregarded us as they talked between themselves.

"I would like to ask the twin questions, my lord." Roget bowed to the Duke. "Would that amuse Your Highness?"

The Duke shrugged his shoulders.

"Is the performing difficult?" Roget asked us, talking loud enough to be heard by the group across the room. "The shows, the crowds . . . ?"

"Any idiots able to flip," Chang said. "Every day living is what wears you out, what?"

The little girls beside the Duke clapped—spontaneously and lightly, in a way that displayed both their appreciation of a humorous mutant and their diamond rings. Roget, meanwhile, walked away, as if trying to slip from our notice.

"And you?" asked one of the girls next to Angoulême. She was addressing me. "Do you find the performing difficult?" I was flustered by these girls, this scene, and so heard the sound of her voice but did not register her words as anything but a meaningless fusillade of noises on some limited musical scale.

All of a sudden—over Chang's far shoulder—I saw Dr. Roget stealing toward us on tiptoes. When he was directly behind my brother, he reached out his little arm and began to tickle Chang's neck.

"Please, stop that!" I shouted. The girls gasped at my outburst. Roget, grinning, tilted his head at me. The woman across the room still did not seem to realize we were there.

(Roget later published an essay that may explain his actions: "The Twins' curious intimacy gives rise to a sanguineous communication between the two. I am satisfied that this creature be guided by a single will; it is said that, upon tickling one of them, the second will tell you to desist, as if this untouched one felt the contact itself." Well, that is absolutely ridiculous; I saw the man. Most certainly I did.)

"And, what, double-boy," Roget was scratching his chin casually, as if he hadn't just assaulted us, "do you think of civilization? Of our fair city London?"

I will escape from your pale world before long, I said to myself.

Chang, meanwhile, was moving us toward the fireplace; he bent us down to procure a deadened piece of coal from the hearth. He held up the gray lump of coal before his eye. "This the sun of London," he said. "This color."

"Fabulous," laughed Roget, and he raised his eyebrows at the Duke, who was nonplussed.

Roget pointed at Chang and said, "This half is fabulous."

And now Roget turned to me, to see if I too was fabulous. "So, lad"—he treated me to an encouraging smile—"you came to the civilized world subsequent to being introduced to an American trader?"

I tried to equal my brother's quip with one of my own (I was young then, and didn't know my limits). "You think he's a traitor, too, then?" I said.

Perhaps my English inflection was not yet as polished as it is today—maybe the distinction between the sound of individual letters was a nicety my intonation could not at that early date support.

Roget looked at me blankly. The Duke stared expectantly, too, as if I was about to continue speaking.

"Why—yes," I answered, softly and yearning more than ever for the social comfort of a Mekong houseboat. "We first crossed the sea with the trader Captain Abel Coffin."

Roget sighed. Chang's expression was similar to the face I must have worn whenever he had one of his onstage extemporizations— openmouthed stupefaction. I felt I was looking at myself, although it was he I beheld. Let my brother be bewildered by my try at repartee, I thought.

"*This* boy seems more imbecilic than the other." Roget nodded at me.

Floundering for the right thing to say, I picked the first anecdote that came handy. "Everything about our birth is known," I began into the story of our origin.

When I finished, I looked up and saw everyone standing around uncomfortably; my narrative had led everyone down the avenue of awkward silence.

"*Il n'est miracle que de vieux saints,*" yawned the Duke.

Hunter took that to be the end of the show, and ran up to us from the other side of the room. "Thank you, Your Highness," he said. "*Pas mal,*" said the Duke. The erstwhile royal opened his hand, palm upward in anticipation, and one of his fawners gave him a little blue pouch.

The Duke addressed Chang and me: *"Pour—"* He cut himself off, and for a moment lost his royal composure. He seemed to be working out a riddle in his head. *"Pour tu,"* he said to us finally, and handed over the pouch.

We opened it and saw a few tiny gold baubles, sparkling against the blue cloth. Hunter looked at the gift admiringly. Chang looked up from the pouch and its gold, and—turning to Roget— he said: "Why the Duke gives us gold, is because he has no crown."

On the overstuffed chair across the room, the red-headed woman's head reared up, like a deer's. Three or four people gasped. Hunter turned quickly to my brother, then back at the Duke. Blushing, our promoter said: "The twin is referring simply to the price of admission."

The air seemed inert, except for the meandering specks of grit that floated brightly along the shafts of sunlight to come to a dusty landing on the floor. The Duke's face, also, remained almost motionless. But soon he began into the slowest of winces. It started in his eye, a dark gloom. Then it slid down his face, capering around his mouth like a bee about a hive, and soon it crept under his flesh and began to disturb the chin. It darkened his whole expression, like the withering of a flower brought into shadow.

The all-but-king merely stood without saying a word, likely wishing he still had the rule of the guillotine. What he still had the power to do was motion for the valet.

The valet turned us around and pushed us to the door. "Follow me, monsieur," he said, exposing a row of childlike yellow teeth. Hunter followed close behind.

Halfway through the doorjamb now, with the valet's hands prodding my brother and me outward, I looked over our shoulders and saw Roget drift toward the woman on the overstuffed chair. The sitting beauty was pursing her lips and scanning the room in front of her in the attitude of a general on his horse. The beauty did not look up to notice our departure, and I had no reason to think we'd ever hear about her again.

Chang and I became the toast of London.

Once Roget published his essay about us, Chang's witticism was at once immortalized in the London broadsheets, and repeated around town as a catch phrase by everyone from shoeshine boys to parliamentarians. At our performances, the increasing number of people gliding by our pen would repeat it in differing variations—e.g., "he ain't got no crown," or, "The regent seems to be one crown short"—and ever more reporters began herding to our cage, as well, busting for another bon mot. I was described as "the one more like a mute."

The strangest of reports appeared in the *Times* of London. Purported to be an "inside account" of our reception in the Duke's drawing room, the story heaped fiction upon fiction. It was entitled "A Harmony in Three Parts?"

It told of a woman that the paper referred to—"for the sake of propriety"—by the "nom-de-amor" of Susannah of the Meadows, a "ravishing red-headed jewel of London society"; she had, according to this rubbish, "by some unaccountable caprice, fallen violently in love with the twins."

After ostensibly speaking with us for "a period that could not have lasted more than minutes," she "loved [us] as one, not as separate men." She was said to be *inconsolable* following our departure from the drawing room, because she knew the "impossibility" of her love.

She hated the thought of our being separated, it was said. "How could I be content with either, were the other dear charmer away?" this beautiful "Susannah of the Meadows" supposedly repeated again and again, over tears, while friends tried to soothe her. The article concluded:

> Situations like this will, considering the sharpness of wit of at least one of this deuce of hearts, occur throughout the expected short life of the double boy. It is not an unreasonable conjecture, therefore, that some female attachment, at a future period, may occur to destroy their harmony, and induce a mutual and paramount wish to be separated; no matter the risks.

This exposé, though a fakery, produced feelings both mysterious and frightening in my brother and me. It touched upon a number of undiscussed resignations. The chance that an actual "Susannah" would ever exist was remote enough, but then, faced with the probability that any such Susannah we'd encounter would never be able to consummate her passion, we had to resign ourselves to a loveless existence. Still, so long as we were trapped in our togetherness, I would never stop hoping that some doctor would one day slice us into sections as keenly as the reporter of that article had divided his last sentence by a semicolon; it was not *I* who feared the loneliness, and the risk. As a man blind from birth cringes from the light upon the sudden gift of his vision, my brother dreaded separation because it represented the unknown. Not I.

After our visit to the Duke's drawing room, and others like it in Britain and Europe, we toured the Continent with Hunter, the months advancing as the shows kept coming, every night another show. Back in England, we met little Victoria, the soon-to-be queen who described us as a "delight" and a "true medical treasure." She was twelve.

But there comes a time when reputation reaches an unrealistic level, and the anticipated thing is not so much welcomed as taken for granted. In St. Petersburg, an imposing city with an elegant stillness unknown in America, Tsar Nicholas clapped politely at us, and he gave us a present in two parts. But he was not enthusiastic about it. And that was when Hunter told us it was time to leave Europe.

Though our manager still treated us like children, we were no longer childlike: now eighteen, we had been away from Siam for four years. With the constant travel, we had had no way to escape, and we decided that when we arrived in New York, we would immediately take our leave. On our next landing in America, we resolved, we would attack Hunter, who had only now just begun to give us any money (we were unsure he had been sending checks to Mother, and he never even returned our pet duck In), and we would demand what was ours. And then, home.

The trip home was again spent in steerage. On a dark night

near the end of the journey, when we were sleeping in our cramped quarters, a young sailor woke Chang and me by shaking us.

"Who?" I said. "Are you?" Chang said.

The young man looked over his shoulder, then thrust out his closed hand in front of us. We looked at his hand, which hovered there in the dark, and for a second the sailor looked at his hand, too, then he rolled his eyes. "Take it!" he hissed.

"Take what?"

He made a clicking noise with his tongue, and then he leaned in close to us—close enough for me to smell his toilet soap. And he grabbed my hand; he placed a note in my palm. Once I took his gift, he looked over his shoulder, then walked away.

We had to wait until the light of morning to read it. "Meet me," it read. And below that were instructions on where and how to rendezvous secretly with Barnum once we arrived in New York.

Two nights later we were back in Manhattan. A crowd of reporters met our boat. Americans did not have the type of confidence that fosters the independent decision-making process, and so it was no doubt the acceptance we had found in England and Europe that prompted our newfound stateside esteem. We were now the most celebrated attraction in the world, more famed than anything in Barnum's show.

Still, we were brought again to Mrs. Sachs's house, as Barnum had known we would be. It was late, a humid summer's twilight. We were on the second floor, in a dark cramped roomlet with one window overlooking the street. We had not slept well; Chang's eyes were red-rimmed, and I would have guessed mine were, too. We had only to decide now whether to listen to the famed promoter's offer, or to try to return home to Siam on our own, which was what I proposed.

"What else we should do?" Chang asked in a whisper. We were standing by the window in our little cubby, looking out at the street below, and we did not want anyone in the house to hear us. A carriage clip-clopped by. "We swim to Siam?" he asked.

I said, "We can demand what we are owed by Hunter—"

"Barnum saying, 'I give you a chance,' " Chang said. "Barnum saying, 'I make you money.' "

"Don't you want to go home?" I asked.

Chang smiled at me like I was a child and he was my father. "Yes, yes, yes," he said. "I wanting that more than anything."

"All right," I whispered. "Me, too."

"We should listen to what Barnum have to say," Chang said. "Then we go home. Soon."

"Maybe Mother has gotten enough from Hunter to pay for our return," I whispered.

"You want to go back to Siam like we just did? Making trip in *steerage*? If we go back like that, we are failure. We go back rich men, we go back winning." With this my brother unfastened and pushed open the small taut window. He leaned us forward, out into the humid night air. We remained like this—in no mean discomfort, leaning out the window so the window stop dug into our chests—and heard far-off conversation, and saw a few twinkling fires in the distance, downtown. A horse and buggy came to a stop at the corner of Forty-second Street, near the Sachses' house.

"We go back to Siam in two, three week," he said.

I have been the more difficult one, I told myself. I know that.

Your brother has been better at finding the best in this, I told myself.

Chang has been the more fit Mekong Fisherman, I told myself. Diminishing the influence of fate. And you should thank him.

"All right, Chang," I said. I held onto his elbow as if he could protect me from falling. "We will listen to Barnum's offer. But if we don't like what he has to say, we will go home immediately." I would not let him look away. "And we will go home within a few weeks, regardless."

"Yes," he said. "Yes."

We hoisted our double-bulk out through the opened window.

Our four hands grabbing onto the sill, we twisted our buttocks and sat—half in, half out, and face-to-face. Then, together, we raised our hands to the window frame over our heads, and we crouched to our feet. Once we had crept out onto the ledge, we positioned ourself side by side, clutching the wall and easing like a double-insect toward the apple tree that was beside the far edge of the house.

We leapt together and grabbed the top branch. We shimmied our way down, and into Barnum's carriage, which was waiting.

CHAPTER FOURTEEN

Adult Contentments

December 6, 1847–April 9, 1860
Wilkesboro

The winter of 1847. A year had passed since I'd held hands with Addie, and I had not had the opportunity ever to repeat that covert activity. She took no note of me now, ignoring my company when we were together as if I were a slave or a tree. Except when she did smile slightly at me from across a table, which was rare and almost more disturbing.

But I became a father.

Poor little Katherine was my first, and the first child born to either couple. Though my marriage was now stagnant, Sarah had continued to want children, as did her sister. And so, as Adelaide and my brother did, my wife and I had engaged in bloodless attempts at baby-making. And so it was that my sad, small Katherine was born.

Wilkesboro's Dr. Cottard rushed over as soon as my wife's water had broken. He did not want to miss a chance to make history, the possibility that he could deliver a double-baby.

It was a cold night. My brother and I stood beside the birthing bed, which was in the secondary bedroom of our house, and Adelaide—who was herself now a few months pregnant—was holding her sister's hand. Sarah lay under the sheet, her thirty-five-year-old belly a globe beneath the white linen. She held her legs raised and bent at the knees, her position making a tent of the bedding that covered her thighs and higher. The cool air was frosting gooseflesh on her uncovered shins. She was crying, from stomach pain or anxiety I knew not.

Even as he was delivering my child, Dr. Cottard stared at us whenever he thought I wouldn't notice, a flicker in his eyes that did not make one think of Hippocrates and the medical arts. In the room's large swinging mirror, I looked a mess, leaning nervously into my brother. A long shaft of moonlight ran from the window to the bed, like an inquisitive apparition.

"Why don't you twins leave us alone in here, now." Dr. Cottard patted Chang on the shoulder. "I know you must be nervous, son, this being your firstborn child," he said to my brother, mistaking Chang for the father. "But men should not be in here, even men such as yourself."

There is the cliché of the nervous expectant father, of the pacing ninny nervously awaiting the birth of his son. But there was nothing clichéd about my fears as Chang and I left the birthing room to walk to and fro in the main bedroom. For the first time I understood the revulsion that others felt toward my brother and me, and it was not a pleasant discovery. As we walked, Chang's feet were getting in my way—when was the last time that had happened? If the baby ended up having no abnormality save a five-inch tangle of cartilage, flesh, and viscera like the one I shared with my brother, that little idiosyncrasy would punish it to a life of the accursed peering eye that never blinks, and to an existence devoid of even a whit of privacy.

"Please do not worry, Eng," Chang whispered. I felt his warmth on my ear. "We work hard our whole life, and long besides. And now your Sarah is having a baby," he said. "Smile, brother. Smile."

"Thank you, Chang," I said.

I walked us back to the birthing room, and we pushed through the door. Cottard noted our entrance with a glance over his shoulder, and then went silently back to his job of bringing my child into this world.

Chang and I came to stand beside Adelaide, who was still holding my wife's hand and whispering encouragement. Five months of pregnancy had given a wonderful blush to my sister-in-law's cheeks, and a fetching heft to her frame. She did not return my smile or even notice me, at least she acted as if she did not. Sarah held her hand. I felt I could not live a minute without looking at Adelaide's blond hair and light eyes, as gorgeous as ever. To conceal my stare only made the state of my emotions more chaotic. Had she cared for me, would she ever?

"Gently, my girl." The doctor sounded nervous now, his hands working under Sarah's sheets. *"Gently."*

"Can you see it?" My wife was panicky and close to tears. "What is it?"

My daughter Katherine was a slight child, and one girl, thank heaven. Nevertheless, she never would approach beauty, nor even fitness: a bony slender neck and soot-colored hair forever in knots, skin like old parchment, and a poor, faint soul—this was my daughter Katherine, slow to grow and needful always of a compassionate word.

I was unlike her, I did not cower when in the presence of people, but I would always recognize my own sorrow in Katherine, in her darting eyes and her awkwardness.

Holding this sad, skinny child, happily bouncing her negligible weight on the band I shared with Chang, I knew my daughter would never grow to be admired, but at least I had fathered a girl who was unconjoined, who looked reasonably American. She would never be hampered from speaking with the one she loved for the nearness of some twin, would not face the accursed peering eye, and she had in me a parent who wouldn't allow a foreigner to take her to a strange land for display. I counted these as blessings. To my everlasting amazement she had whitish skin and round eyes.

In time Katherine, my favorite, was followed by other children: Julia Ann and Roslyn Etta, and Georgianna, each, like poor Katherine, now passed away, God bless all of them; and my surviving posterity James and Stephen, Patrick and Robert, and William, Frederick, and lovely Rosella.

Chang and Addie, too, made a family: Christopher, Nancy, Susan, Victoria (named after the Queen), Louise Emeline (deaf and voiceless), Albert, Jesse (also a deaf mute), Margaret Lizzie, Hattie, and Josephine Virginia, who had the exquisite blond hair of her mother, and who was the only one to die in Chang's lifetime. I loved each of them; in their veins flowed Addie's blood.

But I decided to try forgetting Adelaide's touch. Concentrating my willpower on being a good father gave me new eyes to see the rest of my family, and I dedicated myself to being a better husband and brother.

The birth of our children intersected with an odd time for America. A decade of crisis began with the Compromise of 1850, which was a threadbare patchwork of capitulations that began to fall apart as soon as it was stitched together. The most frayed corner was the concession of popular sovereignty, which made a battleground of each new state. Heedless Northerners, unable to hide from slavery any longer, had to choose sides. Much as enhancements to the telegraph system ran alongside new-built roads and canals and rail lines to shorten the distance between states, these troubles proved that when sections of a nation are perforce tied closely together, one side cannot feign indifference to the other for long.

I was learning of the sure delights to fatherhood, of the specially adult contentments that I would not have known about before Katherine. But—and this may have been the way my father first saw Chang and me—I had trouble regarding this single child as from my own flesh. I knew it was real now, however—my life in Wilkesboro, my connection to my wife, to America, the toils and holds of everyday existence.

When Katherine was still our only baby and the familial revival within my heart was at its highest point, I used to sneak with Chang to look at my child sleeping in her little berth. He and I always did this at night, and always alone. Through the lattice of branches outside the window the moon dribbled glitter on my child, silver pieces winking across her frail little body. "Can you believe that we have done this?" I asked Chang. And he would rub my back and say no, he could not. The small girl seemed a tonic to relieve my grief and longing.

A few years after Katherine's birth, when we were still awaiting our second child, I got to do that which I had been trying not to think about—I touched Adelaide again, once.

It was early one dark morning and quiet except for the chatter of night bugs. Chang was asleep and I had just woken up when I became aware that Adelaide was crying. I do not know how I knew it, she was not making noise enough to rouse me. But I felt it to be true, and when I opened my eyes and looked over my twin's face to see Adelaide in a darkness as pervious as a ratty black veil, my sister-in-law was facing away from us, her leaky eyes pointed toward the ceiling.

My hand was resting on my brother's side, and, careful not to wake him, I stretched my fingers far enough to graze Adelaide's hip. She turned with a start to look over her shoulder, and she gaped at me. We stared, blinking, like two bright-eyed deer studying each other in the heart of a dark wood. She began to smile. Whatever it is you are crying about, I wanted so badly to tell her, I can help. I swear she moved in my direction, and then Chang pitched toward me in his sleep, my hand came off her, and that was that.

Soon Sarah and I had our second child and named her Julia; I watched my brother become a father to babies Josephine and Chris, and our house grew full with these four children.

For a time Chang and I taught Josephine and Chris and my Katherine Gung-Fu on Saturday mornings. Katherine was now about five, Josephine four, and plump Chris a blotchy, almost neckless three. In the grass behind our home, under a river of fine sunlit mist, the children fidgeted like timid echoes of themselves, a row of three youngsters challenging their legs with the low postures of the "horse-riding" stance, which had them all squatting atop imaginary midget horses.

"White Crane spreads wings," I commanded in a tone that pleased me, a tone that reminded me of both my father and who I was when I had affection for myself. My brother and I were in the Seven Star stance, shifting our weight to our back legs and holding all four of our hands in front of our faces.

The children brought their right palms up, facing outward, while swinging their left hands toward the ground. Katherine lost her balance like a fledgling chicken that hadn't yet found its equilibrium. She looked at me with those sad eyes and I had to check my impulse to run and caress her. "Now, now, Katherine," I said, remaining in my pose chest-to-chest with my twin.

"Grab the bird tail," said Chang, sounding pleasantly like Father, too. The children stepped to their left and lowered their right hands. They all moved in that way, that is, except little Christopher, who punched to the right and into his sister. "Ow," she said.

From behind us, I heard a feminine voice: "You're going to have them kill each other with that slanty-eyed mumbo jumbo." It was Sarah, my wife, watching us from the porch and smiling at me, which had become a rarity.

"No," I said. It was sunny and I was occupied with happy memories and domestic pleasures, and through that side door, tenderness for my wife sneaked into my heart. "This will teach them *not* to fight, my dear."

"Oh, Eng," she said. I'd forgotten how nicely her face could brighten, and also how good it felt to hold a smile.

Little Katherine got out of her stance when I wasn't looking. "Can we stop now, Mother?"

"You're going to have them kill each other," my wife said with what sounded close to tenderness before she turned back toward the house, "with that slanty-eyed mumbo jumbo." When her gray dress twirled up, it exposed a sliver of the whiskered pale skin of her ankles. Before she reached the door, the children ran inside with her.

Chang and I had now entered our forties, as had our wives. Sarah and Adelaide had grown more plump with the years and pregnancies. What had been a fresh taboo—hand-holding with Adelaide—was now settling into a ritual, never clarified but repeated every few months, whenever we could, until the dawn of the Civil War.

Years passed, and I did not become fettered to the South and her cause until the very day I realized secession was inevitable. It was a man, a stranger I met only briefly, who was to show me this fact.

One afternoon in April 1856, after we had sold two slaves to a local widow by the name of Catalin McAdoo, a still young and wealthy dowager known for her beautiful blond curly hair, Chang and I had to file papers at the Law Office Building in Wilkesboro, and afterward we saw a strong-looking young man standing outside, broad-shouldered in the sun, just beyond the office's pressed metal facade. His red hair spilled out from under the little coonskin cap pulled impetuously over his brow, and though his face was dirty, his mild eyes and the whiteness of his smile suggested the temper of an angel.

He stepped quickly across the open porch and began talking to my brother and me. "You ain't from up North, are you?" His voice was high-pitched with excitement. "Name's Jeff Roda."

"No," we said.

"You sure are a sight." His chin to his breastbone, he gazed at us with a bewildered grimace. "You ain't Northerners, now?"

"No. We is Chang," my brother said. "And Eng," I said. "Of Wilkesboro."

"This is my first trip to a city suchlike Wilkesboro," he said. "I heard about you big-town folk. You'all grow them weird in Wilkesboro, I always knowed it." He had the faint light in his eye of suspicions confirmed. "I can only *imagine* how they grows them up North."

The way this young man plucked at his red hair made me think of the littlest of children. "I like you fellers from the start," he said. "You want to come to Kansas?" He must have seen our apprehension, because quickly he continued: "We're going to Lawrence to set things right in that . . . *hotbed* of abolitionism." The way he said the word "hotbed" made it obvious the phrase was not his; moreover, his dirty face and his manner indicated that he was too poor to have any slaves of his own. But his emotion stirred me. It is not often you know simply by seeing a stranger's face that he would kill or die for a cause or a comrade. And I believe that is how he saw me, and how he saw my brother: As two possible comrades. No one up North had ever shown such feelings of fraternity, or trusted us so quickly. "Could be a time," he said, and I had the irrational hope that he was as immediately fond of me as I was of him.

"Thank you, Mr. Roda," I said, "for your kind consideration." And he smiled as wide as only men unfamiliar with the hardness of the world can.

Chang and I, of course, did not go to fight abolitionists in Bleeding Kansas, but this man Jeff Roda has stuck in my memory, though I never saw him again, because in meeting him I knew both that the South would secede and that I would support it. The hateful so-called Know-Nothings, organized against immigrants, had emerged as a powerful party in the North. The Northern motto—Liberty *and* Union, now and forever, one and inseparable—sounded false and hollow.

A few weeks after meeting that young border ruffian, Chang and I and our wives had our father-in-law over for dinner. A year earlier, the girls' mother had died, and their brother Jefferson, too, from a head injury that came when the boy was clowning and slipped off a fast-moving carriage. Mr. Yates had been visiting quite a bit since then, but rarely for dinner. He'd diminished a bit with the years; his body was smaller now, and stooped, and his voice, too, was smaller.

We all sat around the long dining table. Chang's son Christopher was there, too—already weighing nearly fifty pounds. The other children—Katherine and Julia and Chang's Josephine—were upstairs with Thom, whose main job now was to take care of the children.

The topic of dinner conversation was John Brown, a free-state partisan who had led a small party two days before in a bloody raid upon some Southern settlers, murdering five men and displaying their slashed bodies as a warning to slaveholders. Yates was telling Chang and me that Brown should be killed and strung up in public.

"I think I'd like to witness such a thing," said Adelaide, who sat with her son in her lap. I hadn't had the opportunity to hold Addie's hand in months that seemed like forever. "Such a man needs be made example of."

"Not me, you'all," said Sarah, still not grown too old to make her baby faces. "With my poor stomach, I never would have been able to watch it." She was at this time pregnant with our son Stephen, and her belly was starting to balloon.

Frowning to herself, my wife sat there insecure and less than flourishing. Earlier in the day, Chang and I had come across a frail kitten under a log, its forelegs split and eyes oozing rheum, the little creature mewling in such a pitiable condition that Chang and I asked Thom to put it out of its misery with a merciful blow of a rock to its head. Now as I looked at Sarah, rubbing her belly and plainly agitated, the thought crossed my mind that my wife did not have the stomach for life.

"Are you talking about that caitiff's execution, or his caitiff deeds?" Mr. Yates shook his head, pursing his small mouth. He wanted to pontificate and not be interrupted, least of all by a woman. It had been nearly fifteen years since we had met him; he'd developed a palsy in his left eye.

"I understand what Pa is saying," said Adelaide, a wisp of smugness in her tone. "That old Osawatomie Brown deserves no fate separate than hanging."

"Would you want to see it with your own eyes?" Sarah cringed at the thought.

"I don't directly want to up and go see it myself," Adelaide said airily. "But we *should* maybe all of us see it—this man who sash-i-ates all over wilderness, killing folks—all of us in North Carolina, to remember the facts of our situation."

"I suppose you're right," Sarah said. "Just not me."

Adelaide smiled slightly, and she pinched the cheeks of fleshy little Christopher, who sat on her lap. "Listen to your aunt, now," she said. The boy nodded seriously, then closed his eyes and burrowed his black-haired head into his mother's stomach. Adelaide wore a strange ruffled yellow house gown she had devised for herself. Above the frilly neckline, her chest was more visible than usual, and though the tightness of her skin was not what it had been in her youth, like a young girl she still had a childish little plot of freckles scattered across her collarbone. Her hair was gray, a droplet of perspiration meandered the arch of her neck.

My nephew must have felt the stare I gave his mother, because soon he opened his eyes and made a quizzical face at me. I had been casting the same hopeful glance for years. I did not look away now.

"My point exactly, Adelaide," Yates was saying. "Will Pundyk's cousin was down there in the Bleeding. Poor wretch got chased down to the river and shot like a dog."

"Father," said Adelaide, "the boy's ears may be a little young for this talk."

"And when he tried to stand up above the water"—Yates's eyes were flashing—"someone struck him dead with a club." My father-in-law tried to catch my eye, or Chang's.

"Horrible, indeed," I said. "In fact—"

"Please go on, Father," Sarah said. She was never outwardly critical of me, as I was never to her.

"I even heard that Negroes hold rifles out there." I had rarely heard my father-in-law's voice sound so solemn.

Adelaide brought her hands over her face, then moved them slowly down her neck, the better to deal with the gravity of that statement. Those hands. She shifted the load of Christopher from one leg to the other. "Go upstairs now, son," she said, and the boy went scampering from the room.

"Well," Chang said finally, looking for any path into the conversation, "at least it over."

"*Over?*" Yates turned scarlet and showed the range of his poor man's teeth. "Over?" His eye trembled.

At this point Soren, one of our slaves, came in from the swinging side door that led to the kitchen, and he began to pour everyone coffee. No one spoke as the Negro walked from person to person holding his white china coffeepot. When he'd finished, all eyes followed the slave as he left the room.

Adelaide said to Chang, "I don't know, maybe my husband's from China so you don't know anything about anything." She shook her head. "But around here, that chickenhearted raid is obviously one of the most evil-qualitied things that ever happened." She was growing more agitated as she spoke. "These squirrelly old blackguards think that what they done, they done as a service to God! And you'all call that over?"

Chang opened his mouth to speak, then closed it. He tried again to respond, but lost the nerve. Instead he took a quiet sip from his coffee cup, the steam from which dampened my cheek.

Then Mr. Yates said, "Parson Hodge was saying in his sermon that that's just the way they are, those Yankees. 'What else,' the

Parson says, 'could be expected from someone from the other world, who is colored with "Freeloveism, Socialism, Spiritualism," and all the other isms that were ever devised by man or devil?' "

Adelaide continued to glare at her husband. "*Over,* Chang says."

At this point I think my wife noticed I was looking at Adelaide, because Sarah began to glare at me with a queer cast to her colorless face. There was no way she could have suspected my feelings, of course. But her eyes did make me less than comfortable. As the arc of our decreasing intimacy crossed the arc of my rising passion for her sister, my wife's silence had become more profound, tiresome, almost cunning even. Maybe that is why I was always surprised at how talkative she became when her father would stop by.

After dinner, Mr. Yates left. Our wives went up to sleep, and Chang and I stood on the porch of our home and took in the spectacle of the starry Southern sky. The anticipation of the coming sleeptime with Addie—it was her turn with us that night— gave rise to butterflies in my stomach, but the annoyance I felt toward my brother simply for existing beside me—and toward my wife upstairs, because she existed, too—alleviated almost all my guilt.

Chang held a drink; he was beginning to develop "the taste." At first he had started imbibing small amounts that were not sufficient to intoxicate me, but enough to loosen his tongue to plead with Adelaide when she was cold with him. And so, Chang was now tending a glass of scotch. Ice jiggled in the glass, the only sound save a cricket or two.

Apropos of nothing, Chang said, "I know now my Adelaide will love me again," smiling, his moonshiny breath in my nose.

"How do you know that?" I asked. Was this his desperation speaking?

"I thinking now about me and Adelaide before Christopher born." His smile was that of a happy man taking stock. "And everything was good."

"Was everything"—I tried to steady my voice—" 'good' then, Chang?"

"We will get back to like that, me with Adelaide." He was

sharing what he thought was the irrefutable truth now, and it kept him grinning. "I just be extra nice to her. She love me again soon." He took another sip. (From the Temperance Handbook: "The tainted nectar compels people to chuckle through hardship, permeates their mind with bogus, liquid happiness. It denies the learning that usually chaperones sorrow.")

My brother delighted in another swig of alcohol, and he coughed. I did not like myself for what I thought next.

It is *my* hand Adelaide holds in the dark, I reminded myself. At least she does every year or so.

You do not want to lose her hand, I told myself. Nor the joy of keeping the very secret itself for all this time. Not to this grinning baboon.

"Eng, I love her still." Chang smiled like Father would when he'd pet Mother's delicate head. "Do you understand?"

The word "infidelity" crept into my mind, debasing the feelings Addie's touch had excited in me—and had kept alive with so little to sustain them. I had a pregnant wife. And children of my own. This had never been my intention, this clandestine and utterly infrequent hand-holding with Addie, *his* wife.

I looked now at Chang. I could easily picture him at twenty, fourteen, ten: grinning with his whole face.

"I not believe our good luck still, sometimes." He closed his eyes and took a deep breath as if he was trying to inhale what fortune he had in this world.

I loved my brother; I hated my brother. My act of infidelity had been nothing other than the innocent clasp of a hand—that was not so corrupt, after all, was it? I now believed myself a terrible person. But is there anyone alive in whom a devil does not sometimes dwell?

"Yes," I said. "Our luck."

I even hated Adelaide at that moment, with her long face and wide hips and sharp tongue. She would never have dared to scold her husband as she did if he had been an American man. And holding her husband's brother's hand—how dare she do that to him? All was self-hatred and despair.

I turned to look up at the window of the room where I knew my wife was sleeping. The candle was out, the window dark. I imagined her pregnant stomach rising and falling gently with each breath. Another clink of the ice in Chang's scotch glass, and I wanted to grab my twin and run us to wake Sarah, whereupon I'd tell them both everything—if not divulge *exactly* the extent of my feelings, then I would say I was afraid that I might *be in danger of falling in love with my sister-in-law.* That would give me a chance at least to talk about Addie. Did she care for me at all?

"What is it, brother?" Chang asked, his face gentle with concern. He was the man she had once loved; I doubted whether her feelings were ever that serious for me. Maybe Chang was the true love of her life, and if that were so, she would surely come round to remembering it.

"Are you?" I whispered in my irrationality.

He squinted at me, patted my clammy hair. "Let's go to sleep now, what?"

"I'm sorry, Bean Sprout, you are correct. Precisely."

Of course, my brother was wrong. Adelaide and I continued to hold hands every year or so and she continued to treat him terribly. And Chang began to drink more heavily. Before too much time had passed it had become reckless. Especially when we were touring.

I did not like his burgeoning habit, but at first I did not fight it. Naturally, this was before I knew of the secret evils of alcohol, that it is a baneful unguent, blackening the crevices of your mind; this was before I knew the scientific evidence. But I felt the devil when he drank—that, I knew.

One night, at the Calvary Pine Bluff Church on the mudflats of the Arkansas River, we had reached the portion of our show when spectators ask questions (a new and short-lived addition to our act), when Chang, after only a single audience question, said, "One more asking, then we are finish."

A gangly man stepped forward from the crowd. "You're married—"

"Needing a drink for answering this one." Chang took his flask from his pocket: Wilkesboro moonshine, its smell prickly like a bee sting to the nose.

"I'll answer the question," I said, giving my brother the eye. "Go ahead, sir."

The man fidgeted and looked apprehensive, but he said, "I was wondering if your marriage—"

"No wondering about our marriage," Chang said. I hated the thick way he'd begun to sweat when he drank. "No more talk." He took another swig, and another. It did not escape the notice of the reporters on hand.

This was when I began receiving posts from the North Carolina Ladies for Temperance Society, which at the time was a society of one—a white-haired lady in Winston-Salem named Mrs. Appleby. She wanted to make me an honorary member of her sorority. I ignored her letters—if my brother wanted to sin with drink, it was not my business.

My magnanimity toward my brother's problem came to an end, however, on a fall day in 1857, when we took my daughter Katherine, now not so tiny after all, for a ride in our horse-driven post chaise around the perimeter of our property. She had had a condition marked by inflammation of her liver, and as a result had lain in bed since the end of the previous spring, vomiting and fainting. But by the fall she had gotten stronger, and when she felt well enough I'd wanted to take her out for a ride.

It was warm and bright, and though she was not smiling, and was pale—how odd to me still, a pale-skinned daughter of mine!—she seemed to be enjoying herself. She sometimes would wrap her arms around my chest, jump up and grab me by the collar, and then kiss me precisely on the chin. I never knew how to handle affection shown in that way. (I was not blind to certain facts about my condition and fatherhood. But I wanted to be loved by my daughter.)

The post chaise seated Chang and me comfortably, side by side, while my daughter sat on my lap. Her bony rump on my knee, she was as light as a kitten. "Gid'yap!" I yelled, and Katherine would laugh every time. Our horse was a fat brown gelding we'd named In whose winter coat was about to come in, and it rode us about our land, up a hill overlooking a pasture thick with foliage, and down toward the paddock where we raised our hogs. The landscape was serene; my brother was drinking bourbon from his flask. Addie had avoided talking to him at all at lunch, though he had asked her numerous questions. "Addie," he'd said, "come with us for horse ride?" She'd merely continued to eat her snuff.

Now I tapped Katherine on the shoulder with the hand not bridling the horses and pointed to the paddock. "Do you see the hogs?" I asked, the bounce jolting my speech a bit. "Do you see the shoats?"

"Yes." She had a voice I'd imagine a fly would have, minuscule and sorry even when nothing's wrong.

"Do you know the noise the hogs make, Katherine?" I asked.

"No." She puckered her face.

Meanwhile, our horse was trotting at quite a hop.

"It's a squeal," I said. "You know it; try and make the noise of the pig," I said. Chang's slurping was disturbing me.

"Please, Father," Katherine shook her head side to side. "I don't want to."

I looked at Chang, then at my daughter, hoping that he would understand I did not like him drinking so much in front of her. Of course, he reeked; his breath and skin emitted a more hateful odor after drinking bourbon than after wine.

"Make the sound of the hog, Katherine," I said. "You are able to, I know it." Chang's alcohol was beginning to bubble in *my* encephalon now, and the little globules organized themselves around my brain stem like infinitesimal ball bearings. I hated the feeling, like slipping on ice, that marks the first steps in the march to drunkenness. The reins felt heavy in my hand. The horse In sped up, and I jerked him.

"Chang, I wish you would stop dancing with that Lady Libation," I said, trying to speak in a code Katherine would not understand. The world was starting to skate by.

"This horse bounce too much," Chang sneered, as if the jolting had been a personal insult. He took another swig.

In was riding at an expansive clip now, and I reined him back. The green of the trees and the approaching hogpen were now exceedingly well defined—as if I'd formerly been seeing the world through a milky film without knowing it. Meanwhile, my daughter's bony frame jiggled on my lap.

"Make the sound of the hog, Katherine." I was trying not to

worry about the state of my exploding head. Our post chaise startled a flock of bluebirds out of a walnut tree and into the warm
afternoon.

"Please, Father," my daughter said. "I don't want to."

"I am sick," Chang said. Without warning, he threw his hand
in front of his mouth and puffed his cheeks, but the sick erupted
out of his lips and through his fingers. He strained to his side in
order not to vomit on himself, pulling me with him. I nearly lost
control of the horse, and had to snap Chang back upright while
trying to bring us to a stop. My twin's head crashed into mine. I
held the reins with all my strength, but they began to slip. "Father!" cried Katherine. "Do not worry, Katherine!" I pulled at the
reins. Chang's head banged against my own again and again. His
vomit trailed onto my shirt. I kept on pulling; the horse whinnied.
My head throbbed, and my twin's retching affected my body, dis-
concerting my stomach, giving me chills. But I pulled at the reins.
The world was flying by. The inside of my chest felt like someone
had dragged a match down the length of my esophagus and lit it
at my stomach. I pulled at the reins, and the horse whinnied. He
stopped.

We had come to a rest in the shade of a scarlet oak that had
leaves of a brilliant royal red, and our horse was still but snorting,
raring to trot again.

My daughter looked at pale, shaking Chang with sympathetic
eyes. "Does Uncle also have an inflammation of the liver like
me?" she asked.

For the rest of the day, Chang was ill, and so, naturally, I too
had to lie in bed while he recovered. I stewed in anger that night,
beside my wife and sick brother.

When the next night came, and with it the time for Adelaide
to join us in bed, no one spoke as my sister-in-law climbed under
the covers. She was furious with Chang, more so now than ever
because he was a rummy.

Soon ten o'clock crested and fell, and eleven, too. My brother
soundly dozed. I, meanwhile, watched Addie, who was lying
in bed behind Chang's back, trying to sleep. It freed a deep
memory—as did the nervousness in my heart—and I was remembering my sister-in-law as she had looked years before, at our

double-wedding. The memory had to rise so far to surface! Past those early days when I thought I may have loved Sarah, past the births of my children, the hand-holding, to this night, when plumper, even more beautiful Adelaide slept with her hair tucked behind her ears, with wisps that fell about her cheeks and forehead, falling in the same way it used to, though her hair was not gray then, more than a decade earlier.

Now, this mature, pregnant Addie's nightgown must have been riding up her leg, because I could apprehend over my brother's hip a moon-shaped glimpse of her skin; jagged shadow patterns covered the tender fat of her haunch, cutting dark lines in the near-dark. I yearned to feel her soft gray-blond locks tickling across my neck.

I reached across my brother's tired body and, silently, coolly, touched her hand. Slowly I entwined my fingers with hers.

Though this was the prize I had won after working so dearly for it for years, I was not happy with it now. I suddenly considered that this hand-holding was insanity.

Still, I did not dare shake her fingers from mine.

"Adelaide," I whispered, with a boldness I'd never known in the years since I first touched her in secret. "Adelaide." My elbow rested lightly on my brother's arm. Her hand dampened with sweat; the feel of her skin was pleasant. Maybe she did love me, after all. How wonderful! My heart was a flying fish, leaping about my ribs. "Adelaide . . ."

"*Shh,*" she hissed. And she yanked her hand from my grasp. I went to take it again. She refused it. I lunged at her hand a second time, and she withdrew it fully now, moving both her arms behind her own back. I reached over my brother as far as I could, to try to touch her elbow. She recoiled. "Stop it, Eng!" she seethed. "Never again, do you hear! This is ridiculous."

"Hmmm?" Chang murmured, waking.

And that was that. I was not in a position to do anything more. She hates you, I told myself.

My heart withered. I began to weep silently, with my eyes closed, and my tears ran down the length of my face and onto Chang's.

"What is it?" Chang asked. "What is it, brother? Bad dream?"

"*Shh,*" I hissed. I had been a terrible brother to him. "*Shh.*" Remorse and shame had me by the throat.

The next morning my eyes fell upon Addie's pale, passionless shoulder, illuminated by the hard, melancholy, bright morning sunlight, and I decided that I would do better to find grace elsewhere. That is when Adelaide, I noticed, began to take up crochet seriously, and I joined the North Carolina Ladies for Temperance Society.

CHAPTER FIFTEEN

Barnum and Our Liberty

1833–1838
New York

In the years I had spent as a young man in New York and London and Europe, I'd never tasted a breath of free air until the night Chang and I set ourselves loose from Mrs. Sachs's house, sneaking down her wall and into the safe passage of Barnum's carriage. To this day, I remember the next night clearly, and the party that attended it.

Prickly music from inside Barnum's huge Connecticut manor muddled out along the Long Island Sound, and most of the party guests flitted unnoticed from the rear foyer to the lawn and back again, like anxious spirits looking for something concrete to haunt amid the chatter and the nighttime sky.

His colossal backyard was embroidered with rows of candlelight: tight queues of glowing candlestands that led all the way to the water's edge. Running up and down one of the corridors of light, a troupe of servants faithfully replenished a buffet table laden with foods I didn't yet know by name—bronzed birds of some kind, and glistening desserts the likes of which I had never seen.

This is the first step, I told myself. Toward home and Mother.

Beside the buffet table, at the lip of the twinkling shore, sat a makeshift bar of balsa wood. On the pale, unfinished tabletop lived any number of bottles of alcohol that the smiling bartender would allow you to empty upon request, and for free.

Compared to affairs in the drawing rooms of England, what was most remarkable about this party was not the number of guests; it was the vastness of the setting that made this banquet seem uniquely American. Rather than forty or so aristocrats in an airless old antechamber, here was a swarm of ordinary people under the stars.

An orchestra was stationed inside, near the French windows of Barnum's red Georgian mansion, playing chamber music poorly out into the night, but—to a man—the crew wrangled at their instruments with enthusiasm, and the atmosphere, saturated with liquor, was charitable to the stalled melodies decaying in the air.

I felt extraordinary standing near Barnum under the sparkly needle bed of the night sky. The furious arrogance that had so distinguished this promoter when we had first seen him years before was now remade into good-hearted camaraderie. His sweeping gestures, his laughter served as an irresistible call to friendship.

"So, fellows, do you like my life . . . ?" Barnum said. On his arm clung a ravishing young woman with clammy brown hair. Her actual eyebrows had been tweezed off, only to be replaced by penciled-in duplicates that were—judging by the stubble—more shapely than their natural precursors. The lady, like Barnum, waited for our response. She licked her lips and blinked at us.

Chang lifted his shoulders humbly and smiled. This was his attempt at an answer to Barnum's question. (Chang had developed little tics that he thought endeared him to the public—raising his shoulders and smiling with a dumb, feigned innocence, for example, and also scratching his head and screwing up his face to show that he hadn't quite understood the English of a particular sentence; he began after time, unfortunately, to perform these affected gestures often, from force of habit, even when we were all alone.)

"All right, Lara," laughed Barnum, shaking the girl off. "Leave me and my conjoined friends alone now—but before you're away," he said, reaching in his pocket. "Present for you, my dear." He gave her a closed-up clamshell. The shell hemisected, to the lady's delight, onto a pair of matched pearl earrings. "Take it and be off," he said.

"How did they get inside there?" The woman's mouth was open in wonder.

"Accept the magic and be off." She was out of sight by the time Barnum beckoned us inside. "All in the presentation," he told us with a wink.

We followed him toward his mansion. In the promoter's tanned face, both jolly and all business, I saw nothing unpleasant, nothing to substantiate all the nastiness Hunter had spewed about him. It was Hunter diminishing in my estimation with every inviting smile that Barnum threw our way.

"Cocktail, sirs?" Barnum's butler appeared at our side suddenly, a small man dressed formally, taking steps that artfully matched the pace of our own. His black hair was pomaded, and the look of the tight skin on his wax-figure-like face—it was the color of blond ash wood—made me think he was Chinese, or maybe even Siamese. I tried to place his nationality—or to elicit a companionable smile—but this servant wouldn't look me in the eye. "Cocktail?"

"No, thank you," I said, as we entered the house.

"Yes—drink, please," said my brother to the butler, whereupon the servant, eyes downward, handed him a glass as big as an urn.

Chang took a sip of the intoxicating drink, his first, and I raised my eyebrows at him in astonishment. A sip, and Chang smiled stupidly as if he'd felt truly scared or his glands had begun to overwork. And the butler departed with tactful stealth.

We were deep inside the mansion now, in a high, large room with oak paneling, far enough from the heart of the party that the noise of the orchestra was drowned out.

One din, though, replaced the other. At the center of the room, a woman wearing a blue dress played the piano amateurishly, a few people clustered around her, laughing as she banged away, and everyone drunkenly began to sing.

In the meadows, fair meadows, I loved a girl
In the meadows, fair meadows, I gave her a twirl,

She was blond, she was blond, my heart unfurled
She was blond, my blond love, my meadows girl. . . .

At the same time, a few partygoers filled the plush chairs at the far reaches of the room, sleeping the belching sleep of the inebriated. Barnum stood with us, fashionably in the far corner, removed from his warbling guests. He held in his hands a sketched poster of Chang and me, an example of the printed public notices he would hang all over the city if we agreed to join with him.

It read: CHANG-ENG: THE UNITED SIAMESE BROTHER. Under the title sneered an American eagle with a shield, and, as legend, there was this quotation: "Union and Liberty—One and inseparable, now and forever."

"E Pluribus *Unum*," Barnum said. "Could mean a lot of money.

"Now I mean it, fellows." Barnum leaned in toward us, smiling, creasing his wide forehead. "You need to work for me. Need to. I will deliver you into greatness. No freak act would be bigger. None in the wide world." He smelled like the ocean. Candlelight and shadow bifurcated his face.

More guests, apparently having heard the news that Barnum himself had gone inside, came into this room. Barnum winked at Chang and me and motioned for us to look upon the swelling throng walking in and crowding around the piano. The entering guests pretended not to look at Chang and me.

"All this," Barnum said, and I found myself staring at the woman playing the piano. Fair-haired, she had slender, fluttering arms. "All this," Barnum was saying, and by now the room was filled with people. "All this, I can give you." He rolled up the poster dramatically.

The question of exactly *how much* he would give was on my tongue. But then a commotion disturbed the atmosphere. Surrounded by angry muttering, persons unseen amid the guests were parting the crowd against its will. With a Siamese inflection the butler was yelling: "You cannot come in here!" But the commotion surged on toward us.

Before long, the agitated crowd dissevered before us, opening up and issuing out the cause of the disturbance: Hunter and Mrs. Sachs.

Hunter stepped up and regarded us through his monocle with a giant half-closed eye. Mrs. Sachs stood behind him, nervously looking at the floor and fussing with her hair.

"You!" said Hunter, and that seemed to be all he could say, because he stood with his mouth hanging open for some time. Someone played a note on the piano.

"Mr. Hunter," said my brother and I, politely. "Mrs. Sachs."

But evidently Hunter was not addressing us, because he covered Barnum with his roving eyes. "These are literally *my* Chinamen, Barnum. I paid to bring them here, I had to look on them for the last years, I gave them a home, they are *mine!*"

"In fact, they are my Chinamen now," said Barnum in a soft voice. And then, now our friend, Barnum grinned his best in our direction. The smile was too polished not to have been the result of considerable practice before the mirror; through it Barnum conveyed that he cared more about *you* than the rest of the wide world—more even than he cared for himself—because the smile understood how singularly wonderful you were, understood it better than you did, and it would be there to remind you of that whenever you needed reminding.

I cleared my throat. "As a matter of fact," I smiled, "we are no one's Chinamen." And I puffed out my chest, straining my bond to Chang. "We are from the Kingdom of Siam, and further, we are each our own man." I reached over toward the blinking, open-mouthed butler and took from his tray a huge glass of whiskey.

I drank a sip for dramatic effect—it was the last burning taste of that baneful liquid I'd ever swallow—nearly spat the awful stuff from my mouth, and began walking with my brother toward the exit.

"Where we going?" Chang asked as we pushed through the crowd, him as fresh-faced as he was at five years old. He poured the rest of his whiskey down his throat, and I was already feeling the sharp black bubbles in my chest. My head was light as a balloon.

"We are leaving," I said, and Chang asked: "What? Why?"

Walking into the night, I was happy as I could ever remember being. We were going to return home, back to Mother, back to Siam.

After wrangling with the carriage driver Barnum had hired to bring us here ("Do you think Mr. Barnum went to all the trouble of getting us to Connecticut," I said, "only to make us find our own way home?"), I got the coachman to agree to drive us to New York, though the trip would take all night. Nothing was going to stop me from getting us out of this godforsaken place.

All during the ride back to Manhattan, I could not contain my enthusiasm. Chang wore such an apathetic face as he watched the landscape go by out the window, I wanted to embrace him in my arms.

"What could be the matter, brother?" I pulled lightly on his earlobe. "We are going home." I tugged again and gently. "Home!"

When he turned to me we were nose-to-nose, and in Chang's eyes glittered nothing of the happiness I'd seen in the joyful or those about to set off for the happy unknown—but I did not care, because just then I loved my brother, and felt as close to our Mekong past as I did to his breath on my cheek. Chang had made the best of our exhibited life, I knew that, and I felt new tenderness toward his heart, because it was good, and his soul, which was brave.

"I am not go back to Siam." Chang's whisper had spittle in it. "No—I am not go back."

The carriage windows were open and a wind came in mild as a sigh. In a few minutes it would start to rain.

"You hear, Eng?" he cocked his head, not one of his most dramatic gestures—but a gesture nonetheless. "Nothing for us in Siam." He let a quick breath out of his nose and turned again to the window. He could not stomach the sight of my tears, probably. "I know from the moment we getting off the *Sachem* that Siam over for us." He sounded tired. "You very stupid if you think any different, what?" He turned and looked at me with eyes seven thousand, five hundred and twenty nautical miles from where mine were. "Good luck going back without me," he said.

I had my hand on the back of his neck. I pulled my hand away. The quiet was dense and passion-filled. So he would be the difficult one now, I thought, he and not me. The cruel one. My heart was deflated and lowering.

I could have said, *But you promised*— I could have asked, *Why would you forsake your home, your dignity, your nation for this cold place?* But I did not break the Silence. The movement of our hearts seems not to coincide.

That I was attached to this selfish cheat made me physically ill now.

I could have thrashed Chang then, walloped him, mauled his head—and I wanted so badly to do that. But it was the memory of Mother, the very mother Chang was now keeping me from—and deference to her wisdom—that restrained me. *A double-boy must never fight amongst yourself.* Her voice like a soft and light pillow. *You may as well cut off your own head.* I would never see the Land of the White Elephant again. I had no idea what to do with my towering feelings of disappointment. So I swallowed them. I had no choice but to stay in America.

But we had no place to go in America. After we collected what little we had at Mrs. Sachs's house (two pairs of black suits, and the first installments of the meager allowance Hunter had begun paying us on our return from London), we spent our first night of emancipation drifting past the few pedestrians who were still about at that hour, men who huddled around fires under the gray sky. We wandered streets that were graced by weeping willows, searching for accommodations. We walked all night, in silent lockstep and avoiding the staring pedestrians, until the last straggling citizens had gone to bed.

I hated him.

Relax, Chang told me. People knew our act by name. As adolescents, we had run a duck business. As young men, we could certainly handle our own act, an enterprise for which people were already clamoring.

These were thoughts I was pondering as we strolled dark, emptied Manhattan until sunup: Maybe I could persuade Chang to return to Siam by the following year. Maybe one day a doctor would come along who could cut off my burden from me.

Soon morning had come, bright and warm, but it proved disappointing at first. Though we stopped at every boardinghouse we came across, landlords were wary of us. Finally, though, my brother and I came to the older sections of town, and there we saw a little theater that had a fence on three sides, the Kay Playhouse. It looked more like a two-story home than it did an auditorium.

"Stop here for a minute," Chang said.

"Why? I want to find sleep."

"For just a minute." His smile made me want to punch his teeth out. We walked the footpath to the white-painted door, which was locked shut.

"Stop your knocking!" said a man's voice from behind the door. It was too early for the box office to be open, the voice explained, and in any event the theater did not host any shows until the following Thursday.

We knocked again. I looked at Chang as if he were crazy; I was sure I was going to use the Gung-Fu tiger claw on him in a minute.

"I said to quit that bang—" The man froze when he opened the door. He was white-haired and very short. His ravaged face looked poignantly good-hearted at its confused tilt.

"That twin . . ." he said, and gestured. "Inside, inside."

The theater itself was modest; about twenty seats hunkered beneath a low ceiling, the stage was little more than a soapbox.

"We want to bring show to theater," Chang said. "We are that twin. You heard of Chang-Eng?"

"To bring *your* show to *my* theater?" Mild amusement flushed this man's raw-boned cheeks. He had a fishy body odor that conjured the stink carried up from the muddy banks of the Mekong when the day's catch had been left to molder in the heat.

I came to understand what was happening. "We will split all proceeds with you," I said, "at any rate you deem fair."

"You mean"—he squinted—"you want to bring that show of yours to my—"

"Are you interested in the offer?"

"Interested, yes, sure—sure, I am, I am interested," the man muttered. "It's just, we are a small—"

"Providing, of course, that we can stay here," I said.

"Providing, of course—? What do you mean, stay?"

"Live," Chang said. "For a short time," I added.

"Why, *I* live here," he said. "There's but one small bed in the second dressing room, and I already . . ." The old man scratched his head. Sleep still crusted the corner of his eye. And I just now realized it was a nightshirt tucked haphazardly into a pair of trousers that made his legs seem theatrically undersized.

"We can sleep on the stage," I said.

The three of us turned to look at Chang's and my future sleeping area; it certainly would not be too big a home.

"Pillows," the man said, preoccupied. "I can provide you with some pillows, sure, sure. Blankets. I can live with that. Split the proceeds, you say. Split the proceeds. . . ." He squeezed his eyes shut and licked his lips, no doubt enjoying the new taste of his future. Then he frowned. "Promotion. Getting the word out. You'll have to handle that business, I have no money for it."

Chang said, "Hang sign, people come."

With that, and the pair of handshakes that followed, we began our extended arrangement with Robert Kay, and the Kay Playhouse.

It was there that we truly cemented our professional reputation in America. After a few months of our own exhibitions, my brother and I were the biggest attraction in New York City. Money came in, and we saved it. "One year," I said, "and we go back." He did not answer, which was fine, because I was not asking him.

And then, one wet day, after a few months back in New York, we had a visitor from our past.

Chang and I were alone in the theater, exercising by walking on our hands across the small space of the stage/sleeping area, when someone knocked on the bolted front door of the playhouse.

We opened the door to an old bald little Siamese man. He sported the shoe leather of a Manhattanite, but as a coat he wore a cotton Siamese peasant's frock. "Hello," he said, and his accent was thicker even than my brother's. "Perhaps you no remember me?" It was raining on his head.

It took me a moment to place him, with his weak neck and his now-wrinkled thin face. Our visitor was Dr. Lau, the Siamese physician who had come to our bedstead when we were children. It had been years since we had seen him at the Irving Wallace Medical College, when he and Barnum had interrupted Hunter's presentation. Dr. Lau no longer boasted front teeth.

A hasty step across the threshold, and Dr. Lau, shaking the water from his sleeve, walked past us and into the theater. He halted at the benches in the back row, and spun around to look at my brother and me. The doctor held a black leather medical bag.

"You endure together," Lau said in Thai. "There is power and glory in togetherness, but happiness in liberty." He bent to put his medical bag on the floor.

Light on his feet for an old man, he sprang toward us and laid a hand on our band, which issued between the buttons of our coats. He squeezed it casually, but not without ceremony; he ran two fingers across its five inches. This old doctor had about him the lighthearted gloom of an undertaker.

Neither Chang nor I bothered to ask what he was doing.

"I separate," he said in English without looking up from the band.

It did not take me long to register his words. Yes! I thought. Yes! Daring to ask no questions, needing no explanation, I thought, Yes.

"What?" said Chang, who I hoped would not say anything to dissuade the surgeon, to break the spell.

"Let us talk Thai," said Dr. Lau.

And he told us his story. Ever since Barnum had brought him to the United States to disrupt our meeting with Dr. Rosen, he had been living in New York, tending to the city's growing yellow-skinned population with his brand of ancient medicine.

"Why us?" Chang asked, in English. "Why now?"

Watching Lau narrow his eyes—deciding how much to tell us—led me to remember when Mother had chosen just which facts of the world were appropriate for our four ears half a lifetime ago.

"I came to find you," the doctor said in our native tongue. "I admit I did it because it will make me famous, this hazardous operation."

"Hazardous?" said Chang.

I will not let my brother ruin my chance at happiness, I told myself. I will make sure this happens.

"Brother," I said, "I am positive the doctor knows what he is doing."

"I do not mean that it is dangerous." Lau was rubbing his hands together nervously. "I mean"—he winced—"*tricky*. Medicine has changed since I saw you last." He held his palms up and spread his fingers—a gesture meant to calm us. "I will do it for you, free of charge." How benevolent his smile was! "We both have some Chinese blood, after all."

"American doctors saying it kill us," Chang said in English.

Lau, too, switched languages. "I not American doctor."

"How would you do it?" I tried to cram assurance in my voice, and indifference.

The doctor grimaced. "Let me have a look."

He seized our ligature and leaned all his old weight into it. He held our "*tzon*" as if it were something precious. He tapped the brown leathery birthmark midway across it and ran a finger over the little brown dot to the lower left of the larger discoloration. The birthmark tingled pleasantly. Then he simply cupped the band, kneading the clusters of cartilage below its flesh, patting it as gently as a mother with her baby.

What do you need, Doctor? I thought. I will chew through the band for you.

Lau stared at the ligament for minutes, and with his face gradually falling, he looked like a lover realizing his mistress is unfaithful, but realizing it slowly—

The doctor was muttering to himself, "Hanging from cord, gradually cord cut through. . . ."

Chang asked, "Do you think cutting would kill us?"—I did not want to hear the answer. Hope had come to dangle before me so unexpectedly, so wonderfully. Let the doctor try to dissever. No matter the risks.

Chang smiled nervously at the doctor. Would my twin even want to do it, if it was proven safe? I did not care; I would do it! The very thought of my brother got me so angry I was sort of blinded. I shocked myself: I wished him dead.

Plants thrive when a weaker offshoot is removed, I thought.

Maybe the doctor will stand over us with a knife, I thought. You could grab the doctor's hand, I told myself. You could seize the knife.

It may be that you would gain all of Chang's strength, I thought. Have the energy of two men.

I would never really have done it, of course. We all sometimes have unfortunate thoughts—but they are only thoughts and nothing more, and we are better than them.

"No, no, no—it would not *kill* you," the doctor said, but he stared so sadly at our band, holding onto it with the slightest touch, as if he did not realize his palm was still against it. He looked at Chang and at me, going from face to face—he must have seen one hesitant expression and one overwhelmed by anticipation—and very softly, he said, "It would kill you."

He turned away from us and picked up his bag. "I have wasted your time."

I felt tears gathering. I wanted to do something—but what was there to do?—or at least to say something.

"Have you been back to the Land of the White Elephant?" My voice shook like a schoolgirl in wet weather.

The physician looked at me and chuckled slightly. "No, I have not." He started to walk past us and toward the door. "Not for years."

I began to speak quickly, trying to find some place to put my hope. "Wait," I said. Mother would now be gray-haired and fragile. "Doctor, wait." She would still be lovely. She had been ravishing in our childhood, her teeth excepted, and so petite. How our money would help her!

"Do you know the best way to get in communication with people on the Mekong?" My speech surprised me by being steady. "I want to send a message to our mother."

"I am sorry. Your mother is dead," he whispered. "I saw her soon before the end, but I was not able to help. She died weeks after you came to America."

My arms and legs seemed numb. I said nothing. Chang let his hand touch mine a little. We walked Dr. Lau to the door. I did not open it for him. The doctor opened it himself and left. After a while we went over to the benches and sank down onto one of them.

Alone with my brother in that theater, I could not bear the sight of him. His face was trembling. If he had said anything I might have kicked that face in. All I wanted in life was to be alone. All I had ever wanted. We sat in tearless silence.

We did not stop performing. I had lost my spirit, true, but after a few far-flung theater owners approached us, Chang convinced me that we could take our show to nearly any playhouse we wanted, nearly anywhere in the country. And we did.

And so it went, year after year. We grew rich, and we grew into men, but did not carry on like rich men. We stayed most of the year at the Kay Playhouse, and in low-priced hotels when on the road. Privately I often read books for escape. Though it would be years before Chang would begin to drink, we started to fight more often. I did not know that I could forgive him—I had the irrational belief that if we'd gone back home when I'd wanted, we would have found Mother alive.

Our show visited Europe, on a tour set up by our old acquaintance Barnum. Back in America, we took our spectacle to the Western frontier. And that is how it went year after year until we met our wives.

CHAPTER SIXTEEN

Secession and Reconstruction

November 6, 1860–March 1868
Wilkesboro, North Carolina

Though the breaking apart of the nation had been forewarned in trickles and rumblings, its sudden violence seemed as abrupt and unexpected as would be the ocean across the land after the rupture of a dam.

November 6, 1860.

Seven months after I found out I'd never hold Adelaide's hand again, a Northerner named Lincoln was elected president. He had declared that government could not "endure permanently half slave and half free." I remembered the red-headed Jeff Roda who'd invited us to Kansas, and knew how men like him would react.

We learned of Lincoln's victory when Parson Hodge, wearing a black churchly suit, dropped by to give us the news. He was trying to drum up opposition to the new president from all his parishioners. We talked politics in our living room—in keeping with my recent policy, I did not look much at Adelaide. Hodge was beside us, and our wives sat opposite, while my children Julia and Stephen (my first boy child, he was now six) played with Chang's Christopher, who was nine. The children ran laps around the room as the adults talked.

"Is it as bad as all that, Parson?" asked Adelaide, crocheting something—making one of the pillows that had begun to show up everywhere around our home. She knocked her knees under her dress.

Hodge frowned, creasing his pink cheeks. "They may as well have elected *Greeley*, Mrs. Bunker." The man of God managed to wink at young Stephen as the boy ran by.

And then an odd thing happened. Adelaide smiled all at once in my direction, a very sly grin, I thought, full of more obvious endearment than she had ever before dared to throw my way.

What is she doing! I said to myself. Why is she so bold now?

"You must be fixing to stay out all night, Parson," Adelaide said, "telling everybody about this Lincoln and such." It was not until she spoke that my poor heart realized it was Hodge she'd been smiling at.

"This, this is my last stop," the Parson said. He noticed Adelaide's eyes, too, because he peered at her nervously through his Benjamin Franklin eyeglasses.

"*Well.*" She continued to smile as if there were only the two of them in the house. "We obviously are glad to see you, Parson, we haven't in some time."

I told myself that I'd replaced the hunger I had known for her with the more prudent attachment to the anti-alcohol movment. Addie was still smiling.

Chang looked as if he was dozing. He had a drink in his hand; when a man yearns for an unrealizable love, a jagged black seed sprouts in his head to crowd any sense from him, and he can go either of two ways. He can do what I did, and plunge himself into some alternative pursuit. Or everything may die for him, clearing room for his great sour need. Chang's palm was sweaty on my shoulder.

My daughter Julia, little and wearing pink, tripped over her feet not too far from Chang. Everyone looked at her to see if she would start crying.

"It's all right." I reached out to my daughter. "Come sit with your father and your uncle."

"No," she said, standing.

Chang coughed. And my son came to stand next to his sister. "Stephen," I said.

"No." He withdrew by a step. I looked to my wife for assistance.

"That's all right. Come here, babies," Sarah said, and the children ran to their mother. She sat one child on each knee, an exertion that seemed to exhaust her. She turned back to Hodge. "Makes me sick to my stomach, Parson, literally, this man in the White House." As she spoke, she took her hand from Stephen's knee and rubbed her stomach and pouted extravagantly. "Really, I shouldn't even be talking about it. I'll just cry thinking about this mess, you'all," she said.

"I wish tears would help set things right, Mrs. Bunker." When Hodge frowned, his whole face went to pieces. "But we need more than women's sobbing now. We need action."

Action was forthcoming. South Carolina, Mississippi, Florida, Alabama, Georgia, Louisiana, and Texas all dislodged themselves from the Union, and at 4:30 A.M., April 12, Southern soldiers let the fire of fifty cannons loose upon a U.S. Army fort in Charleston, South Carolina. Soon after, the Confederate States of America was formed—without North Carolina, for now—and Jefferson Davis was named its president. Everyone in Wilkesboro pondered what our state should do.

Meanwhile, this editorial ran in the *Winston-Salem Spectator*:

> Friends, vindicate the Southern character against the
> aspersions cast upon us by our enemies at the North.
> Remember, what is as true of us as of any other people on
> the civilized globe, we must show that we utterly detest and
> abhor barbarity. We talk of fighting for our individuality, and
> we have an unnatural union within the frontiers of our very
> state—in Wilkesboro! A barbarous union can also describe an
> unnatural union of the flesh! Do we not have the duty to
> catechize the validity of all that happens inner to the borders
> of North Carolina, prior to any external unions we may wish
> to reweigh?

Earlier, if I had never been welcomed in the South, at least I had not felt rejected by it ever since we and our wives fought off those ruffians the night before our wedding. Traits of North Carolina—a genius for repose that is not ignorant of current events, a humor that is sharp without stooping to cruelty, and the lovely sense of isolation—had always made the South preferable to New York and her Northern sister cities. I feared that would change with the coming conflict. I feared we might have to fight our own neighbors.

On the seventeenth of April, a general named Robert Lee resigned his commission with the United States Army and assumed command of the Confederate armed forces. On that evening I caught myself looking at Thom while he cleared the dinner plates; he didn't notice my stare. Bent over the dining table, his face black and gaunt like a carving on an Indian's totem pole, the Negro did not look especially unhappy. I certainly did not want to lose his service. I wondered what he thought, or if he thought at all, about Union and freedom.

"Excuse me, master." His face was rigid as he took my plate away from me.

Soon after, President Lincoln issued a Proclamation of Blockade against Southern ports.

At first, the only concerns were selfish ones: Chang and I had had a tour of Europe scheduled to take us to Amsterdam, but under the circumstances we had no way of embarking. That would be a huge financial strain (also, I had wanted to take myself away from the temptation of Adelaide for a time). Furthermore, we had traded in all of our dollars for Confederate money, which proved to be of less value as the years went on. That, however, was not the worst of it.

Because Wilkes County was sheltered from the world at large by the Blue Ridge Mountains—and since our town saw no major battles—it was written that Wilkesboro remained untroubled by war. Like most details published in accounts of my life with Chang, what is on the page does not correspond with reality. Wilkesboro proved a perfect illustration of how the war transformed Southern society into anarchy.

Though North Carolina was slow to secede, her sons were quick to decide not to fight against other Southerners, and so when war came, Wilkes County sent her boys to battle on the side of the Confederacy. The quickly formed Wilkes Valley Guards made camp on the hill above the old tanyard just outside Union

Square (already rechristened "Westwood Park" once the word "Union" fell out of Southern favor) before marching out on the first of May 1861, numbering 200 volunteers strong.

The fear in Adelaide, and it was a fear we all felt for our children and selves, lent my sister-in-law the fetching aspect of someone who has just been jolted awake from a long and stimulating dream. As for me, I was fifty, and I had grown to disdain the man age was making me. Bodily chores brought nervous depletion. Mornings, for example, shaving would tire me, because of the sight of our faces in the mirror, and getting dressed and undressed hit me in the same way at dawn and at bedtime. Our clothes and bedclothes had snared in their fibers the rankness of old men, and also stains of sweat. Moldiness rolled out from my own body, too, from my hollows and underbrush—and the sourness blew worse off of Chang. Unwelcome sniffs of myself and twin disheartened me a few times every day.

Before long, Wilkes County gave 1,500 men to the fight, more than any other county in the state except for Mecklenburg. Only 250 would return alive, and not many of these survivors came home unharmed. Those who fought from Wilkes were rich and poor, slave owners and not, young and not-so-young, soldiering for tradition, and that they did so in such numbers left the town vulnerable.

Union soldiers, escaping from Confederate prisons like the one in Salsbury, often wound up in Wilkesboro, and whichever runaway Yankees who did not skulk in the dark of the night toward the Federal lines in Tennessee lingered to loot our town. In this, the Union escapees were joined by Confederate deserters, who saw in our small mountain community a matchless safe haven. Before long, Wilkesboro became a sanctuary for rogues both Union and Confederate, a tie between North and South.

Meanwhile, I corresponded with the head of North Carolina Ladies for Temperance Society, Winston-Salem's white-haired Mrs. Appleby. This woman, the widow of a well-to-do cobbler, told me my fame would shine a great light of attention on the cause. We wrote letters daily.

I learned from this widow. Dyed in the wool of American life, alcohol is what had brought the nation to war, and led to the ruination of Wilkesboro. Would sober adults have trained their guns on their brothers? The principal cause of war, and also of cowardly desertion, was the self-inflicted state of stupefaction in which men lived. I lent my name to the Temperance Society's literature.

I was explaining all this to my twin and our wives on the morning of the day in 1864 when I was finally to meet Mrs. Appleby in person. Later that afternoon I was to address a gathering she had planned to boost membership in the society. After breakfast, Chang and I and our wives were in the living room facing each other on our two couches. Sarah had our little son William on her lap—he had been born in February 1861, so he must have been about three years old—and she was combing his hair. Since the war had come to Wilkesboro, our income had been infrequent and limited, and taxes were high. The town itself was depleted from the looting. Now even legitimate Confederate troops passing through the area took whatever they needed from the population. One scamp robbed Parson Hodge of his gold watch on his way home from church. Still, I felt good talking about the Ladies for Temperance Society now, better than I had felt about any conversation I had had with Sarah, Chang, or even Adelaide in quite some time.

"It made so much sense, and so when Mrs. Appleby asked me to speak, I answered, 'Yes, yes, anything I can do to help.' Drinking is evil," I said, "a sin, the devil's eructation."

Chang snorted. Sarah balanced our boy ungracefully on her lap and fussed with his hair; her own was a gray-blond tangle. At Sarah's side, Adelaide brought a finger to her mouth and began to chew on its cuticle. With the added bulk of her body, the clean, soft rolls of skin brimming sweetly over the top of her dress were like clouds disappearing into the horizon.

"Sit still now, Will," said Sarah, dragging a comb through our boy's wet black ruff—she was dressing him up to attend his father's speech at the Temperance Society. My son was round, his features still indistinct. "Smile, William," I said, and showed him what I thought a good smile should look like. He continued to squirm on his mother's lap.

"Stop it, Will," said Sarah. "You know Mommy's stomach can't take any rudeness, now."

Adelaide stared at her sister struggling to groom the boy, and I guessed what my brother's wife must have been thinking: Someone as awkward as Sarah has no chance of making her son look refined.

"Will!" Sarah said, pointing in my direction. "Do you want your father to make you stop?" The boy stole a glance at me before looking timidly at the floor. The role of a father is not only to provide, I thought, but to play the frightening villain.

I smiled at William, and tried without success to catch his eye. I admit that I loved my children unequally. Each successive one dimmed the glow of fatherhood a little. Not that every child at birth was anything less than the root of my attention. I did feel a warmth with each nativity, but as my children grew, their attitude toward me would shade over, their loving faces would take on a disturbed look when they began to realize the sort of father and uncle they had. This change happened every time, to each child. Except Katherine.

"Don't be scared, now, Will," said Adelaide in a soothing voice, taking an interest in her sister's child. "You don't want to make Aunt 'Laide grab you and start tickling." At this, the boy smiled widely. It was one of the few times I understood one of my children fully.

Adelaide, laughing along with William, seemed so perfect for my touch. Do not think of her, I thought. Instead focus on the evils of drink. "Would you like to come to my speech?" I asked.

Chang said, "Oh, I will come." He was trying to be funny. His shoes tapped mine, whether deliberately or not, I could not say.

"Thank you, Chang, very much," I said. "But I was asking your wife." I noticed Sarah had suddenly stopped brushing our son's hair to look up at me.

"Even with little William attending," I said to Adelaide, "the post chaise has room for you." I tried to speak naturally, to everyone in the room. "I'd like as large an audience as possible."

Addie looked for a time out the window at the blue boneset flowers growing beyond our porch. "I suppose I could go with you'all," Adelaide said, with all the warmth of a frosty Northern creek.

Lately, so that we could keep to the safety of our home, we had begun to eat a lot of corn and hogs from our own farm, but recently our Governor Vance had gotten Robert E. Lee to send Brigadier General Hoke's two regiments and one cavalry squadron into the western mountain counties to deal with the deserters and escapees and make the town safer. With the news that a Captain McMillan's cavalry had turned Wilkesboro into an armed camp, Sarah, Adelaide, little William, Chang, and I ventured out into town and on toward Winston-Salem and Mrs. Appleby's Temperance Society. It would take us half the day to get there. Adelaide sat on the far side of me in the post chaise.

We had to ford shallow Cub Creek because the little footbridge had been barricaded by Confederate soldiers. This slowed us a bit, and once we got across Oakwoods Road and onto Main Street we saw servicemen heaping their armaments in the courthouse yard; just beyond that, the whitewashed old jail saw a line of soldiers in front of its thick black iron door, and from its windows jutted the outstretched arms of too many new inmates crowded inside. The army had taken the town back from the looters, but the street was as empty of townsfolk as it had been before the soldiers' arrival.

I barely recognized Wilkesboro. As food and other supplies had grown scant, and the conscription act had taken those few able men younger than thirty-five who had not already joined the fight, crops had gone untended, anarchy had sprouted, and Unionist feeling had begun to emerge in Wilkesboro's dark corners.

And so on this day, the Southern soldiers patrolled the streets of Wilkesboro in their gray uniforms, looking at us with queer expressions on their faces as our post chaise rolled slowly by. The soldiers, known as "butternuts," could not hide their worry behind the long beards they all seemed to have, no matter what age they were—and they were men of all ages. A few of these servicemen carried off goods that were obviously not rightfully theirs. One young Confederate infantryman was lugging a plush red chair along the dusty road, and another, wearing for some reason a

Union soldier's little blue cap, was appreciating some poor woman's necklace against the gray sky.

At Westwood Park, in the shade of the Tory tree—an oak so named because loyalists were hanged there in the Revolutionary War almost one hundred years earlier—several dusky woolen blankets lay covering dead bodies. As we made our deliberate way out of town and toward Cairo, the even smaller community on the outskirts of Wilkesboro, I saw a wounded young man in Union dress bleeding from the head and lying on one of those dusky blankets. He was holding onto the ankles of one of his blond Confederate captors, pulling at the Rebel's pant leg, and I thought of the reports of wounded soldiers lingering on the battlefield for up to five days before being moved to a hospital.

I often had a nightmare about the war. I dreamt of a line of our advancing soldiers twisting away from a storm of gunfire even as they ran toward it, attempting to shield off death with their forearms. In my dream the wounded Confederates did not drop; in the haze of gunsmoke they came asunder: each of the killed stood cleaved down the middle. And those cut apart made their wayward rounds, a gang of halves in a tipsy dance.

At about six in the evening we arrived at the Temperance Society meeting center (also Mrs. Appleby's home) in Winston-Salem, a large brick house approached between a corridor of tall-stalked maples. A wall ran the length of her green property.

Mrs. Appleby opened the door and smiled a curious familiar smile. She had the posture of a sickle, and she searched my eyes for something. She leaned toward me, putting a hand over one side of her face, as if that would shield her near-whisper from my brother's ear: "Mr. Eng, I am pleased you could make it, very pleased." Sarah and Adelaide fidgeted behind Chang and me—my wife carried my sleeping son over her shoulder—and I performed the introductions. Mrs. Appleby looked nervously at Chang.

The living room was spacious and quite dark with the shades drawn. All the furniture had been cleared away. Several rows of lecture chairs looked toward a podium by the fireplace.

The North Carolina Ladies Union for Temperance was ten old women strong: Bible readers and needlepointers, tidy Southern widows without vice, these ladies tapped their laps gently with their pink fans. They wore no jewelry whatsoever, but that may have been due to the war.

"Ladies, this is *Eng*." Mrs. Appleby spoke with the slow gravity of someone trying to impart some message without spelling it out. She looked like she'd been born sometime before Thomas Jefferson took office.

We arrived as the ladies were enjoying their opium tea, which they drank from the Temperance Union's large yellow teacups. One old woman who looked like Mrs. Appleby—small and nervous, bent over—drifted over to us with a tray of teacups. Chang refused. I accepted, as did our wives. After we took her tea, the woman retreated backward, smiling and nodding her head, without looking at us directly.

"I am here to affirm the flagitiousness of alcohol," I said from the podium when it was my turn to speak. To be addressing a crowd, and not because of the accident of my double-birth, was a pleasure. "It does not matter how many livers one has—it is hurtful to drink!" I stroked the back of my brother's head gently, and it gave him a start. He gazed at me under a furrowed brow. I may have bubbled with glee involuntarily.

As I laid out my errorless case against drink, my brother shifted closer to me, to take his arm off my shoulder and play with a strand of loose thread on his coat sleeve. We were nearly facing each other now.

As the lovely tea's relaxant energies took effect, I decided not to mention the new scientific documentation about the influence of ethanol on the brain stem—the black bubble effect. I began instead to recite. A few words by Frances Anne Kemble were among my favorite in the language, and I may have swelled my chest with pride as I declared: "A sacred burden is this life ye bear/Look on it, lift it, bear it solemnly/Stand up and walk beneath it steadfastly/Fail not for sorrow, falter not for sin"—here I intoned deeply for emphasis—"but onward, upward, till the goal ye win!"

The image of Frances Kemble herself floated now before my eyes—I pictured her in a flowery bonnet—and I pointed to the cups about the room as I soliloquized: "Here's that which is too weak to be a sinner—honest water, which ne'er left man in the mire!" I placed my thumbs under the lapels of my jacket, a Siamese version of Lincoln at Gettysburg. I tucked my chin into my chest, I raised a fist and shook it. "And nothing emboldens sin so much as mercy!" I said as Chang extracted from his coat pocket his little silver-plated flask. He was unscrewing the top.

"Maidens of Temperance," I cried, augmenting my words with sweeping arm gestures. "What we needs do—"

Mrs. Appleby, sitting directly in front of the lectern, hissed at me, "Sir, your brother."

I did not look at Chang. Neither did I look at the faces of this modest audience. What I did was close my eyes, and the dark I found on the inward side of my eyelids was encouraging.

"O, that men should put an enemy in their mouths," I was yelling now, "to steal away from their brains!"

The sound of my brother's eager swallowing did agitate me, I confess. As did the frail feminine protesting of the gathered members of the Temperance Society. And also the awareness of the cool metal flask an inch from my cheek I found bothersome. Do not get angry, I told myself. *He* was exactly the kind of man I was trying to save, my poor brother lost to alcohol. To distract myself from the whispers, and to numb my anxiety, I screamed: "Woe unto them that rise up early in the morning, that they may follow strong drink!" My eyes squeezed shut, I was now simply gushing lines, not connecting them, nor worrying about the logic of segue. "He bids the ruddy cup go round/Till sense and sorrow both are drowned!"

At this point a dull knocking sound got my attention. I opened my eyes. An ancient woman of some breeding, her enormous bosom splayed at her midsection, was assaulting Chang with the curved end of her cane. The sun had set on my speaking engagement.

The woman said "Stop" as she swung at Chang, and he was laughing "Stop" as he checked her blows with his forearm. With his other hand, my brother kept the flask to his lips.

Mrs. Appleby and a number of her fellow activists pulled this old woman off Chang and sat her down. Mrs. Appleby waved her fan toward the woman's reddened face, for she looked faint.

My brother was grinning around his flask, but his eyes were

black and sad as those of a gelding, and a shudder passed through him and into me.

"Why are you doing this?" I whispered bitterly.

"I am thirsty."

In the audience Adelaide sat laughing—at Chang or me I did not know. But it was apparent that she did not feel enough of an affinity for either of us even to experience shame at our shame. The women of the Temperance Society ran about fretting and muttering, Sarah was blushing scarlet as she hid my son's eyes from the spectacle, and Adelaide was laughing.

I thought that was the low point of my life in North Carolina. I was wrong.

No matter how often the new government sent forces to extract all the outlaws from Wilkesboro, Northern and Southern renegades would converge again on Wilkesboro as soon as the soldiers would leave, and once more looters would come. We had nowhere to sell our crops.

It was impossible for us to travel away from the Confederacy for any amount of time, and few people in the South were interested in seeing Siamese twins, attached at the chest; the populace had more important concerns. We managed to tour only once in the last three years of the war, and that tour was not lucrative enough to justify its expense.

Nothing that was made outside of the South could be obtained easily, thanks to the suffocating blockade. And Lincoln had declared all slaves in the rebellious states free. In practical terms, this proclamation had no direct impact. Lincoln was sly enough to free slaves only in the Confederate states. Still, we now knew that if the Union won, the abolition of slavery would follow. And after the Battle of Antietam, it looked more and more like the Union would win eventually.

This meant we were certain to lose our slaves, either by governmental decree or simply because we would not be able to afford them for long. And to add insult, the final Emancipation Proclamation sanctioned the recruitment of blacks into the Union army's United States Colored Troops, which gave the uncomfortable impression of slaves fighting their masters. Thom, who tended to our children, never mentioned the proclamation, and neither did any of our other slaves. But everyone knew both slavery and the rebellion were doomed.

By now Adelaide had taken to calling our home "Lonely Trap," instead of Trap Hill. I knew the war would come to affect us personally before long. I wondered if I would ever be brave enough to reengage Adelaide in any way. I realized I had something in my heart like the corked vigor of an unopened bottle of champagne. I did not know if I could keep it down forever.

By the beginning of 1865, all of the Carolinas were demoralized, and the battle was taken to Wilkesboro. The North's General William Tecumseh Sherman battered and burned his way north through South Carolina with an army of soldiers and "freedmen." Even as authentic instruments of communication had broken down—the *Columbia Whig Daily* was burned with the rest of her city—gossip somehow flew about the South, and stories of a South Carolina aflame and demoralized panicked Wilkesboro. We knew the Union was coming, marching through the Salk swamps at a rate of a dozen miles a day, and we thought Sherman would destroy our town and home. He was reducing the South to ash.

The war itself finally came to our home in the name of the Union general George Stoneman, whose directive was to raze the countryside of North Carolina, to destroy rail lines and disrupt Lee's retreat. On March 29, 1865, Union soldiers came riding through the heart of town like a blue windstorm, turning everything upside down, yelling and scaring off the thirty-odd Confederate soldiers who happened to be stationed here. Stoneman's Raiders prowled for goods in every business in town, they burned down the jail, and then they canvassed the countryside. In a timid attempt to gain goodwill, Negro and white inhabitants of Wilkesboro offered liquor to the first Union soldiers marching down Main Street, but that was exactly the wrong strategy, as the soldiers took one sip of that hateful "refreshment" and turned into madmen.

On that March afternoon, I did not know yet that the Union army had stormed into my town. Though evening looked to be coming early in the form of dark rain clouds overhead, Chang and I and Thom and the other slaves were plowing vigorously in the field, trying to extract something from the tired red earth. The air was heavy and wet and silent and smelled of dung. Chang and I were fifty-three years old now. I had grown more than an inch and a half taller than my twin, and our constant leaning on one another had hooked his backbone more than mine. Suffering didn't necessarily give one strength.

First a yell, then the rumble of hoofbeats, and then without warning four Federals thundered onto our property and straight up to us, kicking up a whirl of dust. Their uniforms were divided, especially dark from their waists down to their feet, as if the men had just crossed a river that had been up to their belts. Their horses' legs, too, were darker than the top half of their equine bodies.

When these Unionists came to a halt before us, they sat unmoving atop their horses for a second, silently scratching their heads at my brother and me as if we were talking pigs. I could hear our slaves dropping their farm tools.

"What's this?" One of the soldiers raised his eyebrows at Chang and me. He had a bushy brown mustache that covered his whole mouth.

"I don't know," said another. His horse let out a long breath.

"I don't know," the first soldier repeated through his mustache. He pulled out his pistol and trained it on my brother and me. "What is this?" he repeated, softly to himself. Chang and I both tensed. Over our shoulders sat our house; in that house sat our children, our wives. That was the thought that sat on my mind: Adelaide, and how defenseless she was. And poor Katherine, too, who would be frightened to death if she were looking out the window at this. *Be brave!* I told myself. *Be brave!*

Another soldier, a young pimpled boy with twitching lips, now aimed his rifle at us.

The fourth Union conscript—the only one without his cap— screwed his eyes at my brother and me. "I seen these oddball Chinamen before," he said. "In Boston, a long time ago when I was a kid. They're—"

The soldier with the pistol interrupted: "The Siamese Twins." He did not move his firearm as he talked, and he closed one eye, as if to sharpshoot. "What town is this?" he asked.

It took a while to realize he was addressing us. "You are on Trap Hill on the outskirts of Wilkesboro," I said. Chang looked over our shoulders at the house, and then turned again to the men. He said, "Please—"

"Ever heard of it, Abe?" this first soldier asked one of the others. "Wilkesboro?"

"No." The pimply conscript who held the rifle had a nasal voice. "Look—one half of it acts drunk. What we should do is—"

"Don't *boss* me, I know what to do," the first soldier said, then focused on us again. "You're a pretty strange secesh, aren't you?" His face was covered with a heavy growth of whisker. "Maybe you want to crawl around for us."

Sweaty-palmed, I could feel our stomach turning in our chests.

"I heard it can hover over the ground by mental powers and Chinese spell," said the pimpled one under his breath. "Is that right, can you do that?"

"That's what this double-monster did in Boston, I've seen it."

"Maybe we do that for you," Chang said furtively, his neck thin and creased, his hair thinner than mine. "If you leave after."

"I never saw these two before," the one with the pistol still aimed at Chang and me said, "except could be in a dream." Then, to us: "And what if you *can't* hover by mental powers and Chinese spell?"

We did not answer. The few slaves who had been inside the Negro shanty at the side of our property now walked out into the drab open air.

With their hands visoring their eyes, the Negroes looked up at these less than majestic soldiers like they were gazing into the sun. No words were spoken. The two Unionists who were not pointing their guns at Chang and me rested their hands on their swords. In the silence between the soldiers and our slaves and us there ran a clear understanding. My slaves began cautiously to walk in the direction of the Union men. All of the slaves did this. They were not smiling or laughing, but slowly and soberly walking.

The first soldier, the one with the pistol, glanced at our house over Chang's and my shoulders, and then at his fellow soldiers, and then they all looked to where our wives and children were. The slaves gathered around the horses of the soldiers. And the soldiers, still facing forward and pointing their guns at us, started to back away, their horses stepping gracefully backward. A few of the slaves broke with their brethren to run into the shanty to grab things to take with them, keepsakes and the like, but most of them simply followed the soldiers off our land. Old faithful Thom, who had emerged from the shanty holding only a string of three wooden beads, rejoined the rest, walking off right before our eyes, without saying good-bye.

After the war was lost, Lincoln's coldhearted successors argued that the Confederacy be treated like conquered provinces. With prices in North Carolina so dear after the fall of the South—all told, the cost of many essential items had risen by thousands of percent—and as Confederate dollars became worthless overnight, Wilkes County was ravaged.

Bandaged veterans hobbled about, many simply falling dead in the streets. Families who had lost their homes wandered the once-cheerful open spaces. Sunshine—and it seemed now always to be sunny—sunshine was now more depressing than rain, shining as it did on every misery. The pile of worthless Rebel bills I'd heaped in my stables mocked me every time we went to ride into town. My brother was as poor as I was. How had I ended up in this position—trying to make sense of my accounts, fretting over debts, struggling to support a family in which I often felt like a stranger? Meanwhile, I did not talk much anymore, not to anyone.

Chang and Addie and Sarah and I had never stopped having children, even in the bad times, even when we were older than any other new parents in North Carolina. I think bringing forth babies had almost become a contest to Sarah and Adelaide. As if the number of people involved could make a lonely situation less so.

Our house was too small for the number of children we now had, and our wives were disagreeably assuming all of Thom's child-rearing duties. I was father to seven (Julia, Roslyn, and Georgianna had died from childhood illnesses), and Chang to nine (his Josephine had passed too). My teenage son Stephen and Chang's Christopher lived in the old slave quarters, which we had refurbished with wood we'd chopped from our own land. In the house itself were two bedrooms for the children. Nine slept in beds, the youngest in pallets on the floor.

My poor little Katherine contracted pneumonary consumption and died almost as soon as the war ended, the very same week that my father-in-law died. At first, when the frail fifteen-year-old girl passed, my grief was mild, respectful, an even, vacant dullness I could manage. Then one cold day when Chang and I were riding our buggy into town, I saw a young dark-haired boy idling on a pony near a few roadside bluebirds; as we passed, he yelled "*Gid'yap!*" and kicked his horse, and easily outraced our buggy down the dusty lane. The group of birds took off and fluttered into the warm afternoon, and I was hit blindside by grief. I do not know why it struck at that moment, but I was stupefied by it, and had no one to share it with.

Later that week, Chang and I sat with our wives on our porch eating buckwheat cakes, loitering sadly, the sound of my Stephen and Chang's Christopher chopping wood echoing across our property, and I looked upon my land, my Stephen, even Adelaide, and I wondered how I could ever have derived joy from any of it.

Stephen was a typical Southern boy on the edge of his teenage years—alternately confident and shy, foolish and taken with what he thought was his own wisdom. More than any of my other children, he looked Siamese—and because of that I believed that of all my remaining children, he would grow into a thinking person, as I was.

After the boys had been chopping wood for a while, Stephen and Christopher came to join us on the porch. Stephen was tall, and, unlike I had been, barrel-chested for a lad. My nephew was portly and slow in the ways of the world.

The boys were perspiring. And so, too, I noticed, was Adelaide.

"You are done with the wood?" I asked my son, but not too harshly because he had been working hard at a chore I'd told him to do. And because I was thinking of Katherine and the sadness of fatherhood.

"We was hoping for some buckwheat cakes, sir." Stephen wiped his forehead. What was amazing is that we carried on, still sitting on the porch, still eating buckwheat cakes.

"You *were* hoping," I said.

"Oh, have a cake," said Sarah. "You know your father, Stephen." She gave him a look I had trouble accounting for. She treated me with too much apathy, I thought, at least too much for people who have been married for as long as we had been, and given birth to as many children as we had.

Sarah said, "Oh, Eng, don't go troubling me or my stomach will go off." She was almost laughing. And as Stephen took a cake, he laughed, too, though he was sure not to look at me.

This was a moment, I knew, that had nothing to do with buckwheat cakes. My wife and surviving children had devised a private language of family comedy; they often chuckled about something I was not given the secret vocabulary to understand.

At least, Adelaide—sitting there but not paying mind to any of us—did not take part. I still saw her not as my gray, ever-wider sister-in-law on the porch, but as the exquisite newlywed she was the first night her bedclothes came undone and her eyes said, *I'm wicked.* Memory paved smooth the wrinkles on her face; her eyes were still the wickedest on earth, worlds in which to escape the circumstance of what I was.

But now she was yawning, and her face, as mine must have been, was a portrait of resignation and prospects lost.

Meanwhile, my brother addressed his boy. "You have cake, too, Christopher."

"Thank you, Father." Slow as he was, Chang's son had Adelaide's big eyes, which were happy now and fixed on his father—as his mother's never were on me.

"My son," Chang said. "My good boy."

Christopher's face was filled with gratitude and amity.

"Enjoy your cake, too, Stephen," I said to my son.

Stephen, who had already begun delighting in his meal, turned to me as if I had given him permission to continue breathing. "Yes, Father," he muttered. "Thank you." And he shot a glance at his mother.

This was the state of my relations with my family. Stephen was a talented violinist, and my Patrick liked books as much as I did— I spoke with them sporadically about these topics, but never anything else.

You have failed as a father and a husband, I said to myself. You deserve your heartache.

What have they given me? I said to myself. Any of them?

What have you given them? I said to myself. Not the fullness of your heart, nor honesty.

Do you truly love anyone? I said to myself. Even Adelaide—do you love her truly?

The one responsibility in life, I answered, is to trust in oneself.

By 1867 Chang and I were lucky enough to string together a modest tour of the districts around Richmond.

After three weeks on display, we headed home on a Monday morning. Picturing the house I was returning to put me in a melancholic mood.

Chang and I got home from Richmond late in the evening on a Tuesday. As we brought our buggy to a stop in our front yard, the ruined little moon did not bother to cast its dim light; all the lamps in our house were blown out, and everyone inside was sure to be asleep. That Sarah would be slumbering in bed when I arrived cheered me. I wondered if Adelaide was awake.

Gathering my box of clothes and books from the carriage while Chang lifted out his own suitcase, I stepped down with my brother and walked into our home. Both Adelaide and Sarah were sitting by lamplight in the parlor. Adelaide was holding a little gray cat in her arms, an animal I had never seen before; Sarah was perched beside her sister and laughing happily on our overstuffed red divan. I was surprised not only because it was late for Sarah to be awake, but also because the sisters had not enjoyed each other's company over the past few years. With no slaves anymore, Adelaide and Sarah had had to spend almost every hour side by side— in the kitchen, at the dinner table, cleaning together, tending house—and they had started bickering. That had led our children to begin fighting with one another.

"Well, I'll be," Adelaide said as Chang and I entered the parlor side by side. "Look what's here on my doorstep." I believed she was referring to Chang and me, though she failed to look up from her pet.

Sarah, however, did not ignore our entrance. More than two

decades into this arrangement, her quick blue eyes still darted around nervously whenever I entered the room.

Adelaide turned her broad frame to us at length. "Look at this little critter." She was rubbing the cat's furry little head and rising to her feet holding the animal. "I found her behind the slave house, isn't she precious? Just what this lonely trap needs—and it does need *something*—listen to her purr when I scratch." I had not had a conversation with her in months outside of those of my own imagining, had not stolen a hand-clasp with her in years. Her now-gray hair, the long spear of her nose, the slight trace of some unshared joke behind her smile—

"—And it's obvious she's real affectionate," Adelaide said of the cat. "See, you'all?"

She held the little creature to her face and lovingly brought it to her sweet lips, and the animal could not have understood the pains I would have endured to trade places with it.

"Dirty creature," my brother said, and shook his head. He reached in his coat pocket for his flask, then took a sip of moonshine.

Sarah rolled her eyes. "Adelaide, where in heaven's name do you find these quare things to bring them into our lives?" The exertion of speaking was souring her. She was, admittedly, the gentler one, the more compassionate mother, and after all this time I wasn't sure she had a personality.

"Do you see it's beautiful, my kitty?" Adelaide held the cat outstretched. Her physical characteristics had shifted over time, from soft to hard, from blond to gray, and tight to slack to swollen. This doyenne of crochet and pregnancy was to me one woman and all women, because everything about her was variable, including her temperament. Now she walked in my direction with the animal.

Addie put the cat's little face toward my mouth, and I backed away instinctively. Chang growled as I recoiled into him. "Brother!" He shook his head. "Brother, you spill my drink! Get the dirty animal *away*," he cried.

Adelaide laughed, and drew the pet back to her own cheek. "*I* like nosing him, anyways," she said. "I thought Eng would like him—I *thought* he was the one around here with a sense of things."

She nuzzled her face into the tiny beast's fur, smiling with the bliss of innocent affection.

She should not be doing this, I thought. Should not be exciting my imagination and awakening my heart in such a way in front of my brother and my wife. Did she even know she was taunting me? It was work to stop my hand from shaking on my brother's shoulder.

"I'm going to find a place for kitty," Addie said, and immediately she was gone, leaving the room airless in her absence. I walked Chang over toward Sarah on the divan. We took a seat next to my wife, with my arm atop my brother's shoulder.

Sarah crinkled her forehead as if she were especially interested in the frayed cloth of the divan—she was picking at it. She breathed loudly out of her nose. Chang muttered, "Dirty animal," and then he chuckled bitterly.

Through the walls, the sound of Adelaide rooting around in the kitchen reached my ear.

My wife beside me on the couch must not have been aware that she had a hint of lip rouge on her front teeth. "What is it, you'all?" she said. "What are you looking at?"

Chang held in a belch as I took Sarah's hand in mine abruptly. I had not held her hand in many years. And now I was stroking her palm with my thumb. It was as tender as the wood of a doorknob.

Puzzled, Sarah was stricken with a kind of nervous slouch. She perspired now, and scratched her delicate wrist with her free hand.

I drew her to us and kissed her lips.

"Eng." She jerked back, her complexion turned white as dough. "What has gotten *into* you?" Moist patches of her scalp were visible under her thin gray hair. Already I could feel the black bubbles Chang's drinking aroused in my head. But alcohol was not why I grabbed for her again.

"My *word*, Eng," Sarah said, smoothing her dress. "Please." She frowned as if I'd done exactly what she had been afraid I'd do, which was ridiculous, and made me angry, because it was so unlikely that I would have wanted to kiss her that for her to expect it was an indignity. She rose from the couch and walked off to join her sister.

I could feel Chang's eyes on me. I did not look at him. He put his flask back in his pocket. I could feel the black bubbles. I looked out the window, at the line of mountains. No, alcohol was not to blame for my actions. The sky was getting lighter by this hour; it must have been past midnight. I was too tired to rise from my divan and go to bed. The dusky sky above the tree line winked as birds glided by the moon.

"It cold for this time of year," my brother said.

I did not respond.

"Don't worry." My brother was slurring his words. "Don't worry." He rested his hand on the back of my head and started to pat.

"What did you say?" I did not want his sympathy, his compassion based on what he *thought* I was upset about.

Chang held in another belch, and I felt my own breast churn.

My brother was now as frail as that little kitten, the alcohol having thinned him; he leaned weakly into me. I waited for another tremor from his chest. "So foolish, we were," he said in a whisper.

I looked at him.

"We had never thought women marry us." He reached for his flask again. "Remember—years ago? So *happy*." Bile thickened his voice. "We had *never* thought any would."

"Please stop talking." I said.

He shook his head and muttered, "Never thought . . ." His laugh quavered like a sob before he took another gulp. For the first time, I envied him the counterfeit solace of the flask.

Down the hall, Sarah had united with her sister, and snatches of their unintelligible whispering followed. Many years earlier, at the time of our courtship, and even into the earliest days of our paired marriages, I had found the girls' hushed murmurs appealing. I did not find it so now.

"What you think they talking about?" A chain of suppressed coughs clattered through his body. And mine. "I could put hands over my ears and I still guess," he said. "One spider asking another, 'You making enough string for both?' "

At last we all went to bed. Chang and I were lying face-to-face on the mattress. Outside rain fell lightly and in the bedroom it was dusky and cold. With Adelaide standing over us brushing her hair in the dark, I was thankful for any movement that yielded a glimpse of her face. Bringing her flax comb through her hair, every lift of Addie's meaty arm allowed a view of her nose in the crook between her forearm and shoulder. When she turned briefly toward the window, I saw the flash of her profile—her rousing nose, fleshy cheeks, her high hairline. I tended toward her ever so slightly, and my brother, as drunk as I had ever seen him, did not seem to notice our shift forward. The burden of his weight and how unjust it was that I could not touch her face! The impossible mistake of my position.

Adelaide lowered one knee onto the mattress, then the other. She knelt there, a very full woman. But her heft did not affect the line of her chin or cheek or her pretty neck. "Adelaide." Chang opened his eyes to his wife, his speaking garbled. "Adelaide Adelaide Adelaide—"

The deadweight of my brother falling forward as he reached for her almost pulled me off the bed. Steadying us, I leaned rearward until our shoulders touched the soft of the mattress. I brought my hand to Chang's shoulder and shook him, but he did not awaken. Drool lacquered his chin.

Chang's alcohol was percolating in my brain. I felt swoony. "I cannot believe my brother is so drunk," I said with a stupid laugh.

"It should be obvious to you'all by now," Adelaide sighed, "I don't find it hard to believe." She was facing away from us, pillow under her head and speaking toward the wall.

I allowed myself the exquisite gratification of defending my brother to his wife—knowing what her response would be. "He is witless but kind," I said.

"That rummy Chinaman?" Her sigh was as long as the Yadkin. "Please."

"Adelaide," I said.

Her back made a round lump under the covers.

"Adelaide."

"What?" she said, still not facing me.

"*Adelaide.*"

"What is it?" she looked at me over her shoulder with the grimace of a wearied schoolmarm.

It was at this point I decided to lean across my brother's body to give my brother's wife a kiss.

Nothing could have been less rehearsed, nor riskier, nor any more uncomfortable for Adelaide or me. She turned her head away in quick panic. I kissed her retreating ear—smacked my face against the side of her skull, a sweaty taste to her hair. She pulled her whole body away from us in horror now—slid over the bed as far from me as she could. I had never known such longing.

"Are you cracked?" she whispered harshly, again facing away from me toward the wall, wiping her newly wet ear with her hand.

When she looked at me over her shoulder again, a bead of saliva glistened on her heavy lower lip in the dim light of the moon. She shot an anxious glance at her slumbering husband. "Are you gone squirrelly, Eng? I—"

Meanwhile, I could make out Chang's snoring. I shook him—hard—to test the depth of his sleep. The shake tugged me forward; his head lolled, he gasped slobberingly for breath but his eyes remained closed. He would not wake, that was certain—and just now I did not even care if he did. I was feeling drunk from my brother's alcohol, but I do not use that excuse.

I was shaking; had I not been lying down, I would have been unable to stand. I rolled myself over my brother and toward his wife, and as she was shrinking from me—I think she may have been trying to get to her feet—I lunged for her shoulder with my free hand, and I squeezed it. Her skin was almost as soft as breath under my squeezing fingers. She did not move. She may have been trying to.

I stretched even farther to kiss Adelaide again, with my brother snoring under me. I kissed her shoulder, and when she turned to me to say something—maybe "Stop," maybe something more encouraging—my lips touched hers and her mouth opened to mine with a buckwheat taste. I was half above my brother, who was lying between us; Addie's buckwheat and milk breath spread warmly in my mouth and down my throat. Saliva in the corner of her mouth dripped to wet my chin. There was snuff and buckwheat, milk and fervor in the kiss. My feeling was shock. Two decades of anxiety slipped from my body as a warmth inside my chest emanated out. I was kissing Adelaide over and over in this awkward position, breathing in her scent as she kissed me from over her shoulder; I breathed in the perspiration in her hair. I was unaware of my present state of material being. I did not feel the blankets around me. I did not realize at that moment I had a conjoined brother, and most of all, I did not come near to the thought that I had a wife across the hallway. I did not consider the folly of the situation, nor what would happen next.

Adelaide turned over and inched toward me. She put her arm around me as best she could without disturbing Chang. She got on her knees, leaning over my brother to press her chest into my shoulder, gripping me with sudden agitated confidence, pressing my shoulder to her shoulder as she bent her stomach over Chang's side, and then she lifted herself higher to bring her face to mine, her lips to my lips, to my throat, and she pulled away to look at me with burning shy eyes.

I could not have withstood her rejection at this point. My longing for her had crumbled into an infirmity. I was more sweat now than flesh. I shifted farther across Chang with a good deal of effort—he was lying directly beneath me now—and I lowered my head into the fat of Addie's shoulder as if we were conjoined and I kissed her neck over and over as I began to cry.

"Adelaide." My heart was emptying. "Adelaide."

"*Shh,*" she said. "Shut up."

Chang moaned in his sleep, his breath ruffled the hair on my chest. Addie leaned against her husband to lift my head, and she kissed me. I had never felt this before, a woman insatiate, and grasping. I tried to pull away for a breath, but she held the back of my head and would not let me move. Her fleshy cheek rested against my slumbering brother's ear, her lips were a bit rugged and chapped, but they were moist. A whisper of hair above her lip tickled the upper edge of my mouth.

After each kiss I needed one more, and another, until I began to hope for something more substantial. An odd memory hurried through my head—that years earlier the promoter Hunter had called me the child of two fathers.

I rolled back and canted away from my brother, as far as the bond would allow—Chang and I were now nearly side-to-side on the mattress; he was wincing, but his eyes remained closed, his snoring regular. The trace of a frown crooked his lips. I was holding Adelaide's hand. My heart was pounding madly. She lowered her body onto me, and I felt her. I could not discern her gasp from mine. We lay there like that, not moving, sinfully in place.

I spent the next day in a silent heaven, planning. At breakfast I sat remembering the lovely fullness of her body as she had leaned toward me. And now I barely noticed my brother beside me at the dining table, or Sarah on the other side.

"Not hungry, brother?" Chang asked when I did not touch my hominy. I smiled at him and then at my wife. I was two men, the one seeable by everyone and the shameful hidden self.

In the afternoon, Chang and I and my wife listened as my son Stephen played the violin for us in the living room. He had almond-shaped and -colored eyes, and his complexion was the color of sand. But the turns of his mind were utterly his mother's. He played "I Wish I Was in Dixie," of all pieces. He might have been Niccolò Paganini and I would not have noticed. I was too preoccupied to hear the singing catgut. Still, I closed my eyes and smiled as if I were a musicologist.

She avoided me all day. That was fine; I would be with her one night hence. I had to find a way to do it again, to get my brother drunk enough so that it could happen. I looked at Chang now, sunk down beside me on the divan, my brother so much skinnier than I was, so pathetically undernourished. My wife sat there as well, fleshy and gray. She hated our marriage, too, but I had no idea of her feelings beyond that.

That night, in bed with Sarah and Chang, I was able to sleep soundly and well. If I dreamt at all, it was probably of Adelaide. I was happy, for the last time in my life I was happy.

It was Chang who woke me—screaming "Up, get up!"—and not the stifling heat. Sarah awakened and screamed and ran from the bed. I had not yet had time to get my bearings when Chang jumped us to our feet, yelling, "Everybody get up! Go out of the house!" Flames streamed up the curtains, jumped to the ceiling, and spread over our heads like water pouring down onto a floor.

He and I were racing barefoot across the hall to wake the children, he doing most of the work of running, hurrying as the thick air got hotter and hotter at our backs, the light behind us shining unsteadily, and my heart was pounding now, my head only beginning to clear as I realized my house was burning, and we ran into the first children's bedroom and grabbed four-year-old Rosella and five-year-old Hattie out of their bed, the surprisingly undrunk Chang bending to take his little Hattie by the arm and me gripping my Rosella in the same way. Five of our other children slept in the room, too, all of them a few years older than the two in our hands, and we yelled "Up!" as we got little still-sleeping Rosella and Hattie onto their feet, and the girls—maybe out of instinct, or even fear of the double-father in the dark—struggled and jerked in our grasp, but I had the bunched cloth of Rosella's shirt in my hand. We scooped up the children and began running in the dark, ahead of the smoke and toward the front door, the fire unseen behind our backs, and I wondered, What about Adelaide? Where is Adelaide? as our other, older children hurried screaming by us in a confusion of small scrambling bodies. Chang and I hurried our four mature bare feet upon the floorboards as we carried Rosella and Hattie out past the porch, deposited the kids beside weeping Sarah, and stepped on sharp rocks as we ran back into the house, running up through smoke now and upstairs and across the hall to the other bedroom. We kicked open the door with a double-blow that knocked it off its hinges, but the children had by this time gotten out of this room and I yelled to Chang, "What about your Adelaide?" Smoke streamed into the room. Chang turned and took us down the hall, the thick smoke stinging my eyes as we made our way toward the secondary adult bedroom, arms in front of our faces, the fire cavorting across the wall now. I could not think of anything but Addie in the fire. Her beautiful flesh burning. I did not think of my safety. By the time we got to Addie's room, my lungs felt filled with bones, each breath brought a sharp pain, and my eyes prickled. The smoke and my tearing made it difficult to see if Adelaide was still in the room, but I opened my eyes wider to the smoke, as if my very anxiety about her, my frantic distress and want, would give me sight. "Adelaide!" I yelled; Chang yelled, "Adelaide!"

"Adelaide!" "Adelaide!"

"She is not here!" And I walked us blindly toward the bed, and when we reached it we tripped into it, and onto it, and like attached swimmers we flailed in the sheets as if they were the waves of the ocean, and in the smoke we gasped for air the way divers do. Addie was not in the bed.

Feeling our way, we made it back into the hall. My heart was thrashing and my lungs wheezing. I could feel the heat from the fire on the walls on either side of us. Eyes closed and teary, Chang and I ran to where we thought the stairs were. Once there, we tripped and fell down them.

I bounced and crashed down the stairs with my brother. As we tumbled I could feel his breath in my hair with each groan. We picked up speed, barreling downward. Our spongy exposed band slapped against the wood of the steps at the underside of each rotation, my brother's little mouth emitted a staccato cry that sharpened with every impact, with each crash of his skinny body, and I worried for his health.

We lay there at the bottom, exhausted and bruised. The heat had become onerous, and I had trouble breathing, though it was less smoky here on this first floor. I opened my eyes, and though my lids still felt like they were burning, I could see—Adelaide, coming from the living room and running by our supine bodies and out the door; she was holding the dirty little cat she'd adopted. Sarah was running past her sister at the front door, and once inside, my wife hurried by us toward the living room.

"Get up and help us save things." She did not look at us as she passed.

Chang and I managed to lift ourselves off the floor and scramble to the well across our property, away from the smell of burning wood and into the abundance of evening primrose and farm grass to count our children, and raising a dust cloud as we went. Chang and I got a bucket to put out the fire, but before we had filled it, we realized it was useless. If our wives had not worried about saving *things*, we might have been able to save the *house*.

Sarah and Adelaide rescued most items of worth, and placed our valuables beside them on the grass. The girls were standing before the fire with our children, Chang's Christopher, Nannie, Susan, Victoria, Louise Emeline, Albert, Jesse, Margaret Lizzie, and Hattie; my Stephen, James, Patrick, William, Frederick, Robert and Rosella. They all stood in front of the house, crying.

We could see the bright light in the house rising and falling, slowly, the fire having the same movement as a sleeping man's back glimpsed through a strange window. Some glass was heard to shatter inside the house and something else made a thunderous crash, then it was quiet. I was expecting at any moment for the sky all at once to be infused with light and color shooting toward the vault of heaven in some drawn-out, twisting eruption, dramatic and earsplitting, that would eclipse the moon. That is what I thought the destruction of our house deserved. And I expected neighbors, having seen the fire, to come around to offer help from out past Trap Hill. What did happen, however, was that our home burned to the ground slowly and quietly and with almost prudent confinement.

Had a candle caught on the curtains? Perhaps, but I was sure I'd blown out the wick that sat beside the bed. Even if it had been left lighted, that candle had not seemed close enough to the curtains to do any damage; it was the mystery of our lives, and I did not think we would ever answer it.

Following the blaze, after crowding our now-bickering families for a fortnight into the old slave quarters, Chang and I borrowed money from a New York banker named Babcock Young, taking a loan against any earnings from two tours we set up in haste. And so, as soon as Chang and I had this little money in our pockets, my brother sat me down with our wives and explained in a strained voice that he had a plan that would help us "get along better." He said he thought it would be best, considering the squabbling that had been going on lately between our wives and children, to split up into two residences. "Each wife have her own house, for her and children," he said. Chang and I spent three and a half days in each residence, and I was forced to keep to a strict rule: when I was calling upon my brother's home, I, as a "guest," did not speak unless spoken to, and affected invisibility. Chang followed the same dictum in my house. That way, each brother could approximate unconjoined life fifty percent of the time. That was the goal, in any case.

Both Sarah and Adelaide thought it a grand idea. Adelaide especially seemed enthusiastic about it, and actually looked relieved. "Yes, you boys could spend half a week in each house," she said. (Was it not longing but tedium I had noted in her eyes all these close-lipped years?)

"Why?" I could feel myself swallowing repeatedly. And why won't you look at me now, Adelaide?

"Oh, hush, Eng." Sarah was clapping softly. "It will be so nice to have more space, won't it now?"

I knew the quietude and rigidity of this arrangement would mean the end of my hope of satisfaction with Adelaide. But I could not have said that aloud.

"Why you not like the idea, brother?" Chang asked, blinking at me.

Chang smiled like a man who'd been given back some lost years of his life. I was sure he did not know about Adelaide and me, of course—and I could not understand why he was proposing this foolishness. But then, when had I ever understood the rounds of his perplexing mind?

And so we had matched homes built side by side. What anguish! Each house was two stories, with extra-wide stairways and three bedrooms on the top floor, and each felt much larger and emptier than our old home.

The disadvantages of this arrangement were tremendous, even though it was an attempt at simulating separation. Not that I did not still burn to be separated from Chang; it was that I wanted dissolution so much I would not accept this or any compromise. That was not logic; it was yearning.

Oh, I tried to make do. Sometimes, when in my house, I'd take my flute out of storage and I'd practice, warbling out an invented melody or playing "O, Susannah" with Stephen. Three nights in a row every week watching Sarah brush her hair. Three days away from Adelaide, the merciless tick of the clock, then three days unable to say a word even when in her presence. Sometimes I found myself getting Chang out of bed in the morning and vomiting for no reason. Chang would say nothing—lost, I suppose, in his own Silence.

CHAPTER SEVENTEEN

The Last Journey

August 1873–January 1874
Wilkesboro–New York

The only relief from this double-residence was to tour. And we did that, again. But that was no solace (was it ever?), and then I came home to a life worse than the one that preceded it. When one is forbidden to speak an unsolicited word for more than three days of every week, it is like being dead half of the time, but a death that lacks the halo of eternity. And so, I would sit quietly in my brother's home, following the rules and trying not to be present when Chang and his wife ate dinner, or idled in the parlor room together. But ultimately your desire is inseparable from your destiny, and it becomes nearly impossible to muffle the passion in your eyes by lowering your lids or smiling politely. After a day or two, an urge would come—it would never fail to come—and it was impossible not to talk to Addie about some triviality or another. But she was showing an odd willingness to play the role of Chang's wife, and around me now Adelaide was awkward in the way people feel uneasy when a stranger occupies the empty seat at the dinner table.

The other half of the week, in my house, I had no one to talk to. After a year in this arrangement, I thought my vocal cords would atrophy.

Still, it was in my character always to attend to certain details, even in the worst of circumstances to attend to the fine points. I heard the low-toned voice of my father in these dark times: *A Mekong Fisherman stays abreast of change. . . . Judgment helps one to diminish the influence of fate.*

With our wives one August evening, Chang and I discussed going on another tour, which would be our last, as it turned out. The only time the four of us were ever in the same room anymore was when Chang and I were calculating finances. Chang and I sat at the desk in the study in my house, and our wives stood around us as we looked at the itinerary I had drawn up, figuring out how many days to spend in New York, showing at Wood's Curiosity Museum and Metropolitan Theatre. This would be the most lucrative stop on the tour. I was, however, uneasy about performing at Wood's—which, after fire had razed Barnum's New American Museum in 1868, was in part owned by our old acquaintance P.T.—because that "curiosity gallery" was too close in attitude and arrangement to a circus for my satisfaction. Though Mr. George Wood had written us saying that we could show ourselves at his museum as long as we liked, and each get paid fifty dollars for every five days of performing, I wished only to stay for a single week.

Adelaide wanted no part of my hesitancy. "You said you was 'uneasy' about making fifty dollars a week each?" She was still fervent about things, despite her age. She was now a version of her mother in a one-half scale, her once-fiery eyes now red-rimmed and faint. But she still had something that I took for passion. Maybe it was the suggestion of her former self in her older, wider frame. Her long homespun dress encircled her ankles.

"You may not understand what a Barnum gallery is like, Adelaide." Though she and I were ostensibly adversaries in this debate, I was giddy at the prospect of being able to speak with her. "If one of these 'curiosity museums' found a two-headed Shakespeare," I said, "they would not be interested in whether he could write plays, believe me."

My brother and his wife looked at each other, dumbfounded. Sarah, too, wanted to join in the eye-rolling, but neither Chang nor Addie paid her much mind.

"I like to stay three weeks." Chang leaned feebly into me. He boasted little of the independent brainwork one expects in a sixty-two-year-old man.

"Don't you care about your family," Adelaide said to me, "as much as your brother cares about his?"

"Of course," I said. The joy of talking to her shriveled.

"I haven't asked that much out of either of you in this life, but I've managed to be disappointed anyways," Adelaide said. "At least, look at your brother, he's—"

"I'd rather not," I interrupted.

"—he's, he's . . . but at least he—"

I could not believe it. Defending Chang—and from me. "I don't want to argue," I said. "I don't want to argue with you. . . ."

"Okay," Adelaide was saying to Chang and Sarah, "three weeks in New York, that's what?"

"That's one hundred and fifty each," Sarah was figuring aloud.

"Good, great, and then there's obviously two hundred each for the rest of the trip. . . ."

"It's just," I said, "I feel we are a bit *old* for such a show."

"What in creation are you talking about now?" Adelaide was irritable and as confused by me as a preacher is by sin. "Isn't it obvious, if that Yankee is willing to part with one hundred and fifty—"

"It's not age, it's—well, *I* am what is at issue," I said. "I do not want to debase myself. That is what I am trying to say."

After looking at me a moment, the sisters went on talking and planning the trip with Chang, who was drinking. I sat there, in all respects irrelevant. Out the window, the evening sky was dark enough to make a reflector out of the windowpane. Chang looked closer to me in that reflection than I would have thought.

"I would rather make it two weeks in New York than three," I said. I smiled at Adelaide. I was compromising.

Her face changed, and she showed me a scowl that seemed to begin near her ankles and stretch all the way up to her forehead. Then she said something that would echo through the rest of my days, through every waking hour (and then, of course, there were the nights). "You make me sick," Adelaide said. "I *hate* you, Eng. I really *hate* you." And it was plain on her face, hatred and real disgust.

I did not wither or implode right there, as I feared I might; it was Sarah who gave a start at her sister's outburst. "Adelaide Bunker," my wife gasped. "You liked to have said *too much*." She glared at Adelaide. "That is my *husband* you are talking about," and for some reason she laid her plump bloodless hand on my shoulder. If I had not been so dispirited, I might have jumped when the surprise of my wife's touch bristled the hairs on my neck.

I won this debate about Wood's Museum. Chang and I set up plans to be in New York for only two and a half weeks. It was not out of concern for my feelings that our time at Wood's Museum was cut even shorter than that.

By the end of 1873, the New York I had known had now been subsumed by a taller, blacker place, known far and wide as Boss Tweed's Manhattan. Entering the city on the steamer *Ellenbernie*, we could see the most perverse of New York's alterations: by her southern tip, giant twin columns of what was to be a bridge linking Manhattan and Brooklyn stood facing each other on opposite shores, leviathan siblings across the water, awaiting connection. There were fresh new links everywhere in the city, as telegraph wires crisscrossed Manhattan like arteries in a human body, and the tracks for rail cars slept in the very stone of the streets.

On our arrival, the newspapers were unswerving in their coverage; word had gotten out that we were fighting. There is nothing like conjoined brothers at quarrel to push President Grant off the front pages. Thanks to the newspaper attention, and, as the nation seemed openhearted in mood after the General Amnesty Act had given pardon to ex-Confederates the year before, we'd been drawing crowds in the North as grand as any we'd attracted before the war—everybody came to see "The United Twin, Chang-Eng," and to receive a lithograph of us, arm in arm.

To keep our spectacle modern, my brother and I had been riding two of Michaux's new "bi-cycle" contraptions, pedaling side by side on identical two-wheels—not accomplishing much actual riding within the cramped terrain of our cage. Further, as by this time our constant leaning on one another had hooked my brother's backbone, the large front wheel of Chang's machine would invariably shake, its little hind wheel bobbing and scraping against mine, and we would all but tumble. We abandoned the bi-cycles before we reached New York.

Wood's Museum was at Broadway and Thirtieth Street, and awful as I had feared.

The "museum" was not as degraded as a circus, which is a dusty carousal, an ungodly bacchanal, an animal-reeking, donkey-neighing jamboree encouraging the sort of base voyeurism not seen since the decline of Rome, a nightmare of shrieks, fisticuffs, oddities fornicating in shadows, earsplitting brassy music, drunkards, and, of course, a sea of elephant excretion. Wood's establishment was not as low as all that, but for all its polish, this museum sustained the same sordid instincts as any cheap one-ring out in the Mississippi woods.

An imposing building, Wood's Museum was five stories of marble, brimming with "freaks" brought to America by sea captains or promoters, human curiosities of the meanest kind: Zip, ostensibly a grunting African pinhead who was "Living Evidence of the Missing Link"—he was actually a loquacious and deformed ex-slave named William Jackson; the Howling Human Hyenas, a dirty-faced brother-and-sister act from Australia whose only irregularity was that they shrieked all day long, wore brown cloths about their loins, and kept their hair at absurd lengths (they were also the worst conversationalists breathing, and smelled less than kind); the bearded lady, Virginia, whom Chang became friendly with, but whom I could not look at without feeling odd; and, unseemliest of all, the high-wire acts who slaved for attention above our heads when it was our turn in the "viewing auditorium."

The changing times had had their effect on the audiences, too. Manhattanites seemed an even crueler lot than they had been before the war, as if Yankee victory or seventy years of industrialization had rooted out any vestige of humanity from their hearts. Apparently people thought a 38¾ cent ticket allowed them to curse us. In the harsh light of Mr. Wood's gas lamps, the audience looked like the rabble of purgatory.

When it was time for our act, after the Howling Humans and before Zip, Chang and I, our act softened by the years, would walk out to a checkerboard in the middle of the cageless stage—

walking side by side, then front-to-front, then side-to-side again—and we would call someone up from the crowd to play with us.

On our third night at Wood's Museum, we strolled as professionally as possible out to the board, my brother looking tired and sloping into me, and the crowd laughed at us, guffawed and blasphemed as we made our way before them. An anger festered in their stares, a malediction.

I wanted to pick the kindest-looking spectator I saw to play checkers against, so Chang and I called up a young man—not too young, or he'd be filled with the spitefulness of adolescence, but not old enough for rancor to have set in, either—he was about twenty-four, with an open face and pale clean-shaved cheeks. Looking at him, I would have guessed he bathed and combed his hair every hour.

This young man came to the stage and sat across from us. "You like checkers?" my brother asked him.

"Yes, sir." He was nervous to look at us. He had never been in front of a large group of people before, it was obvious. Meanwhile, a buzzing mosquito annoyed our eyes and ears.

"Beat 'em good, sonny!" "Show those queer birds how to play!" "*King* those Chinamen!"—a few of the shouts from the crowd.

"What's your name, son?" I asked the young man.

"Arlen," he muttered, still looking into the board.

"Do not worry, Arlen," my brother said. "You probably twice the man we are." The old humor. It did not work this time, the crowd was too raucous even to hear his bon mot.

Turning to the game. We were black, the young man red. We gave him the first move, and Arlen bent his head to the board; his pomaded black hair shined. When he finished moving his corner piece, we began with our traditional opening gambit, moving the very middle piece of our front line.

A drunkard's voice form the back rows: "We paid to see a *show!*" Everyone laughed. Then some other voice added, ". . . And not a *game!*" Everyone laughed again.

The young man trembled like a frostbite sufferer.

"It's all right, son." I tried to calm him, though I was stirred by

the madding crowd myself. "Just make the next move, please."
The mosquito whirred by my ear.

Arlen looked as if he were going to cry. And then an invisible
spark acted upon the air, and it was in Arlen's expression, too, and
in the sudden silence of the crowd; even the mosquito seemed to
stop and pay attention. The only sound was the faintly pittering
feet of the tightrope walker overhead.

"Sorry," Arlen said in a contrite whisper. And with a meek
toss, he lobbed his checker piece at Chang and me, hitting us in
the ligature. The crowd underwent a great spasm as one; the
laughter was more of a single loud thundering typhoon than a
collection of cackles.

Arlen stood, his narrow face looking happier, relaxed now, and
he pointed at us. "We want a *show*, not a game!" he cried.

Even at our age, we could have tried to fight; how satisfying to
double-kick Arlen in the head, or to try our hand at challenging
the crowd, which now began throwing pennies and balled-up
newspaper at the stage. But I was too tired, and my brother too
weak, and I suppose age had sapped *me* a bit, too. After a life full
of leering faces and slurs, whenever the fire of rage spread in me
now, my insides no longer went up like twigs and tinder; the
flame just did not catch.

It was with great sadness that I did what I was to do next. As
some unseen hand dimmed the lamps, my brother and I got on
our fours and attempted a handstand. But at our stage of life, and
with Chang's condition, it was impossible to raise ourselves. As we
started to put weight on our palms, Chang shook his head to say
no. Crouched there together on all fours, not knowing what else
to do for the crowd, we began to crawl as one. Happy laughter
and mad cheering from the audience. The proprietor, Mr. Wood—
his shirt tucked haphazardly into an ill-fitting pair of trousers—
stood watching from the very back of the theater, leaning against
the rear wall. From the position of our crawl, he was visible over
my shoulder by the orange-yellow light of his cigar's tip, a tiny
circle of fire under the balcony.

As we made our kneeling way across the stage, the audience
was on its feet, whooping and mocking, and I had not felt this
embarrassed since we'd been made to stand naked for the queens

of Siam—only this was worse; I was now an old man, and knew better than to suffer humiliations. Here I was, however, meek as a martyr. A great wave of complacency came off my brother at that moment, as he bowed and scraped beside me—suggesting something ruined and barren. Maybe it came from his drink-ravaged liver. We were on our knees like that for another five minutes.

Finally the show was over; still, the crowd wanted a last look on its way out the door. The heavy air held tobacco smoke stagnant in that close auditorium, a heaviness on top of everything, even the audience, a tide of hundreds now flooding past the stage, voyeurs of all classes, all ages and both genders, of every stripe, but for all the differences in these people—the many individual cravings and identities alive in such a herd—in every eye flickered the same light, the same insatiable, bellowing curiosity: *I want to see it! Let me get a look at it!*

The Chang of forty years earlier would have crawled around for these morons until his knee prints branded the floor, and look what a lifetime of showmanship had gotten us. Poor Chang—any relic of his charm dissolved away, and with it any humanity. The crowd was whooping. The museum's theater was enormous, but it shuddered and creaked under the commotion, the very walls ready to bend toward the curiosity. Nausea rose in my throat.

"Let's have a drink," my brother said once the theater had cleared out. As was our custom after a show, he and I were still on stage, trying to relax, sitting on our settee side by side, stretching our band and buckling it into a C, each brother draping an arm over the other's shoulder. "Wilkesboro blend," he said, and reached for his flask.

"If you must drink"—I held up the book that I always read after shows on this tour: Verne's *Around the World in Eighty Days*, the literary sensation of the year and a personal favorite of nomads like myself—"at least let me finish this chapter."

For as long, I suspect, as it took his addiction to craft his words for him, my brother stared at me, his eyes dull as Confederate pennies. And he said, "A double, then." His breath was heavy on my neck, he had begun to cough and shake. I could feel his spine tremble.

An intimation of remorse—not unselfish, for it wasn't entirely free of bile—gushed from some artery of my heart. "I'm sorry to upset you, brother, but I can't very well read if you have that drink," I said. "Isn't that right, Chang?"

"Tell me," he asked. "What wrong with one drink to delight the occasion? The show over." His grin was a taunt. "Everyone choosing a drink now and then."

"Alcohol makes people unbalanced." I was too tired for this. "It blackens the crevices of your mind." How many times had I shown him the scientific evidence?

"I am having drink." Even elephants back down. In this way, my decrepit brother was stronger than the mighty beast.

"The black bubbles hinder the encephalon," I said, "and with each of your drunken jumps and hurrahs, with every instance of vomiting and hugging strangers in a saloon, you send out shards of hardened blood, shattering your bowels."

"I not going to hug anyone tonight." His breath was like moldy meat.

Chang called over to Franco Santoro, an Italian immigrant who served as Mr. Wood's assistant. He motioned for Santoro to get him a drinking glass.

"Good," Chang said when the hefty, dark-haired immigrant brought us an oversized glass. I sent the Italian to settle with the ticket booth and to pack up.

I was doubly angry, not just because Chang knew my feelings about alcohol but also because he seemed to be taking pleasure out of irritating me. I controlled the urge to spit at his ugly face.

In a blast of memory I saw Chang as he had been, handsome as a young man, with smooth skin, a rich olive complexion, his hair black and shining. Now his complexion had faded.

Meanwhile, the scotch slid across our connector to work its witchcraft. My brother was drinking more than usual. Already there was the reverberating around the ears like the aftermath of a loud crash. This was the calm that tempts weak souls into the storm.

Santoro returned, and Chang told the immigrant to get him some more alcohol from our dressing room. Then my twin

breathed the sigh of a man who had reached the end of a drawn-
out torture. "Please now, Mr. Santoro."

Chang's eyes followed the shuffle of the immigrant, and
though my brother seemed to be functioning sufficiently, he was
now more a mass of desirous cells than a conscious human. "What
you are looking at, Eng?" he asked. "People would think there
another fire, by your sad face. Chang just having a cocktail, I am
not burning down theater."

After a few duplications of that scene—Chang proceeding to
guzzle, I to sulk, and Santoro returning with more—my brother
grew far worse for liquor. He missed his wife, he said, laughing.
"Can you believe *that*?" (From the Handbook: "The tainted nectar . . . denies the learning that usually chaperones sorrow.")

The air remained heavy and close onstage. The black bubbles
collected like minute marbles around my medulla oblongata, the
world lurched off its moorings. I had never felt this drunk. The
auditorium smelled of sweat, and was completely empty save for
Chang and me.

"I'd like to go to the hotel, please." I began the forward motion
that signaled to my brother I wanted to stand; he sat rigidly. I
snapped back to the settee. My head was lost in inky bubbles.

"Drink with me, Eng. Why won't you? Just once, now what
about that? Would it be bad"—his mouth was hurrying to keep
pace with the effervescence in his brain—"so very much, Eng, to
have some drink with Chang?"

Chang licked his finger and smoothed my eyebrows. The clear
light of the lamps behind his head was clouded as if seen through
waves of cream.

"Your breath stinks of hooch," I said.

"Yours, too." He was grinning like a baboon.

"Is that supposed to be funny?"

Perhaps what I did next was out of guilt—I did not deny my
responsibility for Chang's alcoholism. And so, despite my hatred
for alcohol, and that my brother and I had not enjoyed each
other's company for years, and despite my onetime high honorary
position in the North Carolina Ladies Temperance Society, and
my disappointment that Chang would slight that position by asking if I'd join him for a drink, I said, kindly, for him, my brother,

"All right, Chang." I felt a fondness for his pathetic skinny face. "For you and only for you, I will try a *taste*."

I put down my book, swiveled, and sat face-to-face with my twin. He handed me his glass. I lifted it to my mouth, and when this cup of alcohol closed in on my face, it thrust a thousand tiny pins inside my nostrils and I recoiled, my nose afire.

Chang seized the glass before I dropped it. "Maybe I hug someone tonight, after all," he hissed, and brought the glass before my mouth, tilted it—

When we fell to the floor in a heap, he was saying "Stop, stop," his face growing maroon from the pressure my squeezing fingers were applying to his throat. I accidentally rolled onto the glass.

The pain in the side of my head came as a surprise; he'd gotten me with his elbow. I lost my grip on the choke hold.

We clambered to our feet, leaning on one another, face-to-face, two sixty-two-year-old men swinging ferociously, but in unison. Chang looked frantic with his ballooned, bloodshot eyes. Chips of broken glass stuck to his pants. He was trying the extended-arm, bent-leg fire-and-stones stance—circling slowly to try to fend off my blows—but I was too close to him. Through the chaos of punches, in the smallest part of an instant I caught a look at my brother's wrinkled face, weak, tired, angry. My knee to Chang's ribs threw us backward, his skinny arms flailing.

We crashed together onto the settee, sounding a dull *poof* that echoed across the empty theater. We landed in a tangle, old twins wrestling in unnaturally close quarters. And Chang punched me in the face as we fell to the floor. I had known a moment before he threw it that he would punch me—I simply did somehow.

He shot a knee at my groin, then with his fists he tried to strike my nether half, but he missed, hitting my hips, which caused a blunt pain with each blow. That he was trying for such a sensitive area enraged me; I landed an elbow against the soft bone of his temple, and he moaned, and went limp, bending me back with him. We rolled over, and I grabbed hold of his throat; from below me, he grabbed mine. The force his cold antique fingers managed was surprising; his choke hurt and I was beginning to lose my ability to breathe. I saw his wheezing face only through oscillating black spots. Oxygen could no longer get to my lungs through my windpipe, and I was unable to keep up my own pressure on his throat. He was winning, and I had become the weaker one. I believed it was the end. I felt a chill on the back of my head. I was conscious of each hair on my body and I began to black out.

But, eyes closing, I could actually hear the bones in Chang's neck creaking. His strength had begun to course from him to me, and his fingers lost their thrust, and he could not help but let go of my neck. My grip around his throat tightened.

"P-please," he was saying.

I saw, looking at his gasping face, a scene out of memory: when Chang and I were the littlest of children, we had run along the banks of the Mekong, our first unsupervised excursion to the edge of the river. As I kept the pressure on his throat now, we were again children scurrying along the banks in the sun, in my mind we were children running and catching sight of our double-reflection, it must have been the first time. We bent toward the river together, two little boys in the warm wind, stepping on pink snail eggs, peering at our shared image; Chang appeared more near to me in that reflection than I would have believed, closer than consciousness, closer than a whisper. That double-reflection moving in unison on the blinking water had offered so little information about me. My reflection had not been entirely me.

Now I was putting more pressure on his throat, my fingers slowly sinking deeper into the skin. He had given up fighting back, the only activity in his body was in his eyes, which were pleading for me to stop. I knew I had to let go, but in my brain there trickled something sour that made everything light and clear and I forced the back of my brother's head harder against the floor. It was he who had kept me from returning to Siam, all those years before.

"Aahh, ahh," he said, his face greening.

Tears, spasms, choked whispered pleas came from Chang. I punched him flush in the face, and he writhed and I punched him again, and again, as hard as I could I punched his face. We were a pair of attached sixty-two-year-old men inches apart and rolling on the floor. And over the cries of my elderly brother I punched him again until my hands hurt and I felt something crack in his jaw. I kept on, freer from Chang than I had ever felt. His lips and nose were bloody and he had trouble keeping open his eyes. I even hit our band. "Snap," I said weakly. "Snap."

A croak came from behind me: "Stop—stop what you are doing!" The stout proprietor of the auditorium, Mr. Wood, was running toward the stage through rows of chairs. He was frantic, waving one arm while he used the other to keep his white hat from falling off. "You're grown men!" he shouted around his cigar. Of course we were grown men. We knew that.

I was lying on top of my brother now, spent, chest-to-chest, his sick, labored breath in my ear, a whisper. "I did a wrong to you," he whispered.

Wood ran onstage, and he came to stand beside us, hands on hips, looking down at this aged tangle. "Your brother ain't looking so good."

All the while, Chang was whispering in my ear, "I did wrong. . . ." His murmuring was barbed by such fervor I'd never know for sure whether he was prideful or penitent. With all the emotion of sixty-two years of cinders in his chest, he said to me, "I know everything. Idiot, I knew, I knew, I knew. . . ."

His whole frame trembled. "You five inches from me all the time," he said. "You not think I would have eyes to see everything?" He narrowed those eyes at me, and stared long into my face. Next, his features began to warp. "I do things when you sleeping," he said. "You do things when you think I sleeping."

I looked into his red eyes. I was unable to find the words to say anything. My hand under his head, Chang could not move, but he strained to list away from me. "You kill the home in your way." His voice was not trembling. "I light fire."

Chang had had a stroke. It cost him most of the sight in his right eye and paralysis to that side of his face. The skin of his right cheek hung off the bone like wet dough. With that entire half of his body weakened, he was a deadweight to my left, and I was forced to carry a leather strap that supported his right foot as we hobbled along. Chang's illness affected the workings of his mind, and I began to fear my own dissolution.

We saw the finest doctors in New York; the best prescription they could design was the application of cold water to the face, arm, and leg—and that brought some very little benefit. But with no real signs of improvement, we left for home. In New York Harbor, my feeble limping brother and I boarded the twin paddle-wheel steamer *Northern Beacon*. Chang was laid up in our berth, and I with him, of course. I was healthy for my age. We'll go together, I thought. When it's time for that.

Chang and I never discussed the fire, nor what happened with Adelaide and me that one lovely awful night. On the *Northern Beacon* home, I knew the human fundament of misery. My wife, Sarah, whom I may have loved once, and my twin's bride Adelaide, the woman I have loved more than I thought possible, my children alive and dead, and of course my brother, none of them could I see when I closed my eyes—all these people coalesced in my memory, melting into one form. The one form was that of myself, all I had.

In my way I have been twice most men in that my life has had two meanings—as a young man I craved nothing more than solitude, and in my old age I longed to be less alone and denied the absence of love. But Father's philosophy has proved hollow. Not even a Mekong fisherman can diminish the influence of fate.

Soon the *Northern Beacon* sailed into the port of Wilmington, North Carolina. We were going home together.

CHAPTER EIGHTEEN

Our First Ever Day in North Carolina

Monday, December 10, 1842
Wilkesboro

C hang-Eng," the children chanted. "Mutant, mutant."
Chang and I were thirty-one, and just now coming to the end of yet another tour, exhibiting the bond that the public could not see without assuming we were so very different from everybody else. It had been four years since we'd found out Mother was dead, and it was nearly Christmastime. Chang and I were entering a place I had never been, it was called North Carolina. My ear tingled with the nearness of my brother. I was tired of touring, tired of being irritable.

Why is it *he* never seems unhappy? I asked myself. Chang stays abreast of change, he reacts to it. His dark eyes showed little reflections of me, and he was smiling.

Like my brother without care, I told myself, I need only react to life. That will bring me contentment.

For the first time since arriving in this hard-hearted nation, I experienced a sense of repose traveling in this Southern place, felt the consanguinity between lush, forested Siam and waterless North Carolina, thick with foliage. Appalachia and Siam: sides of the same coin, one dry, the other wet, both green, both utterly natural.

The dust whisked us toward Wilkesboro, a little town where we were to rest for the evening.

"Chang-Eng," the children chanted, trailing our carriage. "Mutant, mutant." Our buggy bounced into town.

If my brother is an amenable person, I said to myself, can I not live that way, too?

Chang had the driver roll us to a stop in Wilkesboro's dusty square, and the people of Wilkes County rushed at us from every direction, cheering our names, which they'd read on the chipped yellow legend marking the side of our wagon. I felt an odd tenderness for my brother as he waved his patented wave at them all. He loved these people, my brother did. Why am I unable to open myself to the possibility of the same emotion, however unlikely?—any love, love of performing, brotherly love, or even something more burning.

Main Street was rounded, with a humped center and sloping edges, and it led us across town. We crossed this dusty street side by side, arms over each other's shoulders, in the calibrated rhythm of our united movement. "Chang-Eng acknowledges you, good people," said my brother. The crowd had begun to follow us, at a distance. A small number of townsfolk did smile openly at us as we passed, and let escape a friendly giggle whenever Chang waved.

"Eng," said Chang. "It is exciting, yes?" With his free hand he smoothed the lapels of his jacket. His face was contented.

I saw only those who taunted us, and so I disagreed. Chang drew himself closer to me, to wave at the people. Everyone clapped. Chang swung around to face forward again with a grin that spread across his whole face.

Main Street came to an end at the Yates Inn, a two-story unpainted log house with eyelike windows and a modest front yard overgrown with chokecherry.

A giant woman sat on the inn's drooping front porch, fanning herself in the skeletal shade of leafless oaks. Two blond women stood next to her—the pair of daughters long-faced, flat-chested, and stepping on worms with their bare feet. It was the tail end of dusk, the veils of nightfall were only beginning to cover the Eastern sky.

The taller sister, I later learned her name was Adelaide, stood just slightly out from under the shade of the porch, and the declining sun shone on her fine blond hair, cutting it into elements of gold and pink gold and shadow. I could have been smitten by either one of them at that moment, but it was the taller Adelaide who took me, standing as she was in the fading light and smiling— at me. She blushed and bowed her head, and I felt no body—not mine or his—no attachment. I did not know if this was hope I was feeling for the first time or an equivalent lightning. Chang turned to me, an entreaty—wordless, but complete—floating in his look.

The smiling girl on the porch moved just to her right to lean against one of the posts. I swore she moved somehow outside the flow of time, leaning slowly, at approximately the pace of the Tower of Pisa—and as she moved, she and her shadow came toward each other to the point of touching. I did not know this blushing woman in the half-light, but I knew I wanted to be like that shadow, beside her. Like a shell opening onto a pearl, my shyness gave way to love. I had a clear sense of who I was, and found myself enveloped in a new-sprung skin of emotion. A bluebird sang in the trees.

"Jefferson," said the mother, a woman of size and optimism. "Go get your father." She removed a little gnat that had flown into her mouth. "Tell him I found a pair of husbands for your sisters."

Both daughters smiled, both exquisite in their way, showing the world the whiteness of their teeth. My cheeks hurt from grinning. And Chang—oh Chang!—my brother's happy heart had thrashed so that I could feel its ecstatic thrumming.

Chang, these memories are yours as well. My poor brother, I am sorry for everything. You are gone now, Chang, and I am no longer incomplete. I love you boundlessly.

I swear the townsfolk cheered.

Epilogue

January 17, 1874
Wilkesboro

*C*hang Bunker has died in his sleep, sometime after midnight in his brother's house. Eng, who woke to the sight of his twin's corpse, has said, "Then I too am done." He has been seized by paroxysms of memory.

Sarah, the elderly wife, hears the moans and runs to wake her son William. She hurries the boy to fetch the only physician in Wilkes County, Dr. William Cottard. But the boy will not reach the doctor in time.

Eng is dying.

Softly, Sarah returns to the frightful bedroom. She comes hesitatingly to stand beside her husband, his chest steeped in sweat. "It will be all right," she tries to comfort him. "The doctor is coming and you can be alone finally and everything will be all right." On the desk sits a gift in two parts from Tsar Nicholas.

His voice a rasp, Eng asks Sarah to rub his arms and legs, which are cold, and she musters the resolve. She soothes his legs, she soothes his arms; she stops. Sarah will not look at him, and then she does. "Would you like me to get Adelaide?" Sarah's voice does not break as she says this. She could not have spoken more clearly, but Eng acts as if he has not heard. He twists away from her—he draws his brother Chang closer to him. Eng takes his twin into his arms: This is the image Sarah keeps of her husband for the rest of her life. Eng dies.

The next morning, Sarah and Adelaide Bunker hire a local tinsmith named Joseph Augustus Reich to build a large metal coffin to fit the twins' immense casket. Cutting thirty-four large sheets of tin, Reich fashions the extraordinary sarcophagus in four hours. Reich is a heavy-lidded young man from Wilkes County, and he wears a proud smile when making the special funerary box. He cannot put his reverence into words, especially when he struggles to lift the Siamese Twins into their coffin; they are interred in black silk raiment with black slippers. Chang and Eng are the greatest human curiosity in the history of the world, Reich thinks, and whoever thought I would be the man to solder them up.

For his sister, because she once visited Wood's Curiosity Museum in New York City, the young tinsmith decides to save a drop of solder that falls from the coffin when he welds it shut.

The twins are buried in a double-plot, under a single large headstone, behind the old Baptist church in White Plains, North Carolina, just outside Wilkesboro.

A NOTE UPON FINISHING THE BOOK

The story you have just read is both true and not. The twins Chang and Eng Bunker, united at the chest, did in fact live between 1811 and 1874, as I have written in these pages. And they did meet the King of Siam, come to America and celebrity, entertain P. T. Barnum, marry sisters, father twenty-one children, and sustain a coupled life as farmers in North Carolina during the Civil War period.

But the book in your hand hopes to be ruled a novel and not a history. Most of its people and situations result strictly from the imagination. Where I have discarded or finessed or invented the details of Chang and Eng's life, it was only to elbow the facts toward a novel's own idea of truth, which is something else entirely.

No definitive record of the twins' life exists; their conjoined history was a confusion of legend, sideshow hyperbole, and editorial invention even while they lived. That said, a number of reference works were essential to my research: *The Kingdom of the People of Siam,* by John Bowring (Oxford University Press, 1969); *An Historical Account of the Siamese Twin Brothers, from Actual Observations,* by James W. Hale (Elliot and Palmer, 1831); *The Two,* by Amy and

Irving Wallace (Simon & Schuster, 1978); *America in 1857,* by Kenneth Stampp (Oxford University Press, 1990); *Entwined Lives: Twins and What They Tell Us about Human Behavior,* by Nancy Segal (Dutton, 1999). I'd like to thank the staff of the Mütter Museum at the College of Physicians of Philadelphia—where the plaster cast of Chang and Eng resides—and Joan Baity, curator of the Old Wilkes Museum, who made me feel at home in Wilkesboro, a town as comely today as it must have been when the twins walked its streets.

And I'd like to express my gratitude to the following: Jonathan Strong, Alan Lebowitz, Jay Cantor, E. L. Doctorow, Peter Carey, and Lee K. Abbott for lessons; Brett Martin, Laurel Berger, Pamela Berger, Chris Noel, Jeff Roda, Doug Glover, and, especially, Susannah Meadows for giving me a read; the New York State Writers Institute; Brian Tart for noticing and fantastically editing me; Carole Baron and the rest of Dutton for bolstering me; and Rob Kraselnik, for lending me some history books.

ABOUT THE AUTHOR

DARIN STRAUSS is a graduate of the New York University creative writing program in fiction, where he was awarded a teaching fellowship. His writing has appeared in *GQ*, *Time Out*, and literary journals, among other publications. He spent more than three years researching and writing *Chang and Eng*, which is his first novel. He is at work on a new novel. For more information about Darin Strauss and *Chang and Eng*, please go to www.changandeng.com